Nam-A-Rama

Phillip Jennings

A TOM DOHERTY ASSOCIATES BOOK
NEW YORK

NAM-A-RAMA

NAM-A-RAMA

Copyright © 2005 by Phillip Jennings

This book is printed on acid-free paper.

Edited by Moshe Feder

A Forge Book
Published by Tom Doherty Associates, LLC
175 Fifth Avenue
New York, NY 10010

www.tor.com

Forge® is a registered trademark of Tom Doherty Associates, LLC.

Library of Congress Cataloging-in-Publication Data

Jennings, Phillip.
    Nam-a-rama / Phillip Jennings.—1st ed.
        p. cm.
    "A Tom Doherty Associates book."
    ISBN 0-765-31120-8 (acid-free paper)
    EAN 978-0765-31120-7
    1. Vietnamese Conflict, 1961-1975—Fiction. 2. Americans—Vietnam—Fiction. 3. Peace movements—Fiction. I. Title.

PS3610.E56N36 2005
813'.6—dc22
                                                                    2004056264

First Edition: March 2005

Printed in the United States of America

0 9 8 7 6 5 4 3 2 1

for

Captain Wayne H. Gentry,
USMC; Air America, Inc.
1944–1970

and

Clinton I. Smullyan, Jr.,
friend extraordinaire

And for all those who proudly served.
And serve.

Preface

I have been blessed throughout my life. It is to my wonderment that I continue to be so. At present it comes in the form of my Very Lovely Agent, Deborah Grosvenor. She did not want me as a client, as novelists are notoriously hard to feed and comfort, and she had already edited and promoted novelists who wrote international mega-bestsellers. Fortunately she had the grace to admit that she laughed out loud when she read *Nam-A-Rama,* and then dedicated enormous effort to finding the right publisher. Thank you.

My editor most likely laughed more frequently before he became my editor. The ineffable Moshe Feder at Forge has at times been almost effable. He made *Nam-A-Rama* a better book. What more can a writer ask? He is a great intellect and a very nice guy who is not working for the Mossad. I have his word on it.

Also a blessing is a tolerant family, Deborah, Jason, Alison, and Coleman (I love them all), who ignored the sight of a man in boxer shorts, flak vest, cartridge belt, flight helmet, and bayonet, ranting about the domicile and trying to call in air strikes on the worthless family animals (one evil dog and two communistic cats) all in the name of research. I will now admit that the slit trench latrine in the backyard was a bad idea.

So much help comes into my life that it is hard to not list name after name, but two excellent writers, Jack Butler and Stewart O'Nan, gave such extraordinary encouragement at the beginning of *Nam-A-Rama* that I have to give them hearty thanks. Bail money is always available, guys. Valerie Vogrin, the world's best writing coach, you were both foundation and muse.

I must thank humankind for its continuing penchant for eschewing common sense and simple decency. Without wars and protracted bloody skirmishes, this book could not have been written. Our pursuit of peace through obliteration seems unabated by our experiences, and the folly is surprisingly easy to satirize. Thank you, civilization.

Not that wars should *never* be fought. As a Marine (once a Marine, always a Marine), I enjoy a good slaughtering as well as the next man. My discourse, in *Nam-A-Rama,* concerns why, when, and how. I am afraid that "if " is not applicable for the foreseeable future. Somewhere, along with crass cynicism and disconsolate despair, however, there must be a descriptive end to bitterness and grief, anger and shame. Laughter, after all, may in fact be the best medicine.

Vietnam was undoubtedly a searing experience. Would that we had cooked it through and through; we might have saved ourselves the decades-long indigestion. But probably not. Americans do not like coitus interruptus, particularly of the militaristic variety. We want to roll over and light a cigarette after a definitive end to things—the vanquished at our feet, or up making us a sandwich.

The Vietnam War seemed to have a venal goofiness unseen since Tennyson's Crimea, or the 3rd Light Horse Turkish shoot at Gallipoli. Festive camaraderie and adrenaline addiction, with weapons and lots of ammo, leads to no good. Those other civilizations—surely they are out there—must be hoping that Earth grows out of adolescence before we shoot our collective eye out.

As presidents and kings and the pretenders to those thrones debate the merits of armed invasion on distant shores, I would pray that they, and we, take the diatribes seriously. My suggestion—that the U.S. commander in chief be constitutionally required to garb him- or herself in full battle dress, replete with facial camouflage and flora-festooned helmet, whilst any U.S. troops are engaged in combat—will most likely not be adopted. Perhaps the requirement that a squad of rabid men run through the Oval Office once a day spraying AK-47 fire above the President's head would add urgency to any settlement talks, but admittedly could play hell with the furniture and visiting potentates.

Contrary to book blurbs or citations for service in Vietnam and Laos, I was not a hero. I belonged instead to that band of brothers more afraid of being a coward than of checking into the Pinewood Hotel. Better dead than look bad, as the Marines would say.

To all the infantry grunts, aviators, doctors, corpsmen, nurses, supply sergeants, and support troops, be they U.S. Marine, Navy, Air Force, Army, or Coast Guard, who served honorably in the theater of Southeast Asia, I offer this book. You were—and are—golden. May God bless you.

PART 1

In politics, stupidity is not a handicap.

—Napoleon

War must be made as intense and awful as possible in order to make it short, and thus to diminish its horrors.

—Napoleon

Them as die will be the lucky ones.

—Long John Silver

1 · Not the Beginning Yet

earheardt and I were having lunch next to a pile of dead Laotians when he came up with his scheme to redeem ourselves with the Marine Corps and settle the score with the Cubans. The sincerity in his baloney-muffled voice made me listen when I knew that I shouldn't. Listening to my best friend had always led to disaster, if not for us then for a number of innocent and perhaps not so innocent bystanders. Gearheardt was one of those people who never looked in the rearview mirror. Causing the Tet Offensive, prolonging the Vietnam War, and getting the President fixed up with the girl who showered in her underpants in Olongopo were hijinks quickly forgotten by the boyish pilot who sat alongside the dusty Laotian airstrip listening to the small-arms fire and distant thump of artillery.

Gearheardt threw the crust of his sandwich away and wiped his mouth with the back of his hand.

"Jack," he said, "this plan will at least get us killed in a real war. Do you want to end up in a pile of dead Laotians?" He gestured toward the pungent stack and grimaced.

"Is that my only choice, Gearheardt?" I asked.

Gearheardt turned toward me, adjusting his shoulder holster and then licking the mayonnaise from the butt of his pistol. His thin blond hair was smashed wetly against his forehead, creases from his flight helmet still visible.

"I'm not kidding, Jack. This is the poorest damned excuse for a war imaginable, and you know it. Look at those poor bastards in that pile. Waiting for us to haul their raggedy asses back to Vientiane so their raggedy-assed families can wail and piss until the government gives them fifty bucks or something. I'm embarrassed to be in this sonofabitch."

"You'd rather be sitting next to a pile of Vietnamese?"

"Wouldn't you?" He was serious.

A mortar round hit the embankment across the runway, blowing dust and grit over us and causing the stack of Laotians to shift and settle. Gearheardt and I ducked and shielded our eyes.

"Jack, this scheme will get us back into Vietnam. I'm sick of this pussy-footing around. We're Marines, damn it. I didn't become a Marine to haul dead Laotians up and down the countryside."

"It's live up, dead back."

"Very funny, Jack. What about my scheme? Are you up for it?"

"You don't have a scheme, Gearheardt. You have an idea," I said.

A second mortar hit in front of us and Gearheardt stood up and peered at the hills to the east. "Isn't anybody going to take that bastard out?" he asked rhetorically, pointing to the hill from which the mortar rounds seemed to be coming.

"A scheme is when there are elements of a plan," I continued. "Like some details of how things are going to get done, you know. That's always your problem. You confuse an idea with a plan." I slid lower against the wall of the shallow ditch. Gearheardt dropped back down beside me. "And technically we're not Marines anymore. I think we belong to the CIA."

He looked at me. "Okay. We take an airplane to Hong Kong. We find that numbnuts Cuban that screwed us around in Hanoi. We shoot him until he's dead. Then we take an airplane to Danang, march our asses up to wing headquarters, and get our commissions back. Those are details."

"You're a planning genius, Gearheardt."

Gearheardt bit his lip and squinted at me, pissed.

"Your sarcasm is wearing pretty thin, Jack. Will you *ever* get off my ass about Hanoi? I'm carrying that to my grave, aren't I? We had the Barbonella plan. Sure it was missing a few details, but if you hadn't lost the damn thing out of the window . . ."

"*You* lost the plan out of the window, jackass. You were supposed to be flying us to Hanoi, not grabassing all over the cockpit trying to eyeball the paperwork."

A volley of mortar rounds hit the bunkers along the opposite side of the airstrip and I heard the CIA officer who ran the war in this part of Laos bellow from within.

"Would *somebody please* call some fire in on that frigging mortar position?"

Moments later the 105 howitzer, almost hidden in its heavily sand-bagged slot behind the command bunker, fired a series of rounds. I watched the jungle near the suspected enemy mortar tube explode and fill the air above it with dirt and then black smoke. My ears rang. Gearheardt shook his head as if he were trying to dislodge something from his ear. The Laotian artillery crew climbed atop the sandbags and began shoving sticky rice balls into their mouths. The little artillery sergeant gazed toward the still smoking hillside and began to pick his nose.

From inside the command bunker the voice of the CIA officer sang, "*Thank* you."

I looked behind where we were sitting and saw the flight mechanics resume refueling the helicopters that Gearheardt and I piloted. Serafico, my flight mechanic, looked my way and gave the thumbs up signal to indicate that we were ready to go. I rose by putting my hand on Gearheardt's shoulder. Standing, I brushed the dust and debris from my trousers and turned to him. He was still staring, unfocused, at the smoke drifting along the hillside. Without looking up at me he spoke.

"Do you ever wonder about the little sonsabitches on the other end of those 105 rounds, Jack? One minute they're finishing a baloney sandwich, and the next they're just meat decorating the trees."

Before I responded about the lack of baloney sandwiches in the North Vietnamese diet, Gearheardt went on. "War is weird shit, isn't it, Jack?" He grinned at me as he stood up.

"Where are you heading, Gearheardt?" I asked him as we walked to the aircraft.

"I'm hauling ammo to that outpost by the old Site 85. You?"

"The customer asked me to take a look over by 110 and see if I • could spot signs of survivors." Site 110, near the North Vietnamese border with Laos, had been thoroughly shellacked by the North Vietnamese two nights before, and the troops that escaped were expected to be trying to make their way to Site 36. The Ho Chi Minh Trail was between them and relative safety, and no one expected many to actually survive. But it felt good to look for them.

Gearheardt grabbed my arm and stopped me, holding my elbow.

"Look, I know you think I'm a screaming asshole sometimes . . ."

"Yes."

". . . and I know you think I'm nuts . . ."

"Absolutely."

". . . but we gotta get back to the Marine Corps and to our squadron. I miss those guys. I miss the real war. And before that, we gotta find that stinking Cuban and kill him. Air America is okay, but we can't have guns—officially."

Some might think that a silly reason not to like flying for the CIA. But I knew Gearheardt. He had thought through the concept of not having official guns in northern Laos, and his statement was solid.

"It wasn't the Cuban that screwed up our mission to Hanoi, Gearheardt. And it wasn't Barbonella, or Whiffenpoof, or that goofy Englishman in Hong Kong. Our 'mission' was doomed—"

Gearheardt jerked his hand away from my elbow.

"Jack, if you say it was because we didn't have a goddam plan again, I'll kill you. I'll shoot you right damn now. We had orders! From the President of the United States!"

"—before we even cranked up. Someone had a good idea, and we tried to execute our *orders* without the foggiest notion of what the hell we were doing or how to figure out if we had done it after we did it."

After a moment Gearheardt turned and walked straight-backed to his aircraft.

Centeno, his flight mechanic, smiled and said loud enough for me to hear, "You and Captain Jack discussing your Hanoi plan again, Captain?"

"Shut up, Centeno," Gearheardt snapped.

He began climbing into the cockpit. As he strapped in he looked over at me and keyed his mike. "You all set over there, Jack?"

I clicked my radio, then turned and gave him thumbs up.

"This war in Laos is no place to win medals. The North Vietnamese and Pathet Lao are kicking the shit out of these guys, and we're just dicking around while they do. Come on, Jack. Let's get back in it." I heard him on the radio and could see his mouth moving under the dark green Plexiglas eye shield on his helmet.

Gearheardt and I had been best friends since flight school. He was a great pilot and a wonderful friend except for his habit of getting us into situations where people were trying to kill us. Besides flying, he loved drinking and whores.

"People think whores are mean, Jack. These girls don't have a mean bone in their bodies," he said.

I sat looking over at him in his cockpit. I felt protected by him, and protective of him. I knew he would give his life to save mine. There were times when I hated him for it.

"When we go to Hong Kong, we can talk about it, Gearheardt. If the Cuban is in Hong Kong, we'll see what we can do. That's the best I can promise."

"You're a champ, Jack. A champ. Wait until you hear the rest of my plan."

I saw the dirt begin to swirl around his helicopter, and he slowly rose, swung the nose of the aircraft around into the wind, then lifted rapidly out of the refueling pits and was gone.

This war *was* sad. The "war junior," Gearheardt called it. A "back fire" to the Vietnam War, fattening up the local populace so that we could feed them to the forty or fifty thousand North Vietnamese troops pushing south through the territory. If we won the war in Vietnam, this place-holding action would deliver a free Laos to the survivors. If we didn't, well, as Gearheardt put it, "They're fucked."

I lifted off and banked low over the command bunker so the customer would know that I was back hard at work even if he wasn't monitoring the radio traffic. I climbed into the cool, fresh sky, circling twice above the airstrip so that I wouldn't pass over the jungle at an altitude tempting for the North Vietnamese machine gunners. A gorgeous day, and the miles of green jungle, punctured by rocky karsts and etched with muddy rivers, stretched languidly in all directions. Full of people ready to shoot me.

At five thousand feet, I could see over into North Vietnam. It seemed crazy that not long before, I had been there.

2 · Hong Kong Hilton No Women in Room

Gearheardt and I made it to Hong Kong. A good thing about flying for Air America was that you only had to dash recklessly around Laos for a couple of weeks a month and then you could go just about any place you wanted if you were still alive. Even Gearheardt grudgingly admitted that was a better deal than the Marine Corps gave us.

On the way over to Hong Kong on Thai Airlines, Gearheardt told me his plan to find an Englishman and through him find Juanton, the murdering bastard Cuban we met in Hanoi who worked for a British beer company.

"I hate to point out to you, Gearheardt, that Hong Kong is full of Englishmen."

"That should make it easy to find one, Jack. You always look at the negative side of things."

"Not all of them are turncoat British agents though."

"Who says?"

Beneath us the hills of Vietnam were full of death, fighting, and skull-cracking boredom. In the first-class cabin the men in suits dozed or ordered refills of their scotch and waters. Ahead of the wing the coast of Vietnam was visible as the Thai Air crew overflew the

Danang, South Vietnam TACAN and turned slightly more northeast toward Hong Kong. Far below and just behind us, in the stumpy hills west of Danang, the sun caught the wing of an aircraft climbing out of a bombing run, and I saw the black and brown cloud rise up behind him. Gearheardt was entertaining the little Thai stewardess by having her guess how much his Air America gold bracelet cost. When she left to refill his beer glass, Gearheardt spoke.

"So you agree with the plan, Jack? We find us an Englishman and hang out with him. We'll tell him enough to get him spooked, and when British Intelligence hears about two American spies—"

"We're not spies, Gearheardt."

"—hanging around Hong Kong after being booted out of the Marine Corps, *bam*, they're on us like ducks on a June bug." He slapped his hands together, waking the fat Chinese businessman across the aisle, who glared at us and then closed his eyes again. He had a mole on his chin with a three-inch hair growing out of it. I had stopped Gearheardt from clipping it when the Chinaman first fell asleep.

"And after we get to British Intelligence?" I said, humoring him.

Gearheardt turned to me and squinted.

"Haven't you been listening? Then we use British Intelligence to find Juanton. When we tell them what we know about the commie network in British Intelligence, they'll piss their pants."

"Why don't we just find the British Intelligence Headquarters in Hong Kong and talk to them? Why all this 'finding each other' talk?" I really didn't want to think about all this and was already sorry that I had agreed to go to Hong Kong. Gearheardt's plan—that word again—was asinine.

Gearheardt stopped his drink halfway to his mouth and looked at me. "Jack, sometimes I think you'll never get this spy business." He paused, then went on. "Someone in British Intelligence in Hong Kong is in cahoots with Juanton. That much we know. We walk in there and start blabbing about killing Juanton to the wrong guy and we're in deep shit." He finished his drink.

"I am not *trying* to *get* this spy business, Gearheardt. You told me that Juanton was in Hong Kong. We're headed to Hong Kong. And there is no shit deeper than what you have already gotten me into." I turned back to the window and stared out.

On the night train from Udorn to Bangkok, where we had caught the airplane we were now on, Gearheardt had elaborated on our movements in Hong Kong. His plan actually was much more thought out than I had expected. I always had to remind myself that Gearheardt was no dummy. He just didn't have a lick of subtlety. Everything was black or white and straight ahead.

When I had first questioned him about his attitude, he'd looked genuinely surprised at my lack of understanding. "We're Americans, Jack. And United States Marines." This was just before he told me he was also in the Central Intelligence Agency. Admissions like that, spilled over beer in the Schooner Lounge on Pensacola Beach, weren't particularly troublesome. I didn't believe him until it was too late.

The way he saw it, we had two missions in Hong Kong. First, we needed to find a way to get close to British Intelligence. Someone there had reported to the bureaucrats in Washington that Gearheardt and I had purposely screwed up the mission to stop the war, and now they wouldn't let us fight in Vietnam. Exposing the Brit who was Jaunton's partner would go a long way toward convincing them we were sincere in wanting to succeed in our mission. Then we needed to kill Juanton, a murdering Cuban bastard who delighted in torturing American pilots in Hanoi and thought he had a lock on the beer franchise that was promised to the good Cuban, for helping us. It was complicated.

"See, Jack, we let the Brits think that we're going to kill Juanton."

"We are," I reminded him.

"Sure, but not until we find out who his boss is in British Intelligence."

"So you think they'll try to stop us?"

"Just the one that gives a damn about Juanton. That's how we know. I don't think the other Brits will care one way or another. Brilliant, right?"

I wasn't so sure, but it did seem reasonable.

I dozed off as Gearheardt was trying to talk the giggling stewardesses to get in the airplane's bathroom with him, claiming it would set a world record and make their parents proud. The bump on the runway at Kai Tak, Hong Kong's airport, woke me, and I was glad that no one was shooting at us as we taxied to the terminal. This was better than Laos. Gearheardt and I had three weeks of feasting, womanizing, fooling Brits, and killing Cubans before we were due back in Laos. He was convinced that was plenty of time. As we left the airplane the captain stopped Gearheardt and told him to never get naked on a Thai Airways flight again. I noticed that one of the stewardesses, nervously laughing behind her tiny hand, was wearing Gearheardt's T-shirt under her uniform jacket. Unchagrinned, Gearheardt told him to mind his own business; it was part of the mission.

It was decided on the way in from Kai Tak Airport that we would put off killing Cubans or finding British spies until after we had relaxed for a couple of days. In fact, I wondered aloud if it might be a good idea to put off killing Cubans altogether, since it really wouldn't help us square things with the Marine Corps.

"Short-term thinking, Jack," Gearheardt said as he ignored the NO SMOKING sign in the Hong Kong taxi. "Sure, we could not kill Juanton. But what about the next Marines that go to Hanoi? And the ones after that? We need to stop Juanton now, or the whole Marine Corps could go down one after another, like dominos. Just because you would rather chase whores and drink beer than do your duty. And I'm not saying I blame you."

There were times when Gearheardt was too maddening to argue with and this was one of those times.

We were in the canyons of Kowloon. Five- and six-story grimy concrete buildings sprouting laundry from every orifice. Through barred windows we saw the mothers and fathers of Hong Kong bar women living their lives under single light bulbs, colorful plastic bowls dominating the décor. Then up Nathan Road, a million light bulbs sold things and advertised where to get them.

We took the Star Ferry to Hong Kong. Gearheardt thankfully dozed. He normally tried to start fights with the crew, who for some reason irritated him. It might have been their sailor suits.

Greeted in the lobby of the Hilton and up twenty-four floors to clean and air-conditioned near-home. Through the black windows sin danced in neon below and across the Fragrant Harbor. Gearheardt knocked on my door. "Let's have a drink." He made his eyebrows dance in a comical way. "These countries have turned their daughters into whores in order to get a better life. We can't humiliate them by ignoring them. This is what they invented war for, Jack."

Annie, the mama-san and proprietress of Annie Lee's Bar & Clean Women, greeted us when we came in early in the evening after a dinner at Jimmy's Kitchen.

"Geelhot," she said over the squeals of the bar-girl fans of my friend, "you come sit here."

"Annie, I want beer and I want girls." Gearheardt was a bit testy because Jimmy had removed the pickled onions from our table after Gearheardt peppered nearly everyone in the restaurant with them.

Annie waved to a plain girl standing behind the bar. "Bring two beers Geelhot and Jack, Jiang," she said.

The plain girl, Jiang, was Annie's sister. Annie had been trying to snag Gearheardt for her sister ever since the first time that he stumbled into Annie Lee's Bar & Clean Women. He had learned to say, 'I need beer and woman' in passable Cantonese. Standing in the door, bruised, near naked, and bleeding from a heated discussion with members of the British Navy, Gearheardt yelled his only Cantonese and caused the bar women to immediately fall in love with him, particularly Annie's shy younger sister, Jiang.

Now, Annie was saying, "My sister you know, Geelhot. Jiang bring you beer all time." She seemed to be trying to read Gearheardt's facial expression. Jiang, having what he called "your little brother's chest," was not going to be snagging the Gearheardt I knew.

"You leave bar-girl alone tonight, Geelhot." Annie pulled up on her sister's shoulders, straightening her stoop slightly. They left, Annie tucking in the back of Jiang's blouse as they walked away.

Gearheardt waved to the covey of young girls sitting in the back booth. Two of them jumped up, but I waved them back down. Their little doll faces frowned.

"Hold off on the entertainment for a minute, Gearheardt." I had been wanting to talk to Gearheardt for the past two days. About what we hoped to accomplish in Hong Kong. When we talked about it in Laos it seemed simple, probably because we wanted an excuse to be in Hong Kong. Now, there were a few troubling aspects.

"Gearheardt, let's say we find Juanton . . ."

"The asshole."

"Yes, but let's say we find him. Do we just shoot him? That didn't work very well in Hanoi. Maybe we should have a clear plan."

Gearheardt finished his beer and smiled at Jiang for another.

"The Brits will lead us to him if he's in Hong Kong, Jack. Then we beat the shit out of him. Then we frog march him into the U.S. embassy and get him to tell the military attaché and the ambassador that we did *not* sell out in Hanoi. Then we take him outside and shoot him." He paused as the beer was delivered, then watched Jiang walk away. "You know, that Jiang actually has a pretty nice butt."

"Here's the problem with your plan," I said.

Gearheardt rolled his eyes.

"No, *listen,* you bastard. *Your* plan for flying to the Moon would be to build an antigravitational device and then fly it there!"

"Sounds like it might work," Gearheardt said absently as he made faces at the bar-girl covey.

"But the *point* is that no one knows how . . . Oh skip it. What do you plan to tell the attaché is the reason that we didn't kill Hoche or the Jeepster? Has that detail of squaring ourselves occurred to you?"

Gearheardt looked at me and seemed sober. "Jack, these dickheads in the embassy won't even *know* what our mission was. We just need them to hear Juanton admit that we didn't sell out the U.S."

He slammed his hands onto the table. "Dammit, I've talked long enough." About three minutes. "I'm getting the girls over here." He grinned in the direction of the back booth and four squealing girls attached themselves to him like nurse fish on a shark. I saw Annie give a dark look at our table.

"Do you girls know how to play Find Stumpy?" Gearheardt asked as the women nestled around him.

Annie looked at Gearheardt and raised a cautioning finger. "You wait one minute. Jiang bring you one more beer you wait."

Gearheardt smiled at Jiang who sat the beer in front of him without raising her eyes. "I need a little excitement," he said. "Got to get my mind off our troubles before we get those British Intelligence folks on our case."

"Gearheardt, you've run fifteen or twenty women through the Hilton, fought with the British Navy, again, and lowered the beer level on Hong Kong Island by fifty percent. Why don't you just take it easy?"

"I know you disapprove of all the women, Jack. But how else will we find out who wears black panties? Research has always been your weak point."

"My weak point has always been feeling like you might know what you're doing and helping you do it. So far, a major weak point. But for some reason I feel the need to protect you in your various missions."

"And don't think I don't appreciate it, Jack. Whatever it is you're talking about. But don't duck the black panties initiative that I seem to be the only one worrying about."

Gearheardt was convinced that Juanton, our nemesis in Hanoi, and his "control" agent in Hong Kong had used black panties as a way to pass messages. Which, according to Gearheardt, meant that Juanton's British contact was either a woman or a male agent who enjoyed wearing black silk women's underwear.

"That eliminates not quite half of the agents in Hong Kong, Jack."

I didn't argue the ridiculous point. Certainly Juanton, the Cuban asshole, must have had a reason to have a drawer full of women's black panties. And we were dead certain that Juanton passed the word to British Intelligence that Gearheardt and I didn't complete our mission in Hanoi because we had been bought off. After that was reported to the CIA and the Marine Corps, Gearheardt and I were brought up on charges so detailed that we knew we had been screwed by the Cuban.

Charge Number Four, Joint USMC/CIA Code of Conduct for Agents DDCIA/ACDC:
Causing with deliberate intent the mastication of testicles belonging to an officer in the Armed Forces of a Country which the United States is not currently attacking with Malice. [Sub-Reference: DDMC 227— Masturbation, malicious]

"See, she goes up there, the message hidden—no, *sewn* into her pants. Maybe even woven into the lace pattern. He yanks off her panties, no one's the wiser."

"You're amazing, Gearheardt." I rubbed my eyes, wishing I were not in the smoke-filled Annie Lee Bar with a lunatic. Half hoping that Juanton was not even in town and that we could just drink and find bar-girls and then go back to Laos.

In the early morning hours of the third night, I woke up in a panic. I had been dreaming that I was drifting through a watery space. Everything I approached shoved me back. I couldn't touch bottom, but I wasn't sinking. I was taking an oath to support the mission of the Central Intelligence Agency in a bar on Santa Rosa Beach.

The sun began lighting the room, and I moved to the window. Hong Kong squatted beneath, head in hand, saying "Oh shit." Its hair was matted and its breath was foul. I remembered that Gearheardt had talked me into drinking harbor water and bourbon as a sign of brotherhood with the town when we were floating with bar-women in the little walla-walla he had commandeered. Just before the Harbor Police gave us a stern warning in Chinese.

In my skivvies I walked down the hall to Gearheardt's room and pounded on the door until I realized it was unlocked. Gearheardt had a fear of being in a locked room.

"Damn it, Gearheardt," I said, leaning over his bed and grabbing him by his shoulders, "what was that you told me last night about the CIA? How in the hell did you ever convince me I was in the CIA?"

"Who are you?" Gearheardt groaned. He turned face down into the pillow.

I clicked on the lamp. Two naked Chinese women sat huddled together against the king-sized headboard.

I began pummeling Gearheardt's back, my voice breaking with emotion.

"How do you always get us into this crap? Why do I always listen to you?"

Gearheardt turned his head and opened one eye. Drool ran out of his mouth and puddled on the pillow. He squinted up at me.

"Am I dead?" he asked. "Are you the devil?"

I slumped on the floor, exhausted by the dream, the hangover, the frustration of having lost my commission in the Marine Corps, and a feeling of failure. Why hadn't I shot Ho Chi Minh? At the bottom of all of my dreams, the question was there.

One of the Chinese women ventured a peek at me.

"You devil?" she asked, peering over the edge of the bed. The other Chinese head appeared beside her. They had evidently slipped to the floor when I was pounding on Gearheardt.

I didn't want to go back to my room, so the Chinese women and I played poker. We sat at the table, me in my skivvies and the Chinese women naked. They were terrible poker players but seemed to enjoy the game, giggling and screaming shrilly each time they lost a hand, which was fairly often since they didn't know the numbers from bird doo.

Gearheardt rolled over near nine o'clock in the morning. He rubbed his eyes like a small child.

"Were you in here last night when some maniac tried to beat the crap out of me while I was asleep?" He reached under the covers and pulled out a beer bottle, holding it up to the light to see if was empty.

"I took care of him," I said. The Chinese women giggled again, and I wondered how much they understood. "It was just the room service guy. Some joker ordered an early morning beat-up. You know how the service is in these hotels. They don't question a damn thing that foreigners ask for. I'll speak to the manager and make sure it doesn't show up on your bill."

The Chinese women were gathering their clothing. Gearheardt sucked again on the empty beer bottle and nodded toward them. "They with you?"

"Have you ever known me to travel without a couple of naked Chinese women, Gearheardt? Of course they're not with me. They were in your bed when I came in here last night."

"It was you beating on me and yelling, wasn't it?"

"Of course it was. I need to talk to you." I paused and indicated the women, dressed and waiting. "Do you owe these ladies money?"

"You mean these women are prostitutes?" Gearheardt almost sounded genuinely distressed. "My God, what have I done?" He pulled the covers over his head.

"It won't work, Gearheardt. I won't have you stiffing these women."

"A tad late for those sentiments, Jack. If you'll forgive the pun. Give them that bowl of fruit the manager sent up."

I shrugged and handed it to the women, who seemed pleased.

"Hell, give them the towels too. I can get more."

The women left with the fruit, the towels, the stationery, the pen, the Gideons Bible, the alarm clock, the telephone book, and, unbeknownst to us at the time, Gearheardt's shaving gear.

"So what is it that you want to know, Jack? You're not the kind of guy that pounds people who are sleeping with two Chinese women."

I stood next to his window and looked below at the grass tennis courts and gardens. Very English.

"I want to know about the CIA, Gearheardt. You talk about them all the time. You claim that we're both part of the CIA. What the hell are you talking about?"

"What difference does it make, Jack? You know that Air America is owned by the CIA, right?"

"I thought that you told me a Texas construction company owned it. But I'm not talking about now, anyway. I'm talking about when we were in Hanoi trying to stop the war."

"I think we should worry more about finding that damn Juanton and taking care of him. Worrying about the CIA is wasting time. It's like worrying about being a Baptist. It's either in your heart or not. What difference does it make who starts wars? People who need a war start wars. It's more a budgeting matter, really. No war, no CIA. No CIA and you've got assassins selling cars down at Bertram Lincoln Mercury just outside of Cleveland. Would you want to buy a car from a guy that would rather be working on the overthrow of some African country?"

"I won't know until you tell me, Gearheardt. You claim you're CIA and that you swore me in, so now I'm CIA. I don't think you can do that."

I turned toward him and found that he had been watching television while he was talking to me, the sound off.

"Damn it, Gearheardt. I can't figure out whether I did what I was supposed to do in Hanoi. It's important to me. Can't you see that?"

Gearheardt came off the bed and stood beside me, gazing out at the gray day, the mist obscuring most of Hong Kong Harbor. Boats appeared from the fog like magic tricks.

"They came to the orphanage after me," he said. "I was the scrawniest kid there. No future. My parents both mad at me. I guess that's why I was such an easy target for the agency. You know which agency I'm talking about, don't you, Jack?" He looked at me.

"Well, since we've been talking about the Central Intelligence Agency for the past five minutes I could take a wild guess. Don't go spooky on me, Gearheardt."

"You're close," he said. "This was an auxiliary organization at the time, just for kids. I didn't get into the real thing until I got into the Marine Corps and flight school. Just before I swore you in."

"I'm not sure most people are aware there is such a thing as a CIA kids' group," I said, reining in my sarcasm. I wanted him to go on.

"It doesn't exist anymore. Not with a Democrat in the White House. Funding was cut way back, and none of the kids could afford their own weapon. And there was a movement to let girls join. They finally just took the kids with a lot of promise and folded them into the senior agency. Luckily, I was one of them, or I'd still be at the orphanage." He shuddered and I didn't know if it was from the chill of the air conditioner—Gearheardt had only the shower curtain wrapped around him—or the thought of being left in the orphanage. "But what does that have to do with anything?"

"Gearheardt," I said, turning to face him as he lay back on his bed, "I would just like to know . . . Why in hell were you in the orphanage? Didn't you just say you had parents?"

"My parents were pessimists, Jack. Didn't think they'd live from day to day. Still don't. They were just being precautious. I'd rather not talk about it. Unless *you* want to." He poked through the ashtray looking for a lightable butt.

"My mother always told me never to think bad thoughts, because they would come true if you believed them," he said. "She was right, I guess." He flicked his flame-thrower lighter.

"She didn't know how to fry chicken like your mother, Jack. That's the difference."

"You're full of crap, Gearheardt."

He smiled and licked a finger and ran it over his singed eyebrow.

"What I want to know," I continued, "is how the CIA influenced our mission to Hanoi. Thinking back, if it hadn't been for that cockamamie story you gave me about them, we might have accomplished what we went to Hanoi to do."

A knock on the door stopped his answer. He opened it to the two Chinese women, who grinned at us over a pushcart. They took the desk chair, the bedclothes, paintings from the walls, the lamp, the nightstand, and Gearheardt's elephant-skin wallet, although, again, we didn't find that out until much later.

"I can't help it, I like enterprising women, Jack. They see an opening and they go for it."

"The hotel will make you pay for all the stuff that's missing. You know that, don't you?"

"Think how much fun it will be arguing with them, though. First, I'll deny it's gone. Then I'll claim that the maid took it. Then they'll have to raise the uncomfortable issue of perhaps there were whores in the room. And you know the Hong Kong Hilton rules, Jack. No women in room. Presumptuous little bastards. As if having women in your room meant you were screwing them or something. I'll claim they were my wife, by God. I'll . . ."

"Save your ravings for the manager. What *about* the CIA? You told me they gave us a chance to be Kings of the Universe. Why didn't they want us to complete the mission? What the President had sent us to do."

Gearheardt sat cross-legged on the mattress in the center of the denuded hotel room. "Who's Tom Dexter, Jack?"

I didn't change expression, refusing to get drawn into his game.

"Tom Dexter is the other you, isn't it, Jack? The you that can do things that Jack Armstrong can't do. Isn't that right? That's why the CIA was involved. So that we could do stuff that Marines couldn't do. Sometimes we have conflicting missions."

"Why don't they just do a little bit of coordination, for God's sake?"

Gearheardt smiled. "Well, we'd all be CIA then, wouldn't we?"

"But the other *us* stopped us from doing what *we* needed, were ordered to do," I said, realizing as I did that Gearheardt had won again.

"That was their job, Jack," Gearheardt said. "Now let's go find something to drink. Maybe today we'll find a Brit." He swung his legs off the bed and began singing "Gonna kill me a Cuban, Gonna shoot him by seven" to the tune of "Got a Date with an Angel."

Of course we didn't find the Cuban or a British spy to speak of. After a week or so of drinking and lecturing bar-women on politics—*"These girls have the right to know the politics of people screwing them, Jack"*—we flew back to Thailand and stayed in Bangkok before heading back up country where Air America awaited our expertise in moving stuff around Laos without looking like we were combatants. Never mind the occasional round through the forehead. I think I knew, flying out of Hong Kong, that we had only been trying to delay realizing the inevitable. We had failed in our mission for the Marine Corps and would fly for Air America in Laos until death or worse.

I had had Ho Chi Minh in my sights, slumped dead drunk in the driver's seat of his Corvette, and I hadn't pulled the trigger. With the leadership of the North Vietnamese army held at bay by the swinging breasts of an American movie star, I'd had the perfect opportunity to do more than my duty, and I hadn't done it. How many men had lost their lives in the war because I couldn't pull the trigger?

Probably plenty, according to the Thai psychiatrist that I sometimes visited in Bangkok when depression kept me out of the bars and massage parlors. My question to the psychiatrist—the cheapest in Bangkok according to the sandwich board on the sidewalk—had been, "Is it only because we don't have a real plan that I don't want to go back to Vietnam?"

"How should I know?" the doctor had answered.

I started seeing a Thai psychiatrist because I didn't like whores. Actually I did *like* them. I just didn't like sleeping with them. Centuries ago, before I left the U.S. for the war, I had been dating Mickey Mouse. Not actually the mouse himself but a girl who wore the outfit at Disneyland. Gearheardt thought that was why I didn't like sleeping with whores. Not that I had been going with someone, but because it was Mickey Mouse, a symbol of something in America. I tried to explain it to the Thai doctor, but it was confusing to him, he said, and it gave him a headache. It was comforting that the psychiatrist's English was poor, and he had an office that was air-conditioned.

"I don't know if I chickened out because I was scared or because I truly didn't think that it was morally right to kill Ho Chi Minh in cold blood when he was drunk," I told him.

"No like chicken." Dr. Boon leaned back in his chair and templed his fingers under his chin. His hands were tiny, and he wore thick gold bracelets on both wrists. Above the door I could see a tiny, gaily festooned Buddhist shrine. On the wall underneath, a framed picture of the King and Queen and beside that a sign for Hires Root Beer. Although I couldn't see it from where I lay, I knew a black and white photo of Dr. Boon holding a skinned cobra, dripping its blood into a glass, hung next to that. It was my favorite.

"Chicken is a term that we use for cowards, you know, like 'not brave.' I mean maybe I wasn't brave enough to do my duty," I explained, not wanting him to think I was crazy.

"Gearheardt say maybe you scare whore. Too much hair. But Thai women—"

"You've been talking to Gearheardt?" I swung my legs to the floor and faced him.

"Gearheardt your good friend. He says you go back Vietnam, everything okay. I fix you pretty soon so you go back."

Dr. Boon's wife smiled up at me from where she sat cross-legged on her mat. She attended all of my sessions and seemed to add an air of domesticity lacking in U.S. medicine. If she had not been Dr. Boon's wife, I might have suspected that Dr. Boon was gay. Every session at some point drifted back to the size of the American penis. An embarrassment in the first session, but Dr. Boon assured me that his wife spoke no English. She was pretty, petite, and always smelled clean.

"Chicken man have no penis, but American man have very large penis, right? Maybe this why you think that North Vietnam Army always no like you."

I sank back on Dr. Boon's hand-tooled almost-leather couch and closed my eyes, wondering if there was a universe somewhere where that made sense. I wished I was there. I felt Dr. Boon's wife remove my shoes and then begin fumbling with my belt. At the end of each psychiatric session she always gave me a bath and massage. Or if she were too busy, she had one of the girls from the massage parlor downstairs come up and do it. After the first time—when I threatened to kill him—Dr. Boon had not tried to get into the bathtub with me. The warm bath and ensuing massage gave each session another element sorely lacking in American mental health treatment. It could be quite nice in that bathtub, being scrubbed by the lovely Mrs. Boon.

It made perfect sense for Dr. Sipsep (Boon) Kulichingchorn to have his office in the Suriwong Hotel, a combination massage parlor and brothel just a block off of Pat Pong Road in Bangkok. On one of my first forays into the enticing cesspools of Bangkok, after Gearheardt and I had been kicked out of the Marine Corps and indentured to Air America, I had stumbled over the sidewalk sign advertising CHEAP PSYCHIATRY HELP YOU. Who could resist?

"I see men all time," he told me later. "They all time dirty or want have sex. I help them. They pay me. Never mind."

His wife, although I did not know she was his wife at the time, was giving me a premassage bath when he slipped into the small, tiled room at the Suriwong.

"You want psychiatly man, chi mai?" he asked. "That me. Dr. Boon Kulichingchorn. Cheapest psychiatly man in Bangkok." He showed most of his teeth and I relaxed. I didn't like having people join me in the bath facilities when women were scrubbing me. But this gentleman seemed comfortable. He was a professional, after all.

"Who told you I wanted a psychiatrist—a psychiatry man?"

"My wife. She say you crazy as loon."

The slight fellow with spotless white shirt loose over gray slacks gestured with a dainty hand, a small fake gold Rolex hanging loosely at his wrist, toward the woman kneeling at the side of my tub. "My wife. She scrub you bath."

I sat up in the water smartly, bringing up a knee to discourage any localized scrubbing activity. "Your wife? This is your wife?" I might have added "whose small perfect breasts are exposed."

"Also nurse and selling man. For psychiatly business."

"Wait. Your wife, who is scrubbing—anyway, she is your salesman for your medical practice? Psychiatry business."

I motioned his wife to bring a towel. She rose and fastened her one-piece cotton wrap, which had somehow come unwrapped. I looked at the doctor.

"Yes, yes. That right. You come lay down new almost-leather couch-bed. I fix you pretty good."

Dr. Boon's wife had pulled the plug in the bathtub when she rose and the empty tub left me cold and naked. Feeling foolish.

"My wife, she office. You come and she towel you." He turned to the door while I searched for my clothes. As usual, they had been sent out to be washed and pressed while I was not needing them. I stepped out of the tub, picking up a magazine that lay on the small table along with various massage oils and powder. The magazine had the graceful flowing complexity of the Thai language on the front and photographs of young Thai women who seemed to have been dressed by the Mad People of Paris. Thai girls loved the latest fashions but never knew when they were being misled by hunger-crazed hermaphrodites.

Holding the Thai version of *Seventeen* in front of me, I followed Dr. Boon down the hall to his office, past a small replica of a Buddhist temple over the Thai-height door, banging my head as I walked in. The almost-leather couch was cold, but as soon as I lay down, the petite and freshly aromatic Mrs. Boon appeared with a warm towel and dried, then covered me. From below, the sounds of an early afternoon bar carried laughter and mellow good cheer to the office. For no good reason, I began to feel sad.

Dr. Boon noticed and leaned forward in his chair. He brought his small hands in front of his face, resting his elbows on skinny knees.

"Is guilty complexion," he said. "You think you hot-ass pilot who can win war. Now you are guilty you cannot."

"Hot-ass," I said. "Is that a medical term?"

"It mean—"

"I know what you meant, Doc."

He grinned, then became serious again. He reassumed his listening intently mode.

I continued, "But you think that I am so depressed because I have a guilt thing? Like a survivor's complex? Is that what you're getting at?" Without real logic, the men who came back could not shake the irrational feeling that they had not done their best, and if they had . . .

"I saying many people die America go Vietnam. Many baby and mother burn and blow up. People have no eye and no arm."

I did not have a great deal of experience with psychiatry, but I was pretty sure there was a method more reassuring than this. My chest grew heavy and a tear escaped my eye and rolled slowly down my cheek.

The doctor began to cry also. "I make you feel bad, Jack. I shitty doctor."

I wanted to comfort him, but I felt too depressed, and he *was* a shitty doctor.

"Jack, you tell me. You tell me story. Then you feel better. I feel better too."

He rested his hand lightly on my shoulder.

"You number one, Jack. Never mind bad luck. You number one. Now you tell me story and I fix wagon."

He smiled now and I felt worse that I needed reassurance from a pidgin-speaking, correspondence-school psychiatrist in an office above a whorehouse on Pat Pong.

I sighed, deciding to not hold back.

"It was Gearheardt. Without him, this wouldn't have happened."

I opened my eyes and looked at the doctor.

"Don't get me wrong, Doc. Gearheardt got me through the worst of it. He's a champ. He's . . . golden."

The doctor sat silent for a moment.

"He same same you, Jack. Gearheardt same same you."

"I know. Great guy. He'd do anything for me." Same same could mean anything from "similar" to "I can't tell you round-eyes apart."

"You sad man, Jack. Geelhot he afraid he make trouble you. You tell me, Jack. You tell me. I fix—not so sad. Okay, Jack?"

His delicate brown face was like a child's, and I did not admonish him for talking to Gearheardt about me once again.

Mrs. Boon knelt at the end of the almost-leather couch and began massaging my feet. Her touch was as lovely and gentle as her smile.

"I guess you might say that Gearheardt did make trouble me, Doc. I don't blame him or anything. He is my best pal. Good guy, you know. Very good guy. Golden."

Mrs. Boon was now massaging my calves. I shivered slightly in the air conditioning; the damp towel covering only a small part of me.

"You tell me, Jack."

It was really quite peaceful in that room. The smell of the new almost-leather, the not-yet-beer-fueled sounds of the bathhouse. Incense burning, pungent and silent.

The now-to-the-knees tender touch of the lovely Mrs. Boon began to loosen my tongue. The story began almost reverently. Love for my country, the Marine Corps. It filled and drew. Images that I wasn't aware that I could create. I felt myself shrinking as dams broke. I extruded and gushed. The sun climbed the wall behind the almost-leather couch of Dr. Boon, cheap psychiatly man extraordinaire.

The flotsam and jetsam of wars and whores rose and spilled onto Dr. Boon's cheap oriental carpet. Hanoi and napalm and the care and cleaning of helicopter rotor blades. Directive 22-7G. The one that directed the pilots to wear camouflage face-paint. (The enemy was never totally convinced that bushes or trees were flying the aircraft.) The dead and the misled, the underfed. Politicians. Morticians. Hits and shits, near-misses, pants pisses, blood, mud, oh fuck, Duck! Oh, my God!

The good doctor sobbed into his hands. The sensual Mrs. Boon buried her face into my towel. A number of the idle masseuses, who had drifted into the room to see the naked American pilot blabbering on about the war and the politicians, held their tiny hands to their mouths, their eyes wide amidst cheap makeup.

My first meaningful session on the couch had most of the brothel staff morose and sniffling in the late afternoon darkness. Beneath us, a Thai band began singing "Raidy Macdonna."

And I hadn't even gotten to the part where Gearheardt and I tried to stop the war!

After that, the sessions seemed to end with Dr. Boon *and* Mrs. Boon crying. The masseuses all watched me get bathed. I didn't even bother to hold the magazine in front of me when I walked from the scrubbing room to his office. Being naked in a Thai massage parlor didn't seem to alarm anyone. And my shame was internal, anyway.

"You no cry long time, Jack," Dr. Boon said as I walked back into his office, trailed by the naked women. (I had made a rule that the women could watch me bathe if they were naked too.) "You tell me story how Geelhot and Jack fuck up."

That stopped me in the doorway and I teared up. Which caused the good doctor and his wife to begin blubbering in earnest. Was I personally creating mass depression in the entire damn Asian theater?

I sat back down, lit a cigarette, and sighed. Then I told him the story. Even the parts that I had to piece together from Gearheardt's tall tales and drunken ravings. How he personally knew the President, for example, and had been there when the war was cooked up.

PART 2

There is no class of people so hard to manage . . . as those whose intentions are honest, but whose consciences are bewitched.

—Napoleon

Never interrupt your enemy when he is making a mistake.

—Napoleon

Here I come to save the day!

—Mighty Mouse

3 · The War Begins
(Cue War Drums)

I *had CIA pizza duty, Jack. They don't let freckle-faced teenagers de-*
liver pizza to the White House, you know. All CIA and FBI, except
that most of the kitchen help at Pizza Joe's were ex-KGB defectors. I
never trusted them," Gearheardt said.

"I was just minding my own business, slicing and pouring, when the
President started whining and complaining to the guys in the room.
Mostly military."

In the Oval Office there were the President, three of his aides,
the Joint Chiefs of Staff, Army, Navy, Air Force, and Marines, and
an Asian guy in a white coat. The President was in his shirt sleeves,
slouching in an easy chair. His aides were behind him, all in dark
suits, perched on the edge of their straight-backed chairs. There
weren't enough places to sit where the President could see you, so
it was kind of musical chairs. If one general got up to make a
point, another general would slide into his seat. The President
looked harassed and tired. He was talking to no one in particular
about his worry that the American people might think he was a
candy-ass.

As the pepperoni was being sliced the President was saying. . . .

———

". . . so everyone thinks I'm just a baggy-assed liberal with all this Great Society horse hockey. I asked you boys to find me a war to run and you ain't found shit."

"Well, sir, we've had some boys poking around in Vietnam for years now as advisers, but they haven't seemed to stir anything up." This from the Army chief of staff.

"I could bomb Naples, sir," the chief of staff of the Air Force said brightly. "I was there in the big one, and the Italians couldn't fight worth a damn."

"Well, that'd be great, General. I kind of had in mind somebody that we could think of some damned reason for bombing. Last I heard Italy wasn't pissing in our mess kit. Ain't there anybody that nobody likes?"

"I meant because of the Mafia thing, Mr. President," the Air Force general said.

The President glared at him and then began pinching his large nose.

The room was silent. Chins were rubbed. Noses stealthily picked. Space stared into.

Finally the Marine commandant spoke up. "What about the queers, sir? We could sure as. . . ."

"For chrissakes, General, what is this fixation you got with queers? Hell, half the damn Navy is queer and you don't see us bombing them."

"With your permission, sir, I could get that started within . . ." the Marine began enthusiastically.

"With all due respect, Mr. President." The Navy chief was on his feet. His seat was immediately taken by the Army chief, who beamed around the room as if he had accomplished a coup. "I deeply resent the implication of your remark about the naval services."

The President waved him down, which unfortunately was onto the lap of the Army chief, who dumped him onto the floor.

"Oh, hell, Sparky, don't get yore dander up. I wuz just kiddin'. You gotta throw the jarheads a bone every once in a while 'fore they get restless on the reservation. Heh, heh." He looked back at his aides, who all went 'Heh, heh'.

The room fell silent again. The President turned to his aides again. He rolled his eyes and shrugged. The aides rolled their eyes and shrugged.

"Anybody want another slice of the mushrooms and peppers?" asked Gearheardt.

"Who the hell are you?" the President demanded.

"CIA pizza man," his top aide responded before Gearheardt could speak.

Everyone ate in silence while Gearheardt busied himself gathering crusts and pouring soft drinks.

Finally the Army chief, now standing—forgetting he would lose his seat—spoke. "Sir, since we already have people in Vietnam, perhaps we should explore that possibility further. The previous President evidently thought the situation there might be exploited if his campaign needed it."

The commandant joined in. "Yessir, maybe the Navy could go over and do that amphibious assault they're so famous for." He giggled into his hand and elbowed the Air Force chief on his left. "Get it, amphibious assault?"

"It doesn't mean what you evidently think it means, you nincompoop," the Air Force general replied without looking at him.

The admiral glared at the commandant, while everyone else seemed to be trying to think of something wise to say to the President.

The Army chief continued. "Maybe we could provoke them if we were to escalate our activity. At the moment we are only acting as advisers in non-combat roles"—all of the military people and Gearheardt laughed—"but we could maybe violate the Geneva Accord that we worked out in Laos. This could destabilize the political situation in the theater and introduce an element of counter-counterbalance whereby the communists would be forced to react with conciliatory gestures or admit to their own hegemony and escalate their own violations of the

Accord. Under each scenario we could sneak in a couple of quick bombing missions and just see what develops."

The President could be heard muttering under his breath something about shutting down the "goddam War College." To the Army chief he said, "Tom, I get that kind of bullshit advice about every three seconds from those idiots over at the State Department. I don't need to hear it from the soldier boys."

The Army chief's uniform suddenly became three sizes too big. He squatted behind the couch, a tear running down his face. He did have the presence of mind to later put out a memo changing his name to Tom.

Just when the entire group was beginning to mentally review their retirement options, the President looked up from his pizza. A string of cheese stretched from his chin back to his plate.

"Where is this Veetnam deal, anyway?" he asked.

"It's in Asia, sir," the Army chief called from behind the couch, a note of hope in his voice.

The President half rose from his chair, startling his aides, who half rose from their chairs, and then dropped back.

"You mean *Chinkville?* Holy shit and firewater, General. Are you suggesting that we actually *try* to piss off about eleventy zillion *Chinks?*"

He looked at his aides and again rolled his eyes. In a stage whisper he said to them, "These boys could get us in reeeel trouble."

Gearheardt noticed that by this time the Asian in the white mess jacket had seated himself behind the President's desk. His feet were propped up on the desk and he was mumbling into the phone something about relatives in Manila.

"Well, technically, sir, I believe a Chink is a Chinese. Although these people are similar in some ways, I've heard they are not actually Chinese, nor are they any great friends of the Chinese." This from the Navy chief. He frowned at the Asian mess boy and motioned silently, with a jerk of his head, for him to take his feet off the President's desk.

"Well if they ain't Chinks, what are they? They got to be something besides normal folks. I ain't stupid enough to get us into no war with normal folks, look like us. Can you imagine me goin' on TV and announcing about how many normal folks we dinged? Shitfire, I couldn't carry the damn pro-Nazi precincts in Chicago."

"I think, Mr. President," the Army chief said, "that they call themselves the Viet Men or the Viet Cong."

The President beamed and slammed his giant hands on the arms of his chair.

"Ookaaay," he said. "Maybe we got ourselves somethin' here. Viet Cong, eh?"

He deepened his voice. "I would like to announce to my fellow Americans that today in Veetnam our gallant troops dinged thirty-five or so thousand Viet Congs." He smiled. "That works," he said in his normal voice. "How many of these Congs are there? Who supports them? Anybody big?"

The Marine and Air Force generals shrugged their shoulders. But the Army general came around the corner of the couch with a spring in his step. "I could ask around, Mr. President. We've had advisers over there for years. Maybe one of them knows something about the country."

"Well, that'd be nice, General. Why don't you scoot on back to the Penteegon and *ask around*. Maybe you could put a note on the bulletin board in the lunch room."

The Army chief made ready to leave. He was pouting again as the President's sarcasm sunk in. He deliberately stepped on the well-shined shoes of the Marine commandant, then saluted and headed for the door.

"Why don't you take this dang boy usin' my phone on back with you?" the President said loudly.

The Army chief stopped and squinted at the mess boy and then looked at the President. "Sir, he's not mine. We have blacks. The Navy has the Filipinos." He left.

The Navy chief leaned forward toward the President. "Sir," he said, "I've got maps and charts over in my office that I could have sent over. The Navy is already patrolling the Gulf of Tonkin."

"The Gulf of which-many?" the President asked.

"Tonkin, sir. It's the body of water off the coast of North Vietnam."

The President's face became suspicious. He narrowed his eyes and glanced at his aides, who all narrowed their eyes too. Then he looked back at the admiral, who was beginning to recoil from the President.

"*North* Veetnam? How many Veetnams are there in this deal, anyway?"

"Just the North and South, Mr. President. You see, after the French defeat at Dien Bien Phu, the Nationalist Vietnamese—"

The President held his palm toward the admiral.

"Spare me the details. I remember this deal now. Damn French sons-a-bitches. Boy, talk about givin' the West a black eye. Are you telling me these are the same guys, these Veet Congs, that I wouldn't let old Baldy nuke a few years ago, when the Frogs got their asses kicked?"

Hearing the word "nuke," the Air Force chief woke up. "Just give me the time and coordinates, sir. I'll have nukes on target in—"

"Calm down, boys. I'm trying to get me some basic info from Sparky here. So, tell me, Admiral, are we for the North or the South?"

"Basically the South, sir. And as to allies, the North Vietnamese pretty well rely on the Russians—"

"I hate those bastards," the President interjected grumpily.

"—for all their military supplies. And the North Vietnamese leader is a man called Ho Chi Minh."

The President's eyes bugged out and he laughed. Then everybody laughed.

"Ho Chee, huh? Well we might have a few surprises for Mr. Ho Chee Cheezit."

Everyone laughed again.

"Who we got leadin' our side? The non-Congs?"

"Sir, a man named Diem or something like that was the leader," the Navy man said.

"Damn? We support someone named *'Damn'*? You know, it's no wonder these countries never get somewheres. What if my name was 'Hell' or 'Shit' or somethin'? I'd still be down in the boondocks shovelin' out the chicken coop."

"Diem, sir," the admiral said softly. "And he's not the real leader right now."

"And why's that, smart boy?"

"He's mostly dead now, sir." He paused and looked around the room at the other chiefs, all avoiding eye contact. "But we didn't kill him, sir."

The President narrowed his eyes and frowned, squinting at the admiral.

The admiral gave a very slight nod of his head and rolled his eyes toward Gearheardt.

"Oh," said the President. "Admiral, why don't you navigate your way over to your poopdeck and get those maps."

"Sir, I could ask—"

"Shake a leg, Sparky. I'm on a roll here."

The admiral rose from the couch and placed his hat on the seat, hoping it would save it for him. He went to the door and hissed at the Asian mess boy, who dropped the President's phone, slowly got up, and followed the Navy chief through the door.

"Gentlemen, if I may interject," Gearheardt said from behind the pizza table, "if you're seriously contemplating action against the Vietnamese, may I suggest that some of my, uh, colleagues might be able to soften up the scene by knocking off some of the leaders. In our opinion, and I'm not talking about the boys down at Pizza Joe's now, this is a golden opportunity to stop communism in its tracks. Assuming it has tracks in Vietnam."

Gearheardt noticed that everyone was staring at him with teeth clenched and hate in their eyes. The President impaled an aide with a look and jerked a questioning thumb toward Gearheardt.

"The CIA pizza man," the aide whispered.

The President drew his still outstretched thumb quickly across his throat and made a gagging sound.

The aide began to tremble slightly. This was the first time that he had ever dealt directly with the President.

"Sir," he said, leaning forward to whisper, "does that mean you're through eating pizza? That the pizza man should not talk anymore? Or that you want us to kill the pizza man?"

His voice broke and the commandant of Marines snickered.

"I just want to be sure, sir," the aide continued.

Gearheardt saved him from further embarrassment. He took his apron from around his waist, wiped his hands on it, and then dropped it on the pizza cart.

"Okay," he said, "I can tell when I'm not wanted. But you'd better let intelligence into your little scheme." He opened the door to the closet, walked in, and shut it behind him. Moments later he emerged and squatted behind a large potted plant.

The Air Force chief raised his hand and waved it like a first-grader. "Sir," he finally blurted out, "if you're serious about nuking those folks, I'd appreciate it if we could do a little conventional bombing first. Some of the defense contractors are complaining that we're not using up their bombs or losing airplanes anywhere near their projections. Their marketing guys see the handwriting on the wall and are on my ass daily." His voice became confidential. "Sir, they are telling me that they can't hold these prices for us. If we get on the shit list, pardon my directness, with our own defense contractors, well . . ." He trailed off.

"I'll keep that in mind, Pappy," the President said wearily, as if he had heard this argument many times before.

"Virgil, sir."

"What'd I just call you?"

" 'Pappy,' sir."

"Are you telling me I don't know the name of my own Air Force chief of staff?"

"No, sir."

"Good. Pappy, why don't you vamoose over to the big hangar and send me an estimate of how many bombs you need to drop and airplanes you need to lose to keep our discount. And I don't want a lot of inflated horse hockey either. That was a goddam Cad-de-lac Deeeville I rode into town, not some turnip truck."

"Yessir, Mr. President," the general said, beaming.

After the Air Force chief left, extending his arms and making jet engine sounds, the Oval Office was quiet again. The President and his three aides sat looking at the Marine commandant, who was cleaning his fingernails with his bayonet.

The commandant started to squirm. Finally he spoke.

"You guys see *Sands of Iwo Jima*?" he asked. "Damn good flick."

The commandant shifted on his chair. He buffed the toe of his shoe that the admiral had scraped on the back of his pant leg, and then crossed his legs. He straightened his seam and picked a tiny piece of lint from his tunic.

The President cleared his throat, and the commandant jumped.

"What about me? sir," the Marine asked.

"You got any info on Veetnam?"

"No, sir."

"You got maps?"

"No, sir. Not of Vietnam, I don't think. No, sir."

"You got bombs?"

"Not many, sir. The Air Force gave us some old World War Deuce crap, but it hardly ever explodes unless we go hit it with a hammer. Hardly worth my men carrying it around."

He began to sweat. He ran a finger around his collar.

"We got a few good men, Mr. President."

"Well, that's mighty peachy, General."

After a moment the commandant began to tap his foot to a tune he was very softly whistling.

The President leaned forward and rested his elbows on his knees, cupping his chin. When he spoke, it was low and conspiratorial. The three aides leaned forward.

"General, I'm thinkin' about a plan that'd be yore fondest dream. You'll be pissin' in yore pants and fartin' Dixie." He smiled and winked over at his aides. One of the aides winked back, then seemed to realize that he was winking at the President of the United States and began winking rapidly as if he had a twitch. The President shook his large, balding head and looked at the commandant.

"I'm gonna have you attack the United States Navy," he said.

Pretty sure that he was the butt of a joke, the commandant maintained his poker face. Then he began smiling, then laughing, then howling, slapping his knee, the tears running down his cheeks.

"Boy, Mr. President, I'd give a year's pay to do that. HA HA HA. Oh, sweet mother." He wiped his eyes on his sleeve. Seeing the President staring at him, he sobered.

"If I can find the Gulf of Tonkin for you, General, do you think you could drive a boat? With those few good men you're so proud of?"

The commandant took a deep breath, adjusted his tunic, looked around the room, stopping momentarily on the face of each of the President's aides, the CIA pizza man—Gearheardt gave him a thumbs up—and finally met the eyes of his commander in chief.

"Mr. President, to get a chance to knock the snot out of those prissy bastards in the Navy, I could drive a covered wagon through the Himalayas." He stood and saluted. "I didn't mean it about the year's pay, though. Little woman'd be on my ass."

"Didn't figure you meant it, Lester. Good luck. My boys here will brief you when we get it all figured out."

"Yessir!" replied the commandant of the Marine Corps, a happy man.

On his way out, Gearheardt stopped him. "General, I'm a Marine," he whispered. "The CIA took me as a child."

The general pulled back and felt for his sidearm but remembered that it had been taken by the Secret Service. "Marines don't deliver pizza, son. Get ahold of yourself."

Gearheardt tightened his grip on the general's arm. "Did the President say anything about my suggestion? You know, the . . ." He made a pistol of his hand and held it to his temple, pulling the imaginary trigger. "I couldn't hear with all your laughing and humming."

The commandant tore his arm free. He just wanted to get away and enjoy the prospect of shelling the Navy. He rubbed his forearm where Gearheardt had grabbed him.

"Damn," he said and backed out of the room.

Gearheardt rubbed his chin. "Diem, eh? I thought he was mostly dead." He turned to the President and his aides. "Sir, if I may interject, when we go to help a country, the boys down at the pizza palace," he winked, "believe it sometimes gets us off on the wrong foot to shoot the leader—"

"Who the hell are you again?" the President demanded.

"Last call for pizza," Gearheardt said, loading his cart.

As Gearheardt left, pushing the cart of crusts and soda bottles, he saw the President reach under the edge of his desk. "Mary Elizabeth," he said into an unseen microphone, "get that wiseass with the slick hair on the phone and tell him to get his ass over here. We got some plannin' to do."

4 · The President Rallies the Troops
(or Tallies the Roops, for Those Reading While Drunk)

Gearheardt and I were at Camp David in the Naval Intelligence tent weeks after he had overheard the President in the Oval Office. The four services (screw the Coast Guard, the orders said) had been directed to send their top men to Camp David for an important briefing with the President. Two or three hundred thousand soldiers, sailors, and airmen were milling about on the grounds. None of the services wanted to have fewer "best" men than the other services, so the number had gotten out of hand.

"Why are we in the *Naval* Intelligence tent, Gearheardt? We're Marines, and all of these damn swabbies are looking at us funny."

"If you mean why aren't we in *Marine Intelligence,* say that to yourself five times quickly. This is the only place we can learn anything. That's why the squadron asked me to pull some strings and get us here." He smiled at the lieutenant commander who was glaring at him.

"He didn't mean you, sir," Gearheardt said, "he meant all of the *other* damn swabbies."

Gearheardt smiled until the commander turned away.

"The skipper knows that the other services will try to get all the good places to bomb, not to mention live and get hooch maids. So he wants us to get what info we can from the Navy. The Marine Intelligence crew lost their orders and went back to Camp Lejeune."

A stage had been prepared for the President and the Joint Chiefs of Staff, who sat sleepily on folding chairs in a semicircle around a lectern and microphone. The President was waiting impatiently under a large oak near the platform. No one had thought to bring musical instruments, so playing "Hail to the Chief " was difficult. Finally the Marine Corps band leader stepped up on the edge of the platform.

"Dut, du du dut, du du DUUHH," he sang.

"Well Lord love a duck," the President said. "Is that it?" Without waiting for an answer from his fear-stricken aides, he strode toward the wooden structure and, proving he was as much a man as any of them, ignored the stairs and vaulted to the platform, almost. He hit his testicles on the corner and fell in a fetal position on the stage, holding his crotch. The Joint Chiefs were too busy saluting to notice, but the Marine bandleader sang "Hail to the Chief " again. Two black-suited Secret Service agents helped the President to his feet, brushing the dust from his coat until he angrily knocked their hands away.

He stepped to the podium and looked out at the sea of faces, the green utilities of the Army, the sharp white uniforms of the Navy, the camouflaged battle dress of the Marines, and the blue-striped robes over light blue pajamas of the Air Force. Having the most airplanes, the Air Force had arrived early and were down front in lawn chairs holding coffee cups, which they raised in tribute to the President as he swept his scowl by them.

"Good morning, military," the president boomed, grabbing his crotch, which strained painfully at the effort of booming. "Shitfire," he said.

"Good morning, Mr. President. Shitfire," the military responded.

"I'll make this quick, men. Then I got to get me a crotch rub." No one laughed.

"I'd better get right to the point, since it appears that the Lithuanian Girl Scouts could march in and take over the country, since the *best* of the military is grab-assing around here right now." He glared back at the Joint Chiefs. Then turned back to the crowd.

"I have called you here today to give you some good news. I have decided and asked the pussies in—I mean the Congress to grant me those powers to do what I have to do. Which is to send you boys over to Veetman to kick some ass! What do you say?" He raised his arms over his head.

"They're all queers in Congress," the Marine commandant said, mostly to himself, since no one else paid any attention to him.

In the silence, an Army corporal near the Air Force coffee station farted. The President turned again to the Joint Chiefs, his arms still raised, his face purple.

"Is this *our* military?" he asked sarcastically. Luckily, Naval Intelligence had figured out that the President had meant Vietnam, not Veetman, and passed the word to the swabbies to start cheering, knowing that the Vietnamese had shit for a navy and that they were not in much danger from any retaliation for sitting off the coast and lobbing Volkswagen-sized shells at native huts two or three miles away. The Army started cheering, probably because the Navy started cheering, and the Marines started yelling for the Army to shut the fuck up, but it sounded like cheering anyway, and it woke most of the Air Force officers and made them spill their coffee. Those with burns were immediately passed Air Medals and Purple Hearts by the administrative staff set up under the stage.

The President faced the crowd, his arms high, the sweat circles in his armpits huge. He launched into a long harangue about the greatness of America, the danger to our Navy from North Veetman boats—this sent Naval Intelligence back to their books—and the fighting tradition of the U.S. military of which he was once a proud member. A few thousand men actually stopped scratching their asses and adjusting their Jockey shorts and listened.

"Men," the President said, "I have gathered you here today so that we, your leaders and I, could share with you the great truths and present dangers of *not* responding to this grave threat." He began to sound like the Baptist preacher he once was.

When at last he paused, he turned to the Joint Chiefs. One was dozing, one cleaning his fingernails with his bayonet, and the other two, the Chief of Naval Operations and the four-star Air Force general, were playing rock, paper, scissors. The president called them to attention. The commandant of the Marine Corps assumed that the president meant everyone, so he screamed out *"Marine Corps, A-TIIINN-SHUN."* The Army chief was trying to convince the President that he had been praying, not sleeping, and the four-star Air Force general was ordering a sergeant to pass the word that attention meant standing up straight and looking straight ahead but he wasn't sure if it meant saluting or not, so every other Air Force guy should salute.

Two or three hundred thousand men were grab-assing around in various uniforms, some at attention, some saluting, and some who had brought guitars were singing "I want to go home, I want to go home, Oh how I want to go home" even though they were just at Camp David and part of something grand in a bizarre sort of way with the sky opening up to blue and burning off the low-lying mist of piss steam, morning farts, and the general belching and braying miasma of healthy young men.

The President returned to the microphone, and after a few minutes everybody quieted down except for the guys with guitars, who were all trying to be the first to think up a song about fighting in Vietnam and how terrible it was and how lonely they were and how the troops knew everything and the officers were dumb shits and trying to think of words that rhymed with "Vietnam," until a few non-commissioned officers ordered some of the soldiers to beat the crap out of the singers and break their guitars, which a lot of soldiers were only real happy to do. Then it was quiet.

"Men," the President began, "that's the spirit. And I couldn't help but notice that over half of the Air Force saluted. I damn sure won't forget that come budget time. Heh heh." He looked at the four-star

Air Force general, who beamed and saluted in a squat, not knowing whether he was supposed to stand at attention or stay seated.

"Now a few minutes ago, I promised a truthful explanation of why I have decided to send the best of America's boys over to some God-awful place to be maimed, crippled, all blown up, and yes, killed." He paused, and the wind could be heard in the tops of the trees lining the parade ground where they were all assembled.

"I don't want any of you—and let's be realistic, there'll be a shit pot full—getting all crippled up and coming back here and saying 'Hey, what the hell. Nobody told me about being maimed or anything.' Okay? Now there's lots of commanders in chief of little pissant countries that send their boys out without a thought of eyes shot out, arms and legs missing, and those wounds you boys always seem to get where you have to carry those little bags around to shit and piss in. Not me, and not the good old U.S. of A." He smiled for a moment as if he thought those little piss bags were kind of funny. Then turned serious again.

"And we'll have our share killed. Make no doubt about it. I don't expect uneducated cannon fodder, and I don't mean you boys of course, but just any old cannon fodder, which is of course just a military expression like latrine or body bag, anyway none of you is expected to understand the historical perspective, and certainly not the global perspective of this action I am taking. That is the job of the President, and I intend to do my duty just like you will intend to do yours. But as I was sayin', the good news is that those that choose or are chosen to be dead will not have to worry about comin' back home and whining about being a cripple or another type of invalid." He stopped and looked at his audience, trying to find someone who at least had the appearance of listening to him.

"Now I'll just ask the Joint Chiefs to say a few words about their views on our excursion to foreign shores."

All of the chiefs tried to avoid eye contact except for the Marine commandant, who had not been listening and was smiling stupidly at the Air Force boys in the front row.

"How about you, General?" the president said.

"How about me what, sir?"

"How about you gettin' up here and saying a few words about why we're going to Veetman."

The commandant slowly rose to his feet, his smile gone. "Was that in those papers you sent over, Mr. President?" he asked.

The President squinched his eyes and stuck out his lower chin. Before he said anything, the commandant approached him and whispered, "Is this about that Navy deal, Mr. President? You told me not to tell anyone."

"It's not about the Navy deal, you horse's ass. Sit down."

The Army general snickered at the bewildered look on the commandant's face.

"Well, since you seem to think it's so funny, soldier boy. Why don't you come on up to the microphone and give it a try?"

The Army general smiled as if holding a secret. He stuck his hand into his tunic, a look of panic on his face when he withdrew it empty. He slapped his pockets.

"General, let's shake a leg," the President said.

"I don't have my notes, sir."

"I don't give a shit, general. Get your ass over here."

The Army general wasn't an Army general for nothing. Quickly pulling himself together, he strode to the podium. He stood there like Patton, waiting, in fact, for a giant American flag to rise slowly behind the stage as practiced secretly the night before. In the quiet of the moment, he heard arguing and cursing coming from below the stage. The Air Force administrative types had evidently unplugged the electric motor that was to raise the flag in order to plug in half a dozen coffee pots. A squad of Green Berets rushed under the stage. Sounds of a beating rose until the Army general stomped his foot on the stage. The beating sounds stopped.

"Men, I know first of all that you join me in thanking our president for giving us the opportunity to show a little two-bit country what good old American boys are made of." He paused and snuck a look at the President, hoping that hadn't sounded like an attempt at a pun. He quickly went on. "Now when you boys get to Vietnam, I want you to keep in mind just two things. And those two things are Hearts and Minds." He stopped and looked over at the President again. The President was staring at a spot about two feet in front of his shoes, biting his lip and shaking his head from side to side. The Army chief tried to dart past him to reach his chair. The President was too fast for him and grabbed his elbow.

"I asked you to tell them why we're sending them to Veetman, for Christ's sake. What was that shit about hearts and minds?" The President's face was glowing in the sun streaking through the trees.

"Well, we're supposed to win them, sir. The hearts and minds of the people. Didn't I explain that part? Did I forget to say that?" He was crestfallen.

"But what in the blasted blue blazes does that have to do with why we're sending them in the first place, you nincompoop?"

"I lost my notes, Mr. President. And the Air Force screwed up the flag. It wasn't my fault."

"That's what the military always says," the President said, pushing him away. "Sit down."

The Army chief stomped back to his folding chair. The Marine commandant, a smirk covering his entire face, looked over at him and whispered loudly.

"Hearts and minds?" he snickered. "You sons-a-bitches in the Army are getting as goofy as the goddam Air Force. You boys holding your secret psy-ops classes together now?" He covered his mouth with his hand and snorted into it.

The Army chief couldn't resist a retort even though out of the corner of his eye he saw the President glowering at him.

"You ignorant pea-brain. The only reason you joined the Marine Corps was that they didn't have an IQ requirement except that it couldn't be over seventy-five. You don't—"

"Naw," the commandant interrupted, "I joined the Marine Corps 'cause I wasn't queer, soldier boy."

The President stomped his foot, drawing their attention. "Knock off the grabass," he said, getting a giggle from the Air Force chief, sitting just to the right of the purple-faced President.

"Your turn, peckerwood," he said, thumping the four-star general on the back of the head.

Before the general could rise, a Secret Service man ran up the stairs to the platform and took the President aside.

"Sir," he said, "the CIA sends word that they are ready to brief you when you arrive at Langley."

"They were supposed to be here, dagnabbit. I ain't drivin' all the way down there to hear them give me that shit about how many people live in Veetman and what the damn crops are. Tell 'em to get their butts up here pronto."

"Sir," the man in the black suit and sunglasses said, lowering his voice, "the CIA said that they couldn't leave headquarters right now. They have word of an impending attack on the U.S. Navy. The Agency is having their top men buy a ship-building yard in Mobile as we speak and will be manufacturing high-speed patrol boats by next weekend. Then they will have covert operatives disguised as boat salesmen working in the Tonkin Gulf by March. That's what they told me to tell you, sir. Oh, and they're out of money. They said you'd know what to do."

The President hung his head. He looked old and tired, and the war hadn't even started. He rubbed his forehead.

"You ready for me now, Mr. President?" the Air Force general asked. He was on his feet and moving to the podium. The President didn't look up but nodded his head yes and gave a weak wave of his hand toward the general.

As the Marine commandant was sneaking off the stage, having overheard enough of the report about the CIA to know he should never have told the bastards, the four-star general of the Air Force looked out over the once tree-covered rolling hills, now denuded of all vegetation as only a quarter of a million teenagers with bayonets and entrenching tools could make them. In the distance the sun shone fiercely on the figures of two Secret Service men staked out on the ground Apache-torture style, having foolishly tried to arrest an Army private for urinating on a presidential rhododendron.

The general lifted his hat, ran his hand back over his gray crewcut, and then squared the hat firmly on his brow. He stuck out his chest and drew himself to his full height. His wings and medals gleamed in the warm sun. A gentle breeze clinked the fasteners against the flagpole atop which Old Glory undulated.

"Bomb the enemy," he said. "Wherever they may be. For wherever bold men come forth to, to . . ." He stuttered and wrinkled his handsome brow. ". . . so we'll bomb to beat the band or else we'll know the reason why . . . in the halls of . . ."

"Shut the fuck up, and give us beer!" a Marine yelled out.

The Air Force band struck up "Wild Blue Yonder" or something as close to it as a band without instruments could strike up.

5 · Mission Imporkable

few weeks before we left for Vietnam, Gearheardt mysteri-
ously disappeared for three days. When he returned, he told
me that he had been to the White House. I didn't believe him
at first, but he had documents that changed my mind.

A letter on White House stationery said, 'Get your ass up here. I
got a job for you.' And it was signed by the President. Gearheardt told
me that his dual role, CIA and Marine Corps pilot, had drawn the attention of someone on the President's staff. They had a plan to end
the war before things heated up too much, and they needed someone
with exactly Gearheardt's qualifications.

When he got to D.C., Gearheardt was met at the airport and taken to
the White House. It was night, and two guys in dark suits and sunglasses practically dragged him out of the terminal.

"You Gearheardt?" one of them asked.

"No."

"You're close enough."

Next thing he knew they were screaming through the nation's
capital in a Ford. Men in a hurry. Driving over curbs, through

flowerbeds, knocking over trashcans. The driver took off his sunglasses, and then they stayed pretty much on the road. The other agent giggled, but didn't take off his sunglasses.

At the White House guard shack, the driver discovered he didn't have his ID so they had to go back to a suburb in Alexandria and wait in the car while he ran in the house and got his wallet. His wife followed him back out to the car giving him a lot of shit for waking up the kids.

They finally got Gearheardt in the White House and led him to a room in the basement. Inside the smoke-filled room was the President, cutting his toenails, while a dozen guys in business suits sat around a table. The men in suits were arguing heatedly and didn't look up as Gearheardt came in. The President looked up, though, and smiled at him.

"You Gearheardt?"

"No, Mr. President," he said, sticking to his story.

"Good. Set your butt down here by me and let me buy you a drink. What'll you have, Gearheardt?"

"A beer, sir?"

"I thought you said you weren't Gearheardt." The President beamed. Three aides appeared behind him and beamed too. "Guess he wasn't so damn smart after all," the President said to them. "Get Gearheardt a beer, boys."

When Gearheardt was seated next to him, a cold Lone Star in hand, the President put one arm around his shoulder and with his other arm made a sweeping motion past all of the dark-suited men arguing heatedly around the table.

"Know what these boys are figuring out, son?"

"I don't believe so, Mr. President."

"Call me Larry Bob, son. Saves a lot of time when you're talking to me. All that President this and President that. Slows down a good confab. Just call me Larry Bob and I'll tell you when to stop." He squeezed Gearheardt's shoulder and withdrew his arm.

"These sons-a-bitches are figuring up how much it's gonna cost to run this damn Veetnam war deal. Some of the smartest boys in the U.S., right here at this table." He looked at him as if expecting a comment.

"I guess they're trying to calculate the budget for the war, Larry Bob. Is that right?"

"Yep, pretty close. These boys are trying to figure how much they can make off it. See that gray-haired feller with the yellow tie? Builds airports. Wants to put military airfields in every Veetnam city that has more'n about two thousand people. Feller next to him is a concrete guy. Over there"—he pointed his long finger—"feller builds ships and is lobbying for us to give some battleships to Veetnam so we can have ourselves a sea battle like we ain't seen since the Big One. I think that little skinny feller is a tire man, but I ain't sure. And, oh yeah, you'll love this one, that fat tub-o'-lard is in the medical supply business. Lookit that possum-eatin' grin on his face. Already made himself a deal with the Rooskies so he can supply both sides."

"Is that legal, Larry Bob?" Gearheardt asked.

"It is if I say so," the President replied.

"You suppose I could have another Lone Star, Larry Bob?"

"I reckon you can. Don't get too familiar with that 'Larry Bob' shit. You're still just a damn Marine." The President signaled by raising his hand, and one of his aides ran over with a beer. He began to whisper in the President's ear. Something about Congress and naked women in the Oval Office. The President excused himself and left the room, carrying one shoe.

Gearheardt sipped his beer and inspected his surroundings. There was no other furniture in the room except for the conference table surrounded by leather swivel chairs and the simpler chairs, evidently for aides, behind them. The ceiling was low; there were no windows. Bright lighting hung over the conference table, leaving the edges of the room in near darkness. Each of the four walls had a door. Gearheardt guessed the room was about twenty-five feet square. He had expected to be in a "war room" with maps, electronic gizmos, telephones, televisions, and transparent boards with grease-penciled aircraft filling every available space. This room was important without looking important, Gearheardt decided.

He tried to concentrate on the conversations going on at the table. They were of little interest to him, but he knew that he was in the presence of America's greatest businessmen. When he tuned in they were speaking in a language that he did not recognize.

". . . short-term returns, my ass. I've got shareholders, you know. You build up faster than I can ramp up, and I'll have to charge the Army double or triple margins." The man, who sounded angry, actually smiled. He was the "tire" guy, Gearheardt remembered the President saying.

"Well, somebody needs to remind old Slickhair that the Street doesn't like surprises near year end. We need to manage the action on a quarterly basis, with the military placing their estimates when it allows my planning boys to get the best spin. Couldn't we allocate the Army on a quarterly basis? If they run out of ammunition near the end of the month, that's their problem. If they see there's going to be a surplus, surely a few big battles can be scheduled without a lot of hoopla. Just to burn up the excess. I would think a quota for each soldier, say 500 bullets a month he needs to shoot, wouldn't be unreasonable."

A skinny young guy that Gearheardt hadn't noticed before popped up near the end of the table. He was wearing heavy black-rim glasses and a gray suit. He waved a tablet of paper wildly.

"TEN YEARS," he yelled.

There was a great deal of consternation around the table.

"Ten years?" asked the medical supply king.

"Hell, I'll be living on a golf course in Florida in less than ten years," the concrete man mused to no one in particular.

"You gentlemen asked me to calculate how long the war had to last in order to get over the fifteen percent hurdle rate. It works out, on the average industry investment that *you gave me,* to a seventeen percent internal rate of return, again on average, if the war lasts ten years and the average soldier shoots three times his weight in bullets, the enemy shoots down an average of three helicopters and two fighters a day, and the soldiers generally ruin any equipment in their possession in, again on the average, ninety days."

The room was quiet while the businessmen doodled on pads that had been placed in front of them and conferred with aides, who now leaned in with earnest brows. The mumbling was subdued. Finally a distinguished gentleman rapped his water glass and cleared his throat.

"Gentlemen, if I can have your attention for a moment. Speaking for the oil and gas industry, I have to tell you that I am concerned. Perhaps disappointed would be a better word." He took a silk handkerchief from his breast pocket and daintily wiped his forehead. Looking at him now in his seventeen-hundred-dollar suit, no one would have believed he'd started in the industry thirty-five years ago as a roughneck on a drilling rig in the Oklahoma panhandle. Worth conservatively two hundred million dollars, he expressed "disappointment" with less anxiety than some would.

"I told the President that I thought we could support his activities in Asia quite comfortably with a return in the neighborhood of twenty percent. Speaking frankly within the confines of this room, I can tell you that my board's patriotism becomes a bit anemic when we fall below that internal rate of return." He smiled around the table, knowing that he was in good company. "Now, I'm not saying that we won't make the investment that's needed to keep this action moving ahead, but if any of you are planning to drive to Disneyland for a little family vacation, I would suggest you fill up your tanks now. How does three dollars a gallon sound?" Since the executives at the table were clueless as to the price of gasoline, there was little reaction.

Another gentleman of the same vintage, but with a snappier tie, chuckled and spoke to the table. "Jim, you boys in the oil and gas business haven't had a creative idea since the gas station. The only thing you *ever* come up with is raising gas prices. You ever think about cutting the price you're paying the Arabs? Why should the damn automobile owners in America have to pay for this war?"

There were a number of "hear, hears" passed around the table after the chairman of U.S. Motors spoke.

The President had returned and quietly taken his chair next to Gearheardt.

"These boys getting it all worked out?" he said, loud enough for only Gearheardt to hear.

"Well, I have to tell you, President Larry Bob," Gearheardt said, "it's a little scary to listen to these men discuss what could be a chance to get my head shot off as if it's just another marketing opportunity." He felt out of his element, but he had been asked.

The President grinned at him. "Oh, you ain't heard nothin' yet. When we put these boys in the Pork Pit you'll see . . . Oh shit, here comes that damn lard-ass from Mississippi. I can't stomach this sonofabitch. And I can never remember his lard-ass name. Where in the hell are my aides?" He propelled himself out of his chair and extended his hand.

"Howdy, pardner," the President said. "How's it hangin'?"

The gentleman from Mississippi took the hand like it belonged to the Pope and put his other hand on top. "Well, Mr. President, I surely would like to know if you've given any thought to my suggestion. Maybe we could go somewhere . . ." He looked down at Gearheardt and then back at the President.

"Oh, this man's okay, pardner. One of my top men. Got pizza deliverin' clearance and everthing."

This last momentarily threw the Mississippian, but he recovered and smiled crookedly.

"I'm sure he's a good 'un, Mr. President. So, have you given it some thought?"

"Won't fly, pardner. Gave it long, hard thought and even talked it over with my boys over at the NdoubleACP. They ain't buyin' it. And might even run into some constitutional problems." The Mississippian started to interrupt. "Now hold your horses, I know most folks don't give a shit. But we get our asses in a sling with the boys in black robes, and it's goodbye Mr. President." He laughed and slapped the man on the shoulder. "Nice try though, pardner. I know I can always count on you for those kinds of ideas, not to mention a sizable donation that I never thanked you for. That bankin' business must be doin' real good. Take care, now. I'll see you in the Pork Pit."

The Mississippian caught the eye of his assistant as he turned around and shook his head negatively. The aide said, "Shit," and slumped back down in his chair.

Gearheardt had missed most of the exchange, intrigued by the timber baron's pitch to the group on the benefit of using wood to build tanks and airplanes. He began to realize that planning a war must be a lot more difficult than the military thought. But most of all he wondered what he was doing in this room. Why had the President ordered him here? He looked out of the corner of his eye and saw the President pinching the bridge of his nose as if to shut off pain. His glasses were pushed up onto his forehead. Without looking up he said. "You know what that crazy sonofabitch's suggestion was, son?" He reached in his shirt pocket and pulled out a folded sheet of paper. He extended it to Gearheardt, who took and opened it. It was on the letterhead of the Bank on the Bank of the Mississippi. This sentence was underlined: "Mr. President, I respectfully urge you to send only Negroes to Vietnam."

Gearheardt looked at the President, as a slight glimmer of understanding of the weight of governing the kooks and cranks in addition to the regular folks began to enter his head. When he had overheard the early Vietnam discussions as a CIA pizza man, he had thought the President was just an idiot.

The President was looking at him. "Yes, sir, Larry Bob," Gearheardt said, not sure what he was agreeing to. He realized the President wasn't looking at him at all. He was actually in a daze or sleeping with his eyes open.

"Mr. President?" Gearheardt said. "Do you suppose you could tell me what I'm here for?"

The President sat up straight and narrowed his eyes at Gearheardt. "I suppose I could if I wanted to. I'm the goddamned President, case you hadn't noticed, son." As suddenly as he had snapped this, he changed again and smiled. "What say we head over to the Pork Pit? That show always lifts my spirits. My aides tell you about this deal?"

He rose and indicated that Gearheardt should walk with him. With a nod of his head he stopped the conversation at the conference table. The men shoved papers into briefcases or the hands of waiting assistants, hitched up their pants, and adjusted their ties tight up around their necks. Their air was of preparing to do their duty, but Gearheardt caught a strange gleam in most eyes. With another nod, this one toward the door at the far end of the room, the President strode toward it as his aides rushed ahead to open it. Gearheardt had the feeling that if the aides had fallen, the President would have walked straight into the door without breaking his stride.

The door was opened and Gearheardt and the businessmen followed the President through it and onto a raised balcony. Before and below them lay a good-sized ballroom, the contents of which resembled a Mardi Gras mixed with an auto dealers convention, without the decorum of either. Temporary booths lined the walls and an island in the center of the huge room like exhibits at a home show, each adorned with the name of a state of the Union. The cacophony of voices and music softened, quieted and then stopped altogether as the crowd below turned their heads to the President. The last moving element to stop was a cavalcade of tiny motorcycles ridden by huge men in cowboy hats wearing bright red shirts. Gearheardt watched a balloon drift slowly to the ceiling above them and bump silently one, two, three times before it came to rest. A moment passed as the President, his hands planted on the railing in front of him, scanned the floor as if he were looking for someone to blame for the mess. Then he smiled and extended his arms wide in blessing.

"Senators," he bellowed, "fresh meat!" He swung his body around to face the businessmen who had followed Gearheardt and the President from the conference room. They had already begun to descend the staircases on each side of the balcony. A roar went up from the floor. The music resumed, and the motorcycles sputtered and jerked forward. The President saw Gearheardt's slack-jawed stare and stepped beside him, throwing a heavy arm around his shoulders. "Figured it out yet, boy?"

"Are those really senators, Larry Bob?" As he looked down, a man wearing moose antlers and snowshoes rushed to the bottom of the stairs and began dry-humping the leg of the gentleman who ran U.S. Motors.

"Servants of the people, Jack. Dividin' up the spoils at the moment."

They went down the stairs, and as they walked through the hall, Gearheardt felt the pull of the President, the aura and power of the man, even beyond the title. There was a sadness in his blustering reply to those who tried to coax him into their exhibits. He dismissed the exhibitors with a skill that left them hope and as much dignity as someone wearing a wedge of cheese or a plastic pig snout on his head could have. The President wore simple gray slacks and a cardigan sweater over his rumpled white shirt. Informal yet elegant in his comfort.

They passed a man dressed as a potato, complete with a large plastic "eye," which followed him and promised low-interest-rate bonds for defense contractors. A booth topped by huge long horns promised cheap Mexican labor and no state tax.

Before they reached the far door, the President took Gearheardt by the elbow, saying, "There's just one more you gotta see, son. At least a couple of these boys got by Barnum and Bailey Marketing 101." They approached a simple, unadorned booth manned by two distinguished gentlemen in blue blazers and gray slacks. They both rose from their chairs as the President arrived.

"Hello, Mr. President," they said in unison.

"Hello, Ben, Dick. Signing any deals?" He laughed as he looked past them to a curtained-off cubicle.

"We'll get our share, Mr. President," the taller one said. "We've got the most liberal incorporation laws in the union. We just like to take our little piece, if and when it's coming to us." He blushed modestly.

"What's behind that curtain?" The President's eyes said that he already knew. He glanced at Gearheardt and wiggled his eyebrows.

"You mean your aides didn't tell you? We got a bit of an advance benefit to give us a little insurance that these gentlemen here tonight don't overlook us and start looking off-shore."

He pulled back the curtain to reveal two young Vietnamese women. They giggled and put their tiny hands to their mouths. They were wonderfully, breathtakingly, and unassumingly naked.

"There's not a product in the world that a naked woman doesn't help sell, Mr. President." The short man dropped the curtain.

"They speak any American?" The President, Gearheardt noted, was taking an increasing interest in the women.

"Not that we can tell," Senator Mutt replied, becoming visibly more nervous at the President's interest.

Senator Jeff lost the foot contest with the President. The curtain parted, revealing the two still giggling women, one behind the other and combing her hair. The President stuck his face six inches from the woman with the comb, causing her to pause in midstroke.

"YOU GIRLS DOIN' OKAY?" he yelled. The women recoiled at the volume but their smiles stayed firmly locked in place. "WE'RE BOMBING THE SHIT OUT OF YOUR COUNTRY RIGHT NOW. YOU GIRLS SHOULD BE ABLE TO GO HOME AND VISIT YOUR FAMILIES BY CHRISTMAS TIME." His watermelon face split in the middle and he licked his lips.

The girls' perfect golden bodies stood out against the black curtain like the tiger painted on velvet he had hanging in his apartment in California. Gearheardt realized that one of the women was smiling at him and he smiled back broadly.

"You numba one G.I.," she said. It embarrassed Gearheardt.

The President was backing off. He took Senator Jeff in a hammerlock and drew him close. "Benny," he said to the struggling man, "you get them women to the Oval Office tomorrow at eleven. That dickhead from Italy is here trying to hardball me on that Navy base deal. I want them women in the office just flouncin' around like they owned the place. That Eyetie won't be able to think his way out of a wet bag. Heh, heh. And there might be a couple of tax breaks your piddly-ass state still ain't got just layin' around the old office too." The President released him and the senator rubbed his neck. He looked angry and nervous at the same time.

"We don't actually *own* these women, Mr. President."

"Well who in the hell does?" The President looked at Gearheardt and shook his head in disgust at the misrepresentation he had caught the senator in.

"The Navy, Mr. President." Senator Jeff inched away from the President.

"*Our* Navy?"

"Yes, sir. Technically the Chief Petty Officers' Credit Union. At least that was the name on the contract."

The President considered this for a moment. He tilted his head and looked at Gearheardt again, lifting his eyebrows and shrugging. He turned back to the senators, now standing shoulder to shoulder in front of the closed curtain. "Well, just get 'em over there by eleven. I'm the damned commander in chief, for chrissakes. And tell 'em to wear some little tiny underwear. It is the gol-danged White House after all."

The President glad-handed his way through the rest of the crowd and reached for the door, which promptly opened before he touched it.

When they were on the other side and the door closed behind them, Gearheardt realized how noisy the room had been. They were alone in a long, dimly lit hallway and their footsteps echoed on the concrete walls and floor. The President was pensive, and Gearheardt began to feel the weight of the White House above them. At the end of the hall they stopped in front of a small elevator. The door slid open, and he followed the President into the chamber. The President sighed and pushed a button marked PRIVATE on the wall.

"You know why that door opened as soon as we got there, son?"

"Guess not, Larry Bob. Mr. President."

"They know where I am all the time."

"Yessir," Gearheardt said, wondering who *they* were.

"Well, son, back to the real world. Oval Office okay with you? I got somethin' to do 'fore I brief you."

Gearheardt knew he didn't have to answer, and they rose in silence from the bowels of the White House.

"How in hell you suppose them Navy chiefs do it? I'm the President of the United States, but if I want somethin' real bad, I always end up talkin' to a Navy chief." He chuckled. "Pretty good-lookin' women weren't they, son?"

"Yessir." He followed the President off the elevator and down a short hall into the Oval Office. Men sitting outside the door who Gearheardt assumed were Secret Service rose as they went in.

"Evening, Mr. President."

"Evenin', Billy." He turned before he closed the door. "You boys didn't see a couple a naked women run through here this afternoon by any chance, did you?"

The men's faces turned red. "Well, sir, they weren't carrying any weapons, that's for sure. And they were with Senator . . ."

"Not a problem, Billy. Just wonderin'. Next time, shoot that damned senator. He don't have any business in here when I ain't here." The President closed the door. "That'll give 'em something to think about. With any luck that prissy bastard will come back and the boys will shoot him," he said to Gearheardt without any indication of humor.

"Take a seat and make yourself comfortable. I have to check my desk to see if anybody declared war on us or anything. This Veetnam deal's got everbody in an uproar. Geez, no one I know could even *find* the dang place 'fore we went over there and started shootin'." He sat down at his desk and began shuffling through papers.

The room was quiet except for his muttered "holy shit" and "stupid sonsabitches." Once he held up a letter and said, "This crazy loon over in the House is worried about the students at some pissant college *mobilizing* against the war. Well, no shit, Red Ryder. Hell, I could get ten thousand college boys *mobilized* to see a fat woman eat a bale of hay if I had beer and coeds. I'll mobilize their asses over to Veetnam they pull any of that shit while I'm President. Where do they get these damned ideas? They must have communists running out the ass on these campuses."

Gearheardt was studying the glass top of the coffee table in front of where he sat. He thought he could make out a petite butt print. He wondered if the President could get those Vietnamese women over to the Oval Office that very night, but he decided he shouldn't ask.

"You ever heard of *Barbonella*?" the President asked suddenly without looking up from his desk.

"Nosir."

"Well, you'll get your chance. Remember that name."

"May I ask why, sir?"

"Sure." The President signed a document with a flourish, dropped it in the out basket, and picked up another piece of paper. He studied it and squinted his eyes, unhappy at the contents of whatever it was. He wadded it into a ball, threw it on the floor, and reached for another.

After a while Gearheardt spoke. "Why, sir? This Barbonella, is that the operations code for—"

"Yeah, that's the one. You'll figure it out in due course, son. Just remember that even the President needs a little cover sometimes. Can't do everthing out in the open."

"I guess that pretty well explains it, Mr. President."

The President looked up. "You sassing me, son?"

Gearheardt saw, from a horrible orange and white football-shaped clock behind the President, that it was almost 4:00 A.M. "Well, sir, if I can be frank—"

"Son, you can be Frick or Frack for all I care. Just let me finish this pile of bullcrap and I'll be with you." He scribbled again. "Seems like every swinging dick in America wants me to give 'em something. Shit, do I look like Santa Claus to you?"

Gearheardt slumped back in his chair. "Nosir."

Finally the President rummaged around in his desk drawer until he pulled out a rubber stamp. He began stamping HELL NO on the papers as fast as he could pull them off the pile. When he was finished he pushed the stack aside, leaned back in his chair, put his feet up on his desk, and pushed his bifocals up onto his forehead. He blew out his breath and looked at Gearheardt.

"Well, son, let's get down to brass tacks." He scratched his nose, and then clasped his hands across his paunch. "I want you to stop this Veetnam War deal."

"I didn't start it, sir."

"Boy, you're a wise-ass little rascal ain't you?" The President dropped his feet to the floor and leaned forward on his desk. "I mean I got a plan and you got a mission. I ain't asking your permission, son. I'm telling you what you're going to do when I tell you to do it."

"Yessir."

"I'm sending you to Hanoi to make a deal with old Ho Chin. How does that sound?"

"Idiocy, sir." Then quickly, as he saw the famous squint, he added, "You have diplomats for that kind of thing don't you, sir?"

"I ain't ever seen a diplomat smart enough to pour piss out of a boot with the instructions written on the heel. Oh, there are some, but those sonsabitches try to think for themselves. Can't count on 'em to just do what I tell 'em. That's what I like about the Marine Corps."

"Sir, didn't you just *get* us into the war? May I ask, sir, why you are already planning on how to get us out?"

The President looked like he didn't like the question. But he shoved his massive hands into his pants pockets and, after chewing on his bottom lip for a moment, replied, "Well, to tell the truth, son, I figured that the Harvard boys knew how to win a war. They backed down the Rooskies in Laos." The President sighed. "Now *I* gotta get us out or there'll be hell to pay. Supposed to be checks and balances in the government. I write the checks and the dipshits over on the hill do the balances. You following me?"

"No, sir."

"S'why I'm President and you're a Marine, son. You see, I start the war, the hawks go apeshit, the left pisses their pants, and I sail on to the second term."

"Because—"

"I step in and work it all out."

"Yes, sir. Why me, sir?"

"Because you're the only CIA pizza man Marine that I could think of." He smiled.

"I'm not him, sir."

"Not who, you little prick?" The President was angry.

"Not Gearheardt, Mr. President. I'm Narsworthy. Gearheardt is my code-person."

"What in the goddam blue billy is a *code-person*?" the President demanded, leaning even farther forward toward Gearheardt.

"When it's too dangerous to be yourself, sir, we use code-persons. That was my code-person. He's not me."

The President leaned back in his chair and replaced his feet on his desk.

"I hate you goddamed spooks. Got a smart answer for everthing, don't you? Now let me tell you how the cow ate the cabbage. You are going to get briefed, right here and now, and then you're going to be waitin' for me to send you a message to do what I tell you to do. Is that about how you see it, pizza man?"

"I'll check with Gearheardt, sir, but I'm sure he'll agree." Gearheardt knew when he was licked.

"You got a backup? Someone you can trust?" the President said, almost avuncular now that he had made his point. "I mean someone besides this code-person."

"Jack Armstrong, Mr. President. He's my best friend in the squadron. Of course that's not his name."

"Of course it isn't. I wasn't born yesterday, son. He speak any Vietnamese?"

"Fluently."

"You understand if you screw this up and somehow live, you'll be eatin' donkey dick and white bread in Leavenworth till Sunday after the Second Coming."

"Jack will do a fine job, Mr. President. Could I ask when he'll, I mean *we'll* be making this trip to Hanoi, sir?"

"Got to kill about a hundred thousand more troops, Narsworthy. Didn't think I knew your real name, did you?" A quick smile. "That ought to do it."

"Ours or theirs, sir?" Gearheardt asked.

"Boy, you are one wise-ass son-of-a-bitch, I'll give you that. Theirs, of course. Got to soften 'em up a bit more. Besides that hard-ass Ho Chi, I hear they got this Gee-ap fellow that would rather fight round-eyes than pull his pecker. Thinks he's this *great* strategist 'cause he chased out a few Frogs and Wogs. Hell, if this was a tal-leywacker measurin' contest, we'd be wolfin' cheeseburgers in down-town Hanoi before Thanksgiving. But these pesky devils are kind of like the little brother of a gal I dated back home. I used to stop by her house to pick her up for some sparkin'."

The President looked at the ceiling and then closed his eyes. "She was a fine lookin' girl, but that dang little brother of hers drove me off. When I was waitin' in the parlor for her to finish get-ting ready, that little cuss would lay into my knees and crotch with a fare thee well. I'd have to stand there grinnin' like a coon with her momma and daddy beamin' at me while my gonads were rang like a dinner bell. Now, understand, I could have knocked the snot out of this runt with my pecker tied behind my back. But how would that have looked to momma? And Daddy always seemed to have a twelve-gauge within arm's reach, and I suspected he knew I was plucking the petals off his little flower. Wasn't nothin' I could do but sneak in a rabbit punch or two when I could distract momma and daddy. But this was one determined little rascal. Don't know why he took such a dislike for me. I finally decided I had to retreat or just up and kill the little bastard and run the risk of daddy trying to dehide me. So, I told Lulu that I had business over in Little Rock that was going to take all my time and just got out while I had some gonads left."

The President sat in silence, looking at Gearheardt. "You get the point, son?"

"If I say no, will I have to listen to the story again, Mr. President?"

The President rose from his desk and came over to Gearheardt. He looked down at him. "You're the son I always wanted, Gearheardt," he said.

"Narsworthy, sir."

"Him too," the President said in the same tone. Then he sighed, walked over to the window behind his desk and stood with his giant hands clasped behind him looking out at the early light. "We got this little riled up sonovabitch doin' a Fred Astaire tapdance on our gonads and those old women on the Hill are afraid that Momma Russia or Daddy China is watching to see we don't hurt him all that much. 'Course Ho Chi ain't too worried about losin' half the damn population." He shook his head. "War of attrition, my ass. I must have been drunk to head us down this road. Goddam Kennedys. Always thought they knew what they were doing."

The room was silent, and the window in front of the President grew slowly lighter.

"How exactly do I accomplish this mission, sir?" Gearheardt asked.

The President returned to Gearheardt's side and dropped wearily into the wingback chair adjacent to him. "When I give you the word, you're going to go to Hanoi, sit down with Ho Chi and make a deal with him. I told you that. You'll get the particulars in the secret code package. Then you just—"

"Will this come in the mail, sir? I just want to make sure I don't throw it away with the junk."

"You ain't takin' this too serious, are you, boy? You're thinkin' that you got me by the oysters since you're a CIA pizza man and a Marine and you're sittin' here in the Oval Office with the President and I'm askin' you to do some secret stuff. Is that about it?"

"Roughly, sir."

"You're forgettin' that if I yell about one word, that man dozing right outside that door will run in here and blow your head off. One word. That worry you at all?"

"Well, sir, with all due respect, I've got two things that worry me. One is the chance that I'll end up being dragged around Hanoi on a long rope after the dinks get through breaking a few rifles over my head. And the other, sir, is that I joined the Marine Corps to kill people, not to be a political lackey. With all due respect, sir."

The President's face reddened. "You insubordinate little jackass. Forget what I said about that son deal. I got a damn daughter braver than you and a whole lot more patriotic."

"Shoot me and send *her*, Mr. President."

"I would, but I'd have hell to pay with her mother. Large woman. Secret Service won't let her in here, or she'd be runnin' the damn place." His anger faded, and he looked at the floor while he chewed on his bottom lip. He took off his bifocals and twirled them around by the earpiece.

"Okay, I know you ain't scared of doin' me this favor *or* of goin' to Veetnam, so what is it you want?"

Gearheardt tried to straighten the trouser seam of the pants he had been in for over twenty-four hours. He pulled his tunic down and rubbed his sleeve across his gold wings.

"I want a case of Lone Star, both of those Vietnamese women, a piece of the Chief Petty Officers' Credit Union, and I want to be a captain." He looked squarely at the President. "And I want Jack to be a captain too."

The President didn't hesitate. "Done, done, done, and as soon as I can get hold of some administrative dipshit over at the Pentagon, done." He smiled and pulled himself out of his chair with an effort. The look on his face told Gearheardt that he had sold out too cheaply. He walked Gearheardt to the door, putting an arm around his shoulder.

"Why didn't you just ask me nicely, son? Shit, I can get all that stuff with one call to the Chief Petty Officers' Club."

"I wanted you to respect me, Mr. President," Gearheardt said.

They were at the door and the President turned him until they were face to face. The President had a hand on each of Gearheardt's shoulders. "You'll do fine, my boy. Just wait until the Barbonella package shows up. Kill whoever gives it to you. Then after you complete the mission, I want you and Jack to meet me in Olongopo in the Philippines. Any questions?"

"Why don't I just go straight to Hanoi, sir? What if I get killed before you send the word to start the mission?"

"You worried about getting killed, son?"

"Not really. But it just seems that with all this planning and—?"

"That's a chance I'll have to take, son. If I went around trying to make sure soldiers didn't get killed just so they wouldn't screw up a plan of mine—well, I wouldn't be much of a president would I?"

The President leaned away and squeezed his hand on Gearheardt's shoulder, causing him intense pain.

"Don't worry your little jar head, son. You just do what I tell you. I'll be back here with that slick-haired car salesman working out the details. We'll bomb till the yellowbacks start sharpening their chopsticks, then we get the word to you." The President seemed to relax as he said it.

"How am I supposed to *get* to Hanoi, sir."

The President chuckled and looked around the silent Oval Office as if to see if anyone was listening in. "The secret way," he said. He patted Gearheardt on the shoulder and pushed him through the door, which opened as if *they* knew he was ready to leave.

6 · Gettin' Out of Dodge

earheardt and I received our orders for Vietnam a few months later. By this time we were in a squadron on the West Coast. As chopper pilots in the Marine Corps, unmarried, yearning for action beyond what we were finding in Southern California, we were excited. The opportunity to go shoot people out of a high-performance flying machine is irresistible of course. And we both liked the name "Vietnam."

I was dating Mickey Mouse at the time, or at least the girl who walked around Disneyland dressed as Mickey. They sometimes use small young men, but Old Mick had to squat to pee during the time that I was dating him, or her. Her name was Penny, and I unfortunately had mentioned the *possibility* of discussing the *chance* of *thinking about* getting engaged. That's why a number of Disney employees, and I assume a fair number of parents and their children, are still talking about Mickey calling a uniformed Marine a thoughtless rotten bastard at the top of her lungs in front of Sleeping Beauty's castle. Of course, now I know I should have waited until she was off duty. When I left the park, Mickey was near the top of the Matterhorn crying and threatening to jump off.

Later I heard that you could still see her in a number of the bars around Disneyland. She wouldn't take the costume off, even though the Disney people sued the hell out of her. She was a mean drunk. Foul-mouthed and quick to throw punches. The letter relating this, from a Marine who had been dating Snow White, had arrived almost at the same time the squadron made it to Danang.

Gearheardt and I packed our gear and marked KILLED IN ACTION across all of the envelopes containing bills and dropped them in the mailbox on the way out of our apartment complex in Anaheim. He had misplaced his car, so he rode to the debarkation area with me. It was in Long Beach at the Naval Ship Parking place, or whatever the Navy called them.

The pier was a grand sight. The ship that we were embarking upon was festooned with pennants and patriotic signage. GIVE 'EM HELL, BOYS and KILL A KRAUT FOR MOM—that one was fairly tattered and discolored—and BENE VALE PUTRIS FAEX, which I assume was hung by some prissy Naval ROTC guy from Princeton. Balloons bobbed merrily from every place you could tie one, and crepe paper ran all the way around the ship, a converted World War II aircraft carrier named the USS *Ike and Tina Turner*. (This was in the time when the Navy, trying to be *with it,* let the men vote on the names of the ships). We were to find she carried a merry crew, except for the twenty-two hours a day they spent pissing and moaning and trying to avoid anything that resembled useful activity.

"You don't like the Navy very well, do you, Gearheardt," I said as he stepped around the Shore Patrol officer who tried to look at our orders.

"They all have beady eyes and wear lipstick, Jack."

"No they don't, Gearheardt."

"Oh, I suppose not. I actually like the way they drive boats. But when they have you aboard ship, they whisper all the time and ring little bells, and loudspeakers are always *now hear this*-ing. It's silly. And they have little sissy names for everything."

He paused and looked up at the ship that was to carry us to Vietnam, by way of Japan and Okinawa.

"In World War II, my uncle was a Marine grunt. He was aboard the USS *Pumice Stone*. When his battalion was ready to hit the beach at Iwo, they loaded into those little Navy boats that drive you up to shore and then the front falls down and you run out and get shot. LSTs or something like that.

"My uncle went down the rigging into the boat, and the coxswain, or wainscoting or whatever they call themselves, was such a sissy that he drove the LST around to the other side of the big boat, away from the beach, and lowered the front. My uncle and his men had to swim eleven miles into the beach."

I couldn't help but wonder if Gearheardt made these stories up as he went along or if he rehearsed them.

Our squadron of helicopter pilots was assembled. A battalion of Marines in full battle gear was in the process of dressing down their ranks, checking their equipment, and getting ready to board the same ship. The officers were yelling at the noncoms, who were yelling at the troops.

I could see that some of the more attractive wives and dates were nervous about getting on a boat with seventeen hundred Marines and were clinging to the men who were trying to get into formation. I think that Gearheardt and I were the only pilots who didn't have dates. Of course, you can imagine the scene if I had had a hysterical Mickey Mouse down among those troops. I was glad that I had broken it off. Gearheardt figured if he could get a woman in Tijuana, he could get a woman wherever we ended up. There was a rumor, in fact, that we were actually going to invade Tijuana.

The sun was rising. The pier was bustling. The bands were playing. If you've never seen your country embark for war in a foreign land, you have missed one of the most stirring scenes known to man. My chest swelled under my Mae West, although it might have been a tightness caused by Gearheardt accidentally inflating it as he stumbled from the car.

Near the defense contractors' pavilions, civilians in white shirts with short sleeves and broad, colorful ties were selling flak jackets and camouflage bikini underwear. The Winchester people were giving out free bullets, although the engraving line was hopelessly long. Gearheardt and I climbed on top of a stack of boxes labeled UTENSILS, COOKING and just took it all in.

We watched the battalion commander, a bird colonel, climb the gangway with a stride that said "Let me at those Cong." Unfortunately, once at the top, he wouldn't salute the little pissant Navy duty officer and say, *"Permission to come aboard, sir,"* so there was quite a scuffle before a corporal threw the ensign over the side and a squad of Marines secured the quarterdeck, another one of those prissy names for the boat's front door.

Finally, the colonel found a bullhorn and addressed the partying mob below him on the pier. "Okay, men, ditch the dates and wives." Much pissing and moaning. "You, the Indian vendors in the back. Give those men back their money. Those eagle feathers aren't going to keep anybody from getting shot where we're going. Come on, men, get those women out of here." He paused and looked leaderly for a few minutes, while the women drifted to the rear and into the cars of the waiting Marines and Navy guys who weren't going to Vietnam and who had come down for an easy score. "Also, men, it has been brought to my attention that many of you are carrying unauthorized items. Please discard the following." He took out a list. "Tennis rackets, golf clubs, pinball machines, lawnmowers, live wolverines, inflatable women, beer kegs, lace or rubber underwear, paint, two-by-fours in excess of four feet in length, and any form of lard. Each and every one of these items will be provided for you when we hit the beach."

The captain of the ship appeared behind him, accompanied by two burly Shore Patrol men with rifles that were all painted up and looked faked. Evidently the story of the duty officer being tossed overboard had reached him. He looked pretty steamed. The colonel ordered the huge, black Marine corporal to toss the Shore Patrol guys overboard and then escort the captain to his quarters. When the captain resisted, they pantsed him, ripping his trousers as they got them over his shoes, and the battalion below roared their approval.

A panel truck carrying a contingent of Colt firearms salesmen roared up. Seeing that they were about to miss the whole shebang, they piled out and began tossing handfuls of bullets at the troops. Moments later, their panel truck on its side and burning, they crawled and limped their way off of the pier after realizing that hadn't been a good idea. The Winchester salesmen hooted at them and shook their fists.

And then it got quiet. The Marines looked up at their leader, standing tall on the quarterdeck, fists on hips, smiling like he knew where he was.

"Are we ready?" He shouted.

"Yeesssss!" We answered.

"Everybody got a gun?"

"Yeessss!"

"Get your asses on board and let's go get 'em!"

"Yeessssssssss!"

The colonel turned to the lieutenant at his side.

"Okay, son, let's head 'em up, and move 'em out."

"What do you mean, sir?" the lieutenant asked.

The colonel was momentarily flustered. He looked over at the major, who was picking fuzz off of his ammunition belt. Then at the sergeant, who coughed into his fist.

"You know, the cowboy guy on TV. That *Rawhide* deal."

"I'm afraid I don't know what you're talking about, Colonel. I could find out and get back to you sir."

The colonel turned back to the rail, grabbed it with both hands and leaned against it. He looked down at the mob, scrambling aboard the ship like British soccer fans.

"Shit," he said.

When we lifted anchor at Long Beach, it was a thrill. If you've ever "put to sea," you know there is nothing quite like it for lifting the heart and freeing the mind. There is a realization that the petty irritants of life, at least a large number of them, can't follow you to sea. The daily influx of bills, the calls from the motorcycle rental place looking for their bike, having to buy gas and food, listening to depressing news, all of that is left behind.

I remember Gearheardt and me standing at the railing at the stern and watching the pier grow smaller, the crowd drift away. There was a sadness, yes, certainly when the quarterdeck sentry had to put a bullet in the knee of Mickey Mouse trying to fight her way up the gangplank as it was secured. There is something particularly poignant about sailing for Vietnam with a giant Mickey Mouse head bobbing in your wake. Even if it is shouting vulgarities. I suppose it's all rather symbolic, sailing away with sailors shooting at a cartoon animal that arguably symbolizes the good nature and optimism of America.

7 · Over the Bounding Sea

So you lied to me about Congress and the Joint Chiefs selecting me personally for the mission, Gearheardt."

"Pretty much. I didn't want to go by myself. Even the President said I needed a backup. And I needed someone who spoke Vietnamese."

"I don't speak Vietnamese and you know it, Gearheardt."

"The President didn't. And it would have been disastrous to go up there without either of us being able to speak Vietnamese, Jack. Think about that!"

"But that's exactly what we did. And it was disastrous."

"Well, that proves it then."

We quickly settled into our shipboard routine. Gearheardt and I were billeted with the other Marine lieutenants from the squadron. We tried to talk our way into the much superior captains' quarters, but convincing the squadron personnel officer that we were both *almost* captains was a lot more difficult than we thought, since he had no earthly idea of what we were talking about and we weren't about to tell him. "Worth a try," Gearheardt said, as the personnel officer wrote "possibly insane" in our medical folders.

The lieutenants' quarters for our squadron were a windowless iron-walled room on the level just below the flight deck in the far front of the boat. We could walk out the door and with a hard left turn be on the forecastle, pronounced "folk-sul" by the prissy Navy guys, with spray in our face and the smell of the sea.

Which was a lot better than the smell in the zoo, an apt name, after the first night. There were fifteen bunk beds, with just enough room in between them for back-to-back footlockers. We had a fellow named Noah Feldonstein in the squadron and we decided to make him "in charge" of keeping the zoo clean and orderly. The biblical Noah, of course, had a much easier task. On the other hand, *that* Noah gave a rat's ass. Our Noah didn't. It was just that when visiting Navy brass would ask, "My God, who's in charge of this damn disaster?" holding a handkerchief to their nose, we could say "Lieutenant Feldonstein, sir," and not look like no one gave a rat's ass. This was how the Marine Corps worked. As long as someone was accountable, you could pretty much do anything.

I sat on my bunk looking at the mounds of combat-colored gear and the joking pilots. I felt clueless and mentioned to Gearheardt that I wondered if we were like Alice, following a rabbit down a hole.

"You mean like that Alice character in *Wonder Woman*?"

"*Alice in Wonderland,* Gearheardt."

Gearheardt, reclining on his adjoining bunk, reached into his footlocker and withdrew his pistol. "Alice didn't carry one of these babies, Jack. A nine millimeter, rapid-fire, fully automatic hand weapon with copper-jacket double loads. I see a damn rabbit or Mad Hatter and they're *wasted*." He dry clicked the weapon and returned it to his footlocker.

"I'm sure it would have been a different story if Alice had been armed to the teeth, Gearheardt."

"You're damn right it would have." He lay back, his hands clasped behind his head, and closed his eyes. "Did you ever wonder what Alice looked like naked, Jack?"

I didn't answer, thinking more about the Cheshire Cat. Laughing at me.

Four days out to sea, the squadron made an important discovery. It was Bearhead who figured it out. No flight operations were scheduled for the day, and we were sitting around on the bunks in our skivvies smoking and complaining. Those who didn't smoke had the extra complaint of having to breathe the smoke. Of course those of us who did smoke had to complain about their pissing and moaning about the smoke. Then there were always those guys who never got into fistfights, and they were always complaining about the fighters knocking over their bunks or stepping on their toes. They weren't really fistfights, just pushing and shoving and wrestling and an occasional punch or two, usually thrown at someone who complained about his bunk being turned over. It was early in the day, and the complaining had not peaked at the fistfight level, which usually came just after lunch.

Bearhead burst in the door. "You know what those fucking Navy guys—"

There was nothing that could cut through the bitching, pissing, moaning, and complaining more quickly than anything that started with "those fucking Navy guys." We were galvanized into a tight-knit, cohesive, combat-ready Marine squadron just by hearing those words.

"I say we kill 'em and take over the ship," Flager shouted, frantically trying to find his pistol in his footlocker.

"Wait a minute." Buzz, the senior, and largest, lieutenant stopped his diatribe against people who don't smoke and complain about those who do and held up his hands. "Let's listen to what Bearhead found out." The zoo quieted and allowed Bearhead to continue.

"You know how it always seems to get so damn rough at night where the boat rolls and pitches till it throws your ass out on the floor? Every damn night! And everybody is throwing up all over the place?" Bearhead dropped to the footlocker that was always in the center of the zoo, usually with a poker game in progress. He lowered his voice as if someone could be eavesdropping through the inch of steel wall in the center of the boat in the middle of the Pacific.

"Last night I got up to take a piss and Weatherly had shut his foot-locker so I had to go—"

"So you're the bastard that's been pissing—"

Buzz held up his hands again, his eyes shut. "You guys can sort that out later. Go on, Bearhead."

"—so I take a wrong turn on the way to the head, and when I open this door there's these Navy assholes with a switch box that says 'pitch' and 'roll' with degree markings and everything and they're laughing their asses off." He paused to see if they got it. "And I heard one of them say *I'll bet those jarheads are puking their guts out.*'"

Dowger was shaving the hair off his forearm with his K-bar. "So what's your point? Everybody pukes their guts out every night in here. Damn deck looks like a giant combination pizza in the mornings. So what's with the switch box?"

Bearhead was happy that he was the only one smart enough to figure it out. "Don't you get it? Those fucking Navy guys have got the zoo on a hydraulic platform. The sea doesn't get rough at night like those assholes told us. It's them! Dicking with us!"

"Let's kill 'em and take over the ship." Everyone ignored Flager this time because he had already lost his pistol. Losing your weapon was not good in the Marine Corps.

"Shut the fuck up, Flager," said Bearhead. "Listen guys, we can't let them get away with this. Buzz, what do *you* think?"

Buzz was strangely contemplative. He scratched his nuts and stared unfocused at the bulkhead. "I'm not so sure, Bearhead. How would they get all that gear rigged up? Just to screw with us? That would be a substantial undertaking. A feat of engineering that could require considerable forethought and exquisite execution." It was rumored that Buzz had actually gone to a private school, or at least not a state-chartered university. Around him the other lieutenants sat or lay on their bunks talking among themselves. Buzz scratched his chin and then began again on his balls. "The chiefs," he finally said. "That's how they could have done it." Now that he had pronounced that Bearhead was right, the atmosphere in the zoo became charged.

"Flager! Go find your gun!" Weatherly shouted. He seemed to get a kick out of Flager rummaging frantically through his footlocker. As I had seen Weatherly throw Flager's pistol overboard the first night out, it was pretty certain the idiot wouldn't find it and start shooting.

The room erupted in a barrage of threats against the Navy. The idea of setting fire to the ship and flying off in the helicopters seemed to be taking hold when Peters shouted everybody down. "Hold on!" He was a well-respected officer and the best fighter in the zoo, so everybody quieted down. "First of all, the helicopters won't hold enough fuel to get us back to land. Second—"

"We're all going to die!" Butler screamed. He had been screaming this ever since the squadron received its orders to Vietnam, so no one paid much attention except Peters, who punched him out for interrupting. I respected Peters even more and winked at Gearheardt, who was in his footlocker drinking a beer and peeking out through the barely open top. Alcohol was not allowed on board ship, and Gearheardt only drank in his footlocker. I never figured out where he stored his stuff. He stuck out his fist and gave me a thumbs up, and then let the lid close back.

". . . and second of all, we've got to quit letting these Navy assholes know they're getting to us."

"This isn't one of those 'turn the other cheek' speeches is it, Peters?" Buzz asked. "You the chaplain now?"

Everybody laughed, even the chaplain, who was lying in Gearheardt's bunk in his skivvies, trying to be one of the boys. His name was A. G. Thomas, which before he could explain otherwise, we decided stood for "Assistant God."

Peters was a blond surfer type from Southern California, a lot smarter than he looked. He actually looked like an All-American boy, which was why everybody thought he was Jack Armstrong. Everybody but me, of course, because I *was* Jack Armstrong except when I was Tom Dexter.

"No, this is a 'lie low and get 'em when they least expect it' speech. Don't any of you assholes know anything about tactics?

Here's the plan. Nobody say anything to any swabbie. Act like nothing is wrong. In fact, we're going to have to eat our vomit so they won't even know they've been making us sick."

A couple of the younger lieutenants, Daniels and Becker, threw up.

"Pritchard! Eat your own!" Peters grimaced and turned away. Pritchard had a fine coat of red hair down his back, and everyone knew he was dangerous. "The next thing we do—"

"ATTENTION ON DECK."

The XO of the squadron bounced into the room. We had called him Pepe since he first bounced into the Three-sixty-three ready room just before we got our orders to Vietnam. Our old executive officer had given the obligatory Friday afternoon Don't Drink and Drive lecture to the squadron, then tanked up at nickel drink night at the O club and wrapped his car around the sentry shack at the main gate. The group docs had grounded him to teach him a lesson. The new XO, Major Gonzales, had this bubbly kind of personality usually only found in high school cheerleaders and people on drugs. We suspected he was both. But that wasn't why we hated him. We hated him because he always brought bad news. And you could tell he loved doing it, hating us equally. He was short and wiry and had thick, black, curly hair and a black curly mustache.

"A very good morning, men. Listen up. You can be at ease." He stood on a footlocker so that everyone could see him. The lieutenants went back to lying around and scratching their nuts. "Flight operations tomorrow. It should be a beautiful day for flying." Loud groans and a couple of "aw shits" from the back of the room. "If you're on the schedule, breakfast, I hear there'll be French toast with real maple syrup, at oh-five-thirty, brief in the three-six-three ready room at oh-six-thirty, launch at oh-seven-hundred. Any questions? Good. Next . . ." He consulted a clipboard. "Next, the skipper wants everyone in the ready room this morning at eleven hundred. He's going to cover some rules of etiquette for our stay in Japan and Okinawa on the way to Vietnam. Beautiful countries, and I know that you all will be entertained. Also I will announce the results of the 'name the squadron' contest. A disgusting affair, I'm afraid, but more on that later. I will also give the rules for the 'name the enemy' contest, which is the last one before we get to Japan. I think that you'll all agree that the skipper's games have made the trip go faster." The major pulled nervously on his black mustache. "Any questions?"

"Yeah, are we almost there?" Harrington asked it every chance he got.

The major ignored him. "Any complaints that I could pass along?" He assumed a majorly stance, hands on hips, and methodically looked from face to face. He stopped at Pritchard's. "What in hell is that dripping down your chin, Lieutenant?"

"Becker's puke, sir."

The XO swallowed hard, and it seemed he was searching for a response. Then he bounced down off of the footlocker and through the hatch without looking back. "Eleven hundred hours in the ready room!" he yelled over his shoulder and disappeared.

"Thanks, Pepe!" Weatherly shouted in a falsetto voice.

Buzz and Peters faced each other in the center of the zoo. There had been a rivalry for leadership of the lieutenant pilots since the two joined the squadron. Nobody really gave a damn except for a few of the junior second lieutenants. I certainly didn't. Not only because Gearheardt and I were *almost captains,* but also because I didn't see how it would affect my life in the slightest. After a moment Buzz grinned and walked over to his bunk. "Okay, Peters, we'll go with you on this one. No one set fire to the ship, boys."

At eleven hundred hours we were all in the ready room. The three majors sat in the front row, the captains behind them, and then all of the lieutenants. Maps, charts, briefing boards, photos of airplanes, and all sorts of aircraft paraphernalia hung from the steel walls. Helmets, kneeboards, and pistols in shoulder holsters hung from the pilots' seats. The ceiling was low and crisscrossed with pipes and tubes; all painted gray and labeled with stenciled letter: P-I-P-E, 78935. USN, or B-L-K-H-D, SEC. 2-G, USN.

At eleven hundred hours and one minute the Skipper walked into the ready room.

"ATTENTION ON DECK," the XO yelled.

The Skipper, Lieutenant Colonel Bradley J. Coats, strode through the squadron and faced us from behind the briefing podium. "At ease, men," he said, and smiled. He was a distinguished figure, with prematurely gray hair, a neatly trimmed gray mustache, and an equally trim five-foot-eleven, 170-pound frame. He had been a fighter pilot in Korea. He had a tendency to be rather aloof and had never, to anyone's knowledge, spoken to a lieutenant in the squadron, except in the cockpit, where he jabbered like a gibbon. We all liked him and respected his apparent disdain for us.

He fidgeted with a notebook on the pulpit-like stand before he looked back up at us, all seated again. "Good morning, gentlemen. I'm sure that Major Gonzales has alerted you to flight operations tomorrow. We will also commence night operations tomorrow evening at nineteen hundred."

There was a collective, muttered *"Shit."* The dickhead major had certainly not mentioned it, probably fearing for his life in the zoo. The craziest bastard in the squadron wasn't crazy enough to like night flying off the carrier. Maybe nonpilots thought that it was easy in a helicopter. It was anything but. You had to get down close to the water, which you couldn't see, and when you came back aboard by matching your speed to the boat and moving sideways onto it, you completely lost sight of the boat until you hit it, one way or another. Baxter used to say the only good thing about night flying off the boat was that it gave him a chance to shit his pants and not get teased about it.

The murmuring quieted down, and the Skipper continued. He picked a memo from his pile and held it chest high, looking as if he were trying not to squint as he read it. "You men in the zoo should be prepared for a couple of new pilots that will be joining us in Japan. This directive says four, but I believe that it's in error. Three-sixty-three will receive two Negro pilots, one Jewish pilot and one American Indian pilot. That's what the directive from HQMC says."

He looked around the room and found Captain Shinn, the squadron administrative office.

"Captain, don't we already have a Negro pilot and a Jewish pilot? Didn't you get back to HQ with that word like I asked?"

Captain Shinn jumped to his feet.

"Yes, sir. The colonel is correct. However Directive 33-71, the latest, says that our table of organization has to have a spare Negro pilot. I have requested a Negro Jewish pilot, since we would have to get rid of one of our current pilots in order to billet two new pilots. Lieutenant Bearhead qualifies as our American Indian pilot, and I have notified HQ, sir. The American Indian awaiting our arrival in Japan will have to find another squadron. 33-71 does not call for a spare American Indian pilot."

The Skipper looked confused. "So we will have how many pilots joining us in Japan? Not counting the American Indian. That's two Negro and one Jewish, or just one of each?"

Lieutenant Feldonstein jumped to his feet. "Sir, I could stay in Japan with the Indian and let the new Jew come on board." Noah Feldonstein was always nervous that people would discover that he wasn't Jewish. His family name was originally Feldon but had been changed to Feldonstein to sound more Jewish, since the family had been persecuted for generations for no good reason.

The Skipper, bewildered, looked to his staff sitting in the front row. "Who in the hell is that?"

"Lieutenant Feldonstein, sir. Goes by Sky-Kyke. He's been the squadron's Jew since last April. Good man, too. Keeps the zoo shipshape, I've heard." Major Bartly, the squadron logistics officer, had never been to the zoo.

Now the Skipper was clearly pissed. He had probably only read the directive to the squadron so that he could appear to be in the thick of things running the squadron, and now he was lost.

"Okay, listen up. Next item."

Feldonstein slowly sat down, a hurt look on his face. A self-effacing fellow, it was he who had given himself the Sky-Kyke name and had drawn the Star of David with wings on the back of his flight suits. A nice friendly kid who would later make the fatal mistake of flying a burning helicopter upside down with bullets in his body.

The Skipper droned on through the bulletins that poured forth daily from the ship's communications room. A nervous Headquarters Marine Corps giving last-minute instructions to its boys heading for war. Care of the rotor blades. Care of the engines. Care of the feet, hands, back, neck, and head. Logistical minutiae. Bulletins for flight operations, field kitchens, latrine construction and maintenance—the list went on and on. Bulletins correcting or amending previous bulletins. When the entire squadron was asleep behind their dark aviator sunglasses, the Skipper paused, sat back on his captain's stool, and dozed off himself.

This was the way that Major Gonzales found the squadron when he returned from his mission to try to placate the ship's captain, whose tiny room sink had been shit in—again. I had awakened when Pepe gently closed the door. Fifty sleeping men sat in the room, the Skipper in front reflecting them from his aviator glasses. The major cleared his throat loudly. A few of the lieutenants stirred. The Skipper started and dropped the bundle of memos and directives he had in his lap. I wasn't sure whether he had actually been asleep or was just afraid of being the only one awake. He spotted the XO in the back of the ready room and beckoned him to the front. "Take over, Major," the Skipper said.

The XO bounce-walked to the front of the room and took the podium. "Men," he said, "this afternoon at fourteen hundred, the Skipper will lead the discussion on the treatment of women in Japan, Okinawa, and Vietnam. You will all attend. Any questions? No, not you, Harrington. A number of you have not been out of CONUS for any extended time, and the Skipper feels he needs to give you some guidelines and instructions. If there're no questions, we'll get to the 'name the squadron' results and then on up to chow."

Major Gonzales reached to the inside pocket of his leather flight jacket and pulled out a folded legal-size paper. His face darkened as he carefully smoothed it out on the lectern. He finally raised his eyes to look at the roomful of pilots. He took a deep breath.

"Very funny, gentlemen. Very funny. I would have expected this from a group of high school boys. But from commissioned officers in the U.S. Marine Corps, well, I am disappointed." He looked back at the Skipper, who was playing with the zipper on the calf of his flight suit.

"Just get on with it, Major," the Skipper said.

The XO set his jaw and narrowed his eyes toward the squadron. "First of all, I want to congratulate you all for taking the time to submit your choices." He was still so new to the squadron that he thought someone might give a shit. A number of the pilots applauded, the sarcasm too subtle for those who believed defecating in the captain's sink was a clever practical joke. "Knock it off!" the major growled.

"I won't read the results in their entirety. They speak volumes of your intellect, your spirit, and your love for the squadron." He held up the legal pad and shook it at them.

"Let me read some of them to you. Fucking Ravens, Fucking Flying Dicks, the Fucking Assholes, all of these got five votes. Next we have the Shitheads, the Dickheads, the Fuckheads, and the Fucking Shitheads. Those all got two votes. One vote apiece for Greasy Assholes, Cunt Lickers, and my personal favorite, the Fucking Dickhead Greasy Asshole Pussy Lickers. You men should be proud of yourselves. Oh yes, there were four ballots that just said, 'Fuck You.' I have chosen not to take that personally."

He folded the yellow paper and put it away in his pocket. "After consultation with Colonel Coats, we have decided to call the squadron the Purple Tigers." A number of the pilots groaned. Pepe continued, "And we also decided not to—"

"Why *Purple* Tigers?" Lieutenant Bensen asked.

"Yeah," Lieutenant Crowley chimed in, "why not just call ourselves the Lavender Gay Guys With No Dicks? That would save the other squadrons the effort of thinking of it."

"Two Sixty Four got to call themselves the Rat Bastards. Let's vote again." This from Winston, the lieutenant everybody called Fatass because he had an enormous ass.

"Knock it off. We're the Purple Tigers. I don't want to hear any more about it. I've warned you about excessive profanity. I certainly won't, or I should say the Skipper won't have it in the official squadron nickname. And as I started to say, the 'name the enemy' contest is not going forward, although I can imagine what you men would have come up with in any case." There were quiet boos from the back of the room. "Okay, knock it off. The Skipper has decided, upon my recommendation, to go with the official enemy name from Directive 17-55, Victor Charlie, or Charlie for short."

There was a stunned silence in the ready room. Finally Lieutenant Harrington raised his hand. "Sir, could I ask a question?"

"It better not be 'Are we almost there?,' Lieutenant. That joke is getting old."

"Yes, sir. I wanted to know if Charlie is a Vietnamese name. It doesn't seem right to have an enemy named Charlie."

The major smiled. "The name is from the phonetic representation of Viet Cong or VC. It isn't really a name." He laughed nervously. "This is no big deal. Now the next item—"

"Can we call him Bruce?" someone shouted from the rear of the room.

The major frowned. "Very funny. That's enough about the name. Now at fourteen hundred—"

"How about Fucking Bruce?" It was another voice, and the major didn't look up quick enough to see where it came from.

"Knock it off! No more names. I'm not going to—"

"Bruce the Dickhead!" Shouts of agreement.

"LOOK. I don't give a DAMN what you want to call the enemy. THE OFFICIAL NAME IS CHARLIE. NOW, NO MORE ENEMY NAMES!"

The Skipper stood and stepped to the major's side, putting a friendly hand on his shoulder. "Calm down, Major," he said with a chuckle. "The men are just playing with you because they think you're an asshole." He patted the major's shoulder again and gave him a little shove toward the front row of seats. "Okay, gentlemen, let's drop the crap about the squadron name. We'll call ourselves Rat

Bastards and call the enemy the same thing. How's that?" No one spoke. The Skipper aimed his reflective lenses around the room. "Settled then."

Major Gonzales couldn't let it pass. With an aggrieved look he stood up and addressed the squadron commander. "Sir, I think you may have misunderstood. Two-sixty-four are the Rat Bastards. Plus, it might be confusing to call ourselves *and* the enemy by the same name."

"Well, we're all called Marines. No one seems to be confused by that, Major."

"Yes, sir, but the point of naming the squadron is to distinguish ourselves from the others." He struggled to keep the anger from his voice.

The Skipper didn't. "Damn it, Major. You may want to distinguish yourself by calling yourself a Piece of Dipshit or whatever it was you suggested. But as long as I'm commander of this squadron, we're not sinking to that level. It's Rat Bastards and that's enough about names."

"But, sir."

"Let's hit the wardroom, gentleman. The Navy doesn't like us late for chow." He stepped quickly toward the rear of the ready room.

"Squadron, attention!" the operations office yelled.

Gearheardt and I started to follow our squadron-mates out of the ready room. I was hungry, and Gearheardt felt he needed to line his stomach before he began the afternoon's experiment in drinking aviation fuel distillation mixed with grapefruit juice. Just as we reached the hatch, another Navy term we had to endure, Major Gonzales caught up with us.

"You two, you're Gearheardt and Armstrong aren't you?"

Gearheardt was about to give a wiseass answer but I felt sorry for the XO after the name fiasco. "Yessir, that's us," I said.

"You two need to be in the captain's quarters at thirteen hundred. You know where that is?"

"No sir, and I don't know where his sink is either," Gearheardt answered.

"This has nothing to do with that," the major said dismissively, indicating the meeting was on far more important things. "Be there at thirteen hundred." He stepped through the hatch and his flight boots clomped down the steel deck in the passageway.

Gearheardt grabbed my upper arm before I could follow the major. "Look at this," he said, holding out the yellow paper that I had last seen go into the major's flight jacket. I took it and read the agenda for the meeting just held, including the list of suggested squadron names. Gearheardt's finger directed my eyes to the bottom of the page. The last item listed was "Barbonella." In my head, full of hundreds of movies I'd seen, dramatic music came up. In my skivvies, my sphincter tightened.

I looked at Gearheardt, who shrugged. "I would imagine that someone has found out our plan and has decided to kill us."

"We don't even have a damn plan! What the hell are you talking about?"

"I've found it's best to always assume the worst and then just go with it." Gearheardt was incredibly exasperating when he was sober.

At 1300 hours, full of chicken chow mein, the two of us stood outside the stateroom of the ship's captain. Gearheardt started to knock on the bulkhead but I stopped his arm. "Listen, pal," I hissed in his ear, "none of your wiseass stuff. Maybe this isn't even about Barbonella. Let me do the talking unless they ask you a direct question. Got it?"

"Be my guest." He rapped three times on the bulkhead.

"Enter." A deep voice from behind the door.

Gearheardt stepped through the door and came to attention. I fell in beside him.

"Almost Captain Gearheardt reporting as ordered, sir." The asshole, I thought.

"Almost Captain Armstrong," I said, not very loud.

"At ease, gentlemen," the ship's skipper, Captain Rex Sand, said. "You men know your CO and XO, of course. This gentleman is Commander Flynn, my intelligence officer, and that gentleman," he nodded toward a stern lieutenant commander sitting to the side of the room, "is my assistant something or other."

Captain Sand was a stocky ex-Academy man. He had a gray crew-cut and bushy eyebrows, which were still half-black, drawing your attention to them. The other two naval officers could be described best as nondescript. Neither wore lipstick as Gearheardt always claimed they did. The cabin was spartan by any standards except how the rest of the men on the ship lived. A built-in bunk, desk, chair, trashcan, and just about everything else in the room were gray. Like the ship. Over the shoulder of the captain I could see a bookshelf containing tomes on everything from driving a ship to painting an airplane. I thought I saw a copy of *Panties on Priests,* but when the captain swiveled around to face us, his shoulders blocked my view. I decided that I'd better tune in to what was going on.

"Gents," the captain began with a pleasant, friendly tone, "best place to start is at the beginning. What the hell are you two up to?"

Before I could formulate a reply, Gearheardt spoke up. "Sir, I'm afraid that's classified. Almost Captain Armstrong and I have no orders and can't tell you about them. The only part that we can tell you is that we're almost captains and we're on your side, sir."

The silence in the room hurt my teeth after a while. Our five superior officers were inhaling air and exhaling hate and noxious gases. Gearheardt had left me no wiggle room with his answer.

At the count of fifty—I was counting to myself to take my mind off Leavenworth—the captain quit staring at us and looked at our squadron CO. "Is this more of that Marine Corps bullshit, Colonel? I'm so tired of that damned attitude I could puke."

Our Skipper shrugged and held his palms up. "Captain, I don't know a thing more than you do. The scuttlebutt we got was that these two were asked by the highest authorities to stop the war. The Barbonella plan, according to my sources. The Marine Corps has a man stationed permanently in the shitter at the White House and this is the info he passed on."

"In the shitter?"

"We've had a man taking a piss since 1962. No one goes up to a guy at the urinal and starts a conversation. So, he just stands there

holding his dick and listening to the staff drift in and out, talking."
He smiled. "This is all highly confidential of course."

"You mean this Barbonella plan that we—"

"No, the shitter detail. We're about to bust an Air Force guy that's
been taking a crap for about two years now. We think he may be a
plant. The Marine Corps has the exclusive rights to the White House
plumbing. The son of a bitch in that stall better be constipated or
he's in a world of hurt." In answer to the six heads turned toward him
the colonel went on. "I just got off of the White House guard detail.
Great duty. My replacement keeps me informed."

During the small talk among the senior officers about past *cream* assignments, Gearheardt whispered to me, "Let's just blow out of here."

Captain Sand leaned back in his chair. "But bottom line, do you
expect me to believe that two green lieutenants have been given a mission by the White House to end the war in Vietnam? Does that make
any sense to anybody?" The captain shook his head. He looked back at
us and tried to assemble his most stern look. It worked pretty well.

"One last time, *Almost* Captains—whatever the hell that's all
about—what's this Barbonella mission? Because if it's really about
ending the war, you can goddam just forget it. We've geared up for
this thing and gone to one hell of a lot of trouble. I, for one, could
use a little combat time"—the Marines gave a quiet "Hear, hear,"—
"and I don't mind telling you that I won't take lightly to a couple of
jarheads shortening my career path. I suggest you men go on over
with the rest of us and do some fighting. None of this pussyfooting
around with Barbonella plans or anything. You read me?"

I was going to heartily agree, when Gearheardt spoke up. "We
don't know what you're talking about, Captain. So of course we can't
agree. If I did have orders I know that one of them would be to kill
whoever had unauthorized information about anything called Barbonella. I am assuming, sir, that is not the case here." It dawned on
me that my friend had been in the CIA since he was eleven years old.

The captain was on his feet, little pearls of spit forming at the
corners of his mouth. He leaned over his desks bracing himself on his

fists. "Listen up, Almost Captain Gearheardt. I don't care if your orders are to cut off your dick and call yourself Nancy. If you try to stop this war, I'll personally have the skin off your ass for a lampshade. Do I make myself clear?"

I gave Gearheardt no time for the snappy response I could see he wanted to make. He was enjoying this. "We understand perfectly, sir. I think there's probably been a mistake. We want this war every bit as much as you do. Will that be all, sir?"

"Get out of my sight!"

Gearheardt started to reply, and I grabbed him and shoved him outside, closing the door behind us. He smiled like we had found a whore's purse.

"Can you believe that?" he said. "Those bastards are scared to death of us. We really do have a mission that comes from the top. They don't know shit or they wouldn't have called us up here. We're golden, Jack. We're golden."

My problem is I always want to believe the best. As we strolled back to the zoo, I figured, what the hell, we're golden. It would occur to me later that there was a leak. Someone knew about Barbonella, certainly more than *I* knew, and wasn't happy about it.

8 · Asia Ahoy

First stop for the carrier was Japan. For refueling and, I can only assume, to get the Skipper laid. Lots of decisions are made this way in the service. It's worked okay so far.

Fatass was the first one to spot Japan on the horizon. We had been at sea for eleven days. A couple of those days were spent cruising around practicing helicopter operations, and I suspect one or more of them got scheduled because Bearhead had shorted out the ship's navigation system, flooding the electronics rooms by redirecting the urinal drains. The zoo was more stable at night after that, too.

Fatass was on the forecastle of the ship when we sailed into Tokyo Bay. He had been out there all night after making the mistake of suggesting the boys in the zoo sing some whaling songs to pass the time after evening chow. We locked him out, and he got the privilege of alerting us to the green, silent country as the fog lifted in the early morning. I went out on deck as we passed a colossal stone Buddha nestled in misty pines, facing the sea lane with the patience of the ages. I recall shuddering a bit as I gazed at it, thinking, inexplicably, that we might not be prepared for Asia. Most of the zoo, fifteen or twenty pilots, stood at the railing, their khaki uniforms crisp, shirt sleeves and trouser legs snapping in the breeze over the bow, staring at the shore. The solemn silence told me that the quarter-century link to our Marine heritage was sobering. U.S. Marines in Tokyo Bay. Our fathers and uncles would not have believed it.

Nor did Butler. "It's a trap!" he screamed, scaring the hell out of all of us at the rail. "We're all going to die!" He emptied his .38 at the receding Buddha. I saw tiny sparks fly as the bullets struck the stone. It didn't seem like the thing to do, but no one moved to stop him.

"THIS IS THE CAPTAIN. STOP FIRING. REPEAT. STOP FIRING." The ubiquitous speakers of God boomed "Now hear this! The individual or individuals firing weapons at the Japanese property report to the bridge at once! Repeat. Report to the bridge at once!"

Butler looked confused. "What did he say?" he asked Fatass. "My ears are ringing." He fumbled new rounds into his pistol.

"He said the Navy doesn't think you can hit the eyes."

Which is how Butler became the first U.S. Marine to be keel-hauled on a U.S. naval vessel in almost two hundred years. We could have stopped it, but most of the guys had never seen a keelhauling, and few liked Butler. He had the not terribly endearing habit when he was drinking of pissing wherever he happened to be, not taking into account where *you* happened to be. It wasn't technically a keelhauling, anyway. We just helped some swabbies tie a rope around him so he could be dragged behind the carrier through Tokyo Bay.

Before we docked, actually at Yokosuka not Tokyo, I grabbed Gearheardt and shoved him against the bulkhead in a quiet passageway. "We need to talk," I said. He tried to spin away. "I mean, right now."

Gearheardt smoothed the front of his shirt and straightened his wings. "I know what you're going to say. But I don't think there's a problem. If the Skipper or the boat driver knew anything more than just a rumor, they'd have our asses on the end of that rope with Butler." He laughed thinly.

I stood eye to eye with him. I couldn't see any fear, but he broke first. "Let's go get ready to go ashore," he said, twisting away.

I grabbed his shirt again. "Look at this." Pulling a folded piece of paper out of my breast pocket I stuck it in front of his face.

WE KNOW WHAT YOU BASTARDS ARE UP TO. FORGET BARBONELLA OR DIE. PLEASE PASS THIS ON TO GEAR-HEARDT, THE SQUADRON'S COPY MACHINE IS DOWN.

Gearheardt took the paper and wadded it up after reading it. He tossed it over his shoulder.

"This is a joke, Jack. You don't think they could have copied the thing by hand if they'd wanted to? I think you're overreacting to the meeting in the boat driver's room. They have a vague idea that we are up to something, and if they find out what it is they're going to kill us. I think that's all this means."

I could never tell with Gearheardt. But we were closer than any brothers. We'd been together since flight school.

"That's my point, you prick! We *are* up to something! And they *are* finding out! I didn't join the Marine Corps to be killed by my own squadron-mates for Chrissakes!"

Gearheardt was calm, probably because he already knew I was one of *his* squadron-mates and I wanted to kill him.

"Jack, remember that Brigadier Bittersly said—"

"Gearheardt, you jerk, we made Brigadier Bittersly up in a bar in Huntington Beach. Don't quote that crap to me now."

"Jack, I just think that sometimes we are called to do more than just follow the orders of the Marine Corps. Sure, we could just go over and have a good war and come back home. But *this,* this is a chance to change the course of history. This is a chance to be famous. Besides, the commander in chief has ordered us to Hanoi. Are you suggesting that we ignore that?"

Not one hundred percent sure just exactly *what* I was suggesting, I hesitated. Gearheardt put his arm around my shoulders and started us moving down the passageway. When we rounded the corner, we almost ran into Peters. He stood in the passageway, his arms outstretched, hands against the bulkheads, blocking our path.

"What are the Bobbsey Twins up to?" he asked. "I'm getting a little worried about you two. You're not goin' Navy on me, are you?"

"Get lost, Peters," I said. I outranked him, though only by date of rank at this point, and for some reason I thought his show was all bravado. The only guy he ever punched out was Butler. And Butler liked it and never punched him back.

Gearheardt had a slightly different reaction. "Bearhead is taking your wife's letters into the shitter with him, Peters." He pushed by and continued down the passageway.

I turned to follow Gearheardt. When I caught him my anger was gone. I felt fearful, let down.

"You know, Gearheardt," I said as we walked toward the zoo, "I had really been looking forward to this war. Now you're ruining it. Some cockeyed orders from the President. Threatening letters. Peters obviously suspects something."

Gearheardt shrugged.

I continued, "I have to admit that you threw him off. He won't remember what he was suspicious of for a long time, knowing how his mind works."

"Your paranoia is showing, Jack."

"Gearheardt, people are threatening to kill us right and left. That can hardly be called paranoia."

"You're the one with all the education, Jack. If you say it's not paranoia, I'll believe you. Whatever it is, I think it's wise for us to be on our toes. You need to be more careful."

"*I* need to be more careful? Gearheardt, you drive me goddam crazy. If I remember correctly, you somehow got us into this situation— the boat driver and the Skipper and the XO warning us and threatening letters from our squadron-mates, who by now think we're homosexuals. This is not a good start to this war."

We were at the zoo. Inside, a scene of hellish frenzy replaced the normal trash-strewn landscape as the occupants prepared to go ashore for Cinderella liberty—everyone back on the boat by midnight. Gearheardt was asked by several lieutenants to join their shore party as he made his way to his bunk and footlocker. These small gestures began to convince me that perhaps the entire squadron was not aware of Barbonella. Maybe I *was* getting paranoid. I began to feel a bit better but still wanted to place a phone call to the White House when we got ashore. If there was *any* chance that we were going to get killed by *our* side, I at least wanted to hear about Barbonella from the President himself. Gearheardt agreed. He also suggested that we check in with his superiors at the CIA.

"What? The CIA? What in the hell do they have to do with Barbonella? I thought you said this wasn't an agency deal." Gearheardt and I were alone in the zoo. When the first liberty call came over God's speakers, the zoo emptied like the time the Navy pukes announced 'nickel beer and free pussy on the flight deck' over the speakers when we were first aboard and didn't know that they were screwing with us.

"I had to at least inform them, Jack. They're the ones that got me out of that orphanage, and I do owe my second primary allegiance to them. And don't forget that you're a part of the agency, too."

"So what did they say?" I ignored the comment about my alleged agency affiliation.

Gearheardt sniffed at the armpit of a civilian shirt and began to put it on. "They didn't like it very much. Thought the whole Barbonella thing was idiocy and ordered me to stop it."

"They *what*?" I rose up from my footlocker, where I was rummaging for a polo shirt.

"Oh, not us, they think that we're Narsworthy and Dexter. They want us to stop Gearheardt and Armstrong."

"That's us too, you jerk. How did I ever let you talk me into this 'two person' crap? Who does *the President* think we are?" I felt myself going crazy and thought it was just as well.

"He thinks we're Gearheardt and Armstrong primarily." Gearheardt pulled on his prized elephant-hide cowboy boots, tucked his slacks into them, and stood up. "We're just going to have to kill Narsworthy and Dexter. Or at least let the agency think they're dead."

"How do we do that?" Going along with this wasn't nearly as exasperating as arguing logic with Gearheardt.

"You'll think of something, Jack. In a pinch, you always do. That's why you need me. To get you into pinches." He waited while I slipped on a civilian shirt, and then we proceeded to the quarterdeck to check out for liberty in Yokosuka. It was early morning and our plan was to visit the U.S. consulate, call the White House, and by noon be discovering and exploring the sights, smells, and sounds of Japanese bars. Then if we had any time left we would see a bit of the Japanese countryside. Observing the Marines gathered near the gangway, jostling each other for position, I felt somewhat uneasy at the thought of unleashing this horde on the unsuspecting populace of Yokosuka. Even if these people were the direct descendents of the guys who suckerpunched Pearl Harbor, it seemed pretty cruel to turn loose hundreds of Marines into their midst. When I voiced a bit of this sentiment to Gearheardt while we waited our turn, he pointed out that the area immediately surrounding the docks of most ports in the world didn't usually house the virtuous and saintly. After a final speech over God's speakers about respecting the Japanese people and their customs, the men began to stream ashore and were swallowed up by the pimps, prostitutes, touts, louts, crooks, charlatans, madams, thieves, and others who made up the welcoming committee.

Gearheardt and I shouldered our way through the crowd. At the main gate we jumped into the back seat of a small taxi and Gearheardt screamed at the driver, "TAKE US TO THE AMERICAN CONSULATE."

Luckily the driver, a bespeckled, pockfaced Japanese with a shaved head, spoke almost perfect English. "Hey, fuck you consulate. No have here fucking Tokyo. Want pussy. One thousand yen. No have local beer, make sick. Fucking good American beer buy from chiefs. Five hundred yen. We go pussy now." He popped the clutch and shot away from the curb.

Gearheardt, who constantly amazed me with his grace and flair in handling unexpected situations, got the driver's attention by taking off his shoe and smashing it against his right temple.

"No pussy, you Japanese asshole. Take us to the U.S. consulate right now or I'll goddam kill you. Kemo sabe?"

The driver slowed down and rubbed his temple, peering at us in the rearview mirror with new respect. "Hey Marine, you take easy. Consulate closed. What you need consulate?"

"We need to call the President of the U.S., you nosy bastard. Now take us there and it better be open or we're going to skin you. Comprende?"

"Call to states included price of pussy in number one club. My brother own club personal friend of President. We go now. Have American beer and girls many girls love Marine."

Of course the sonofabitch was lying. Gearheardt and I dropped about a hundred bucks on beer and women before we finally decided that the club owner was dicking with us. He would hand us the phone and then express amazement when the President wasn't on the other end.

We took a taxi back to the Navy base and went into the administration building to find a phone. We found plenty, but when we asked the Navy operator to hook us up to the President the line always went dead—sometimes immediately, sometimes after some pretty vile comments. By noon we were sitting on the steps of the admin building smoking cigarettes when a guy in uniform, himself smoking a thin cigar, spoke to us without turning.

"You boys want to make a phone call?" he said and drew on his cigar.

"We're not boys, asshole. We're almost captains. Don't make me come over there and shove that cigar where the sun hasn't shone since the last time you and your boyfriend were at the beach." Gearheardt was *not* in a good mood.

The guy just laughed. "I may be an asshole, but I know better than to pay a hundred bucks for pussy and a phone call to the President. You damn jarheads shouldn't be on the streets without keepers. Anyway, you want a phone call, see Chief Utterback in 336. It's up the stairs, third door on the left."

"Thanks, Chief," I said. I got up and Gearheardt followed.

In 336 the pudgy, jolly telecommunications chief was playing chess with a seaman third. When we came in he dismissed the seaman, who closed the door behind him as he left.

"You boys need a phone call, right?"

I put my hand on Gearheardt's arm and held him back. "It's okay, Gearheardt," I said. "It's the chief's territory." I couldn't stop his mouth as easily.

"Yeah, fatso, we need a phone call."

"It'll cost you. You want an open line or you need secure?"

"I guess the secure line is a bit more expensive, right?" Gearheardt must have thought that biting sarcasm was landing on someone that gave a damn. I knew better.

"I got costs at the other end of a secure line I gotta cover," the chief said reasonably.

Even I could smell a rip-off. "There's nobody *at* the other end but the President, Chief."

The chief shrugged and held up his palms, his eyebrows arched.

"Hook us up. And we need a room to make the call."

The chief took a phone out of the desk and plugged it in. "When you lift up the receiver and dial your number the President will be on the line. Leave two hundred bucks in the drawer."

"What if we don't?" Gearheardt was still upset at the lack of respect.

"That would be pretty stupid considering where you're headed. I could make it hot for you down there." He put on his cap and walked to the door.

"In Vietnam! You could make it hot for us in *Vietnam*!" Gearheardt was almost beside himself. "You fat prick! I'll make it hot for you—"

I cut him off by slamming the door as the chief left.

"Gearheardt, we don't give a damn if the chiefs are running the war. It's either them or the gunny sergeants. What difference does it make? Get the President's number out here and let's get this over with."

The best thing about Gearheardt was he never carried an emotion further than he absolutely needed to. The chief was forgotten as he pried a small slip of paper from between the layers of the heel of his right shoe. He read it and tossed it on the desk. When he finished dialing he held the receiver at an angle to his ear and motioned for me to draw close to him so we could both hear. I heard the tail end of a ring that sounded like "Hail to the Chief" and then a man answered.

"President of the United States speaking and this better not be that goddam siding wiseass."

"Mr. President, it's Gearheardt sir."

"Gearheardt! Where in the hell are you, son?"

I already had heard enough to know that Gearheardt—and by association me—really did have a secret mission from the President of the United States.

"We're not supposed to tell anybody where we are, sir. But I'll give you a hint."

"Hell, I was just being sociable, son. You're in room 336 of the admin building at the Yokosuka Naval Yard. Tell Chief Utterback he's a bit overdue. But never mind that, what can I do for you son?"

"Sir, Almost Captain Armstrong is here with me, Mr. President."

"Hello, Almost Captain Armstrong. Ngnh quih!"

"Bless you, Mr. President."

"That was Vietnamese, boys. Thought you spoke it like a native, Jack."

Gearheardt was nodding his head quickly, wanting me to agree. I caved.

"Of course, Mr. President. I was just kidding. Quang nhat song binh." I made up some gibberish on the assumption that he had shot his wad in Vietnamese.

"Heh, heh, don't have the foggiest what you're saying, Jack. But I know Vietnamese when I hear it. Glad you're on the team."

"Mr. President—" I began.

"Call me Larry Bob, Jack. Gearheardt knows I ain't too formal with my team. Now what seems to be the issue? By the way, sorry about that siding salesman thing. Brother-in-law of mine in the business sicced a salesman onto me Thanksgiving. Sonofabitch is persistent, I'll give him that. So to what do I owe the honor of this call? You ain't getting cold feet, I hope."

"No, sir," Gearheardt volunteered. "Jack just kind of needs to hear the mission straight from you, Mr. President. And I do have to tell you that we have had a few indications that Barbonella is out of the bag."

The President listened without comment as Jack described the scene in the ship captain's office and the warning note that he had found on his bunk.

Then the President spoke. "Well first off, the cat ain't out of the bag as far as Barbonella is concerned. Some boys have heard some scuttlebutt and are trying to make something of it. That's a game the military plays about twenty-six hours a day. I could start a rumor the Pope eats poontang and find twenty thousand new Catholics on the cathedral doorstep tomorrow. No, the thing—"

"The Pope eats what, Mr. President?"

"Never mind, son. As I was saying, the thing we might have to be concerned with for a while is this shitter detail here in the White House."

"Surely you can send a Secret Service man down to stop that leak, Mr. President, no pun intended." But Gearheardt laughed and gave me a thumbs up. He was enjoying this.

"Son, we got a turf battle in that shitter you wouldn't believe. Normally the Marine Corps has first rights to the info they can get. But Air Force Intelligence somehow got a man into one of the stalls, and now the whole damn thing is over at JAG trying to get straightened out. Sometimes I think the commandant has the right idea."

"What's that, Mr. President?" Gearheardt was professionally curious.

"Same answer he has to everything. This time he wants permission to stick a flame thrower under the stall door and let her rip." The chuckle that followed made me think the President liked this solution also. "The Marine Corps don't take kindly to the Air Force moving in on their territory."

"So, Mr. President, if I may get back to the reason we bothered you, why is it that you are so sure that Barbonella isn't blown?"

"Mainly 'cause there's just you boys, me, and Barbonella knows anything about the whole shootin' match, and I don't think she's of a mind to tell anyone."

"Barbonella, sir?" Something about this was upsetting to me. Who *was* Barbonella? I had thought it was just a silly code word.

"I told you before, boys, that I can't keep all my eggs in one basket. Too damn important. Your mission is just one element of Barbonella. You boys hold on a moment." There was a pause, and then the President came back on the line. "Hold the phone away from your ears a moment, fellows."

As we did so an ear-splitting *AHOOOOOOGGAA* filled the room. After a moment we put the phone back up to our ears and heard the President laughing. "One of the chiefs got me this dive horn off a submarine." He laughed again.

"Boy, I love that part. Hear that clicking and scratching? That's the spooks and kooks trying to get their listening devices working again. Let me fill you in quickly while they've got their fingers poking in their ears. You boys are carryin' the iron fist to Hanoi, but I got a sugar pot goin' up there at the same time. Gonna hit ol' Ho Chi in the head and gonads at the same time. Hee, hee. You boys see *Barbonella* like I tole you to?"

"Mr. President, the best we could find out was that *Barbonella* wasn't even made yet, that is, if you're talking about the movie that—"

"That's the one. Hell, it's made, all right. I got a script in my desk right— *Son of a bitch!* My copy's gone! I'll have someone's ass or my name ain't Mr. President." He was quiet for a moment and we could hear the sounds of drawers being pulled out and rifled. Finally, he came back on the line. "Yep, found the damn thing. I put it into my briefcase to take up to my bedroom and just plumb forgot. Anyway, the movie is made, and I've seen it in the White House screening room, but not whatchucallit, where they send it out to the picture shows. Seems there's a big hoopla over releasing it. The star sobered up and about went apeshit when she seen what she'd done. Pretty ugly Hollywood deal." The President laughed.

"Just a few copies exist right now, but the dang Cubans been makin' sure that their pals get one. Let me jump to the short hairs here. I'm going to play a tape that was smuggled out of Hanoi last month. You'll see what a golden chance this is. Hold on now, I'm fixin' to play this back if I can get this doohickey fired up." Pause. "Here we go."

Low static and then a crackle and popping noises. A man's voice, hushed like he was afraid someone would overhear him. A desperate voice. Only a few words could be made out.

". . . nearly mad. Uncle is smitten with . . . every day . . . sometimes five or s . . . Barbar . . . obsessed . . . and out of control. He suspects that I am not . . . repeat Barbonella opportunity must be . . . Nearing end. Made me watch. Horrible. Horrible. . . ."

The President came back on. "Now you get it, boys?" he asked. "See the deal?"

I started to say that I wasn't sure when Gearheardt interrupted.

"Almost Captain Armstrong has it completely. We await your further instructions, sir."

"When I get the star to get her butt up to Hanoi, you boys be ready to go in behind her. She's your cover. Be ready." He paused.

"And boys, when you get there, you'll find the poor bastard who made the tape, or he'll find you. He should identify himself as the Whiffenpoof. When he does, you may have to kill him."

Even Gearheardt was silent. After a moment I said, "I think I understand, sir. From the tape, he seems to have gone, well, he's just not much good, burned out, wouldn't work back in civilization. Maybe an embarrassment to the U.S."

"Oh, naw, I just never liked the little prick. Tryin' to screw me on a beer deal," the President said. "Always pullin' my chain. Just do me a favor if you see him."

"Sir, how will we know that the *star,* I mean how do we know when she'll be in Hanoi?" I didn't want to take anything for granted. Maybe the President thought we were a lot better than we were.

"Well, son, you'll be told the day. If you think you can miss the news that an American movie star with legs all the way up to her ass has parachuted into downtown Hanoi carryin' a banner that says 'Ho Chi for Me' then I reckon I got the wrong team. She ain't sneakin' in, you are."

I heard a phone ring in the background.

"Hold on a minute, boys," the President said. "Goddam help around here thinks I got nothin' better to do than answer my own phone."

Faintly I heard the President say, "Hello, oh, just a minute, sweetie, be right with you."

He came back on our line. "Now, boys, the boat will pick you up at the mouth of the Black River and get you up to Hanoi. From there—"

"With all due respect, Mr. President," Gearheardt interrupted, "I'm not riding any *boat* up to Hanoi. We're pilots. Let us figure out a way to fly a helicopter to Hanoi."

"Pilots, eh. Okay, that sounds like a plan. Yeah, wait a minute. That *is* the plan. Had you mixed up with someone else." I heard him say something to the person waiting on the other phone. Then he came back again. "You'll get the rest of your instructions when you're in Vietnam, boys. Good luck. Say hello to 'Gon' for me." He hung up.

I realized that I was bathed in sweat. The chief's room was not air-conditioned, which meant that it probably wasn't his real office. But it wasn't the heat that was getting to me. The mission that my drunken, carefree, clumsy best friend and squadron-mate had gotten me into was real. Really real. And I had just spent ten minutes on the phone with the President of the United States. I let out a deep breath and looked at Gearheardt. He was rifling through the chief's desk drawers.

"Who is the hell is 'Gon'?" I asked Gearheardt.

He didn't look up from his rifling. "How the hell should I know? Maybe that Whiffenpoof guy. Gon Whiffenpoof." He held a document up to the light.

"I don't think this is Utterback's real office," he said. He tossed the papers he was holding back into the drawer and shut it. "Well, what do you think, Jack?"

I took another deep breath and let it out slowly. "Let me ask you, Gearheardt. Do you think that our orders will be to kill Ho Chi Minh? I know you said that we were supposed to make a deal with him, but that 'iron fist' thing and just the whole, whole *feeling* I get about this . . . Making a deal doesn't make sense." The crazy thing was that I felt uncomfortable at the thought of killing Ho Chi Minh and yet had never given much thought to heading to Vietnam and contributing to the death of countless unknowns.

"I'm not going up there to give him an enema. And sounds like the President's got the fornicating covered. So I'm pretty comfortable with what's left we could do to him. Jack, you got to learn to roll with the rain off your back."

I stood up. The military issue wall clock read 14:30.

"Gearheardt, it's amazing how much you know for someone so damned stupid."

Gearheardt grinned. "Thanks, Jack."

I went on. "Let's go get ourselves a quick beer, and then hire a taxi to show us some of the countryside. We may not be back in Japan anytime soon."

Just outside the front gate of the Yokosuka Naval Yards was a bar called Clover Leaf Bar. It had shamrocks painted on the windows. Gearheardt and I stepped in for a beer at 1445 and at 2350 were rousted out by the Shore Patrol so that we could get back on ship by midnight. And we would have made it except that Peters and his crew had somehow gotten the head squid at the naval hospital drunk enough to quarantine the ship for bubonic plague, and it took until about four in the morning to get everything straightened out. Gearheardt and I agreed that the little black flag looked good flying next to the Stars and Stripes. We saw Captain Sand running around flailing people right and left with a cat-o'-nine-tails, but he was too drunk to really hurt anybody, and after he was pantsed he didn't look much like an authority figure anyway.

I woke up before dawn in my familiar bunk in the familiar zoo. I jumped down to go take a leak and landed on Gearheardt, who was out cold on the floor beside his footlocker. On the footlocker was a scrawled letter that I took to the head to read. I had read some of Gearheardt's letters to his left-behind sweethearts, and they were always entertaining. The letter began:

> Dear Mom,
> Jack and I were in Japan today. The country is beautiful and the people seem nice. Not all of them wear the colorful costumes, but the more traditional people do. Jack and I are together in the squadron. Don't worry about me. Jack will always . . .

I didn't read on. I had this feeling that I didn't want the responsibility of a brother in Vietnam. Just one more thing to worry about. What if he didn't make it? Gearheardt shouldn't have a mother or a brother.

PART 3

In war, the moral element and public opinion
are half the battle.

—Napoleon

In war, three-quarters turns on personal
character and relations; the balance of
manpower and materials counts only for the
remaining quarter.

—Napoleon

I yam what I yam.

—Popeye the Sailor Man

9 · War at Last

We had flown into Danang from Okinawa. The squadron was loaded into C-130's, and we just went there. Not much ceremony. Some of the logistics guys had gone down early to get the area ready. We took over a camp from the squadron that we replaced, at the southwest corner of the Danang runway. Someone had thought we would like living in tents where we could enjoy the ear-splitting runups of jet engines only a few feet from our cots. I think it was the F-106s headed north about 0530 every morning that some dumb grunt general thought we pilots would especially like.

We were all on edge as soon as we landed in Danang. When the ramp at the back of the C-130 opened, Flager ran out and shot an airman in the knee and wounded two water buffalo and a kid selling Pepsi before Major Jamison was able to knock him down. Everyone was surprised Flager had a new gun.

Most of us just sat in the airplane looking at one another, not talking, until Peters said, "What the fuck are we supposed to do now?"

Everyone was quiet until Butler mumbled, "It's a trap. We're all going to die." Then we all got up and walked down the ramp and stood around on the tarmac getting our eyes adjusted to the sunshine.

It seemed incredibly bright. We could hear artillery rounds head out-bound, and then small thumps as they landed in the distance. As we stood waiting for the trucks to haul our gear and us to our new home, it struck me as how *American* we looked. As new guys we were apart from the activities of war going on around us. Clean, fresh, and with a look of wonderment almost hidden behind aviator sunglasses.

Bearhead stood away from us. The Skipper had given in and al-lowed him to tie an Indian band around his forehead. In place of the survival knife issued to and worn by the other pilots, Bearhead wore a tomahawk, its handle stuck through his pistol belt and trailing a small feather. It was a gift from his tribe when he had left the reservation school to join the Marine Corps. The Skipper had at first insisted Bearhead wear "none of that native shit," but the group public rela-tions officer had convinced him that this was the kind of *color* that at-tracted television cameras, and there was nothing short of the Medal of Honor that the Skipper wanted more than coverage of his squadron on television.

Bearhead slowly turned to survey his surroundings. He paused frequently as if memorizing the terrain or the considerable U.S. forti-fications built up around the fighters lining the runway. Toward the west he had to shield his eyes, and I saw the heritage of plains war-riors in his profile. I looked where Bearhead was looking and was aware that the squadron was in a bright bubble of dust, heat, and noise. Outside the bubble, the low, cool, green hills of Vietnam stepped up into the Ammonite Mountains behind.

Gearheardt walked over and stood next to me.

"Well," he said, "we're not dead yet." He put his hand on my shoulder, and I saw Peters look at us and raise his eyebrows.

"Look at old Bearhead over there," I mused, "surveying the land that he knows he will fight over. He's kind of a dipshit for the most part, but I have to admit he looks like a warrior right now."

"You ever fly with him?" Gearheardt asked.

I shook my head no.

"Don't, if you can help it. He may look like a warrior, but he's got to be the biggest plumber in the squadron when he's in the cockpit. As a pilot the man is a waste of good sky. Bad enough just trying to keep straight and level, in an emergency he tends to want to smash the instrument panel with his tomahawk and get inverted. I hate him."

"Then I hate him too," I said. "I hate everybody that's incompetent."

"Kind of a pretty place, don't you think?" Gearheardt said, indicating the mountains and then the South China Sea beach across the runway from us. "I hope we don't have to do our Barbonella thing before we get a chance to kill something. I just want to strafe. I've always wanted to strafe even if it's in one of our damned helicopters with door gunners. Not exactly an F-4, but at least we're slow enough we can see what we're hitting."

The six-bys arrived, and we loaded for the ride to our new tent homes. The few remaining pilots from the squadron that we were replacing tried to sell us useless junk that they were leaving behind: ashtrays made of coffee cans, cheap fans that didn't fan, and bookcases made from ammunition boxes. We bought all of it. We were the FNGs, and we had to play our role, just like the old salts had to play theirs. Of course the old salts, the guys that had been in country longer than we had, even if this was fifteen or twenty minutes, had horror stories for every situation. Like when you went to take a piss, down an empty rocket pod stuck into the ground or a half-sunken fifty-gallon barrel with screen over the top, was when the snipers always got you. And there was always a guy in another squadron that went out to take a piss and the VC had booby-trapped the pisser, so they found the guy's hand out by the runway still holding his dick.

We were the Fucking New Guys. Ready, willing, and able to kick Cong ass.

"Open your eyes! Open your eyes, damn you, or I'll pull this trigger! You crazy bastard! You'll kill us! OPEN THEM!" We hit the ground, bounced once, and then settled. The Marines bailed out the side, past the door gunner, who was illegally firing (it was not a designated "return fire zone" due to a typo in the ops order) over their heads into the tree line. Seconds later we were airborne again, the helicopter leaping without the weight of the ten combat-dressed Marines. I slumped back in my seat and gulped the air flowing in the open window, my pistol dangling loosely in my hand. The adrenaline began to wear away, and I became aware of the ungainly gaggle of machinery in a slow climbing turn out of the jungle and back toward the coast of Vietnam. Flying co-pilot on strike missions, inserting Marines into suspected enemy troop concentrations, was below Dante's bottom circle. You were helpless. You were sure the idiot in the right seat, the pilot, was the most incompetent son-of-a-bitch in the military, and you had to let him kill you or be court-martialed—or at least written up for insubordination. When we began to let down into the landing zone, when the shooting started, the co-pilot was to rest his hands lightly on the controls so he could take over if the pilot was hit. That was the fondest dream of most of the co-pilots. And Barnes was the worst pilot in the universe. He couldn't *spell* "sky."

I keyed my intercom mike. "You do that every time, you bastard! I'll never fly with you again. You close your damned eyes every time we head into a hot zone! Why do you do that?" I took another deep breath and realized that we had already begun to let down into the pickup zone to load another stick of Marines. Fear made my voice husky and breathless. "Oh God, not another trip back to that zone. Shit, shit, shit."

"It scares the heck out of me to land when people are shooting at me." Barnes's voice was calm, reasonable. "I can't help it, I just shut my eyes. It's kind of like when someone is taking your picture I guess. You know how you don't want to shut your eyes but then—"

"*What about us, you prick?* You think it doesn't scare the crew and me to fly into that landing zone knowing you have your eyes closed! Jesus, Mary, and Joseph. Let me fly the damned thing. Please, Barnes." I looked over at the ugly, screwed up, shit-eating half-face that I could see below his green Plexiglas visor. I wanted to kill him. I added him to the list of the people that I wanted to kill since I had gotten to Vietnam, none of them the enemy.

"I can't let you fly because you're not a designated wing leader yet, Jack. You know that."

I strained against the shoulder harness. "So you'll just fly with your eyes closed and kill us all in the landing zone, you dim-witted, crazy asshole! Let me out! Goddam it, I'm jumping out of here as soon as we touch down."

Barnes gave his maddening little snort out of his pig nose that stuck out just beneath the visor. "You say that every time, Jack." He actually smiled over at me. "Okay, Gunny," he said to the crew chief behind us, "let's get 'em in and get 'em ready."

We dropped down over the tree line, into the semi-dry rice paddy filled with Marines divided into small fire-teams, waiting to be lifted into the jungle. Ahead and behind us, the squadron touched down almost at the same time.

As we loaded the Marines for the flight back to the strike zone, I looked at the scene in a daze. The Marines, most of whom looked just barely old enough to drive, were solemn and pale beneath a hell's wardrobe of weapons and ammunition. This operation was three days old and had already chewed up half a battalion of troops. Barnes was calmly eating sunflower seeds and spitting the shells in a cup, rather than spitting them out into the mud and muck a few companies of Marines and a squadron of helicopters make of a landing zone. He appeared unconcerned that he would very shortly be heading back to the terror that caused him to close his eyes and put all of us in mortal danger with or without any enemy participation. It was becoming too easy to say; I hated him. Because he was three months senior to me, he had the right to crash and kill me if he was incompetent enough, without fear of retribution. My choice was to get yelled at and have a bad fitness report or to die.

10 · The Leaping, the Gaping, and the Flaming

I hate this fucking place."

"Thanks, Adams, you're so nice to wake up to." I threw my boot at him. Of course it was the Air Force F-4s hitting afterburner down the runway that had awakened us, but Adams was closer and I really was getting tired of hearing him every morning. Everybody was getting tired of Adams, in fact. Bearhead threw his tomahawk and barely missed Adams's head but hit my boot. Adams threw my boot back at me, but hit Buzz. Buzz jumped up and stumbled over Fatass, who was kneeling down trying to find his shower shoes. Fatass didn't throw anything at anybody, but the sight of a gigantic butt inches from his face caused Flager to begin screaming and then lurch off his cot toward the tent door. He knocked down a pole and collapsed the front half of the tent down on Butler, Peters, and Zimmerman. The "Fuck yous" filled the morning air like bees pouring out of a busted hive.

"What in the hell are you men up to in there?"

Someone was scratching at the canvas, trying to lift it where it had collapsed. "Let's knock off the grab-ass, lieutenants. We've got a full schedule of flying ahead of us today. Butler, are you in there?" It was Major Gonzales.

"No, sir."

"Very funny, Butler. Get your butt out here in a flight suit right now. Collins is sick and you've got the perimeter run with Askins."

After a moment the major said, "I know you're in there, Butler. I'll see you at the ready room in five. Shake a leg."

"The perimeter run is a trap, sir."

"I am tired of that trap shit, Butler. Everything is a trap to you. Now get your butt out here."

"I'm trapped, sir."

The major began talking to himself. "Why did I get in this damn outfit with the loonies? Isn't there anyone in this squadron that just wants to do his duty?" He had lost some bubbliness in the past month or so.

"I'll take his place, sir." It was Gearheardt, who slept in the next tent.

"Good man, Gearheardt. Get your gear and I'll see you in the ready room. And you see me in my office in thirty minutes, Butler."

As the voices retreated I heard Gearheardt begin to lobby Gonzales for permission to strafe everything that moved. He had told me that firing the tracers down through the morning ground fog was the coolest thing he had ever seen. "Shakes up those fucking grunts too. Sonsabitches are mad as hornets when we finally land with their hot chow."

Butler really was trapped. The tent pole had fallen across his legs and somehow leveraged itself against the side of the canvas so that Butler couldn't get out of his bunk.

"Don't worry about me," he said. "Save yourselves." He began giggling and I heard him light a cigarette.

"I hate this fucking place," Adams said.

I climbed out of the jumble of tent canvas and upturned cots, grabbed a flight suit, my helmet bag, and my boots with the tomahawk slice out of them and caught up with Gearheardt and Major Gonzales.

"I'll fly with Gearheardt, sir. On the perimeter run, I mean. I'm sure Askins won't mind."

"I'm sure he won't. Okay, Armstrong, you and Gearheardt know the drill. Baker's your wingman." He peeled off toward the admin tent while we continued ahead to the ops tent. "And Gearheardt," he said, not knowing whether or not he was in on the joke, "none of that strafing stuff."

"Aye, aye, sir." Gearheardt gave a half salute to the major's back.

The run consisted of turning up and hopping over to the 1st Battalion/9th Marines headquarters, loading pots of steaming oatmeal, then proceeding to each of the outposts that the Marines manned around the Danang perimeter. Headquarters thought it was a great morale booster to give the grunts hot chow every morning, and it also served as an inspection of the area in case a regiment of North Vietnamese had managed to sneak in next to us during the night. It was a pretty good routine, except that the grunts hated the oatmeal and the pots usually returned still full. The choppers would normally take ground fire going in or out of the landing zones. The ubiquitous VC snipers would crank off a few rounds, resenting their nights crouching in the undergrowth or up in trees. They probably liked oatmeal more than the grunts. That was what made the perimeter run so dreaded by the pilots. No one wanted to buy the farm delivering oatmeal. Gearheardt didn't care. He would fly anything, anytime.

Approaching the zone, Gearheardt called the Marines.

"Good morning, Slick Baby. You read Purple Tiger?"

Clicks, static, more clicks.

"We read you, Purple Tiger. This is Slick Baby."

"Purple Tiger is inbound your LZ with hot oatmeal. Request permission to strafe the perimeter."

"What? Purple Tiger. Say again perimeter strafing?"

"Roger, Slick Baby. Understand you are requesting Purple Tiger strafe your perimeter."

"Uh, wait one, Purple Tiger."

A long pause while we approached the LZ.

"Purple Tiger, this is Slick Baby Six. Gearheardt is that you, you rotten bastard?" Six indicated the leader of the unit.

"That's affirm, Slick Baby Six. Your radioman evidently heard us taking ground fire on our approach to your LZ and has requested we hose the area."

"Bullshit, Purple Tiger. You try that every damn time. We got friendlies around here. They don't appreciate having their wakeup call being a goddam Marine helicopter shooting up their village. Knock it off. And take that oatmeal back to HQ and drop it on them from about five hundred feet. Slick Baby Six out!"

"Roger, Slick Baby. Have a good day, sir."

We dove at the landing zone, where Marines stood watching us.

"Gunny, I'm making a low pass over the LZ. Get those oatmeal pots in the door and when I give the word, kick 'em out. Then we'll commence strafing on the far side of the LZ. You think I don't know where the darn friendlies are?"

"Those are the ones we have to bury when we kill, aren't they, Skipper?"

"Don't be a wiseass, Gunny."

The crew chief door gunner answered with two clicks on his mike.

Looking over at a grinning Gearheardt I keyed my mike. "Why do you torment these grunts, Gearheardt? Look at that, their mortar pit is about knee deep in oatmeal. Oh, shit, they're shooting at us."

"They don't really aim, Jack. And I torment them because it takes their mind off the war. These sonsabitches have a shitty job out here, you know. They hate aviators anyway. Okay, Gunny, let 'er rip. Fire up those M-60s and see if you can at least hit dirt today. That's it, that's it. Get that tree there. Come on, Gunny, you're blind. You'd miss the air if I didn't make you practice. Now you got it. Okay, cease firing."

I shook my head. "You're nuts, Gearheardt."

"I just like the sound of those guns and the way the shit down there jumps when the rounds hit. Come on, Jack, we gotta have *some* fun, or what's the use of being here."

We had this discussion almost every day. "Gearheardt, we've already lost Kirby and Johnson. You've been shot down twice. We pick up about a dozen kids a day all shot up, and Charlie Med is full of wounded troops. This war doesn't exist for your personal enjoyment, damn it."

"Well, someone should have thought of that before they invited me, Jack. Whose enjoyment should I worry about? Huh?"

"You know damn well what I mean. Whoa, whoa, Gearheardt, watch where you're heading. Oh no you don't. Let me have this thing. Goddam it, give me the controls! You're not going to buzz the squadron again. It blows the shit out of everything. The Skipper is going to have your ass, buddy. Oh shit!"

Gearheardt was leaning out the window looking back at the tents we had overflown, less than twenty-five feet above them. He was laughing.

"Oh wow, Gunny, look at Sanders! We must have blown the top off of the shitter! Oh man, there's toilet paper everywhere. Hold your fire, Gunny! Might stir them up!" He laughed, and I realized that the gunny was as crazy as he was when they were in the air.

Gearheardt climbed to five hundred feet and leveled off. We swung toward the coast and I could see the small fishing boats heading out to the sea. I took a deep breath and tried to relax.

"Purple Tiger Two, this is Lead. I'm heading out over the water to check my instruments. We'll be near the beach and won't need an escort. See you in the barn."

"Purple Tiger Two, rog. Too chicken to land and face the music, Gearheardt?"

"Gearheardt's on R&R in Bangkok. This is Narsworthy, Tiger Two. Land before we shoot your sorry ass down."

We heard two clicks and our wingman peeled away. Gearheardt spoke to the gunny and the side gunner. "Gunny, Almost Captain Armstrong and I are going to discuss top secret women. You and the kid will be off the intercom for a bit."

Two clicks.

"We're getting kicked out of the squadron, Jack."

"What?"

"Hold on, let me finish. The Skipper is sick and tired of my shenanigans. Every grunt in South Vietnam has reported me as a flying maniac. And I've complained to the chaplain about the food. Even wrote my congressman about it."

"The food? Gearheardt, have you completely lost your mind? What has the food got to do with it? You dumb—"

"Hey, anybody can be a wildassed pilot. The Marine Corps is full of 'em. But everybody hates whiners. Especially official whiners. Like me. I told the chaplain that the food was so bad that I couldn't believe in God anymore. He's pretty upset. Hey, let's buzz that boat." He took off power and put the chopper in a sharp descending turn. The boat below us was round. It looked as if the two Vietnamese men were fishing from a giant straw Frisbee. "They won't jump out, you know. I think they know that if we dive fast enough and low enough we won't be able to pull up and we'll crash into the water and die. That's why the sonsabitches won't jump out of their boat. Hold on, Jack! Oh wow, there they go over the side!" We pulled up hard and Gearheardt looked down behind us. "They love this shit, Jack."

"Somehow I don't think so, Gearheardt. But don't change the subject. Why are we getting kicked out of the squadron?"

"The Skipper told Group Headquarters that we were disruptive to the war."

"He told them *what!*"

"God, it's pretty here. Look at that beach. And the deep blue water, green mountains in the distance. Jack, you have to admit this place is gorgeous. The Skipper had to tell them something. He'd look like a big pussy if he told them that I was just too wild for him to handle. So he told them that I demanded better food or I wouldn't be responsible for my actions. Interestingly enough, when the chaplain looked into the food thing, he found out that they were feeding us scraps from the ships those Navy pukes are floating around on out here, and sometimes the leftovers from the Air Force parties. Makes sense of all those little square crackers with cheese we get all the time, doesn't it, Jack? That's why I stick to C-rats when I can. There, you know what you're eating."

"Why are *we* getting thrown out of the squadron? You're the one flying around strafing everyone and flathatting your ass off. You're the one evidently pissing and moaning to your congressman about the chow. So why is it *we*?"

"I told the chaplain that you're masturbating all the time, Jack. I hope you don't mind, but I had to think to think of something, and I knew that would make him so uncomfortable he wouldn't dig into it. He went to the Skipper and supported the idea of throwing you out of the squadron too." He was looking down at the approaching beach, straining his eyes to see if any of the bodies lying out were nurses from the Air Force medical unit. He looked back at me. "Okay, I can see you're pissed, Jack. I don't know why you make such a big deal out of these things."

I keyed the mike and let it stay open, the loud irritating hiss fitting the moment, before I began talking. I was trying to keep from pulling out my pistol and shooting him in the leg.

"You don't think it should upset me that my record will show that I was kicked out of my squadron in Vietnam for excessive masturbation? You miserable—"

"Naa. I'm just pulling your chain. You're so gullible, Jack. When the Skipper was chewing me out for blowing down the chow tent, I just mentioned that he didn't have the balls to kick you out along with me, and he took the bait."

He was looking at me. "It's part of the plan, Jack. Did you think that we would just skate up to Hanoi and everyone would wonder where old Jack and Gearheardt were? If we screw up the squadron's records, we're really in deep shit."

I found myself foolishly relieved. That was probably the point of Gearheardt's little masturbation joke. "When will all this happen?"

"The President said that—"

"You *talked* to him?"

"I'm trying to tell you, Jack. I had a beer with him in Saigon last week when I flew down on that Air Force bird. He was on some kind of a big deal ASEAN thing. Drunk as a hoot owl when I saw him, but he gave me the word. I don't think he was as drunk as he was pretending. Probably doing some plausible deniability for the little woman. Anyway he said it should be within a couple of weeks. We got the body count he's been after—you know how many of those little suckers we've killed so far?—well anyway, he's ready, but the *star* is balking at the nude parachute part. Some kind of professional pride thing. But the President says it's a deal breaker. I have a feeling that he's promised someone a nude leap and he's not backing down. And he says she has tits that'd make Mrs. O'Leary's cow lay down and cry, and he wants 'em flapping in the breeze as she drifts over Hanoi. He's about to persuade her it's for her own protection, and I think he's right. No AA crew is going to blow free tits and twat out of the sky."

"Let me get this straight. You and the President were sitting in a Saigon bar last week talking about the star's tits drifting over Hanoi. Right?"

He nodded, looking perturbed that I would question him.

"Why didn't you say something to me?"

"I just did. I had to figure a way to get us kicked out of the squadron before I discussed it with you. I knew that you'd have a damn conniption fit and want to do everything by the book. Now, it's all fixed. We'll get thrown out when I give the Skipper the word, after the President gives us the word."

"The Skipper is in on this now?"

"Oh hell no. But he'll do what I ask him to do. He came into the club in Saigon when I was huddled with the President. He can't figure it out, but he knows better than to dick with someone that drinks beer with the President of the United States in a strip joint in Saigon. Also, the Skipper was with the lovely Mrs. Taylor when I saw him. You know, the Mrs. Taylor he sent back to the States a while back."

The Skipper had come storming into our tent one evening soon after we had started operating at Danang. He never entered any place. He always *stormed* in. It was late in the evening. Everybody was lying on their cots, reading or smoking and shooting the bull, scratching their nuts.

Everybody but Taylor, who was in his sleeping bag even though it was about a hundred degrees. The Skipper stomped over to Taylor near the back of the tent next to the runway.

"Taylor, is your wife here? Don't lie to me, Lieutenant. I'll have your ass for breakfast if you lie to me." Peters and Butler snickered, and the Skipper glowered at them, then turned back to the cowering Taylor. He was the wimpiest of the lieutenants. Small, quiet, a decent pilot who never missed a mission. He had sandy hair and soft moist eyes. He seemed happy all the time, which didn't really go with the rest of his personality, but the squadron had decided that he was probably just retarded.

"No, sir," he said. He lay on his back, his sleeping bag pulled up to his chin. His small head looked childlike above the substantial body filling the sleeping bag.

"Did you or did you not buy a box of Kotex at the Air Force exchange this morning?"

"The Air Force exchange has Kotex, Skipper?" Butler asked from the dark of the front of the tent. "No one told me."

The Skipper looked as if he were going to reply to Butler then thought better of it.

"I don't remember, sir. I don't think I did," said Taylor.

"You don't remember whether or not you went over to the Air Force exchange this morning and purchased a box of Kotex feminine napkins? Son, I'm not going to be the laughingstock of the—"

The tent door was pulled open, and Major Gonzales strode into the tent. He stopped beside the Skipper.

"Sir, Group just called, and the Colonel wants to see you up there right now. I think it's about Gearheardt again."

"You mean Almost Captain Gearheardt? Our Gearheardt?"

"Yes, sir. And, sir, in Korea we didn't have almost captains. I don't think we should humor him and let him—"

"Major, I've been in *two* wars. Three, counting this piece of shit war. The first two I could kind of figure out. They were in iambic pentameter, if you know what I mean. This war . . . this war hasn't any rhythm. Unless you count that goddam godawful music the enlisted men play twenty-four hours a day. And we fly around with our thumb up our ass here and . . ." He stopped and looked around the tent as if waking up from a bad dream. Then he shrunk as if he had sprung an air leak. He sighed deeply, motioned for Major Gonzales to leave, and indicated that he would follow soon. "Get a jeep and a driver, Gonzales," he said loudly. Then he turned back to Taylor, whose large eyes peered up at him from the top of his sleeping bag.

"Mrs. Taylor," he said. Quiet but firm.

"Yes, sir," the sleeping bag replied.

"You know that you can't stay here with your husband. You know that don't you?"

A muffled reply that sounded like a resigned yes.

"If the Marine Corps had wanted your husband to have a wife here, they would have issued him one. You know that too, don't you?"

"Hmmmphhuuuh."

"Tomorrow morning, Mrs. Taylor, I'm going to personally escort you to Saigon and see that you get a ride back to the States. You understand, Mrs. Taylor?"

"Hmmmphhuuuh."

The Skipper took a deep breath and looked around the tent at the men, who were trying to act like they weren't listening. He leaned near Taylor's head.

"Taylor," he asked quietly, "is your wife naked in there?"

Taylor nodded.

The Skipper shut his eyes and sighed deeply. Then he straightened up and stormed out. Peters groaned, and Zimmerman stumbled out of his cot and out the front tent flap, a copy of *Playboy* clutched in his hand.

"And I ran into him in Saigon," said Gearheardt. He was flying lazy circles over the spot where he had chased the fishermen out of their boat.

"Wait a minute. That was a long time ago when the Skipper took Taylor's wife to Saigon," I said.

"It seems the Skipper's idea of getting her back to the States included finding an apartment for her in Saigon and going down to see her every week. She's probably still down there. Boy, she was a good-looking little woman."

"Let's head back, Gearheardt."

We started a gentle turn northwest toward the Danang airbase and our camp. Gearheardt flipped on the intercom and spoke to the gunny. "We're back up, Gunny. You guys okay back there?"

"Yessir," the gunny replied. "Request permission to test fire my guns, sir."

I looked below us and saw a fleet of Vietnamese fishing boats. Off to the other side a small U.S. Navy craft sped toward the Danang harbor.

"Permission denied, Gunny," I said, even though Gearheardt was technically the aircraft commander.

Gearheardt smiled and keyed his mike. "Pussy," he said.

11 · Viet Nam or Vietnam
(We Were Never Sure)

Armstrong, grab your gear. You're going on a little trip. Lucky guy, you're the new forward air controller for the First Battalion, Eighth Marines. Can I have your air mattress when you're dead?"

It was Taylor, who had turned into a real prick after his wife left. As assistant operations officer, he got to inform everybody of the crap details they were assigned. He openly admitted it was the part of his job he liked best. Now he was standing at the foot of my cot, where I had been relaxing after a morning flight. This announcement to me was clearly a high point of the day for him. Becoming a forward air controller for an infantry unit was pretty much like being convicted of murder and moving in on death row. The difference was that on death row you had good chow, a bed, and people weren't trying to kill you all the time. And, given the appeal process, you had a better chance of not dying. When the action was too heavy for the ground troops, they would call in air support. The trick was that the FAC needed to be where he could observe all the action as well as where the aircraft were striking. Taylor knew all of this, which was why he stepped briskly aside when I lunged off my cot and tried to sink my teeth into his neck. Even though I knew he was enjoying it, I began my groveling.

"Send Adams, send Zimmerman. No one likes Zimmerman. Everyone wants to screw Johnson's wife. Send him. All of those guys would be better FACs than me. Send Feldonstein. Everybody hates how he always eats one thing at a time off of his food tray. Send him. Jews like being FACs. He told me he wanted to be a FAC. Really. Come on, Taylor. Why me?"

Taylor beamed at my performance. He was almost happy again when he got to do something like this.

"Major Gonzales said to send you. Of course, he thinks you're Gearheardt. He can never get you two straight." He held the clipboard toward me so that I could initial beside my name that I had received my orders. I spit on it and tried to tear the paper off of the board.

Taylor laughed. "I already signed your name on the paper back in the office. I just like to see how people react." He laughed again and started out of the tent. "Be ready by fourteen hundred. Askins is going to fly you down to Chu Lai and drop you at One Eight headquarters." He stopped. "Is that your coffee can ashtray?"

I didn't answer, and he left. I got dressed and found Gearheardt in the motor pool tent having a beer with the motor pool gunnery sergeant.

"Here comes a dead man." The gunny smiled and saluted me with his beer when I walked in the tent. "Welcome, Almost Captain Armstrong. We heard about your good fortune, sir."

Gearheardt was leaning against the fender of a Mighty Mite, one of the few mini-jeeps that the squadron motor-T sergeant had not traded off for comfort items such as walk-in refrigerators. I expected to see the familiar grin spread across his face as he listened to the gunny jibe me about my death sentence. But he looked worried. Now I knew for certain that this wasn't somehow part of the Barbonella plan.

"Shit," Gearheardt said, handing me a warm beer.

"No shit, shit," I said. I slumped down onto the ground, leaning back against the tire.

Gearheardt spoke, looking at the gunny as if to confirm what he was saying. "The gunny talked to a Navy chief pal of his. He thinks he can trade you to the Army if you're willing to be a second lieu-tenant again."

"The chiefs can *trade people?*"

"Could you let me have a moment with Almost Captain Arm-strong, Gunny? Thanks. And we'll get back to you on the trade idea. I don't think it's going to work, but I'll talk to Jack here."

When the gunny left, Gearheardt slipped down the side of the mini-jeep and sat beside me. "I think that Gonzales did this because of Barbonella," he said. "He thinks this will throw a crimp into our plans."

"He knows our plans?"

"Probably not, but that dickhead Skipper might have let him in on a bit. Just enough to get Gonzales suspicious."

Gearheardt was quiet and I knew that I was doomed. I had wanted to believe that this was somehow part of the plan. Gearheardt and I sat smoking in silence, finishing the warm beer and not looking at one another.

"Why does everyone want to stop us from stopping the war, Gearheardt?" I asked. "Isn't stopping wars usually a *good* thing?"

I wasn't expecting an answer, and Gearheardt didn't appear to have heard me. He flipped his cigarette butt through the tent flap. "The piece of Man that God can't touch," he said finally. "The church has a lot invested in wars."

I looked over at him. This didn't sound like Gearheardt.

"At least that's what the chaplain told me," he said.

"The Assistant God has too much time on his hands to think," I said.

"Look, Jack. I'll try to get in touch with the President. He's prob-ably the only one that can help us now. I promise you I'll get you back in the squadron. Try to stay alive until I can get to him. Okay?"

"I'll try to be the worst damn FAC they ever saw. Call in air strikes on the HQ. Stuff like that."

"Everybody does that, Jack. But do what you gotta do. I'll get you back."

At the headquarters of the First Battalion Eighth Marines I reported to Major Finch. At least I reported to his administrative officer's assistant's secretary, Corporal Downey. Downey was pretty much what you would expect to find in a hot tent in the middle of suburban Doc Quo, Vietnam: disgruntled and near-terminally addled and anxious.

"You Lieutenant Armstrong?" he asked, reading the copy of my orders that I had just handed him.

"No," I said, trying one of Gearheardt's tricks.

To my surprise and discomfort, Downey began to cry. He sat down heavily onto the folding chair and laid his head on his small wooden desk. "Why do I have to put up with all this?" he blubbered into the crook of his arm. "All of you lieutenants give me nothing but shit."

He sobbed for a while as I shifted back and forth, peering occasionally out of the tent flap to see if anyone was nearby. Finally I spoke up. "Okay, I *am* Lieutenant Armstrong, if that's why you're crying. Who ever let you in the Marine Corps?" This last under my breath.

Downey straightened up and smoothed my orders on his desk. "Sorry, sir," he said. "I'm a bit touchy today. I got a Dear John letter this morning." He sniffled and I hoped he wasn't going to begin bawling again. He was a Marine in a combat zone, for chrissakes.

"Tough luck. Maybe she wasn't . . ." I paused. "Could you just process my orders and tell me where to find my crew?"

I was entitled to a radio operator and a runner slash backup. My success, and my life, depended on us working together as a team. I knew many FACs had grown terribly fond of their team in the field. I stepped outside of the GP tent and watched the young Marines go about their business. Smoking, lounging, and pissing and moaning. They looked strong and cocky, and I began to look forward to getting my team and beginning the training that we would need to function effectively in the field. This rear area, where the Marines cleaned themselves and their weapons and recuperated, was in a valley formed by two sizable sand dunes. The South China Sea was just beyond the runway that served the A-4 squadron and the metal mat that served as a landing pad for the chopper squadron. Presumably I had friends in the chopper squadron and made plans to visit them when I got squared away in my new home with the grunts.

"Who the hell are you?"

A redheaded major who couldn't have been more than five and a half feet tall bumped into me as he rounded the corner of the tent. He looked as if he'd invented the Marine Corps. A tattoo of the Eagle, Globe, and Anchor on his forearm told me he was a mustang, a Marine who started as an enlisted man and had made it up through the ranks.

"Almost Captain Armstrong, sir." That damn Gearheardt.

The major let it pass. He stuck out his hand and nearly broke my fingers in his handshake.

"Welcome aboard, Armstrong. I assume you're the new FAC. Last one wasn't worth shit, no offense to the dead. You met your team?" Without waiting for an answer he stuck his head inside the tent. "Dooley or whatever your name is, get your ass out here."

The corporal immediately appeared, squinting in the bright sun.

"Get this man's team rounded up and get him squared away."

"Sir, his team is burning the shitter. Do you want me to—"

"Get someone else to burn the shitter. We got a mission tomorrow, and this man's got to get snapped in. I'm not heading into that goddamned area without boo-koo air support." The major smiled at me and grabbed my arm above the elbow. "G-2 says the North Vietnamese got .50s, antitank guns, and are dug in like gophers. Gotta have lots of air support or we'll get creamed."

"Sir, I don't think I'll—"

"Ain't paying you to think, Lieutenant. You just get those Phantoms on station tomorrow with lots of goddamned bombs and shit. Good man." He squeezed my arm and left. I briefly wondered what Downey would think if I used his desk to cry. My only hope was that my team knew what the hell I was supposed to do.

"Sir, there's your radioman and humper. The bumper is the guy that carries all your gear," Downey explained when I looked puzzled at the term.

I should have known that the battalion wasn't going to give me their top men. A quick look at the two Marines strolling casually toward us between the tents pretty well confirmed it. The taller of the two was at least six and a half feet tall and weighed maybe one hundred thirty pounds wet. He bent over at the neck as if his dogtags were pulling him down. The Marine beside him appeared to be some sort of simian in uniform. The effect of a widow's peak, which met a single dark eyebrow above his eyes, gave him a strange owl-like appearance without any hint of intelligence.

The fact that my life was no doubt in the hands of these two scrambled my thought process momentarily. When I recovered, they were directly in front of me, saluting. Their names were Barker, the tall one, and Granger, the Neanderthal. After I returned the salute, Barker spoke. His voice was a high screech as if someone had recently hit him in his incredibly prominent Adam's apple.

"Why'er we took off shitter burning detail, Lieutenant? Sergeant said we could have shitter burning detail till the cows come home."

"You're Barker, right? Well, Corporal Barker, in the air wing the latrine burning detail is about the lowest job you can get. Why are you asking?"

Barker looked down at Granger, who shrugged. Then he narrowed his eyes and looked back at me.

"You ever been on a FACing mission, Lieutenant?"

"I attended forward air control school last year. But no, I haven't actually been on a mission in country."

"Well, sir, on shitter burning detail Granger and I get to go into the battalion four-holers, about eight of 'em, and roll out the fifty gallon drums of piss and shit. Then we haul 'em over yonder against that dune and pour JP-4 into 'em and about half the time when we strike a match they blow like a bastard 'fore we can run off, and shit and piss goes everwhere. Then we haul 'em back to the four-holers and crawl under them and re-install the barrels whilst a bunch of damn Marines try to shit on us. Then the end of the day, we clean up so we's can start all over the next day. So the thing is, Lieutenant, Granger and I'd just as soon stay on shitter burning detail than go back out there to that FACing, if it's all the same to you." The primate nodded his head in agreement.

My mind was trying to process this while dealing with the very strong aroma of four-holer. Fighting back the nausea, whether from fear or shitter fumes I wasn't sure, I took charge.

"Barker, I don't intend to become the first lieutenant in the U.S. Marine Corps to personally handle latrine burning detail. Since we're a team, that leaves me with only one choice, handling the forward air controlling for the battalion. And that's what I intend to do. You and Granger get your gear, your radios, your whatever else we need out there, and report to me in thirty minutes. We're going to go through a quick FAM session, get a briefing from G-2, and then begin lining up air support for tomorrow. Any questions?"

Corporal Barker shook his head, no. Private Granger, who had not moved a muscle since he had appeared in front of me, didn't move a muscle again. In fact, he didn't appear to be breathing. I put my face closer to his and saw his eyes move.

"Granger, can you hear me? Is he deaf or something, Barker?"

"Nossir. He just cain't open his mouth. Grunt told him that shitter molecubes floats all around and that breathing is just like eatin' shit molecubes. So Granger don't open his mouth all day. He told me he can breathe through his ears. I reckon he can."

I straightened up and decided that I didn't care if Downey saw me cry. "Okay, men. See you in half an hour at the operations tent."

Barker and Granger turned and started away. I called out to Barker.

"Son, how many FAC missions have you been on? With the other FACs, I mean."

"Ain't been on many, sir. Lieutenant Wilson, he's the lieutenant before you and after Dobson and Kramer, he said if I showed up on a FACin' mission again he'd tie me in a knot with my dick. I love that Lieutenant Wilson. Saved my life. I'se the one that gathered him up and put him in the bag, sir. If you don't make me go on this FACin' mission, I'll do the same for you, sir. Cross my heart."

Tears welled in my eyes. "How about Granger? Has he been on a mission?"

"Oh you bet, Lieutenant. He's been on all of 'em for this battalion."

Granger grinned, the first animation I had seen other than walking and saluting.

"So you know all about this stuff, Granger?"

He shook his head, still showing his large yellow teeth.

"Why is it that he's survived, Barker?" I asked, assuming that Granger wasn't ready to open his mouth just yet.

"Beats me, Lieutenant. Ain't never heard him talk about it. Reckon he's just real careful."

"Well, at least he looks like about the best humper a team could get, Barker. He could carry a tank out there I'll bet."

Barker laughed, and then covered his mouth as if embarrassed. "He ain't no humper, Lieutenant. He's your radioman. I'm the humper."

"Of course," I muttered to myself as they walked away, their smell parting the chow line ahead of them.

I hadn't had butterflies in my stomach for a long time, but when the choppers carrying the company that I was attached to fell toward the strike zone at 0730 the next morning, the butterflies were giant fanged bats fighting each other. The world was shooting, and I couldn't tell which was friendly and which was enemy. In the helicopter a kid in a helmet ten sizes too big for him sat on the bench across from me pumping his knee up and down and fingering his M-16. He looked like he was the last kid on the bench and the coach was about to put him into a game with the varsity. He saw me looking at him and gave me a thumbs up. I wanted to stay in the belly of the chopper, knowing I could plead with the pilot to let me ride home with him. Except when it sounded like some asshole began beating on the side of the chopper with a ballpeen hammer—it was so hard to believe that someone was actually trying to shoot you—and I could see little bits of sky through little holes that were opening up in the sides of the aircraft, I wanted off.

When we hit the ground I jumped out and landed on top of a Marine who had been shot in the throat. I tried to avoid looking down at his face, because I didn't want it to be the kid with freckles and a nervous knee. Blood pumped up over my boot and pant-leg, and then I was past and headed for the shallow indentation in the field that provided the only cover. Barker and Granger were right on top of me, literally right on top of me as we dove into the ditch. When I looked back, I saw the crew chief jump out, pick up the Marine shot in the neck, throw him into the chopper in one swift motion and then they were gone.

"Barker, get that gear set up! Granger, get Red Hat on the horn and see what we've got on station!" I found that I could actually function, a tiny life-sustaining cell structure in my brain sending the message that if I thought about what the hell was going on I would lose all control. Unfortunately, the same structure was not working with my small team. They lay comatose beside me, Barker jabbering unintelligibly about the noise and Granger lying on his back smiling at the sky in what seemed perfect contentment. Had not the air been heavy with "molecubes" of sound and fear, I'm sure I could have heard him humming.

The last of the choppers disgorged their troops and left the zone. Now only the steady, rapid, death-carrying crack of the small arms and the thumping of the heavy machine guns sucked rational thought out of your skull. I could actually hear the air parting above me as the metal bullets, ours and theirs, crisscrossed the football field-sized landing zone. I knew that the green tracers that occasionally sped by were from AK-47s, and it incensed me that the crazy little bastards in the treeline would try to kill me. The tracers were the most real thing about the zone. They moved at their own speed. They owned their space. I thought about how pretty the zone would look at night with their green tracers and our red tracers crisscrossing it and believed that I had become, with very good reason, crazy as a loon.

My mind raced around, trying to think of something, but no thought was sticky enough.

I raised my head in time to see a Marine look over the paddy dike, empty his M-16 into the treeline ahead of him, raise himself up to get a view of his target and then slowly let himself back to earth, a red spot spreading on his chest, and a jagged tear in the back of his flak jacket. I had been in the zone for about twenty seconds. When I looked at my "team," Granger was ready. I took a deep breath and closed my eyes for just a moment, searching for the Marine inside.

Granger handed the radio handset to me. "We got two flights of Phantoms and a flight of A-4s, Lieutenant." He showed his big yellow teeth. "Phantoms are Camelot Lead."

"Camelot Lead, you read Fish Barrel?" Some asshole at Group HQ probably thought that call sign was funny when he assigned it.

"Roger, Fish Barrel, Camelot Lead on station. We have two napes, eight five-hundred-pounders, and all the 20 Mike Mike you could ever dream of. You got a target?"

"That's affirm, Camelot. I'm popping purple smoke. Got us in sight?"

"Got the purple smoke, Fish Barrel."

"Roger, Camelot. Let me have the napalm in those trees at one o'clock from the smoke. Stay in the trees. We have friendlies fifty yards from them. You copy?"

"Roger, Fish. Camelot lead is rolling in with 20 Mike-Mike. If I'm on target give me an Affirm and Camelot Two and Three will drop the napalm."

I heard him before I saw him. The Phantom came across the zone at a shallow angle and the treeline began disintegrating with hundreds of small explosions as the twenty millimeter cannon in the F-4's pods roared like machinery.

"Camelot, that's affirm. You're dead on."

"Roger, Fish. Camelot Two and Three let's get the barbecue lit."

"Camelot Two in." A roar overhead and then the treeline was fire. Hot, boiling, black, oily fire. I gasped for air, rolling over on my back.

"Camelot Three in." Another roar and the fire became more, hotter fire. I couldn't breathe, and it was impossible not to think about the bastards crouched in the treeline in their stinking black pajamas becoming standing rib roasts. I was glad.

The black smoke rose above the trees and had just begun to dissipate when the rib roasts began firing at us again, the first fusillade taking down the gunny and a dumb-looking kid from Brooklyn who had gone up on one knee to watch the napalm.

I hated those rib roasts with everything I had. They had just been *napalmed* for God's sake! The rotten little bastards still wanted to shoot us. Stupid asshole shit-brained dick-headed slopes.

Barker was still blubbering, but Granger had turned out to be a champ. He was on the horn before I even asked him, bringing the other aircraft into position over our zone, giving battle damage reports to the departing flights, and grinning with those big yellow teeth.

The Marines were now organized in the LZ. We were taking heavy small-arms fire from three sides and the Marines were returning it and lobbing round after round of 40mm back at the trees. It occurred to me that we were pinned down. There obviously were a hell of a lot more NVA surrounding us than we expected, and I gave a moment's hatred to the dumb assholes somewhere who'd decided it would be a good idea to land us in the middle of a bunch of enemy. What *were* good ideas in war? Why *am* I lying in a dry rice paddy surrounded on three sides by people whose names I couldn't pronounce willing to have their meat charred off their bones just for a chance to get me in their sights and put two grams of metal through my head? I am crazy as a mule on locoweed. I directed two flights of Phantoms and a flight of A-4s around the zone, feeling the dirt and debris fall on me after their bombs hit in front of us. I was mad at them too, the A-4 pilots.

The NVA seemed to increase their fire after every bombing and strafing run. I prayed that we did not have some loony company commander who would decide we should charge the treeline. I called Red Hat, the airborne command aircraft, and told him to get more help on station.

The redheaded major crouch-ran over and fell down beside me. He looked like Yosemite Sam. The hair on his neck and arms gleamed in the sun.

"I picked a fine fucking time to go into the field with one of my companies, didn't I, flyman?" He adjusted his body so that he could peer up over my indentation at the treeline in front of us. "Captain Howard was feeling poorly, and I decided to lead the boys myself. Battalion is going to have my ass when I get back."

I took comfort that he had actually said something about getting back.

"Lieutenant, we need to get some support in here. I've radioed HQ and they're sending another company. And they're putting another company behind that ville." He pointed to the remains of a village through the trees to our left. "Be sure and tell the fast movers that we'll have Marines over there. And we need some ammo in and medevac out. Can you get that for me?" He left, crouch-running like a cartoon, with tracers, red and green, crossing above him. I called in the mission requests.

We were in stalemate. My first damn mission as a grunt and we were stalemated. The firepower of the aircraft kept the NVA in the trees, but we couldn't advance and couldn't pull back. I lit a cigarette and looked at my team. Really looked at them for the first time.

They were two of the ugliest human beings in the world. Barker had stopped blubbering long enough to dig a small foxhole for himself, and he crouched in it, reading. Reading a paperback. He picked his nose and wiped it on his pants.

Granger was dozing, his yellow teeth to the sun in his open mouth. Drool ran his down his cheek, a trail of pale skin showing through the dirt. He had been wide awake minutes before.

I didn't want to die with these men. And they weren't anybody whose picture I wanted on the bookshelf beside the fireplace in the den, their arms draped over the shoulders of their lieutenant, grinning in their combat gear, funny haircuts, and hat-hair. Me with a cigarette in my hand and no shirt.

I felt strangely calm. I was scared silly, but I also felt amazingly safe in the midst of these Marines. Around me they performed whatever tasks were at hand professionally and almost matter-of-factly, directing concentrated fire by means of a few hand signals, moving forward when directed without questioning the sanity of the order, and treating the increasing wounded with the reverence of sacred religious icons. The Navy corpsmen assigned to us crept to every post and pillar of our assembled group, giving medicine and comfort to those unfortunate few who took hot metal into their bodies.

The groundfire, which had slacked off, picked up again, and I decided to believe in God. He would get me out of this. I decided that He would be more likely to listen, since I hadn't been in contact in quite a while, if I just asked for a couple of small favors. I would stay in Vietnam if he would just get me back to the squadron. I didn't want to be a grunt anymore. These poor bastards had to do shit, whoops, sorry God, stuff like this every day, and I just had better things to do. I had all that pilot training. I promised God that I wouldn't bitch if I got killed as a pilot.

It was about a million degrees. Between directing flights of fighters we lay in the sun in the LZ. Heat waves rose up between us and the treeline, which now danced the hula when we tried to spot targets. I tried to trick God by asking Him only to let me see the cool water of the South China Sea again, nothing else, knowing that if I could see the water I would not be pinned down in this stinking hell with a stinking floor of dirt mixed with human waste carried over the centuries to these fields for fertilizer, and a ceiling of a devil's patchwork of lead in invisible angles and patterns stitched together with more flesh-seeking lead. I ran out of water and would have stolen Granger's, but he had forgotten to bring any. Why couldn't I remember that I had the two biggest fuckups in the battalion? Of course he didn't have any water. I made Barker give him some of his. They began arguing about who was going to do what when they got back on shitter burning detail. We had about twenty minutes before any other aircraft could be on station. We rested.

_____

God was leaving to play golf. He had on a lovely beige cashmere sweater over chinos. I mentioned to him that His alligator golf shoes were exquisite and wondered briefly if it would be considered rude to ask Him how much He paid for them. "Could we just talk for a moment before you go, God? I've really got a problem and I need Your help."

He looked at his Rolex and smiled. It was a beautiful smile, and I noticed how much he looked like my father, particularly around the eyes. "Son," He said gently, "I've had this tee time for six months. Now isn't very convenient. I am truly sorry."

An angel landed on His shoulder and whispered in His ear. He raised His eyebrows and shook His head slightly. "Stay a grunt until I get back." He left, and I hit the angel. It fell and I began kicking it as it tried to roll away.

"Lieutenant!" It was Granger, holding the radio handset up to my face. "The Sandys are on station." Sandys were A-1s, the most beautiful, wonderful thing in the whole world, prop planes that could get low and slow and pound the enemy with individual attention. They each carried more armament than a B-29 in World War II. Now we would teach those bastards in the trees. I directed the A-1s pass after pass. It was now *two* million degrees in the landing zone. The choppers came up on Guard and let me know that they were a minute out of the zone with ammo. They wanted me to pop smoke where they should land to pick up the wounded. I threw green smoke and they said they had it in sight. The Sandys unloaded the last of their ordnance into the treeline and pulled off. Four Marine Cobras began low passes, strafing and firing rockets. Behind me just above the horizon I saw the H-34s begin their descent into the zone.

Then the rotten, God-forsaken, cock-sucking, mother-humping, shit-headed, dick-brained, asshole-licking, fucking *GOOKS* began dropping mortar rounds into the LZ. One after another the explosions walked toward the green smoke lingering in the still, scorched air.

How did the bastards know that the choppers would land no matter how hot the landing zone was from small arms, but they couldn't land during a mortar attack? I saw them abort their landing just short of the zone, peeling off to the south and west in pairs. Around me the Marines who weren't face down in the dirt trying to escape the shrapnel flying through the air looked at me as if it were my fault the choppers were hauling ass without picking up the wounded or dropping ammunition.

"Fish Barrel Three, Jelly Belly lead." It was the lead chopper.

"Go ahead, Jelly Belly."

"We'll hang around southwest of the LZ for a while, Fish. Can you get some strikes on those mortar tubes? You must be taking ten rounds a minute. How're you holding out?"

"Jelly Belly, I'll try to get more fast movers and Sandys up here a-sap. We're . . ." I thought better of what I was about to say, "We're making out okay. We would like you to get those wounded out of here if at all possible. Fish, over."

"We'll do our best, Fish. Get rid of those tubes."

I received word of two more flights of fighters on station and began directing them. Wing asked me over and over how many flights I thought I would need, and I finally told them to go fuck themselves, I had no idea. I was beyond all fear of authority, all fear of man, God, and anything else I should fear. I knew that I was going to hug dirt in this paddy until I could silence the mortar tubes, which were now dropping rounds every thirty seconds into the zone. Surely they would run out of ammunition. I called for more Sandys. The Cobras came back, sniffing like terriers around the treeline until one of them jerked up suddenly and then cartwheeled into the edge of the LZ.

A Marine lying near us, hugging his M-16 alongside his face like a favorite teddy bear, looked over at us during a lull, when only the almost peaceful popping of small arms was in the air.

"How many strikes will they send, Lieutenant?" He seemed fearful of my answer.

I looked at Granger's notebook, required to be kept for the operations officer to pass back to the air wing. It recorded each sortie and the amount of ordnance expended. The notebook was torn, filthy and full. Granger was keeping record on the back.

"They'll never, ever quit, Marine. They'll send strikes for goddamned ever."

Late in the afternoon the choppers landed. Not only did they bring ammunition, they brought fresh troops who joined our company as we slowly advanced on the treeline in front of us, the incoming fire decreasing noticeably with each rush the Marines made. Before dusk they were in the treelines. An occasional crack was heard when they encountered a sniper and flushed him out.

In the landing zone, I sat on my helmet and smoked a cigarette that it had taken me three attempts to light, each time the shaking of my hands extinguishing the match before it reached my cigarette. To keep my mind off of the immediate past, I wrote up my after-action report while waiting to be lifted back to the base near the beach. Barker and Granger lay sleeping in the late afternoon sun. Barker had already asked me if he could not have a medal but just get shitter detail forever. Not being all that used to combat, he fully expected that he was going to get a medal for cowering in a shallow ditch blubbering for a day. I asked God—why did I think of him in loud pants and a pullover?—if He would forgive me for wishing that Barker had been shot.

Yosemite Sam walked over to where I was sitting and waved me down when I started to get up. I tried quickly to think of how to appease him so that he wouldn't report me to the battalion CO as a sniveling weasel. I hoped that the LZ had been chaotic enough that he had not heard my wimpful pleadings with the saints and goblins to kill everybody but save me. Maybe he hadn't noticed that I had often directed bombing runs far beyond their target until I was more certain of my ability to bring them in close.

"Thanks, flyman," the major said as he stuck out his filthy hand. "You saved our ass on this one. We'd a been a fucked duck if you hadn't stayed on that horn all day. Most of the FACs are back there with me in the center of the zone. You've got balls laying right on the perimeter, son. But that was goddam fine air work." He let go of my hand and motioned for me to follow him back to the center of the LZ to be picked up by the choppers.

I looked at the slack-jawed faces of Barker and Granger.

"What were we doing out here on the perimeter?" I asked, for future reference.

"What's a perimeter, sir?" Barker asked. Now that the action was over, he was becoming the more animated of the two. Granger was sinking back into his silent state. I looked at his idiot face and knew the meaning of "dumbfounded." I also knew why he had survived all of the other FACing missions. He was too damn dumb to be shot. Shooting him wouldn't make any sense. But he had saved my ass today, and that's the way it was.

I learned something that late afternoon when the sun came thinly through the trees, the trees almost devoid of branches and leaves, the quiet so pure that you could hear a Marine scraping the bloody mud from the soles of his combat boots, the hesitation of the knife as pressure was applied near the heel and then the release as it moved the gore to and off of the toe. A skinny corporal came shyly up to the major, who was sitting beside me writing his after-action report. The corporal was stripped to the waist and had a sunken chest.

When the major looked up at him, the corporal nodded over his shoulder toward the thirteen bodies. "When do you want to load the meat, major?" he asked.

I looked at the major to see his reaction. He didn't look up.

Where was Gearheardt when I needed him? I did not want to be a grunt.

At the base I had an attack of nerves as the adrenaline wore off. After I stripped off my clothes, I had to sit on the side of my bunk for a while before I could stand up, let alone walk to the shower.

Cleaned up and feeling better about myself, I decided to drop by the troops' chow hall to check up on them. If the major thought I had done a pretty good job, maybe some of the troops wanted to say something to me also. Before I reached the door, I saw a number of the company lounging in a circle next to the water buffalo, sipping beer and smoking.

"What the fuck was the point of that little excursion?" one of them asked rhetorically.

I tried to enter into the discussion with the grunt lieutenants in the O Club tent, but it was another day at the office for them. I couldn't let down to that level and knew that I would embarrass myself. I kept walking and sipping warm beer hoping that what was waiting for me in my tent would go away.

And what was waiting for me was the sight of the thirteen dead marines that were lying in a neat row in the center of the landing zone when I finally got there to be picked up. The company had no body bags, so the kids were lying on ponchos with tent halves on top of them. When the first chopper landed, it blew the tent halves off, and we had to look at the mostly naked bodies. Three were whole and the rest had grotesque shapes with missing body parts. One had only half a head.

When I finally had nowhere else to go, there was a Captain Fowler waiting impatiently on my cot. "Where the hell have you been, Lieutenant?"

"Fuck you," was the only reply I could think of. Luckily he was an administrative pogue and that was the only response I needed.

"The major said for you to write the letters to the next of kin." He stopped and held up his hands toward me. "You don't have to have known them. Just write the letters."

He thrust a file into my hands. "Here are their names and addresses. By the way, that shithead humper of yours, Barkley, or whatever the hell his name is, wrote the last bunch, but we can't send them. He wrote a bunch before we read any, but that can't be helped now. You can redo these we caught and send all of them at once. The major wants them to go out tomorrow. We care about these kids, you know."

When he was gone, I dropped to my cot and rigged a lamp so that I could read and write from my bed. The thirteen names and their next of kin were on the top of the folder, held there with a paper clip. I took it off and straightened it, marveling at the mundaneness of it. Then I picked up the first of the letters that Corporal Barker had written to wives and parents, the letters that Fowler had said weren't to be sent.

Dear Mr. and Mrs. Jackson
Yore boy is dead. Land mine blowed his legs off and maybe his arms to.
I am sure he is happy dead cause he don't have a dick or nothing after
steppen on the land mine. I didn't know yore boy so I cant say if he was
queer like Davis says. I think you get some money but not a hole lot. Bet-
ter then nothing. And the skipper says to tell you that he was one of the
finest young men he ever saw. Ever one killed that day was to. Also some-
thing about him helping his country but Davis was maken stupid noise
and I didn't hear everthing. Davis didn't like yore boy but at least he is
dead now.
Yore friend

Corporal Frederick W. Barker US Marines

Oh my God, I thought. How many letters had that dickhead Barker sent out before someone thought to check them? I looked up and Barker was standing in the tent-door.

"You send for me, Lieutenant?" he asked.

"I didn't, Barker, but I'm glad you're here. What in the hell were you thinking with these letters? Are you a complete moron?" I sat up on my cot.

Barker took a step back as if I had hit him.

"Lieutenant Caldwell told me I was to write those letters since he knew I liked readin' and everthing. He told me that the mommas and daddies needed to know how their boys died and everthing so they could feel better. He said you cain't just have 'em thinking they went to shit and the hogs et 'em."

I grabbed another letter and read from it.

"I think yore boy was screaming mostly cause his guts was hanging out and maybe ants was eatin on them. He was sure enough a loud screamer. Davis said to shoot him our ownself but Davis don't like anybody and nobody likes him.

"Do you actually think that some parent is going to feel *better* after they read that?"

"Lieutenant, that was Freedman. He got hit right over there by the fence by a mortar. I *heard* him, Lieutenant. He screamed about all night before someone could get out there to him."

"That's not the point! Oh, shit, never mind, Barker. What did you want? You know damn well I didn't send for you."

"Sir, they's making up the shitter burnin' detail this evening. Me and Granger—"

"Get out of here, Barker. Tell your pal that he doesn't have to worry about getting aced off the shitter detail. I'll take care of it in the morning."

I wrote for two hours. Every letter made me harder, less compassionate. Afterward I sat alone in the dark tent, smoking and thinking. I couldn't handle any more warm beer or company. I had to decide if I had the balls to suck it up and bury all this shit. It was a choice between John Wayne or lipstick and a purse.

The next day we were off the rotation to go out into the boonies. But the following day we made an assault at the base of the first range of hills to our west, and the enemy was dug in deep. We lost "only" three men. Over the next few weeks, we averaged losing about four Marines a week. I became numb, rising and riding the choppers into the landing zones, calling down fire from above, and hugging the shit-packed ground for all I was worth. I wanted to be back in the squadron so bad that I forced myself not to think about it, imagining that I was serving a sentence of some kind. I thought of Gearheardt back in Chu Lai, about thirty miles north of where I was now. I wondered if he was worried about me and was surprised that he hadn't figured out a way to fly down to see me.

I got rid of Barker but kept Granger. He never changed. A mute at the base and a competent, mechanical radio-man in the landing zones.

At three weeks into my time with the grunts I passed Barker in front of the chow tent one evening.

"Hey there, Lieutenant, you ain't dead yet?" he asked. "You gonna beat Lieutenant Vervack's record near four weeks pretty soon. The gunny tole me he already lost a bunch of money on you."

In my bunk I told myself that Barker was an idiot. Taking care of yourself, doing a good job, being with good men was how you stayed alive. Statistics didn't matter in individual cases. Then I put my head under my pillow in case the shakes came back.

Gearheardt stuck his head into my tent.

"Olly, olly, ox in free, or something like that. Hey, pal, you don't look so good."

"Take that flashlight out of my face, Gearheardt. I am statistically dead."

"Heard you were a big hero around here. Kill anybody we know?"

"I'm telling you, Gearheardt, it's not funny. What the hell are you doing here anyway?"

"I got your papers, my friend. The President said my buddy Jack needs to be with his buddy Gearheardt. In fact I asked him to get the orders cut to say just that. Here."

He held up a document and pointed his flashlight at it from top to bottom. Amid all of the official SecDacNavDD118cc crap a single sentence read, "Lieutenant Armstrong needs to be with his buddy Gearheardt."

"That sent 'em through the roof up at Wing HQ, I'll bet. And look at this."

He held up a copy of *Stars and Stripes,* the armed forces newspaper. On the front page a headline read POLL SHOWS PUBLIC TRUST FADING.

"Listen to this, buddy. 'In a poll released today by Apgard Polling, it was revealed that the U.S. public by an overwhelming margin would prefer movie stars run foreign policy. Mickey Mouse was the most trusted public figure again, followed by Mickey Rooney, Mickey Mantle, and Mikii Tita, a Las Vegas dancer.'"

"What the hell is that all about, Gearheardt?"

"Don't you get it, Jack? President Larry Bob, not his real name, is covering his ass again. Before this is over, they'll have Mickey Mouse strapped in Old Sparky, and the Prez will be totin' tacos on the Mexican Riviera. America is fried, and the Prez's future is lower than a short order cook."

I sat in silence for a moment. I could see Gearheardt outlined against the tent opening.

"Compared to that, the war seems almost sane in light of what happens in the world. Maybe I want to be a grunt. At the end of the day, if you're alive and can feed yourself, you're happy." I paused. "Is that so bad?"

Gearheardt grew serious.

"I've got to get you out of here, Jack. You're going nuts."

While I was musing, Gearheardt was throwing my gear into a parachute bag. He tossed it out the door and turned back to where I sat on the edge of my cot.

"We can go right now."

We left and walked through the night toward the sound of a helicopter idling. When I looked up I saw its running lights and it felt good. The rotors were stopped and drooped awkwardly. A giant exhausted insect.

At the last row of tents, Gearheardt stopped and shined his flashlight on a sign that hung from the last of the last. It was the tent where the bodies that hadn't been flown out yet were kept until they could be shipped to the big walk-in reefer in the sky, as the troops called it. The sign was new and hand painted. It read, NO SNIFFING THE DEAD.

"When I was walking up to your tent some beanpole was hanging that sign. What the hell is it supposed to mean?"

I sighed and moved him along by the arm. Goddamn Barker.

"It's because dead men have molecubes floating around them and it's like eating the dead if you sniff them."

Gearheardt said, "Oh."

12 · Roll Out the Barrel, We'll Have a Barrel of British Spy

Gearheardt and I found our contact, or rather he found us, in a small bar near the Air Force hospital in Qui Nhon. The squadron had moved there, settling in semi-livable huts alongside the runway, to support the Korean troops who had arrived, evidently to bring a taste of barbarism to *our* side. One of their tricks was sending their Viet Cong prisoners back for interrogation inside an empty 55-gallon gas drum. Three or four to a barrel. Unsurprisingly, they were quite ready to be turned over to the Americans or South Vietnamese for questioning when they were unloaded.

"You know, Jack," Gearheardt said, watching the South Vietnamese soldiers pry the lid off a barrel just unloaded from his helicopter, "you paint those barrels yellow, add some wheels and an ooga horn and you've got yourself a circus act."

"Seems a bit cruel, Gearheardt," I said, watching the groveling prisoners unravel from the knot.

"They should have thought of that before they became Vietnamese, Jack."

We were relaxing in the stolen-air-conditioner comfort of Mama-San's Number One Beer House when the contact came out of the pisser. He stopped by our table and smiled at Gearheardt.

"Devil of a war, ain't it mate?" he said.

"Yes," Gearheardt answered. He sipped his beer. He hated to be disturbed when he was off the flight schedule and only had a few hours to drink beer.

The contact seemed uncomfortable for a moment, looking around the dark room as if seeking assistance. All we knew was that the President had told Gearheardt that a contact would find us in Vietnam. There was a password, but Gearheardt had forgotten it.

"Yes, certainly the devil of a war," he said again, sounding British.

I have always liked the British. They have this tendency to say things like "Hello. What's this?" when their arms are blown off or they spot a farthing on the sidewalk. Even with his nervousness, the man carried that British ability to make the rest of us seem under-dressed or in the wrong place. He was sloppily clad in a dark suit, a striped tie hung loosely from the neck of his damp white shirt, and black lace-up shoes bereft of polish completed the outlandish garb of a gentleman in a whorehouse in a war zone. Gearheardt was in a camouflaged flight suit, the front zipper undone down to his pistol belt. I had on a new lightweight jungle-green flight suit that the gunny had stolen from the Air Force and traded to me for a forged pass to Na Trang.

Now the would-be contact lit a bent cigarette and, after putting the blown-out wooden match in his side coat pocket, cleared his throat.

"Yes, well, devil and all that."

"Are you the fucking spy posing as an Australian weapons dealer that we're supposed to meet?" Gearheardt asked suddenly.

The man straightened himself and again glanced around the bar. None of the Marines or whores seemed to be interested in the conversation.

He pulled a chair out from our table and sat down.

"Actually, Mr. Enderby sent me. From Hong Kong, you know. He said you would be expecting an Australian gentleman. Mr. Enderby said that the *devil* greeting would be the sort of—"

"Password?" I finished for him.

The man smiled at me, acknowledging my presence for the first time.

"Oh, jolly good, yes, the password. Are you Narsworthy or Dexter, sir?"

Gearheardt became alert.

"I'm Almost Captain Gearheardt. Never heard of those other guys. Maybe Mr. Enderby of Hong Kong sent you to the wrong Qui Nhon. There's one in Oklahoma, you know. Goddamned Okies, but salt-of-the-earth people." Gearheardt was in one of his moods.

"No, I'm quite certain that I am in the proper Qui Nhon, Almost Captain Gearheardt. I am also aware that you, sir, are Narsworthy, and this must be Almost Captain Armstrong, known to the CIA as Tom Dexter. Am I correct, sir?" He smiled at me, and I thought I saw the flash of a gold tooth.

"Buy this man a beer, Jack, I mean Tom," Gearheardt said. "He can't help where he was born. Can you, Mr. . . . . Mr. . . . ."

"Oh my, rude of me. Yes, I am . . . Gon."

Gearheardt snorted. "Well we are . . . here."

Gon shook our hands, knocking over Gearheardt's beer glass.

"Oh, dear, let me buy you another beverage. Seems appropriate, doesn't it, Mr. Narsworthy. The spilled American beer, I mean." His smile was becoming a bit irritating as he flashed it at Gearheardt who looked at me and raised his eyebrows in the universal sign for "watch my six." He motioned for me to lean away from the table and brought his head close to mine. "Give us a minute, Gon," he said.

"Jack, you notice anything funny about the British accent?"

I started to reply, but he went on, looking back at Gon.

"The guy is a fucking Mexican."

Now that I looked closely, I noticed that Gon's face was brown and he had straight black hair. A gold tooth flashed as he smiled back at my rude stare.

"Why would they send a Mex . . . ?"

"Goddam spies can't do anything without jacking around. I would imagine that Taco Tom here just needed something to do." Gearheardt held up his finger toward Gon, indicating we would be with him in a moment. Gon was picking his teeth with the corner of the menu and nodded okay.

"All we need is for this guy to tell us the name of the beer. We were supposed to give him a contract, which we don't have, and then he would help us in Hanoi, where we are going but don't know when. The President blames the delay on that dope with the greased-back hair. He says Nixon has found himself an advisor with the curliest hair above waist level and—"

"Gearheardt, could you just stick to the current situation and tell me about your conversation with the President later?"

"Can do, Jack." He straightened and turned back to the table.

"I'll tell you what, Gon old pal, I have no idea what you're talking about, but we'll pretend to be Narsworthy and Dexter, who are code-persons for me and Jack and who are supposed to meet a Brit MI6 guy sometime before we go on the mission to Hanoi, which I am awfully anxious to do if the President would get off his ass and get the orders to me. Now are you happy?"

One of the interesting things about Gearheardt was that he would sometimes wake up in a funk (this was one of those days) and not be able to tolerate beating around the bush.

After a moment, Gon answered. "Yes, quite so." He leaned back to allow the shriveled mama-san to place the new beverages in front of us.

The Mexi-Brit leaned forward and rested his arms on the table.

"So then, gentlemen, I take it from that remark that you do not have your orders yet. Nor, would it seem, do you have in your possession the contract. Would I be correct in that assumption?"

I had no idea what he was talking about. Of course I was aware that Gearheardt was also a CIA agent and had supposedly sworn me in and that the CIA was somehow involved in the mission to Hanoi. But contracts?

"Don't jump to any conclusions, Gon," Gearheardt said. "Jack here doesn't have pizza clearance. Maybe you and I should have a chat while Jack amuses himself with one of the better-looking women of this establishment."

"I have no intention of screwing one of them, and I think polite discussion is out of the question, Gearheardt. Just because you—"

"Fine with me, Jack." He turned to Gon. "What say we just go ahead and chat about this *contract* that I am unfortunately missing?" He winked at me as Gon once more surveyed the sad Third World bar, sad war-torn people, and happy, gun-crazed warriors.

"Yes, Captain. First, I must tell you that I am Cuban. After the Bay of the Pigs, the Americans promised me a job spying for the British. I have spent my years in the Cuban jail learning a British accent. To get ahead in this world, one must . . . but that is another story. I am your contact and the contact for the mad Cuban in Hanoi. That is why that—"

And we might have found out a bit more about what the hell we were supposed to do in Hanoi, but the door burst open and six Air Force officers, in stunning jungle fatigues, ties with matching breast handkerchiefs and Italian leather flight boots, stumbled in. They were a couple of Jolly Green crews, also stationed in Qui Nhon, to provide Search and Rescue for the A-1 fighter/bomber squadron there. From the look of them, they were well oiled and besotted. One had a bandage around his head, blood seeping through, and blood besmirching the front of his tailored fatigues.

"Have you boys been fighting?" Gearheardt yelled above the noise they brought in with them.

They stopped, turned their heads like drunken bovines, and spotted Gearheardt.

"GEARHEARDT, you rotten bastard!" they all cried at once. It was pretty much his full name outside of his small circle of close friends.

The Air Force pilots would have attacked him in force but evidently couldn't figure out how to get around the table and chairs blocking their way. Two of them sat down heavily and began to draw a flight plan on the table top. One was trying to get his emergency radio to work as another, evidently not quite as drunk, was trying to convince him that calling in an air strike on Gearheardt wasn't possible at the moment. The remaining two, including the one who looked like the flute player in the revolutionary war painting, just grinned foolishly and weaved.

"Look at that disgusting sight, Jack," Gearheardt said. "Grown men acting like grown men."

Gearheardt and the Jolly Green pilots had a wary respect for each other's flying ability and mission. That was not why they hated him. They hated him because he had tried to use their air-conditioned, tiled, and always freshly cleaned shitter, complete with uniformed attendants. They caught him on the pot, newspaper scattered, cigarette butts strewn about, and tossed him out on his ass. "Took five of them," he said.

Now they suspected it was Gearheardt who had poured Agent Orange on the putting green that the Air Force had painstakingly constructed and nurtured behind their flight line. It was. He carried a putter over to their flight line for weeks after it had become black sand, asking the duty officer, "Okay if I use the putting green, Lieutenant?" I had no idea where Gearheardt got a putter.

The Air Force crew had aroused the other patrons, and the Number One Beer House was rocking. The air circulated by the grunting air conditioner was mostly smoke. The jukebox suddenly came alive with Chuck Berry singing "Maybelline." The voltage differential had him singing it chipmunk style.

Gon leaned toward Gearheardt and cupped one hand beside his mouth.

"*Do you know Battambang?*" he yelled in Gearheardt's direction.

"Town in Oklahoma?" Gearheardt yelled back.

"*Forget the Oklahomans, Captain. Battambang is beer we will represent. Named after . . . where I meet Rico . . . can't impress you eno . . . must tell Juanton to . . .*"

I could make out only so many words, and I could tell that Gearheardt wasn't even listening. Sounded too much like directions or something, probably. He looked at me and shrugged his shoulders.

The Mexi-Brit grabbed Gearheardt's arm.

"Please listen, Captain. I need to give you some information."

A slow, mellow ballad by a Vietnamese singer started. It sounded like someone playing the musical saw, but conversation was possible now.

"The British team in Hanoi has been compromised. They—"

"Got caught screwing a woman?"

Gon ignored him.

"They are expecting the contract from the President."

"Last one I signed got me sent here," Gearheardt said.

"Would you shut up and listen, Gearheardt?"

"Quite right, Almost Captain Armstrong. This is important." He reached into his rumpled but nicely tailored suit and drew out an eight-by-ten photo. He unfolded it to reveal a glossy shot of an extremely attractive and scantily clad young woman. The photo was creased and worn.

"You haven't been yanking your crank with that thing, have you, Gon? What are all those spots and—"

Gon blushed. "No, Almost Captain Gearheardt. Those are simply . . . That isn't important. This is the woman that you are to meet in Hanoi. This is Barbonella."

"The broad parachuting into the commies' HQ?"

"The same. She is instructed to eventually get you to your meeting. At that time, the—"

"Any chance of holing up with her for a while? You know, just to do spy stuff. Right, Jack?" He was grinning and holding the photo up to see it better.

"Please be serious, Captain. There are a number of very powerful businessmen and government officials who have been—"

"Trying to hole up with her? I'll bet they have."

Gon deflated and sat back in his chair. After a moment he shrugged. "Perhaps we will meet in Hanoi."

"Vaya con Dios, señor," Gearheardt said.

"Gracias," Gon replied, and then grinned sheepishly. He rose and adjusted his tie.

I tried, he seemed to say. He retrieved his cigarettes from the table and left the bar. Later we would learn that he had attempted to drive to Battambang from Qui Nhon and experienced an unfortunate run-in with the Korean troops, who mistook him for a Mexi-Russian. He was "barreled" with two Viet Cong for half a day until the Koreans needed the fifty-five-gallon drum to construct a piss tube and let him out. He was bent double and close friends with the two enemy soldiers, although he hadn't caught their names.

"I would imagine *he's* a barrel of fun," Gearheardt said. But I was still worried that we didn't get any helpful information from him that we might need.

"Jack, trust me. We're getting full instructions from the President of the United States. I was warned that the Brits would try to horn in on this deal. I was just trying to confuse him."

"I hope it worked on him as well as it did on me."

On the way back to the Marine hooches, I tried to find out more from Gearheardt about the "beer" issue and the British participation in our Barbonella mission. I had taken some comfort in their involvement. The British seemed more serious about things and less likely to go off half-cocked.

Gearheardt ignored me.

It was getting dark and as we passed the flight line we saw Grady, one of the junior pilots in the squadron, putting away his mess gear and tidying up the cockpit of the H-34 where he lived. He had been late for three flights in a row, and the Skipper had ordered him to move his gear into the aircraft and live there so he could be on time for any launch that might come up.

"Any action out there, Grady?" Gearheardt asked, looking up at the lieutenant as he brushed his teeth.

Grady spat into his canteen cup and smiled down at us.

"An ARVN unit is getting the shit kicked out of them somewhere on the road to An Khe. They have about a dozen Special Forces guys with them."

"Did the squadron try to get any of them out?"

"Murph tried a medevac about an hour ago, but couldn't land because of the fifty cal fire. I think we're going to stand by until morning and hope they make it through the night."

"Let's go over to the operations hooch, Jack. This sounds like a job for Super Pilot."

"You're drunk, Gearheardt. They won't let you fly. And you're not on the medevac schedule anyway."

"The day they won't let you fly night medevac drunk is the day we throw in the towel," he said, dodging Grady's emptying of his canteen cup. He took off for the operations hooch.

Inside, another new pilot, Lieutenant Ross, sat at the desk listening to the ops radio. It monitored most of the channels in the area. He looked up as Gearheardt and I approached.

"The answer is no, Gearheardt," he said.

"He can have my job," one of the flight crew lounging on the reclining chairs in the ready room called out. "I was hoping not to die tonight anyway."

"See, shithead," Gearheardt said to Ross.

I already knew that Gearheardt would end up on night medical evacuation duty. The thought of missing action was more than he could take. And if Americans were wounded, he would fly a rickshaw through a monsoon shitstorm to get the troops to a med station.

After a moment of haggling and threats, Gearheardt and I went to the back room and retrieved our flight gear. We were replacing Tooms and Woods as one of the two crews on standby.

"Now we get to fly together, Jack. No one is going to go wake the Skipper and tell him we've taken over night medevac. Anyway, they probably know we don't have our orders to go north yet. Suspicious assholes." He was smiling, as he always did when he sensed a bit of action.

And we got it.

Around 0100 the squadron received a request to extract two of the Special Forces troops from the An Khe road battle.

Lieutenant Ross, still yawning after the loud phone buzzer on the ops radio had awakened him, briefed us.

"They got a couple of guys with wounds that they don't think can wait until morning, Gearheardt. One guy has a head wound and the other a sucking chest wound and a bullet in his spine. You game?"

"Give me the fucking coordinates and call signs, Ross. You know we'll go."

A shaken backup crew stood behind us. New guys who had had just enough taste of night medevacs and stories of Gearheardt's escapades to wish they were somewhere else.

"They're on the side of a hill, Almost Captain Gearheardt," one of the pilots said. "You'll have to hover to load them. No landing spot." This turned out not to be true but just a report from an earlier crew that had been lost and making up excuses.

Gearheardt was eating it up. He liked nothing better than a challenge to his flying skills, danger to his life, and a bunch of pilots scared shitless surrounding him.

"You ready, Jack?" he asked. "Did you copy down all that call sign and coordinate crap?"

Walking in darkness to our aircraft which the alert ground crew had preflighted and started, Gearheardt stopped and listened for a moment, "Do we really want to stop all this, Jack? What will we do next?" It was rhetorical, and he hurried to the side of his helicopter.

A gentle rain was falling and affecting my sphincter. Night medevac in the rain. Damned Gearheardt.

It got worse. As I reached the flight line, I heard an argument between Gearheardt and one of the other pilots. Gearheardt's position was that the flight was too hairy for the new guy and that I should take his aircraft so that we would have both choppers piloted by more combat experience. Gearheardt was probably right, but I would have preferred flying with him. I realized, however, that this new arrangement meant that I probably would not be required to make a pickup. Gearheardt could get both wounded, while I circled comfortably out of range of ground fire. I enjoyed the adrenaline rush of combat flying almost as much as Gearheardt, but unlike him, I didn't crave it or seek it out like an idiot.

Gearheardt won the argument and I strapped into the pilot's seat of Papa Tango Three Six, with Lt. Brown as my co-pilot. Bunting climbed into the co-pilot's seat in PT Two Two with Gearheardt.

In the blackness we taxied to the runway and rolled down it for takeoff. Easier than lifting off as we normally did. I followed the flame coming from Gearheardt's exhaust and joined him in a climbing turn over Qui Nhon and then inward toward An Khe.

Each of us had two crew on board, manning the M-60s. This was one of the crappiest jobs in the war, riding around in the belly of choppers piloted by wild-assed Sky Kings. They had to keep the aircraft running, shoot back at whoever was shooting at us, help get the wounded into the aircraft and, if possible, attend to their wounds as best they could on the way to the medical units. They all loved the job.

"Papa Tango Three Six, you back there?" Gearheardt radioed on the squadron channel.

"I'm right behind you, Two Two. Are we lost yet?"

The rain was not heavy but it made it more difficult to see anything on the ground. We had instructions to basically follow the Qui Nhon highway (which we couldn't see) until we intersected the 245-degree radial off of the Chu Lai ADF. The battle should then be underneath us.

"Monitor Guard on the UHF, Jack. We'll use 131.8 on the squadron radio."

I clicked my radio twice to acknowledge that I understood.

"Three Six, I'm going to turn on my running lights. I know you're blind as a bat, but try to keep me in sight."

"How do you intend to find the LZ, Two Two?" I asked on 131.8.

"Jack, there's nothing out here that's over a hundred feet until we get ten miles inland. If we hit a mountain, we've gone too far."

"Two Two, watch out flying over Pigville. They're sure to lob a few rounds up at us."

A few days before, Gearheardt had been taking a four-hundred-pound sow to a village on behalf of the USAID folks operating in the area. The animal had broken loose in the chopper, and Gearheardt gave the word to boot it out before it ran back into the tail cone of the aircraft and caused severe control problems. They were at five hundred feet.

"I was right behind him when that pig went out," Johnson had related in the officers' club tent that night. He had been flying wing on Gearheardt. "Man, those little pig feet were a blur. Count on Gearheardt though. The thing made a perfect arc down to the ground. Right in the center of the village."

Gearheardt had been unchagrinned. "I normally prefer a lower level pig launch," he explained to the beer-chugging pilots in the tent. "The forward speed of the pig will cause it to bounce along the ground before it explodes. You can skip it right into the mouth of a VC cave if you practice. We had a lot of experience in the Boar War."

"Papa Tango Lead, you read Cricket on Guard?" said a calm and collected voice.

"Hello, Cricket, I read you. How're things at ten thousand feet?" Gearheardt answered.

"Is this Gearheardt?" the overhead command ship asked.

"The one and only, Cricket. You got me on your scope?"

"We have you and your wingman about five clicks east of the LZ. Say your altitude."

"Two Two and Papa Tango Three Six are at one thousand feet, Cricket. You got any help for me down here, or are you just cruising for chicks?"

"Two Two, be advised that the dinks are over-running the LZ. Too close for any air support, Gearheardt. You still planning on going in?"

"Does the pope shit in the woods, Cricket?"

A new voice on the radio broke in. "Two Two, this is Playboy Lead. You read?"

"Now the Army wants in on the act! I read you, Playboy. What's your position?"

"We're just lifted off of Qui Nhon, Two Two. Be there in about five."

The Playboy aircraft were Army gunships, sent up from Saigon to support our squadron at Qui Nhon, as the Marine Corps was woefully short of attack choppers. They were good guys—crappy pilots, but fearless.

I had little to do but try to keep Gearheardt's running lights in sight. It struck me that the United States had about twenty million dollars worth of aircraft and half a dozen flight crews heading out to try to rescue wounded Americans. I prayed that Gearheardt, at center stage, wouldn't attempt a suicide mission, that he wouldn't be shot down if he did, and that I wouldn't have to go in and try to get him out if he *was* shot down. I decided to let God try to figure out whether I was on the right track or not with the prayers. I left it to him to deal with the guys in the landing zone.

"Three Six, you read Playboy?" Gearheardt asked me on the squadron channel.

"I read him, Two Two. I think I see him hauling ass up behind us. Two of them. You taking them down with you?"

"I would imagine I couldn't stop them. Medal-hungry assholes.

You just keep me in sight, and if I can't get out of the zone, try to come in and get the wounded. If we can make it over to your chopper, we will. But get the Special Forces guys."

I clicked my squadron radio twice.

I began to worry about finding the battle zone in the rain and clouds (at least I told myself I was worrying about it), when I saw the parachute flares ahead of us.

"There they be, Three Six. See the flares? Let's go down to five hundred feet. We can keep them in sight now. Playboy, you caught up?"

"I'm just above you, Two Two. We'll head on and take a closer look."

I saw them then. Two Huey gunships, rockets and M-60 machine guns mounted on their sides. They pulled ahead and descended below us.

"Cricket, Papa Tango Two Two. We have the LZ in sight. Tell Laura I love her."

"Two Two, say again the last."

"Never mind, Cricket. Hang around up there until we're out of the LZ. We may need help finding the medical ship."

We had been instructed to take the wounded offshore to the Navy hospital ship when we got them out of the LZ. I didn't want to think about finding it and landing on it at night. I was sure Gearheardt was looking forward to it. He had never landed on it without claiming engine trouble so that he could stay on board and try to screw the nurses.

"Three Six, let's go down to a hundred fifty feet. I'm turning left here so just stay with me. I'm going up on the HF to try to get someone on the ground talking to me." He paused, his radio still on and hissing. "Not much trouble finding the zone, is there?"

The battle was not difficult to keep in sight. In addition to the flares being dropped continuously over the area by Air Force aircraft, there were numerous explosions and hundreds of tracers crisscrossing what must have been the commander's headquarters. My HF radio was not working, so I concentrated on following Gearheardt's aircraft as he descended in a tight left turn.

He came back up on the squadron channel.

"Good news, Three Six. The bad guys haven't overrun the zone yet. We can still get in and out if we come in from the north and go out the same way. Most of the enemy troops are attacking from the south. Good deal, huh?"

I clicked my radio again. Damned Gearheardt.

"The Playboy ships are about to take a quick pass over the zone. If they can find a spot they'll bend back around and lead me in. Laying some rocket fire on the south. Sound okay?"

"Two Two, just let me say for sanity's sake, that this zone is way, way too hot for you to get in and out of. We all want to save those guys, but we've got our own crew to think of. Take a look over there. That zone looks like a two-sided firing range on Uncle Sam's birthday. When the Playboys get—"

"Oh, Three Six, they have four more badly wounded Special Forces guys. I can't get all of them. You come in right behind me. That's better than trying to go in one at a time, don't you think?"

Damned Gearheardt!

"Two Two, this is Playboy, we just came out of the zone. I only took about twenty or thirty hits." He laughed and I knew it was that damned Capt. Vance—crazy as a loon, crazier than Gearheardt. "My wingman, the pussy, had a chunk of his cockpit shot off, and he's headed back to Qui Nhon. I'll hang here with you and lead you in. Come in from the north and as hot as you can manage. You'll never be able to turn around in the zone, so just take off straight ahead. I'll try to keep their heads down."

"Playboy lead, any chance of getting more gunships out here?"

At least Gearheardt had a tiny lick of sense.

"What for?" Vance, the dope, would always prefer solo performances. It kept the medal count up.

"Let's go, Jack. You got me in sight?"

I clicked again. On the aircraft intercom I checked with my crew.

"You guys set? Probably can't use the guns once we get down close to the ground. At least the mortar fire is lighting up the area. We should get three guys. Stay in the ship if you possibly can, Gunny. If you have to get out to help them load, tell me and then hit my leg when we're ready to lift off. All set."

"Fuck me," was all I heard, I think from the corporal who was the side gunner. Lieutenant Brown, beside me in the cockpit, was bouncing his knee up and down with an increasing rhythm. He clicked his intercom, looking straight ahead.

"Hit the lights," I said to him. He dimmed the instrument panel lights and checked to see that the running lights were off. There was no need to advertise our position on the way in.

We circled far to the north of the battle and went to treetop level, keeping our speed at about ninety knots. It was dark below us, but the fighting ahead kept the cockpit lighted. Brown adjusted his shoulder straps. I pulled the clear Plexiglas visor down over my face.

Ahead of me I could see the outline of Gearheardt's aircraft against the light of the battle, and ahead of him a shape that was the Playboy gunship. When I saw the rockets leave the pods on the side of the gunship, I knew that we were approaching the zone. Tracers began appearing from the darkness between Gearheardt and the landing zone. They came up in graceful, swooping arcs, curving away and behind us as we sped by. The crack of small arms fire and the thump of larger machine guns now began to grow louder.

"About ten seconds, Jack," I heard Gearheardt say. We usually abandoned the call signs when the two of us were on a mission together. It saved just a split second of thinking time.

I heard the first round hit my aircraft and began my trick of counting them. Simple thinking told me that any round that I could hear hit us wasn't one that would kill me. Then the next rounds hit, two and three, quickly together. As I saw Gearheardt begin to flare his helicopter to slow for landing, the rounds began hitting my aircraft in bursts that took away a large part of my ability to think. I heard the gunny shout something on the intercom, and Brown jumped as a round came through the windscreen and smashed the first aid kit between us. I felt a sharp pain on my neck.

The gunny was shouting almost continuously now and I made out that our gunner had been shot in the stomach. I raised the nose of the aircraft to bleed off airspeed as we came over the trees at the edge of the landing zone. Gearheardt had come to a stop in front of me and I had to adjust at the last moment to keep from hitting his aircraft with my rotor blades. I touched down roughly.

"Get 'em in! Get 'em in, Gunny!" I shouted, not using the intercom. The radios were all but useless as everyone was screaming at once. The mortar barrage, which had let up, now began in earnest, and explosions walked across the zone in front of me. I heard and felt the blasts. Outside of the helicopter, scores of troops swarmed, hunched close to the ground. The light of the flares and explosions put everything into silhouette.

"Skipper," the gunny called on the intercom, "they've got to bring the wounded over here. It's going to take a couple of minutes. What do you want me to do? There's a shit-pot full of ARVNs trying to get on board."

"Keep 'em off, Gunny! Do what you have to do!" The Army of the Republic of Vietnam had an aversion to dying unequaled in Southeast Asia.

We sat in the zone with the war going on around us. A bullet or shrapnel clanged through the aircraft about every ten seconds. Only a few in the cockpit, as the enemy, blessedly, normally aimed for the bulk of the bird, behind the cockpit. I saw Gearheardt's crew chief on the ground beside his aircraft, trying to help lift a stretcher into the cabin. He went down on one knee as a black spot appeared on his thigh, then recovered and helped a shirtless soldier with a head bandage climb up also.

"Where are those fucking guys, Gunny?"

"The sergeant says to wait one, Skipper."

"How's Porter?" I yelled.

There was a pause. "Not good, sir."

Porter was the gunner. A pudgy kid from Nebraska.

An American soldier climbed up the side of the aircraft and

grabbed my arm through the cockpit window. He leaned his mouth close to the side of my helmet.

"Thanks!" he shouted. He gave a thumbs up with his free hand.

"Jump in," I shouted. "Let's get you guys out of here before the ARVN bolt!"

He leaned closer. "Can you move over toward that treeline?" he yelled. "The guys you need to load are there. We're having to drag them. Can't stand up. You get zapped."

I looked where he was pointing, about twenty yards away. It was closer to the treeline, where most of the small arms fire was coming from.

"Okay," I shouted to him. "Get some fire going—"

The soldier shrugged. "Get my wounded out. We'll be okay." Or something that sounded like that. He jumped back to the ground.

I pulled the chopper into a hover about five feet above the ground and moved sideways across the zone, thankful for something to do. Two more brilliant flares popped open above me, relighting the zone.

My downdraft blew the cover off of a line of dead soldiers. The light so bright there was no shading in the zone. White or black. The soldiers looked eerie. Black eyeholes and bloodless faces. They were all Vietnamese.

When we sat back down, I could hear the rounds hitting the sides of the aircraft again. A bullet came through the cockpit and Brown and I both jumped back. I heard or felt it passing.

"Skipper," the gunny shouted into the intercom, "Porter's bleeding to death! Gutshot, sir!"

He wanted me to do something.

Goddam it! I wasn't the one fucking around trying to get the wounded over to the aircraft! Goddam it! What the hell was *I* supposed to do!

I keyed the intercom mike. "*Does everyone have their head up their ass?* They knew we were coming for these guys!"

The gunny, I assumed, clicked his intercom mike.

A blast landed between Gearheardt's aircraft and mine, and I looked across Brown to see if Gearheardt was still in one piece. I saw him looking back at me, his face a black place inside his hardhat.

"This is the shits, isn't it?" I heard him say to me on the squadron channel.

"They're in! They're in! Go! Go! Go!" The gunny was slapping my leg from below.

I called Gearheardt. "We're all set. Let's get the fuck out of here!"

As Gearheardt lifted from his spot and lowered his nose to gain airspeed, he answered, "Now Jack, is that the kind of language that your mother would wo— Oh shit!"

I saw his aircraft lurch up as a mortar exploded underneath. The small arms fire begin to pound my aircraft again as I climbed to where more of the enemy could see me. I pulled hard right to avoid running into Gearheardt and then we were in darkness again, the light and tracers now coming from behind us.

"You okay, Gearheardt?"

"I got red and yellow lights all over the damn place, but I'm running fine. How about you?" We leveled at five hundred feet and Gearheardt turned on his running lights.

"Porter is hit. Bad. The aircraft is okay."

"You want to go to Charlie med"—the medical unit near Qui Nhon—"or out to the ship?"

"I've got two head wounds, a spine shot, and the gunny is holding Porter's guts in. Let's head for the hospital ship."

"You go ahead in. My guys can wait. Another minute or two won't matter." He switched to UHF. "Cricket, you read Papa Tango Lead?"

"We read you, Papa Tango. We are to advise you that Backbiter Six says to not, repeat *not* land in the zone to pick up the wounded. You copy?"

After a moment, Gearheardt replied. "These guys are going to be awfully disappointed that I have to take them back and drop them off, Cricket. Could you pass on a message from me to Backbiter Six? Tell that dumb cock—"

"Drop it, Gearheardt." I needed the channel. "Cricket, we'd like to have a heading for the *Hope*. And we need it right now."

The drop of the wounded on the USS *Hope* was as uneventful as a night landing on the back of a small bouncing platform can be. Gearheardt actually did have engine problems and spent the rest of the night aboard the ship. Porter was dead when we offloaded him, but the Special Forces guys were all still alive.

My co-pilot, Lieutenant Brown, turned in his wings the next day. I had not realized that the mission was his very first in Vietnam. It was just too much for him, he said. Strangely, no one razzed him. I felt bad for him, knowing that I should have communicated more with him in the cockpit, given him something to do.

The gunny spent the morning washing the blood out of the cabin, even though his rank would have excused him from that chore. I hung around the aircraft for a while also, having trouble letting go.

Gearheardt came back from the hospital ship the next afternoon. I expected him to have lurid tales to tell. But he didn't tell them.

"Not a lot of sex available there, Jack. Couple of cute corpsmen, but the women docs were bitches. They had locked up the nurses before I landed." He smiled, and I wasn't sure which parts of the story to believe. He went on. "So I went to the radio room and called the Prez."

"About our mission?"

"Naw, just to shoot the shit about football. Of course it was about the mission, Jack. That damn Brit didn't clear up anything, and the squadron keeps getting more suspicious. We need to move things along."

"And there are those nights like—"

"Yeah, I knew you'd say that, Jack. We gotta stop this shit or we're going to get creamed."

That evening I faced what all of the officers dreaded, and usually passed off to someone in the squadron administration—the letter to the parents or wife, the next of kin. The NOK on the form that we all filled out.

I couldn't help but think about Barker's letters, the idiot, and knew that I could craft decent, helpful, compassionate letters to grieving NOK. I thought about the letters that I had written about kids that I didn't know. Now that seemed immeasurably easier.

I sat with the pad and pencil and couldn't. There was no way to start. I fiddled with the pencil, tapping it on the paper until Gearheardt loudly cleared his throat. We were in the hooch, Gearheardt's cot directly across from the foot of mine. I was supposed to write the letter in the admin office so I could use the typewriter. But I didn't like being in there.

I couldn't get beyond the salutation. Maybe we did need brainless idiots to write these letters.

"Jack," Gearheardt said, "maybe you're putting too much emphasis on just the dead son and NOK's part. Whatever you say, they'll still be whining and moping around the house, forgetting to feed the dog. And the kid will still be dead."

When I didn't look up and encourage the asshole, he went on.

"In fact why don't you send the Next of Kin a bill? For the shipping charges. Your son shows up C.O.D., and that gives you something to think about, Jack. I think the NOKs would appreciate having something to take their minds off of the loss of the kid. Maybe the cost of his uniforms and guns and things, too. You know, *Your son did not complete his contract to spend a year in Vietnam. We must ask you to remit the sum of $3,500 to the U.S. Government, care of the Secretary of Defense.*"

"I don't think so, Gearheardt," I replied through my clenched teeth. "I'm really not needing your bullshit right now."

He thought for a minute. "Yeah, you're probably right. Just tell his folks he was the greatest fighter since Audie Murphy, and without him we might have lost the war. That's the best you can do, Jack. Tell 'em the son-of-a-bitch was a fighting machine."

I looked over at him, lying on his bunk with a coffee-can ashtray balanced on his chest. He raised his eyebrows.

"I didn't start this damn thing, Jack," he said. "Maybe we ought to go up to Hanoi and stop it." He smiled the Gearheardt smile.

I lay back on my cot and closed my eyes. After a while, I began reliving the five minutes in the LZ where I had lost Porter. His last words were "Fuck me."

I had done well. The adrenaline rush had been exhilarating, climaxing when we entered the darkness climbing out of the zone and I knew I was going to live.

The truth was that Captain Glassner wasn't the screaming asshole I always mentally called him. After every mission where we lost pilots or crew, he came into the officers' club and announced, "God has made his selection! And it was a good one! Fuck the dead!"

I began to drift off. The adrenaline was almost out of my system after twenty-four hours. Was there really a mission to Hanoi?

I started to ask Gearheardt, but he was reading letters from his girlfriends and humming. The tune was "Fascinating Rhythm," but I knew his new words were "Parachutin' Pussy."

There had to be a plan.

13 · Heaven Is an H-34 in Vietland

O kay, gents, let's synchronize our watches. Shit, what happened to my watch? Major, give me your watch. Okay, thanks, I've got zero six forty-three and thirty seconds. On my mark, we'll set to zero six forty-four."

He stared at his watch. "Major, is this damn thing working? Oh, there it is. Shit, now it's zero six forty-four and fifteen seconds. What the hell is this little gizmo over here, Major? I thought that was the second hand. Okay, coming up on zero six forty-five, on my mark. Mark. Everybody got six forty-five? Of course it's past that now, but you know what I mean. What time do you have there, Major? Oh, this is your watch? Now we have to synchronize with the artillery battalion. How do we do that, Major? It won't make much difference if the squadron is all on the same time if those goofballs over at artillery are slow. They'll still be shelling the zone when we're trying to land. We don't want that."

Major Gonzales stepped to the front of the briefing tent and handed the Skipper a watch. "This is your watch, sir. I took it to make sure that we were synchronized with Group, the Air Force, and artillery."

The Skipper looked at it. "This thing is two minutes off from the one we just synchronized to, Major. Now we have to do the damn thing all over again." He grabbed the watch the major held out. He stood looking at both of them draped over his large hand. They were the same Marine Corps issue, black-faced with olive drab canvas bands. After a moment of concentration he said, "Which one was the one that was synchronized with the artillery?"

Major Gonzales made a face but didn't let the frowning Skipper see it. "Here, sir. I think it's this one. We can check it because it will be the one that is *not* in synch with the squadron. Or if it is, then it doesn't make any difference."

"Huh?" the Skipper said, looking an awful lot like a man who left the officers' club tent at 0330 that morning.

"Captain Shinn, what time do you have?" the major asked.

"I don't have my watch, Major. I think the hooch maids stole it. Sorry."

"How about you, Adams. What's the time exactly?"

"My watch is broken, Major. I think the Skipper said it was about six forty-five."

"How many of you have your watches on, gentlemen?" the major asked nastily.

No one raised their hand or looked him in the eye.

"Do you mean to tell me that we have been dicking around with the damn time for the last thirty minutes and not a one of you is even wearing a watch?" We knew he was mad because he never cursed even a little bit. We also knew that Group was on his ass because the squadron had been late the last few strike missions.

Adams raised his hand. "I'm wearing mine, Major. It's just broken. I think that Fuller dropped his—"

"Shut up, Adams. I could care less how you broke your watch." He turned to the Skipper, who was still staring at the two watches in his hand as if the Oracle of Gidema was going to rise out of them and give him knowledge. "Skipper," he said, "we should get on with the briefing. We need to be in the air by zero seven fifteen. I'll worry about the time, sir."

"Well, get it right next time, goddamn it. Group is on my ass. Put out a squadron order that no one is to wear a watch until I say so. I'll have the official time, or at least you will, and the others can just ask. I'm fed up with all this watch business. Let's shape up, Major. Get on with the briefing." He stormed out of the tent. After a moment he stuck his head back in. "Is this where the strike briefing is to take place?"

"Yes, sir."

"Okay. I thought this was just where we were fixing our watches." He stepped back in. "Where are all those charts and maps and things? Vervack, get your ass up here and start the briefing." He took a seat in the front row of folding chairs.

The squadron intelligence officer, who was not a pilot, strode confidently to the front of the tent. He set up a large map on an easel and then turned to the squadron. He had a long, handlebar mustache and beady eyes. The middle of his face would have fit comfortably on a ferret or a wolverine. He didn't like pilots.

Sometimes after a strike mission where we had gotten totally shot up, we saw him go behind the debriefing tent, and his thin shoulders would shake as if he were laughing. We had decided to kill him long ago, but he was rumored to be "connected." We weren't sure what that meant, and I assumed that it was just our excuse not to kill him.

He put his hands on his hips and surveyed us all. His utilities were starched and crisp. His first lieutenant bars danced in the morning light when he moved.

"The squadron is going into the Cau Cau Valley this morning. We will be joined by 361, 364, and an Army Cobra squadron flying escort; 261 will be providing medevac as well as search and rescue."

"We will be airborne at zero seven fifteen. We will proceed by flights to LZ Blue, where we will pick up our troops, who are from First Battalion Ninth Marines, Charlie and Delta Company. At zero seven forty-five we will be airborne again, rendezvous with the Cobra escort at Checkpoint Alpha, the mouth of the Ng Thrin River, and then proceed to the strike zone to arrive when the artillery lifts at exactly zero eight hundred hours." He looked around, hands still on hips. His tight smile hadn't wavered, yet.

"Any questions so far?" he asked.

"Yeah," Buzz began, "who's this fucking 'we' you're talking about?"

"Whether you like it or not, I am a member of this squadron, Lieutenant Eckerd."

"Well, this turd is a member of my body until I can get to the four-holer, Lieutenant Vervack."

Major Gonzales stood up and faced the squadron. "That's enough, gentlemen. Get on with the briefing, Lieutenant Vervack." He frowned at Buzz and sat back down. The Skipper sat beside him admiring the two watches he was wearing on his left wrist.

Lieutenant Vervack continued, uncowed. "You have the coordinates of the pickup zone and drop zone on the handouts for your kneeboards so I won't cover that unless there are any questions. We don't expect there to be many enemy in the strike zone—"

"Good, let's not go there." It was from a lieutenant at the back of the tent.

"—after the bombing missions from zero seven hundred to seven thirty, and the artillery barrage from zero seven thirty to zero eight hundred."

"If we got zero enemy at zero eight hundred why don't we zero go?" It sounded like the same guy.

Major Gonzales stood up again. "I said knock it off! We are going to finish this briefing, get in those helicopters, and fly those troops into the strike zone. I don't want to hear another wiseass word out of any of you. Do you read me?"

Vervack walked to the easel and took out his famous red pencil. He began drawing symbols on the map in the area of the strike zone. "We can possibly draw fire from here, here, here, and you should watch your departure over this area here. Mostly small arms, with some light machine gun. No reported fifty-caliber but we won't know until we get there. They usually keep their heavy stuff as a surprise for us." He turned from the map and smiled. Buzz mouthed, "We, you asshole?" but didn't say anything out loud.

"We could possibly encounter some really heavy stuff, say thirty-seven-millimeter, if we wander too far off of the flight path and get over by this ridgeline. Let's try to stay away from there."

"*I'll* sure try," said Flager in a high voice, but nobody laughed. Thirty-seven millimeter would put a hole in you about the size of a basketball.

"If you're shot down and can't get onto one of the SAR choppers, hook up with the Marines in the zone. If you should get separated, head for this village," he pointed to a black speck on the map, "which is reported friendly."

"Let's attack *them*."

The major snapped his head around, but no one was smiling, and he turned back to the front.

"That's about it. Any questions?"

Major Gonzales stood up and faced the pilots. "Okay, gentlemen. You have your flight and aircraft assignments. Let's try not to botch this one up."

I was fairly calm. The first few missions after I got back to the squadron from being a FAC were easy and relaxing compared to the ground war. Then, near Bong Nhgn, Bootig's aircraft exploded as we headed into a hot zone, killing the crew and eleven Marines who were on board. The next day, Brown, and a kid I didn't know very well, lost an engine on takeoff and plowed into the aircraft taking off next to them when he tried to turn back to the LZ—a no-no with an engine failure at that height, but who knew what else was going on in the cockpit with all the groundfire coming through the formation— and set a new squadron record of eight crew and ten Marines on the ground killed. Still, this morning's mission was not unusual or particularly dangerous. As bad as the zone was, at least I wasn't staying behind in it.

Gearheardt and I sat side by side near the rear of the briefing tent. Gearheardt was his usual self, grab-assing with the other pilots and making fun of the major and the intelligence officer. I was more subdued, still thinking about the dead rat that I had found in my sleeping bag when I returned from my brief tour with the grunts.

The rat had not died of natural causes, and I couldn't help but think it was tied to the Barbonella mission. Gearheardt took it in stride, assuring me that it only meant that someone or ones in the squadron was on to us and that they thought we were rats and were going to kill us. I had run out of responses to his logical acceptance of the bizarre.

At the front of the tent a huge wail went up as Tilton was selected to fly co-pilot with the Skipper. Tilton seemed oblivious to the fact that the Skipper was sitting five feet from him as he lunged at the operation officer.

"I'm not flying with him, you bastard!" Tilton yelled. "The Skipper can't fly a helicopter to save his ass, but he never gives the co-pilot the controls."

"Somebody has to fly with him," Captain Reynolds said calmly. He went through this every mission and was not easily moved. Rumors that cash could get you out of the Skipper's aircraft were probably untrue, since once assigned, everybody in memory had flown and actually survived. Gearheardt, of course, was always volunteering to fly with the Skipper, so they never let him.

There was no doubt that it *was* a challenge to your nervous system. I had had my share of hops with him and come back wringing wet and exhausted. The Skipper, among other irritating characteristics, had a habit of lighting a cigarette as soon as he got airborne and keeping one lit for the whole flight. He would squint over the smoke drifting up into his face as he struggled to keep the aircraft moving in only one direction, a massive feat for him. To make matters worse, he constantly keyed the microphone, intercom or the squadron channel, it didn't matter, and muttered to himself.

"Goddam thing. Whoa, hold on. Oh shit. There you go, baby. Watch it, watch it. Oh boy. Oh boy. Down, you bastard. Goddam sonofabitch. There we go. There we go. Oh shit, watch it."

Meanwhile the chopper would be lurching about the sky, one moment drifting toward a terrified wingman, the next minute plummeting toward the earth, crabbed so that the rushing air would sent dirt, maps, and anything loose billowing around the cabin. On the ground in the zone, no matter the groundfire or mayhem, he lectured his co-pilots on cockpit procedure and explained in detail why he had made the bizarre and engine-damaging power adjustments on the way into the zone. Once, when he had made a landing so hard that the tailcone broke free of the helicopter, he explained to his co-pilot how he had detected a fire in the tailcone and broken it off to save the rest of the aircraft, which was then abandoned in the LZ. Invariably the co-pilot had to take the rap for any damage to the aircraft, a career-shortening entry into a pilot's logbook, which was about the last straw for most of them.

Tilton was now reaching the point of making a fool of himself, crying profusely, slumped in the front row of folding chairs. I knew that his wife had recently had a baby. I heard him tell the XO that he had just shown a picture of his newborn girl to Adams, which was one of the signs that he would probably get shot down and killed now. He didn't mind taking normal risk, but he couldn't fly with the Skipper. Meanwhile the Skipper was writing on his kneepad, copying the radio frequencies (he never remembered them and always used Guard anyway) and the landing zone coordinates (his co-pilot had damned well better know where they were all the time) and humming, occasionally turning his wrist so that he could view his two wristwatches. He was a great CO actually—if you stayed out of his way and didn't have to fly with him.

Gearheardt tapped me on the shoulder. "Who's your co-pilot?" he asked.

"Winston," I replied.

"You and I were scheduled to fly together. Someone changed it."

"What does that mean? Crew schedule changes all the time."

"Have we flown together since you got back?"

I thought about it. "No, I guess not."

"They aren't going to let us get in the same aircraft. They're afraid we'll head north. I think they know the time is near." He smiled and patted my knee.

"Who are *they*?"

"The ones that don't want us to go."

"Is the time near?"

"We'll know more tonight. I have a call in to Larry Bob, and I think he's going to give us the word. He didn't go to all the trouble to get you out of that FAC job for nothing."

He chuckled to himself and said, "By the way, you know who they got to take your place as the FAC?"

"I heard it was Cobb. Wasn't it?"

"Naw, Cobb ran off and shot himself in the big toe. You remember Jensen, the pilot that hung around Group headquarters and was pimping for the Wing hotshots?"

"*Him?*"

"Colonel Garrett caught something that turned his dick black. Blamed Jensen. So now Jensen is a FAC."

"I never was a fan of Jensen, but I have to tell you that I pity him with those poor grunts."

"Don't pity Jensen. He's the FAC, but he's running the show out of some massage parlor in Bangkok. Has a telephone hookup and a big map. Just calls in air strikes by the grunts reading him coordinates. They love him, by the way. Bombs the shit out of everything in sight. What does he care, he's in Bangkok."

Around us the last of the pilots were grabbing kneeboards and helmet bags. Most had put on flak vests, though few wore the flak diapers that were supposed to protect your family jewels. The aircraft had armor plating under the seat, at least. Tilton had resigned himself to flying with the Skipper and was getting briefed by the ops officer, the intelligence officer, and Major Gonzales all at once. Each was afraid that Tilton might screw up and not bring the Skipper back, and the squadron would get an asshole for a new skipper. They patted Tilton on the back, grabbed his arm at the biceps, rubbed the back of his neck like a prizefighter, and carried his gear outside to the helicopter. I heard a loud sniffle as he passed by the side of the tent where Gearheardt and I still sat. Alone now.

"You're calling the President? Today? After we get back from this strike?"

"I'm not eager to stop the war. I kinda like it, you know. But I'm tired of waiting around for orders, and the other day I even had a chance to strafe and didn't take it. I'm telling the president to shit or get off the pot."

"You better watch it or the President could send you to Vietnam."

"Exactly. Let's get this thing on the road. If we're ending this thing, I hate to just keep blowing the hell out of the countryside." He got up and I followed him. "See you after the strike."

We walked toward the flight line. Ahead of us the pilots were finishing preflight and climbing into the cockpits. Faces were getting serious now. I punched Gearheardt lightly on his arm and turned toward my aircraft. He stopped me.

"Where is it we're going this morning? I was dozing through Vervack's briefing."

"Your co-pilot knows. It's a piece of cake. We took a strike in there a couple of weeks ago and didn't find anything."

The squadron lost Downing, Gaines, Webster, and Kinkaid in the strike zone. Brewster and Flemming managed to get their ship airborne, but only made it halfway back to the pickup zone. They were picked up by the SAR ships and taken to Danang med, where Brewster was operated on for a head wound and Flemming lost his leg. Tilton and the Skipper were shot down in the LZ, and Tilton attacked the Skipper with his fists and then his kneeboard when the Skipper insisted they go through the engine shutdown procedures before they left the burning cockpit. We never saw Tilton again. The rumors were that he either defected or was AWOL and selling burgers at Marineland of the Pacific. The Skipper inadvertently had listed him as KIA on his after-action report, and that was as good as a get-out-of-jail-free card, since *no one* was allowed to question the Skipper's administrative action forms, and certainly not his after-action reports. The Skipper's crew chief, transferred shortly thereafter to the USO in Bangkok, later wrote and said that the Skipper hadn't been shot down but had crashed in the LZ while trying to synchronize the two watches on his arm and fly the aircraft at the same time.

When we debriefed after the strike, the Skipper was pumped up.

"Fantastic job, gentlemen. Our squadron showed the others how to do it today. I've been given word by Group that we got more Marines into the LZ than any other squadron. Well done."

Captain Reynolds, always a stickler for details, stood up. "Begging the colonel's pardon, sir. The message from Group said that we *left* more men in the LZ than any other squadron. I think that they were referring to the fact that we lost three crews, sir. I'm not sure they meant it as a compliment."

"Well, damn it to hell. There always has to be something. Before we leave this Godforsaken place I'd like to see this squadron fly one perfect mission. I suppose Group will be on my ass again. Major Gonzales, get the names of those men who we left in the zone. Also put out the order that the new squadron superstition is that you need to wear two watches on your arm for strike flights." He held up his arm showing his two. "I got the shit shot out of me but still made it out, and I'm wearing two watches. The news boys love this kind of stuff. You got that, Major?"

Major Gonzales slowly got to his feet. His face looked pained. "Sir, I have the names of those crews we left in the zone. What do you want me to do with that list, sir? You do understand that—"

"For God's sakes, Major. You mean you don't even care about those men we lost? I'm shocked, but war is a strange business and affects us all differently. Take today. It left me exhilarated and those other men dead. Can't get much more different than that. Very well, gentlemen, carry on with the debriefing. I have paperwork to do."

The squadron sat in stunned silence after he left. Even the craziest of the pilots felt loss. Finally Major Gonzales looked up from where he had been staring at the floor. His gaze drifted around the room, stopping briefly on the faces of those who tormented him most frequently. "I think that the Skipper has taken the concept of detachment to its ultimate utilization," he said evenly. "Command affects all of us in different ways. I can tell you that the Skipper doesn't approve of the conduct of the war and is struggling to do his duty." He sighed, and I almost felt affection for him. "You men heard the new squadron superstition. See Captain Beavers in S-4 and get new watches. Let's not let the Skipper down. Those of you who bunked with the pilots we lost today, see me after the debriefing to talk about personal effects. Now Lieutenant Vervack will ask you a few questions about what you saw out there this morning—armaments, bunkers—you know the drill. Then you're all dismissed." He turned away and then looked back. "The squadron did okay today. Those of you that helped get the bodies out of the zone will be remembered." He left.

Lieutenant Vervack went forward and repositioned his charts and carefully exposed a new quarter inch of red wax on his marker by unrolling the woodpaper around the end. When he turned back to the pilots, there weren't any.

14 · South Vietnam Adieu

The beginning of the end of my tour in Vietnam was on my birthday. Traditionally, the squadron operations officer didn't schedule you to fly on your birthday unless it was absolutely necessary to winning the war. Because the new squadron operations officer—Captain Shinn had augered into the side of a hill on a night medical evacuation attempt—was a complete prick, we were all flying on our birthdays. Captain Wilson, the new ops officer, decided that flying to Danang to bring back barbed wire was of vital necessity to winning the war and that I was not to be excused just because I was turning twenty-four.

"I'm not going to fly today, Captain. It's my birthday."

"Happy birthday. Now get your butt into that cockpit. Winston is your co-pilot. Buckum and Sterling are flying wing. You don't hear any of them pissing and moaning about flying on their birthdays."

"It's not their birthday."

"I don't give a damn. Drop the concertina wire at these coordinates when you return. Then you can have your cake or whatever it is you think you're entitled to." He thrust out the frag sheet and I took it. I had always thought not flying on your birthday was a bit silly anyway. In fact I had decided that I would *prefer* flying on my birthday because it decreased the odds of me being killed since the chances of being killed on my birthday seemed statistically much lower than *not* on my birthday. When I expressed this to Gearheardt, he disagreed vehemently.

"War and especially death in war is about irony," he reasoned. "Therefore it is a waste of death not to die ironically. It deprives your survivors of a great opportunity to wail '*And it was on his BIRTHDAY*' as if your cold, head-and-armless body would have been less gruesome were you zapped on one of the other 364 days of the year that weren't your birthday."

"I'm sorry I brought it up, Gearheardt. I should have known you would have some bizarre—"

"What's bizarre about it?"

I thought about it. "I suppose you're right. Where do you come up with these notions? You never struck me as a barracks philosopher."

"AG."

"The Assistant God tells you these things?"

"Sure. He's writing a book about dying in combat. Called *Better Them Than Me*. Whenever he gets a vision that someone is going to die on a mission, he interviews them to add irony to their death. He says that those dying on their own, not on their birthday, or Christmas, are perpetrating undue misery on their loved ones, and his job is to lessen the pain. He's decided that Labor Day and other little pissant holidays don't count, by the way. The only biggies are your birthday and Christmas, unless you're Jewish."

"So if you are, then dying on Jewish holidays—"

"Sky-Kyke filed for non-flight status on 324 'Jewish holidays' so far and kind of ruined it for everybody else. The four days in May that Jews aren't supposed to let their feet leave the earth—called 'shuffalom'—was a new one to AG and he's still researching it. He's trying to contact the chaplain in wing headquarters who is really a rabbi, but so far he hasn't had any luck."

"Almost Captain Armstrong, are we going?" Winston was impatient. He stood in the door of Gearheardt's hooch in full cockpit regalia, including flak diaper, which made it appear he was in some sort of remedial potty training. I grabbed my helmet bag and flak vest and stood up.

"So I'll see you in a couple of hours, Gearheardt. Don't go to any trouble for my birthday when I get back." I strapped on my shoulder holster and pistol belt with the Randall knife dangling from it. It was specially made for me with my name on the blade.

"I was going to have a little get-together but couldn't find anyone else who wanted to." Gearheardt always told the truth.

"Just as well. I hate guys that drink themselves silly in my honor, except you of course, Gearheardt." I lingered a moment while Winston started toward the tarmac to preflight the helicopter. No one else was in Gearheardt's hooch. I sat back down beside him on his cot.

"Are you sure President Larry Bob said it was this week?"

"You heard him."

"Let me hear the tape again. I want to make absolutely sure. I was going to do it later, but I didn't realize that Captain Asshole would have me on the flight schedule today."

Gearheardt reached behind him and grabbed a small tape recorder. The tape he took from the toe of a well-worn flight boot stuffed with socks. Someone who was looking for the tape would have had to brave the smell of rancid cheese. He slipped in the tape and after a couple of false starts, the deep sonorous voice of the President and our responses were clear on the tape. It had been made on the day that the squadron had set the Group record for most crew lost on a single mission.

". . . I don't let my boys down. You tell Almost Captain Armstrong—"

"I'm here, sir."

"—that I've got everthing under control and he needs to quit bein' such a goddam pussy about it. Tell him to kill somethin' while he's waitin', for God's sakes. 'Swhy we gave him a damn gun."

The President had been defensive and irritable from the moment we got him on the phone at wing headquarters by bribing the wing telecommunications sergeant. From his ramblings, it was clear that the "star" was still giving him trouble, now about how cold her ass was going to be drifting down from ten thousand feet over Hanoi.

"I told her that the boys in Korea were a hell of a lot more cold than her ass was going to be. She made some wiseass remark about this being Vietnam, but I finally got her to shut up and strike a deal. Damn preemer donna. I had to send 'Slick Hair' on a night mission to strike a deal that she gets to fire one of them anteeaircraft guns the Veetnams have. Lord love a duck, why a woman would want to straddle twelve feet of hot steel pipe shooting lead a mile up in the sky is beyond me. But we got the deal done. Hope she don't hit anybody on our side. Someone'll have my ass if it gets out."

Gearheardt and I had exchanged looks when we first heard this, and now we did again.

". . . so you boys be ready. It's a go on the twenty-seventh."

"That's my birthday, Mr. President."

"Who's that? That you, Gearheardt?"

"No, sir. It's me, Almost Captain Armstrong, or Tom Dexter, for the CIA guys listening in."

"Oh, there ain't none of them smartasses workin' tonight. I threw 'em a beer bust and let 'em dress the State Department secretaries up like Rooskies, and they get to interrogate the hell out of 'em. Highlight of their year, let me tell you."

"Anyway, this alright? Doin' this on your birthday? Don't misunderstand, I don't really give a shit, but I didn't get to be President by not actin' like I did. So, it's the twenty-seventh."

"Could I clarify one thing, Mr. President?"

"Is this that dang Almost Captain Armstrong again? Gearheardt, did you tell me he was a whiner 'fore I let him into this deal?"

"He's okay, Larry Bob," Gearheardt said, giving me the signal to "get with it." "He just wants to make sure everything goes according to Hoyle."

"Hoyle?"

"Never mind, Mr. President."

"Mr. President, this is Armstrong. When we get to Hanoi, the secret way, and I need to ask you about that before you get off the phone, are we to make a deal with Ho Chi Minh, kill him, get him a date with Barbonella, or what? I think that we should be absolutely, perfectly, and unmistakably clear on this aspect."

"Couldn't agree more, Armstrong. And I agree with what yore sayin'. Let me put it this way. You boys have the full power of attorney for the United States of America, ain't ever been given to any jarheads, I can tell you that, and you got guns and knives. I can't make it any clearer than that. Now get your asses up there on the twenty-seventh and get this damn war stopped."

"But, Mr. President—"

"Gearheardt, old buddy, I trusted you on this boy. What's his problem?"

"No problem, Mr. Larry Bob. Jack and I are practically on our way."

Gearheardt was grabbing my arm and twisting with a strength I hadn't expected.

"Look, boys, the pressure is on me on this one. You do this for me and yore careers are golden."

"Mr. Larry Bobident, you are going to be able to count on us to help you stop the killing and bloodshed that is—"

"Oh hell, son, don't be naive. There'll always be killin' and shit like that. I got to stop it now 'cause this Nixon asshole has come up with his own plan, and he's toutin' it all over creation like it was the greatest thing since tits on women."

"Nixon has a plan, sir, to stop the war?"

"We had a copy of it 'fore the ink was dry. His plan is to 'cut and run.' Now there's a helluva plan. He's hired himself this curly-headed foreigner guy to outline it in ten-dollar words, but best I can tell, if Nixon gets in he'll just have the boys high-tail it out as fast as their eleventy-jillion-dollar-a-copy airplanes will carry 'em.

"Boys, we just got to get outta this deal as best we can. Reminds me of when I was a little feller and we had this big old ugly snake coming around stealing eggs and chickens and whatnot. Scared the piss outta my little sister. So one day my daddy said,

" 'Son, this here's gone on long enough. You need to find that dang snake and kill it.' Sure enough, about noon I seen that snake wiggling cross the dirt near the barn, and I commenced to hit him with a club, and then I pounded him with a rock, and finally went in the barn and got me a shovel and chopped him all to pieces. My daddy walked up as I was grindin' parts of that snake into the dirt and looks down and says, 'Son, about five minutes ago me and yore mama took up on the snake's side.'

"I think folks are just getting tired of seeing these little bastards takin' a good poundin' no matter how ornery they might be."

Gearheardt and I looked at each other and frowned. This didn't sound good.

"What about the Vietnamese, sir?" I asked.

"Who?"

"The Vietnamese, sir."

"Well what about 'em? I ain't too worried about the sonsabitches we're bombin'."

"No, sir, I mean the *South* Vietnamese, the ones on *our* side. Are we just going to abandon them to the communists?"

"I'll have to get back to you on that, son. The important thing is that Nixon ain't in yet, and we need to fix this war. How're you boys doin', by the way?"

"We had a pretty bad day today, Mr. PresiLarry Bob. We lost Downing, Gaines, and—"

"Spare me the details, Gearheardt. If I had to listen to everbody that died in Veetnam, I wouldn't get my presidentin' chores done till midnight. If yore worried 'bout them Veetmese folks, you better get somethin' done up in *Han*oi on the twenty-seventh. Heaven help us if that lying Nixon bunch gets in here. Again, boys, you got the full faith and credit of the U.S. of A. behind you, whatever that means. Now you have yore instructions. Go get 'em."

Gearheardt tore the tape out of the machine, dropped it in a number ten food can that he used for a wastebasket, and set fire to it. "We won't be needing that again."

"Except in our court-martial as evidence that we shouldn't be shot," I said.

"Oh shit," Gearheardt said, "you're right. Well, too late now." With his K-bar he lifted the black, curled ribbon of charred tape.

I stood up to go again and was hit at the hooch door by a charging Buzz followed by Adams and Zuder, his two main henchmen. I fell back against Gearheardt's cot and stayed on it.

"Not so fast, *Almost* Captain Armstrong," Buzz sneered. He motioned for Adams and Zuder to stand outside the tent and not let anyone else in.

There wasn't any doubt in my mind what this was all about. Lieutenant Buzz ran the squadron lieutenants, knew all that was going on in the squadron, and was rumored to write the menus. It was significant that he had never confronted us about Barbonella. At the very least he had to have heard the rumors that Gearheardt and I were under some kind of secret orders.

"I know your plan, gents," he said as he pulled up Gearheardt's footlocker and sat down on it. "I beat it out of your pal Flager." He lit the short butt of a cigar and blew the smoke toward us. He flipped the burnt wooden match expertly through the door.

"Flager wouldn't know a plan if it bit him, Buzz," I said, hoping that he was kidding. I had always kind of liked Flager. I was afraid of him because he was crazy, but I liked him.

"No shit?" he said finally. "And I suppose you're not planning to hole up in a massage parlor in Bangkok with aliens either."

"Hadn't planned on it, Buzz." Gearheardt, who didn't much like Flager, was smiling.

Buzz yelled out the door of the tent. "Adams, go tell Gomez he can let Flager up out of the four-holer pit." He turned back to us. "For some reason I believe you, gents." He turned around again.

"Zuder, go on with Adams and help him clean up Flager. Take him down to Charlie Med if he needs it."

Buzz pulled his footlocker closer to our cot and lowered his voice.

"You know why I believe you, gents? 'Cause I got your orders here." He reached inside his flight suit and produced a manila envelope, popped it open with his thumb, and pulled out the contents: four pages of DDs and 1196s and serial numbers, stamped at the top with a red, half-inch-high BARBONELLA.

Gearheardt and I took the pages and began reading. They were the orders that we had been expecting.

"You know it's a court-martial offense to open some one else's orders." I was calm only because I had somehow suspected this would happen.

"No it isn't. I'm the squadron mail officer, the squadron admin officer, the squadron assignments officer, and the squadron bully. Any questions? Good. Now here's what you don't know." He leaned forward even closer, and Gearheardt and I leaned our heads toward him.

"I knew Flager didn't have a thing to do with it. First of all, I just enjoyed knocking the snot out of him because he shot up my stereo last month. But most of all it was just so the other dipshits in the squadron who suspect your mission now have something to think about. Gents, I'm on your side."

Gearheardt put out his hand and Buzz took it. I wasn't so sure and hung back. Buzz noticed and frowned, his eyes piercing.

"Look, dickhead," he said, meaning me, "I got my own theories about this two-bit war. Strike or hike, is my fucking plan. We either nuke the north or get our asses home to mama. We put big fans on the DMZ and blow the radiation into China. They got more people than you can shake your dick at anyway. And not enough Uncle Ben's to feed half of 'em. Stop 'em before they come over and get two million deep at the Dairy Queen lines, if you get my drift."

"Gee, Buzz, you're a humanitarian."

Buzz glared at me. "You know why nobody likes you, Armstrong?"

"I was hoping you'd tell me, Buzz."

"Cause you're a wise-ass." He paused and drew on his cigar. He leaned back away from me as if he had made his point.

"Somebody needs to tell 'em we're not as stupid as we look. Old Ho Chi already said that we couldn't win a war of attrition because he was willing to sacrifice ten of his men for every one of ours. Is there a swinging dick stupid enough not to believe him? What does he give a shit? Afraid he'll lose the next election in Hanoi? Somebody better get real in this damned war, or there'll be people hurt."

"Tell who?" I said. When Buzz wrinkled his brow, I went on. "You said 'somebody needs to tell 'em.' Tell who?"

Buzz's smile was to cynical as stink is to shit, as the President would say. "Well, that's the question, isn't it? Who in the hell in the chain of command has the balls to say 'Fuck this shit, we're invading North Vietnam or we're going home.'"

"Eloquently put, Buzz. I particularly like the fan on the DMZ idea."

Buzz looked skeptical.

Gearheardt was taking all of this in with what would be called a bemused look. He didn't dabble much in the philosophy of combat or politics. He tried to keep his life simple, except for when he was pulling the chain of the Assistant God. Then he pretended to be interested in religion.

Buzz looked a little embarrassed after his last outburst. "Not that I give a shit about them, but I got little brothers need to go home to Mama. My army brother even has a wife and kiddy and he's humping around the Delta. The rest of those Army dicks can—"

"So you're going to help us get to Hanoi?" Gearheardt said suddenly, reminding me of how this all started.

"I don't know about that, but I'm going to try to keep that bastard Wilson from killing one or both of you. This barbed wire trip he has Armstrong on is a crock of shit. You think the squadron is going to frag two choppers to fly to Danang to bring back a roll or two of barbed wire? Get serious. Check the tail number on the bird they got you scheduled to fly. Yankee Romeo Three Four. Guess where that

came from? I'll tell you. It's the bird we stole from that South Vietnamese squadron that was up here last week. And the coordinates
where you're to drop the load? Nowhere, man. Out in the damned
boonies. They got lots of call for barbed wire out there. Like I said,
get serious."

I wasn't sure what to make of all of it. Buzz seemed sincere. Gearheardt had the same half-smile on his face and was humming very
softly. It was hotter than hell in the tent, and outside I heard the
squadron drifting down to the chow tent. A hooch maid in black
pants and white ao dai, a straw "wok" on her head, looked in, saw
Buzz, and hurried away.

"My crew? The other chopper?"

"My guess is they don't know shit. Winston is probably just ex-
pendable. No one likes him anyway, and it's only a matter of time before he augers in. Fucker can't fly. The rest of them are the squadron
dregs and shitbirds anyway. Don't ask me who knows and who
doesn't. The best I can tell, you pissed off some chief in Yokosuka
and you're screwed."

He stood up and stretched. "Trying to stop this war is the dumb-
est idea I've ever heard, but it's a shitpot better than what we're doing
now. Personally, I just want to go back to Bangkok and screw my
brains out for the rest of my life. But I promised Mama I would help
my little brothers, so I'll help you." He went to the tent door and
looked out.

"You're going to have to get your ass in gear before they come
looking for you. Gearheardt, you should take Winston's place. Charlie and I will fly the backup bird on your wing. When we get to
Danang, have your crew chief and gunner refuel you before you go to
pick up the load. Then when both of them are out of the aircraft, get
the hell out. Charlie and I will cover for you as long as possible, but
you're basically on your own. You may not have enough fuel to get to
Hanoi, but that's something you'll have to figure out. In your orders,
it looks like there are a couple of ships off the coast that maybe you
can get fuel from. I don't even want to know."

Buzz started outside. I looked at Gearheardt, who shrugged and grabbed his helmet and a parachute bag full of gear already packed. My heart was racing, and I thought of a million things I wanted to do before I left, none of them possible. I did stop by my tent and throw a few items into my parachute bag. Fatass saw me and waddled over.

"Good luck," he said. He stuck out his hand.

"What do you mean?" I asked. What did *he* know?

"What does good luck mean? I thought it meant that I was wishing that something bad didn't happen to you. No one ever talks to me. Are we supposed to be wishing bad luck instead? Like that break a leg thing for actors? Why doesn't anybody ever talk to me? Is it because I'm fat?"

"Yep." I didn't have time for Fatass.

15 · Vietnam at Escape Speed in My Rearview Mirror (in G)

We made it to Danang without a problem. Captain Wilson tried to stop us, but Gearheardt decided that he couldn't possibly get into any more trouble than we were heading into and punched him out. As most of the squadron had been wanting to punch out Captain Wilson because he had been a grunt before he transferred to the air wing, it caused no real stir, and he was lying peacefully on the tarmac when Gearheardt jumped into the pilot's seat, making me co-pilot even though I was senior. Winston was glad not to have to fly with me, and Buzz, true to his word, flew on our wing.

Ten minutes out of Chu Lai, a flight of Army Cobras attacked us, but they didn't really press and we evaded them easily. Buzz had warned us that there were a few die-hard units that the chief had probably gotten to. We knew that not only had Gearheardt insulted one too many chiefs in Yokosuka, but that they had a number of long-term construction contracts that were going to be in default if the war was over sooner than planned.

"You can't blame the chiefs," Gearheardt said as we pulled into a tight diving turn to allow the Cobra rocket to miss us. "They got inventory up the ying-yang and were in the middle of shifting from

LIFO to FIFO. No wonder they're pissed that we're heading out to stop the— Whoa." We were at treetop level, and he narrowly missed an antenna. We were nearly to Marble Mountain, south of the Danang airbase.

"Does everybody in the whole country know about this, Gear-heardt?" I asked. "What happened to our *secret* mission?"

"Hold on, Jack. We're there." He flared and touched down. Buzz flew low over us, waggled his rotors in salute, and turned back south.

"Gunny, you and Winger hop out and get the concertina wire ready to pick up."

I heard two clicks on the intercom and the chopper moved slightly as the crew jumped out.

Gearheardt pulled in power and lifted off almost immediately.

"We're on our way, Jack. Onward to immorality."

"Immortality, Gearheardt. What's that clicking sound on the radio?"

"The squadron channel is off. I don't want to listen to a lot of threats and bullshit."

"Well, something is clicking on the intercom then."

Gearheardt looked down and behind him out his window.

"Oh shit, the crew chief is hanging on to the damn step."

In the belly of the chopper I saw the crew chief's head pop up beneath the cargo door. I unstrapped and lunged for him, nearly falling out myself, caught his shoulder holster and dragged him inside. He lay gasping for breath on the floor, his face red and twisted. His radio cord had kept him attached to the chopper when we had lifted off, and when it didn't automatically unplug, he had grabbed the step-bar to keep from being strangled.

I plugged my headset into the outlet on the bulkhead.

"We got company, Gearheardt. Gunny Buckles seems to have come along for the ride."

The Gunny was now looking alert. Alert and puzzled. I leaned over to where I could yell in his ear.

"We're on our way to Hanoi to stop the war." I decided the truth was the best. *Anything* I said was going to sound crazy.

God bless gunny sergeants. He looked up at me and gave me a thumbs up. Then closed his eyes and continued rubbing the red welt around his neck.

I climbed back into the co-pilot's seat and plugged in my headset. "What about those fighters that were scrambled to chase us?" I craned my head around in the cockpit expecting to see tracers or the flash of a Sidewinder just before it hit us.

Gearheardt laughed. "Turn up your UHF so you can hear the broadcasts on the Guard channel. You'll love it. So far the Air Force has scrambled two flights of Phantoms with orders to shoot us down. Then the Marine Corps diverted a flight of F-8s and two flights of A-4s out of Chu Lai to shoot down any Air Force aircraft that fired on us. Now the Navy is trying to get into the act. They've given kind of a goofy order, first sending some F-4s off the *Oriskany* to fly cover for the Marine F-8s, but that was evidently before they were attacked by the Marine A-4s. Now they're busy defending themselves."

I was silent as I tried to digest the enormity of what we had caused and what we were attempting. Below us the water became greener as we got farther from the shore. Our fuel tank was full. Four-plus hours of flight time. Gearheardt had produced a map, with all French notations, showing North Vietnam. Hanoi was circled. My stomach felt like it was full of dry ice. The noise in the cockpit of the H-34 was its normal ear-splitting roar, but I could tell that Gearheardt was humming as he made calculations on his kneeboard after measurements on the map. He looked happy as a pig.

I lowered the sun visor on my helmet, thinking no one could recognize me. Gearheardt and I now both looked like grasshoppers in the cockpit. He had folded the map away after offering it to me, then smiled and began humming again. I recognized it as a song that I had taught him. "Wings over Mexico." Each verse and refrain were the same, "Wings over Mexico," sung to the tune of "Here Comes Santa Claus." My career was behind me. In fact probably 99.9 percent of my *life* was behind me. My best friend and I were at fifteen hundred feet over the South China Sea, within sight of the Vietnamese coast, shimmering in the haze to our left. We were going the "secret way" to Hanoi.

I began singing out loud and Gearheardt joined in.

Wings over Mexico, Wings over Mexico, Wings over Mex-i-co.
Wings over Mexico, Wings over Mexico, Wings over Mex-i-co.
Wings over Mexico, Wings over Mexico, Wings over Me-hex-i-co.
Wings over Mexico, Wings over Mexico, Wings over Me-hex-i-cooooo!

16 · Feet Wet—North Vietnam

ow exactly is this supposed to work, Gearheardt?" I asked.

We were down to less than a thousand feet above the water. The sky had grown overcast, and the water looked cold and menacing, unlike the friendly blues and greens of the water off the coast of South Vietnam. We reasoned that a low-level flight, while not fuel efficient, would give the North Vietnamese less warning of our approach. But then, that was my question, what *was* our plan of approach?

Gearheardt studied the water below us. Whitecaps appeared farther out to sea on our right. Through a light mist on our left, I could intermittently see the coast of North Vietnam, sinister and foreboding, although it was exactly the same coastline as that of recent sunbathing expeditions in Danang. The engine noise had numbed my eardrums, and it was almost peaceful in the cockpit. Gearheardt spotted something on the water and began to grin. He took off power and shoved the nose of the chopper over into a shallow dive, coming over the top of a fishing boat at less than one hundred feet.

"Flip it on," he said.

"Grow up," I answered. "This is serious, Gearheardt."

"Come on, this is the last time."

I flipped on the outside speakers, rigged on the Vietnamese helicopter to use in their psy-ops, as Gearheardt keyed his mike.

"NO FISHING. REPEAT. NO FUCKING FISHING. RETURN TO SHORE AND TURN YOURSELF IN TO THE AUTHORITIES. SHAME ON YOU. THESE FISH AREN'T YOURS. THEY BELONG TO THE GOVERNMENT OF FRANCE."

"They don't even speak English, Gearheardt."

As we passed over the boat I could see five or six small figures looking up at us. One was shaking his fist. Gearheardt grinned and pulled his head back into the cockpit.

"Yeah, it would be a lot funnier if they could understand us. But I like doing it anyway."

"Look, we're heading for Hanoi. Do you even know how to get there?"

"Haiphong. Turn left. Follow the river. Satisfied? Surely they've got a water tower that says 'Hanoi' on it. We land there."

"And how do we plan to get our asses in to see Ho Chi Minh? Did you have your secretary call ahead?" I thought maybe the sarcastic humor routine might work for me, too. I looked at the map of North Vietnam I was holding, and the shaking told me it wasn't working quite like I hoped. At least Gearheardt was right about the river from Haiphong up to Hanoi. Of course that wasn't exactly what I meant by my original question.

"Did you forget about our package of orders?" Gearheardt's voice was irritating, but the message was welcome. I *had* forgotten it. Shuffling through the map case beside my seat, I found and opened it.

"Great, here's a map. Like we didn't have any maps." I imagined the President or one of his numbnut aides assembling the package back in D.C. "Fantastic, a list of hotels in the area. Okay, here's a list of contacts. Holy moly, we have this many agents running around Hanoi? There must be fifty people on this list. Here's a great one, Gearheardt, 'Gon Norea.'" I was babbling, and I took a breath to calm down.

"Keep up the running commentary and sarcasm about the contents, Jack. It helps me to concentrate."

"Don't get snotty with me, you bastard. This is one of a long line of screwed-up situations that you got us into, without giving a thought to my life or limb."

"So we have a list of contacts. What else? I had to go through the package in a bit of a hurry when Buzz gave it to me."

"Contacts, addresses. Here we go, an envelope marked Top Secret, Eyes Only."

I took it out of the package and noticed that the seal on the back of the eight-by-eleven manila envelope was broken. The name on the front of the envelope was "Gerard Finnigan Gearheardt (Narwsorthy) Special Agent & Almost Captain USMC 087863." I put the rest of the packet away and started to open the envelope.

"Gerard Finnigan?" I said.

"Give me that, you aren't the Eyes Only the President had in mind." Gearheardt was smiling, but he grabbed at the envelope and yanked it from my hand, back over to his side of the cockpit, where it continued out the side window, quickly disappearing in the airstream.

"Oh, shit," Gearheardt said.

"*Very* nice. In fact, that might be the nicest move that you have made in our too-long friendship. Was that cute? Ripping our orders out of my hand? Did you get a kick out of that?"

"Knock it off, Jack. Sarcasm won't really help here."

"And what *would* help, Gerard Finnigan Gearheardt?"

Gearheardt actually growled. "Only my mother calls me that. And she only did it once."

"Is that when they took you to the orphanage?"

Gearheardt was silent for a moment. He didn't like to talk about his folks dropping him off at the orphanage. Before I could apologize, another voice was heard.

"If you don't mind me saying so, sirs, you're not giving me a lot of confidence that you know what the hell you're doing on this so-called mission."

It was Gunnery Sergeant Buckles. I had forgotten that he was in the belly of the chopper. Now he had awakened and obviously was plugged into the intercom.

"Hello, Gunny. How are you feeling?" Gearheardt asked.

"Not bad, Almost Captain Gearheardt. At least I thought—"

"You can drop the 'almost' Gunny. Just call us 'Captain.' We'll be dead or captains when we finish this mission."

"Thanks, Captain. Anyway I thought I was doing pretty good until I heard you and Captain Armstrong discussing what we were doing. Now I'm—"

"Don't sweat it Gunny. Captain Armstrong is just upset that our instructions flew out of the window, that we barely have enough fuel to get to Hanoi, and that there's a strong possibility that they're going to chop our nuts off when they catch us."

"When who catches us, Captain?"

I could answer that one. "*Whoever* catches us, Gunny. We've pretty well managed to alienate everyone. We're on our way to Hanoi with a vague notion of meeting with Ho Chi Minh and making a deal with him to stop the war, or perhaps killing him. I was foolishly hoping that the orders that Captain Gearheardt threw out the window might fine-tune our options a bit. To say nothing of perhaps providing a kernel of a clue as to how we hope to accomplish all of this."

Gearheardt keyed his mike as soon as I finished. "Captain Armstrong has a tendency under pressure to speak in sarcastic tones, Gunny. I don't think our situation is quite so, so—"

"Fucked up?" I suggested.

"You really are getting negative, Jack. It's not becoming for an officer in the Marine Corps. And you seem to be wanting to take your anxietal anger out on me. Your best friend and the one that saved your career from going down the tubes on that excessive masturbation charge."

"YOU WERE THE ONE THAT MADE UP THE DAMN CHARGE, GEARHEARDT. YOU SILLY BAS—"

"Captains! Could you stop the bickering for a minute and discuss what we might do? I assume that turning around and heading back to Danang is out of the question?"

Gearheardt was calm, but he wouldn't look me in the eye. "Probably not a good idea, Gunny. There were two or three dozen fighters trying to shoot us down when we left."

Mr. Voice of Reason. I hated him.

"Sounds like we're headed for Hanoi then, Captain. Well, if it's any help, I speak Vietnamese."

Tears came to my eyes at hearing *any* good news. "That's great, Gunny! I didn't realize you'd been to language school."

"Haven't, Captain Armstrong. But I've lived outside of Danang in a whorehouse for the last couple of years. You pick it up."

"Well then, okay. I mean that's great. Look, gents, I need to think this through. Give me a minute here." Having an interpreter was a definite advantage, but I needed to think through a plan. Gearheardt's idea was to always just push ahead and see what happened.

"Well, at least we have an interpreter, Jack." Gearheardt was happy again. It didn't take much.

"Yep. Now when they have us upside down and they're starting to pour hot lead down our assholes, we'll be able to understand that they're saying 'Now this may hurt.'"

"You're a pessimist, Jack. I never knew that about you."

"Please, Gearheardt. Let me think for a moment. Let's have at least *some* plan of action."

"I'll go for that, Captain Armstrong," Gunny Buckles said.

I read and reread the remains of the package that had contained our instructions. The addresses of contacts, their names, their affiliations. I had a French map of Hanoi, and I plotted the addresses on the map, using code in case the map fell into communist hands. For example, if the name was 'Lars,' the address was marked four blocks away from the actual location. It wasn't a brilliant plan, but in a helicopter offshore from North Vietnam with a couple of hours of fuel remaining, you did what you could.

"Gearheardt, you need to angle over nearer to the shore. I have to try to spot some kind of a landmark to get us situated on the map. We'll need to skirt Haiphong. And forget your goofy plan to fly over the ships in the harbor and harass them with the loudspeakers. No, don't give me that shit, I know that you wanted to do that. Anyway, if my calculations are right, we should be getting close to the time we need to go 'feet dry.' You set, Gunny?"

"If you mean am I set to head overland into North Vietnam, assuming that's what 'feet dry' means, I guess I'm as ready as I'll ever be. Do you want me manning this M-60 down here, Captain?"

"Absolutely," said Gearheardt.

"Not," I added. "Gunny, we don't have a high probability of pulling this off, and we don't have the firepower to take on the North Vietnamese. I can't see any benefit to pissing off any more folks by shooting at them as we fly over." Gearheardt was pouting. "You understand, Gearheardt?"

He clicked his mike twice.

We were nearing the shoreline. Rain was making it fade in and out of our vision, but I saw a village on the north bank of a small river and was pretty sure I knew where we were. "Head in north of that village, Gearheardt." He adjusted the turn and angled toward the shore, dropping down to five hundred feet above the water.

"Gents, here's the plan as I see it. I'm going to take us up this area here, all the way to this spot south of Hanoi. That way, we don't get near any large towns, any major roads, anything that the North Vietnamese should feel they have to defend heavily. Then we land in this area wherever we can find a clearing and hide out until dark. It's only about three miles from there to the neighborhood where Gon Norea lives. He's noted as one of the most reliable of our agents. From there I'm not sure what we'll do, but at least we can hole up, and maybe he can help us get to Ho Chi Minh. How does that sound?"

"So far so good, Jack. But what about the folks looking for the chopper that is buzzing around the countryside? You think somebody might bother to report us? And then have a shitpot full of soldiers looking for us? What about that?"

"You're a pessimist, Gearheardt. I never knew that about you."

"Go to hell." But he smiled. "But, seriously—"

"I'm pretty sure that there will be an air strike scheduled for this afternoon. One more chopper buzzing around the countryside won't be cause for *extra* searching. It isn't a chance that we can avoid anyway."

"How about ditching it in the river?"

"And fishing it out so that we could escape in it if we have to?"

"Sounds dumb when you say it like that. It was the gunny's idea, anyway."

"Leave me out of this, sirs. I'm down here pretending I'm not in the belly of a chopper about to head unarmed into North Vietnam and piloted by the Battling Bickersons."

"The Battling—?"

"Never mind, Gearheardt. Remember, after the air strike we have the famous—"

"The Parachuting Pussy! I had almost forgotten."

"The what?"

"Never mind, Gunny. We'll explain it later. Right now we're about thirty seconds from 'feet dry' and the beginning of my plan to get us into Hanoi undetected."

And about thirty-five seconds before they shot us down.

17 · North Vietnam in Your Undies

W ell, here's another fine mess you've gotten me into, Gear-heardt!"

"Hold on, boys. I'm putting her down in the rice pad-dies. YeeeeeHaaw!"

We had seen the tracers at the same time we heard a loud thunk up and behind us in the transmission area and multiple clangs in the engine compartment in front of us. You can screw around with engine trouble for quite a while, but we both knew that if you took damage in the transmission you were flying a Volkswagen. The instrument panel lit up and I smelled burning fluid. The engine coughed and the nose began to swing to the right and I knew that we were ground bound. Gearheardt almost did his usual masterful job of guiding us to a gentle landing. At the last minute the engine coughed and quit. The chopper lurched and threw my head against the radio panel. I must have blacked out for an instant, then I heard the M-60 crank off a long stream and knew the gunny didn't need instructions from us.

"Hey, Mom, I'm home!" was the last thing I heard from Gear-heardt before we tore off our helmets and headed out the cockpit windows. Squatting in the rice paddy I saw a group of folks running along a paddy dike carrying weapons.

"Okay, this doesn't look good," I said. I had my PPK in my hand, but it gave little comfort. I remembered my mother's caution—never squat in a rice paddy in North Vietnam.

The Vietnamese hit the deck as the gunny searched for them with another burst from the M-60. Then it was quiet.

"What now, pal?" I asked my squat-mate.

"We rush them," Gearheardt replied, as if answering an annoying child.

I grabbed his arm as he duck-walked by me, heading to the other side of the chopper.

"We what?"

"You got a better idea? We need to take the offensive. It pisses me off that these little bastards shot us down and now run out here like they owned the joint."

I wouldn't let go of his arm. "Gearheardt, we just flew an armed chopper . . ." But then I realized that it wouldn't do any good to point out the obvious to Gearheardt. He was in his "We're American Marines" mode.

"Jack, if these guys had jack-shit they'd be all over us by now. I think they're just poorly armed villagers, probably as scared as we are."

"They're all pissing their pants then."

Gearheardt smiled and patted my hand before he pried it off his arm.

"You'll never make Almost Captain with that attitude, Jack."

He stood up and told the gunny to fire a long burst in the direction of the men crouching behind the paddy dike.

"Let's go, Jack." He began running toward the dike, shouting and firing his pistol. I followed, as always, shouting and firing, thinking briefly for the hundredth time how much safer my life would be if I shot Gearheardt instead. Naturally, Gearheardt tripped and fell, leaving me running, shouting and shooting wildly all by myself, now almost more embarrassed than scared.

The villagers dropped their weapons and stood on the paddy dike, even more embarrassed than I was as I stopped in front of them. They were the original motley crew. Six of them—four pre-teens and

two with prostate trouble—stared at me and the approaching Gearheardt with hateful faces. Their discarded weapons lay at their feet,
an AK-47 with a broken stock and bent clip, a flintlock rifle last seen
in the hands of a Pilgrim, a club, a pistol, two spears, and a baseball-
sized rock still in the hands of the oldest warrior. He threw it and hit
Gearheardt in the chest.

"Ouch." Gearheardt rubbed the spot and kicked the rock away. It
rolled near the ancient one, who picked it up and threw it at Gearheardt again, hitting him in the arm.

"Damn it. Knock it off," Gearheardt said. He pointed his finger at
the old man, who promptly pointed *his* finger at Gearheardt.

"That guy is pissing me off, Jack."

"He's an old man, Gearheardt. And we've just invaded his village.
Give him a break. What do we do now?"

"First we find the weapon in the village they must have used to
knock us down. It wasn't any of this crap," he said, motioning toward
the hardware on the ground.

The gunny arrived carrying the M-60.

"Ask them if there are regular troops in the area, Gunny," I said.

I felt vulnerable in the rice paddy. Five hundred yards away, I saw
what appeared to be the huts of the village. The quiet was as suffo-
cating as the smell. In the distance I saw misty hills.

"Nggh, noying luga luga nihg nygeegoegg?" the gunny asked.

The old man began a rhapsody of Vietnamese, spittle and gibberish flying in all directions as he waved his arms and made every ges-
ture but the peace sign.

"He says that the Army left last night to go fight the Marines
down south, and as soon as they return they'll pulverize us and then
sew our tongues to our assholes."

Gearheardt laughed. "No shit? Did he say that? Boy, how'd you
like to eat your own—"

"Shut up, Gearheardt," I said. "Gunny, we get the point, whether
that's an accurate translation or not. We need to vamoose. Got any
ideas?"

Gearheardt stopped his pantomiming of the old man's torture description and became serious.

"These boys are going to drive us to Hanoi, Jack. We can't make it on our own, and I think we can control this crew. Surely they have an old truck or something around here."

They did.

In the village, under the stunned and angry eyes of the women and even older men and younger boys, we uncovered an ancient Russian truck, rusted and dusty. It had a covered wagon arrangement on the flatbed. In the cab were upturned barrel halves for seats.

"Hey, this is nice," Gearheardt said to the scowling ancient. "Gunny, get the crew rounded up. Don't take any kids, but try to find the chief of the village and maybe one or two old guys with sons in the army."

"You got it, Captain. And the chief is right there by you—the rock thrower. It sounds like his son is off fighting the Marines." He began talking to the villagers who stood in a half-circle around us, murmuring and spitting on the ground. They were mostly older women and a few teenagers.

Within minutes the gunny returned. I didn't like the look on his face. With him were three elderly men, a young Vietnamese woman, and two Chinese midgets.

"Holy shit, Gunny. What's with the little people?"

"The best that I can make out, Captain, is that they are with a psy-ops troupe who were performing in the village when the word came for the soldiers to get their asses down to Quang Tri to fight the Marines. They're stuck here, and this young lady is the manager of the troupe. The only thing she would tell me is that we're taking her back to Hanoi." He shrugged and threw the responsibility to Gearheardt and me.

The midget male in the Uncle Sam suit was pretty obvious. I was still trying to figure out who the female midget was supposed to be. I decided that she was Queen Elizabeth—a pink hat, pearls, and small black purse my clues.

"Captain," said the gunny, "I don't think we have as much time as we thought. This girl seems to think that the soldiers are already on their way back. Maybe we'd better di-di out of here."

The young Vietnamese woman stood in front of me, defiant. I couldn't help but notice that she was one of the most attractive Vietnamese women I had seen. The top buttons on her shirt were undone and I saw the gentle rising slope of her breasts. Déjà vu was around me like the aura of a migraine. This was the other thing my mother had warned me about.

"Wake up, Jack," Gearheardt said. "We're loading up these villagers and heading for Hanoi. Right now."

"What about her?" I said, motioning with my head.

"She only has one eye, Jack. In case you hadn't noticed. Besides, I'm not hauling a freak show around the countryside. Invading Hanoi in this rust bucket of a Russian shit-truck is bad enough. If we wait, the soldiers may be on our butt. If we go in the daylight, a flight of A-4s will probably blast us off the highway. I prefer being killed by my own, so let's head out."

"She seems pretty damn insistent. Gunny says she has lots of pull in the village. She's the propaganda officer or the political officer or something like that. The villagers, even the chief, are afraid of her."

"Jack, I don't care if she's the one-eyed Queen of Sheba. There is no fucking way I am taking that crew to Hanoi."

We left about fifteen minutes later, compromising by having the Chinese midget in the Uncle Sam suit ride on top of the cab. Gearheardt wasn't happy, but at least he had a reason to back down.

"Saber Lead, this is Saber Three. I've got a Russian truck in sight. Request permission to fire my rockets."

"Wait one, Saber Three. Isn't that a Chinese midget in an Uncle Sam suit on top of the cab? We'd better get permission from wing HQ before we take the truck out."

Across the sea, Oval Office.

"*Sir, the Air Force requests permission to fire on a Russian truck in southern North Vietnam. There is a Chinese midget in an Uncle Sam suit involved.*"

"*Well, son, how 'bout checkin' the record? Did I declare war on Chinese midgets? Tell the damn Air Force to hold their fire and lay off the local beer for God's sake.*"

"*Heh, heh, heh,*" he said to himself. "*Sounds like Gearheardt's made it to North Veetnam.*"

After his hat blew off in the first five minutes, the midget took off his blue waistcoat and looked just like any other Chinese midget in striped pants, and we were strafed repeatedly by Air Force jets. They missed, causing Gearheardt to jeer and shake his fist at the rotten marksmanship of the Air Force.

The road was a series of potholes tied together by small strips of dirt, gravel, or, very rarely, asphalt. Conversation in the cab of the truck was mostly "umphs." The barrel top was biting into my butt with a vengeance, not helped by thirty-five pounds of Chinese midget riding on my knee. Beside me the Vietnamese troupe manager sat stoically, not even umphing at the most breathtaking of the potholes. I was in love with her.

On her other side, the gunny rode shotgun, cradling the M-60 in his lap. The driver, next to me, appeared to be either severely retarded or a large eleven-year-old. Maybe both. He grinned foolishly at all times, particularly when a pothole dropped us into butt-hell and bounced us back to the roof of the cab when we came out the other side of the hole.

Gearheardt sat in the back with the five prisoners. By the end of the first ten butt-busting, gear-screeching miles, he had his "prisoners" laughing at his card tricks. Before late afternoon they were singing "Wings Over Mexico" until I shouted back for them to knock it off. A truck full of Vietnamese singing fraternity songs might just arouse suspicion, I argued successfully to Gearheardt.

The plan was to reverse roles and act as if *we* were the prisoners if stopped by anyone. We were being taken to Hanoi to be turned over to the authorities. I was pretty certain that the villagers would behave; the gunny looked menacing with the M-60. I wasn't so sure about my one-eyed girlfriend, but Gunny assured me that he had informed her that if she gave us away, I would shoot the midget.

"I'm not-*umph*-usually-*umph*, *damn*-the kind-*whoa, umph*-guy-*holy shit*-that shoo-*umphs*-oots midgets-*ouch, whooooa, umph*," I tried to explain to her.

She had to turn her head toward me completely to see me with her good eye. Her left eye was mainly whitish with a blue-gray swirl.

"You shoot midget, I cut off balls, GI."

I was amazed that she was able to talk without umphing with the bumps, and that she spoke passable English. This was a woman that I could take home to mom.

Gearheardt stuck his head through the canvas flap behind the cab and gave me the thumbs up. "Jack, we're golden. These guys don't care for Ho Cheese any more than we do. They heard that speech about losing ten men for every one of ours and said "Fuck that shit" or the equivalent in slope talk. No offense intended," he said over his shoulder.

Then he turned back to me. "These guys aren't as dumb as they look. But if the soldiers get back to the village and find out we took their fathers, we're probably going to get the shit shot out of us when they catch us." He paused and looked at the gunny, the girl, and the midget, then back at me. "But this is going pretty well except for that and the damn U.S. Air Force trying to blast us, don't you think?" He ducked his head back through the canvas flap.

In a moment he reappeared.

"Jack, I promised these guys we'd stop and pick up some beer. What do you say?"

I adjusted the midget on my knee and looked back at him. Uncle Sam, now off the roof, stuck his head through the flap alongside Gearheardt.

"No way, Gearheardt."

He disappeared again, and I heard the unmistakable sounds of piss-ing and moaning in English and in Vietnamese. I tuned it out just as we plunged into the mother of all potholes and hit bottom with spine-shattering force. The midget queen of England's head drove back against my teeth with a crack. The driver laughed out loud and drool flew from his mouth. The girl's leg rubbed against mine as we careened out of the hole. This was the most romantic moment of my life.

I fell asleep just after we stopped to get beer for Gearheardt and his pals in the back of the truck. When I woke up my head hurt like a bastard.

The gunny was talking to the girl.

"She says that we are nearing Hanoi, Captain. How are *you* feel-ing, sir? I think you must have taken a bit of a bump in the shoot-down. Your eyes were dilated this afternoon, and to tell you the truth you seemed a bit goofy, if you'll pardon me."

I drifted off again, the headache blissfully disappearing in a foggy half sleep. It was almost gone when I awoke and looked through where the windshield should have been.

We had seen bomb damage in the countryside, but now it became increasingly evident. Crater upon crater around burned out buildings, and rings of berms that looked to be anti-aircraft gun emplacements.

When we heard the air-raid siren we knew that we were nearing Hanoi proper. The sound was faint, but moments later we heard the thump, thump of bombs exploding in the distance. Our driver grew somber, and the gunny quieted as he listened to the departing Amer-ican aircraft that came over us. I had filled him in on all that I knew about our mission and Barbonella. He took it the way that Hannibal's men took the decision to cross the Alps on elephants; nothing was too bizarre for officers and politicians to dream up for the grunts. Finally he had said, "Well, I'm proud to be part of it."

I sat up suddenly.

"What happened to the midget? And the girl?"

"They hopped off just when we hit the outskirts of Hanoi, Captain. You don't remember all of that?"

"Did she say anything? The girl, I mean. Did she—"

"For a Vietnamese, she spoke pretty decent Spanish. She lambasted you and Gearheardt pretty well. She knew I was just a poor pawn of the rich." The gunny smiled.

"Spanish? What in the hell—"

"You'd better hope that you don't run into that one again, Captain. She's a girlfriend of a Cuban, Juanton something, and tough as nails."

Late in the afternoon we stopped alongside the road. The gunny, seemingly the only one of our entourage with a lick of sense, felt we should wait until darkness to enter Hanoi. Gearheardt and his new best friends sat in a small circle passing around a huge bottle of Vietnamese beer. I sat with my back against a tree and tried not to think about the folly of rolling into the enemy city armed only with an M-60, a vague sense of mission, and a crazed Marine pal who believed in himself more than he believed in all of the dangers in the world. It was almost peaceful.

Gearheardt, more alert than I would have thought, heard it first.

"Jack," he said, "do you hear that? I swear it sounds like a C-123 coming overhead, low and slow. Do you suppose it's some kind of rescue mission for us?"

"We have no one *wanting* to rescue us, Gearheardt."

He stood and made his way to the edge of the trees where he could look up toward the southeast. After a moment, he pointed.

"That, my pessimistic friend, is a C-123. And, if I'm not mistaken, it has Air America painted along the side."

I moved to see where he was pointing. The silver aircraft was cruising as if it were flat-hatting over an Iowa cornfield. Although it was too high for me to read the letters, I could see the outline of an insignia where I knew the Air America logo usually was painted.

"Those CIA pilots may be rotten bastards, but they have some balls," Gearheardt said, respectfully. "If they aren't looking for us, what in the hell do you suppose they're doing up here in the land of the ack-ack?"

—which at that time opened up all around us with a roar that sent me to the ground and the villagers under the truck.

Gearheardt held his ground, watching the tracers arc over and behind the C-123.

"Jack," he shouted above the din of the 88s and 37mms, "they aren't shooting at the damn thing. It's like they're giving a salute. A major fix is in, Jack. Major." Rather than being curious, Gearheardt sounded in awe.

I joined him at the treeline in time to see the rear cargo door of the aircraft fall open as it passed overhead. A lone figure catapulted from the door and a parachute popped open almost immediately. All of us, villagers, the gunny, the idiot truck driver, and Gearheardt, watched openmouthed as the paratrooper drifted slowly downward.

Gearheardt grabbed the Japanese binoculars that hung around the neck of the village chief. After a moment of adjusting and swearing a smile came to the lips below the eyepiece.

"Naked as a damn jaybird, Jack. Those straps must be hell on her crotch, but that is one fine pair of tits."

Although he supposedly spoke no English, at the sound of "tits" the ancient villager grabbed the binoculars from Gearheardt's hands and jerked them to his face. After a moment of adjusting and even more apparent swearing, a smile came over his lower face that exposed his molars.

We watched the woman—she was decidedly that, even without binoculars—drift near the dry rice field, touch down with her feet, fall on her face, and bounce over onto her butt, on which she was dragged a few yards until the parachute collapsed.

She rose and unbuckled, looked at the hordes of North Vietnamese bearing down on her, and spoke loudly enough for us to hear, two hundred yards away. We couldn't understand much, although Gearheardt said he could make out "motherfucker" and "agent" in the late-afternoon blue air.

In one of the only times he retreated from a naked woman, Gear-heardt turned and grabbed the truck driver, whose shirt front was soaked with drool.

"Everybody get your asses into the truck. We still have a few miles to go and two beers to drink before we get to Hanoi."

The gunny herded all aboard. As Gearheardt jumped up into the back he looked at me. "She's got legs all the way up to her ass, Jack. This is our chance." He closed the cover, and I heard him uncapping more beer bottles. His seriousness had lasted almost a minute.

It turned out to be more than a few miles in to Hanoi. As we drove, we observed troops and civilians streaming toward the area we had departed as if a giant Vietnamese-magnet had landed. We drove two or three miles, having no one challenge us.

"Damn, Gunny," I said, "maybe something is finally working like it was supposed to."

At that moment, a troop of little angry men in green uniforms and pith helmets stopped us. My heart raced as they surrounded the truck, waved their weapons, and shouted. Indicating that we should get out of the truck, they gave us no chance to further the ruse that we were prisoners already under control of some authority—which probably wouldn't have worked anyway. Gearheardt and three of the villagers were standing pissing out on the road when we looked around back of the truck.

Gearheardt grinned when he saw me and said, "Are we almost there?"

We got the whacking that we evidently deserved before a sem-blance of order was restored and we convinced them that we weren't a crew shot down in the just-completed air raid. It seemed to make a difference in the general hubbub, which included some pummeling of the villagers also. Finally the gunny got a conversation started with one of the officers. He argued that Gearheardt and I were on a special mission and that we needed to be taken to see Ho Chi Minh.

That brought about another round of whacking and kicking while the soldiers stripped us of our flight suits and boots. We stood in our skivvies beside the road. By this time a crowd of cranky Vietnamese had gathered, and it was evident that they thought we hadn't had near enough abuse. Gearheardt didn't help things by his constant grin and tiger-striped skivvies. I could have whacked him myself as he continued to antagonize the soldiers and the gathered crowd.

The soldiers found the letter from the President in Gearheardt's flight suit, and the gunny tried to point out the presidential seal, but the troops didn't seem to be impressed. The gunny turned to me.

"Didn't you gentlemen have some sort of plan?" he asked.

"You mean besides flying all the way up here to get beaten to death by this crowd?" I replied.

One of the soldiers stepped forward and raised his rifle to strike Gearheardt. Gearheardt's look stopped him for a moment, and behind us we heard the soldiers that had been rifling our gear let out an exclamation. The one who was in charge came over to me and held up a photo. He looked at my face, back at the photo, and then spoke to the gunny. The photo was from my wallet. It was a picture of Penny and me, with Penny in full Mickey Mouse regalia, enormous head and all. The North Vietnamese seemed unsure of themselves now.

"They want to know if you know Mickey Mouse personally," the gunny said in a low voice. "That's you in the picture, isn't it?"

It was getting dark and I was getting cold in my underwear. Of course it was me in the picture. The gunny confirmed that it was, and the officer struck a match and held it to my face and then to the picture. He grinned.

"Mick Mou," he said. "You." He pointed to me and I nodded my head.

"Donald Duck is married to my sister."

"Shut up, Gearheardt," I said. "Just let this goon get everyone calm. I'm not up for another round of bashing, if you don't mind."

"How's your head?"

"Shut up."

"Gee, I was only asking."

The gunny and the Vietnamese had a moment's conversation, and then we were given back our flight suits. Our boots were already on the feet of soldiers. We saw them clomping around the truck, and I cautioned Gearheardt with my eyes to leave well enough alone. After another round of shouting and pushing, the soldiers let the villagers load back onto their truck and leave. One of them gave Gearheardt a thumbs-up as the truck drove off.

We were loaded onto another flatbed truck, hands bound behind us, and we drove slowly through the crowd of fist-shaking people. I wondered briefly why no guards were in back with us and quickly decided no one wanted to brave the spit, bottles, bricks, trash, and sticks thrown at us by the anti-Disney group in the crowd. We were out of range soon, and I looked over at Gearheardt trying to dislodge a large tree branch from his shoulders. His head was bleeding but no serious wounds were evident. The same with the gunny, and I didn't feel too much the worse for wear. I let out a breath that it seemed I had been holding since the troops had ordered us out of the first truck. The streets of Hanoi were narrow and dark, looking no different from the streets of Saigon for the most part, absent the color of advertising, rows of strip joints, and people. We saw almost no one while the truck sped toward the center of the town, throwing us dangerously near the edge of the flatbed when we rounded corners.

The gunny scooted next to me and leaned into my ear.

"You still have that map. I can see it sticking out of your flight suit. I'm going to move around and try to get it. Stick your knee out this way."

When he had it in his hands, behind his back, he turned back to me. "We may not have much time," he said. Gearheardt leaned toward us so that he could hear also. "I'm going to roll off this truck. If I can get away, I'll find one of the contacts on that map and then we'll find you. Whiffenpoof, Gon Norea, *somebody* that can help us."

"I'd suggest putting on a hat," Gearheardt said. "Walking around Hanoi in a flight suit with your hands tied behind your back could raise suspicions. I've noticed a lot of these people are not six feet tall with blond hair. Just a suggestion."

Not having suffered five years of Gearheardt's sarcasm probably kept the gunny from resenting it. Almost.

"I'll take that into consideration, Captain. I realize it's not as well thought out as your plan of dropping in on Ho Chi Minh unexpectedly, but I'll work on the details later."

"Gunny, do what you have to do. Remember we lost the *plan* out of the window before we read it. Hopefully, someone on that map has some knowledge that will be helpful."

"It's also helpful that I speak Russian, and if I can get a dark suit that doesn't fit maybe I can pass. I always have the advantage of being unexpected. How many Marine Corps gunny sergeants do you think they see walking around the streets up here?" He moved toward the edge of the bed. "And if they stop me, I'll probably end up wherever they take you anyway." When we began to slow for the next corner, he was gone.

The truck turned onto a wide boulevard, trees on an island running down the middle, dark and shuttered shop houses lining both sides. Gearheardt and I sat with our backs against the cab, both silent and looking up at the moonless, dark sky. I had to think about what kind of a naive, trusting, dumb, romantic sonofabitch would find himself on the bed of a truck in downtown Hanoi without a clue as to what he was doing. And who was the one-eyed Vietnamese midget manager with sloping breasts? We hit a bump and I banged my butt down hard on the wooden bed. Gearheardt, the bastard, was humming "Wings Over Mexico" or "Here Comes Santa Claus," I couldn't tell the difference, although he always said there was one, and it dawned on me that my friend might have lied to me about a lot of things.

Just as we pulled to a stop in front of an ominous building with guards outside and bars on the windows, Gearheardt nudged me. "Has it occurred to you that Gunny Buckles might be a spy?"

At least I could still feel cranky. "What in the hell do you mean by that?"

A guard appeared on the street beside us and motioned menacingly for us to shut up and get down from the truck. Gearheardt ignored him.

"He shows up, gets a ride to Hanoi, and then disappears. You have to admit that seems a little strange. I know that you were spilling the guts of our plan to him all the way to Hanoi. How trustworthy can a guy be if he's running a whorehouse in Danang when he's supposed to be killing people?"

"Our plan? Our *plan?*" I shouted at him even as two soldiers appeared beside the first and began to drag me off of the truck. "And just what *plan* is that, Gearheardt? The one—"

"Hey, knock off the earheardt-Gay. I told these guys my name was Narsworthy."

I really, truly wanted to cry. How had I let myself believe this idiot was doing anything but winging it, just to have an adventure, thinking that because we were Americans, we would somehow prevail, or win, or save the day, or . . . my mind began to stutter. I didn't know what to think next.

And I didn't get the chance to think anything next except how incredibly painful it was to be dragged backward by my bound hands, up two steps, through a door, down a wooden-floored hall and then, after having our hands untied, thrown down a flight of concrete stairs. Gearheardt landed beside me, groaning and cursing. The door was closed at the top of the stairs and we were in darkness.

"You can bet I'll be telling Mr. Minh about this treatment as soon as I see him," Gearheardt shouted.

"Oh shut up, Gearheardt," I said.

"Where in the hell have you two been?" a voice asked out of the dark behind us. It was a woman's voice. Pissed.

"Who's that?" Gearheardt asked. "Who's in here?"

"Who is the hell do you think it is, you nincompoop? How many American women do you think parachuted into Hanoi this evening?"

"You must be Barbonella," Gearheardt said.

"Thank God you're here," I went on. "We saw you land."

"No, you can thank that smooth-talking son-of-a-bitch in the White House I'm here. I doubt if God has ever talked anyone into jumping naked out of an airplane."

"I just meant that we were supposed to hook up with—"

"Are you still naked?" Gearheardt asked.

"Don't get any ideas, soldier boy. Let's cut the crap. What are we supposed to do now?"

Of course Gearheardt and I were silent.

"Don't tell me. You two don't have the foggiest idea. Great. Cowboy Larry Bob tells me that you two will meet me and take it from there. So here the three of us are in some spider-infested stinkhole in downtown Hanoi, with our tits hanging out."

I heard Gearheardt groan.

"There's spiders in here?" I had feared them since childhood, more than anything else on the face of the earth.

"Oh, brother. You're worried about spiders and your pal is about to pop his wad. This is the worst nightmare since that space movie idea. Shit, shit, shit."

"Gearheardt, damn it, that's *my* leg. Get your ass off of me. Ouch! Hey! Jesus, let go of my hair! Damn it you two, back off."

I listened to heavy breathing on either side of me, but at least sensed no motion.

"Both of you calm down. We're officers in the United States Marine Corps, for God's sake. At least two of us are, and you, Barbonella, you're . . . well, whatever you are, attacking Gearheardt isn't going to help things. Besides, he likes it. Oh, crap. Barbonella, did you just spit on me? Come on, now. We've got a mission to carry out. We need to be resourceful and just figure out how to do it." Silence. "Have either of you got a flashlight or maybe even a match?"

"Did you just fall off the turnip truck? Why would I be sitting here in the dark if I had a flashlight? I've got squat." She began mumbling to herself. "Why didn't I just let them release the damn movie?

A few bad reviews, a new husband, and I'd have my career back."
Then louder. "Let me give it to you again, soldier. I did my part.
Stripped down and jumped out of the airplane. You and your pal
were to be on the ground to meet me with Ho Chi Minh holding a
dozen red roses. Instead, I hit on my ass, bounced twice and then the
People's Revolutionary Dickheads grabbed me and brought me here."

"I thought that Ho Chi was supposed to be in love with you," I
said.

"What? Who told you that? He's never even seen me."

"He's seen *Barbonella,* the film. The Cubans got a copy for him."

"And he *liked* it?"

Gearheardt finally spoke up. "What's with the People's Revolutionary Dickheads? I thought you liked these people. Whose side are
you on anyway, Barbonella?"

"Quit calling me Barbonella. That was what Elmer Fudd in the
White House called me. My name is Betty." The way she pronounced
it, very dramatically, it came out "Butty."

"Okay, Butty. Look in case you two haven't figured it out yet,
we're not getting much done here. Butty, what *do* you know about all
this? We've got to be honest with each other or we'll just rot here."

I heard her take a deep breath. In the silence I heard the clomp of
boots on the floor above us.

"Come on, now. They may be coming back to get us. I'll go first.
The President sent Gearheardt and me up here to make a deal with Ho
Chi Minh to stop the war. We understood that he had some kind of—
of *thing* for you. You were to distract the locals while Gearheardt and
I slipped into town. Unfortunately, we were shot down earlier today."

"Jack," Gearheardt growled, "you may be talking to the enemy."

"At least he's talking, you moron. And don't think I don't feel you
sliding up next to me."

"Gearheardt, I'm not going to warn you one more time."

"Good."

"Butty, you were going to say . . . ?"

"The President told me that I could have a part in bringing the war to a close. You two were to give me a package that I could give Mr. Minh if I got close to him, which he assured me I would."

"Probably rubbers."

"Ignore him, Butty. What did he say about us?"

"That you were going to try to negotiate something also. That I was to cooperate with you and help you get next to Mr. Minh."

"The four of us in bed. That'd be cute."

"Anything else?" I asked.

"That I would get to shoot an anti-aircraft weapon."

"At one of our *own* planes, you ditz."

"Not if they would stay away from us and quit bombing, *Almost Captain Gearheardt.*"

"That's the way you fight wars, *Barbonella.*"

"How about any other names, any contacts?"

"Whiffenpoof and Gon Norea. Whiffenpoof is British, I think. And Gon Norea is Mexican or from Panama or somewhere."

"Whiffenpoof is British? I had the impression that he was an American agent," Gearheardt said, making me think that he was more into this conversation than he let on.

"Never mind, Gearheardt. Look folks, we know two things. First, we're here on the same mission, to stop the war. Second, our only chance seems to be to contact Whiffenpoof, or Gon Norea, or hope they contact us. And maybe, just maybe, Gunny Buckles will find them."

"Gunny Buckles?"

"Jack, are you wearing a pith helmet?"

"No, Gearheardt, I am not wearing a pith—"

"Get your damned hands off of me."

"Jack, she's wearing a pith helmet and she's fully dressed. You lying—"

"I never said I was naked, twerp."

The door at the top of the stairs opened. In the light that came down, I saw Butty sitting next to me, her back against the wall, dressed in a North Vietnamese army uniform, complete with pith helmet. Gearheardt was close beside her.

"Mick Mou, you come." I could only see a dark silhouette against the bright light.

"I'm sorry. I don't speak Vietnamese," Butty answered, her voice sweet and respectful.

"He means me, Butty. Mick Mou. I'll tell you later." She didn't have to know everything. I began to crawl painfully toward the stairs. The soldiers hurried down and grabbed me, pulling me to the top.

"What about us?" Butty asked plaintively. "I'm not staying down here in the dark with Romeo."

As the soldier closed the door to the basement, shutting off the light, I heard Gearheardt. "So what's your sign?"

"Shut the fuck up, you moron."

"Oh, a spirited wench." He was giggling.

18 · Hanoi—Torture Lite

I was taken to a room in the back of the building. The room was dark except for a light shining on a chair in front of a plain wooden table. At the table sat three grim men, two in uniform and one in a Mao jacket that was about three sizes too big for him. No one said anything, so I took my place in the interrogation chair. I was prepared not to piss anyone off, since so far I hadn't really been treated too badly. The light was only moderately bright, and I could see the faces of the three Vietnamese. We stared at each other for a moment and then the civilian spoke.

"What you leg?"

I wasn't too sure what that meant, but pointed to my leg. After they had a short whispered conference, he asked again in a slightly elevated voice.

"What you leg? Mick Mou?"

"Oh are you asking my name? Sorry, I thought you said, 'What my leg.' My name is Almost Captain Jack—no, make that Almost Captain Tom Dexter. Shit, pardon me, you already have my I.D. I was right the first time, Almost Captain Jack Armstrong."

The interteam conference was slightly longer and seemed more heated.

"Mick Mou come Ho Chi Minh?" the civilian said, moving his head as if his collar was tight. Not likely in that suit, which must have belonged to the largest Vietnamese in the world.

"You'll have to pardon me again. See, I don't speak Vietnamese. I'm not Mick Mou, I mean Mickey Mouse. He is actually a cartoon character. The thing is that my girlfriend, Penny, works as Mickey Mouse part time at Disneyland. Maybe I shouldn't be telling you all this, but I can't see how you would get much military intelligence advantage by knowing that. But yes, we have come to see Ho Chi Minh. That part is right, if that's what you're asking. Do you suppose that I could have some of that water?"

I leaned forward to reach for the bottle of water sitting next to the larger of the military interrogators. He jumped up and knocked over his chair.

"Whoa. You don't need that gun. I'll get a drink later."

When everyone was seated again and I had leaned back in my chair, the civilian called a conference and the three put their heads together and began whispering. The military duo seemed upset at the civilian, who had assumed a very defensive posture, if body language was the same in Vietnamese. He cleared his throat.

"Chicago bad car?" he demanded.

I looked at him with my most sincere look, as if I truly wanted to answer him.

"Yes, the traffic can be bad in Chicago, or they do have bad cars there if that's what you mean."

"Chicago me," he said pointing at himself.

"You've been to Chicago?" I pointed to him and raised my eyebrows.

"Chicago," he said. He smiled at me and at the two military men. I took that to mean, "Now we're getting somewhere."

"What you leg?" he asked, his voice gruff again.

"Look, don't any of you speak English? This interrogation is not going to get us anywhere if we can't find a common language. ¿Habla español?"

"Chicago you leg."

I sighed and leaned back again. This was getting us nowhere.

"Parlez-vous français?" I ventured.

Now everybody smiled and spoke at once. They all seemed to know French. Unfortunately I didn't.

"No speakee. No *oui, français.*" Even to me that sounded stupid. "English *solemente.*"

We sat in silence for a long moment. The smaller of the military men began to pick his nose. It irritated me. This was my first interrogation after all.

"I'll try again. I am here on a mission to see Ho Chi Minh. It is very important that I be taken to him. Could you find someone who speaks ENGLISH? I think that would speed things up. SPEAKEE ENGLISH. I don't mean to be rude, but people are dying. This is very, very important. From the President of the United States. Are you getting any of this?"

I pointed at the water bottle and slowly moved my hand toward it. No one objected, and I opened the bottle and chugged it down. The non-nosepicker picked up the empty bottle when I sat it down, looked into it and held it out to the other two, beginning another long conference. I felt guilty, knowing that Gearheardt was probably still in the basement, dying of thirst. For the first time I noticed that there was a tape recorder on the table, the tape slowly revolving—the only working thing in the room. It was almost funny. I was in a shabby building in downtown Hanoi in my flight suit and sandals that hurt my feet. This did not seem a historic moment.

The larger military man got up and walked behind my chair. It made me a little nervous but I tried not to look at him. I could hear him breathing and smell whatever he had had for dinner. I hadn't eaten in at least a day, but it still didn't smell very good.

They tried a new tack.

"Bom hospiter." It sounded like an accusation.

"No bom hospiter."

"BOM HOSPITER." He was working himself up.

"NO BOM HOSPITER."

I decided that was a mistake at the same time that dinner man whacked me on the side of the head. It hurt like hell, but I didn't look up at him. He whacked me again, and my ear started ringing. The nosepicker was smiling, and I realized this was the part of the show that he had come to see. I wanted to rub my ear but didn't want to give him the satisfaction.

"Bom hospiter?" the civilian asked. It sounded hopeful, and the civilian raised his thick black eyebrows as he asked it.

"Name, rank, and serial number, pal. I know my rights. Jack Armstrong, Almost Captain, 087862. That's it, if that's the way you want to play it. Name, rank, and, OUCH. Holy shit. That hurts." Now I looked up at dinner man, and he backed away. "Give me a damn break! You wouldn't know what the hell I was answering anyway." I scooted my chair farther away from him. He drew his revolver and pointed it at me. "Don't look them in the eye" came back to me from long-ago training.

I ignored him and looked back at the civilian. His lower lip was trembling. He began a long tirade during which I heard Chicago, hospiter, Mick Mou, bomb, and a lot of ngyning and nahnging. I wished Gearheardt were with me so I could strangle him.

Finally the civilian, who had gotten to the point that his spit arched through the light regularly, stopped and slammed the table with his fist.

"Yes," I said. I didn't give a damn. "Yes, I have done all those things and more." They had broken me with stupidity, and it had only taken fifteen minutes. Probably a new record for a POW interrogation. If there were a POW Hall of Fame, I was sure to be in it. At least I still had my fingernails.

Dinner man took his place behind the table to what I took to be congratulatory smiles from his colleagues. Nosepicker pushed back, rose, and came around the table, stopping beside me.

"Don't even think about it, asshole," I said.

I wasn't sure whether it was my tone or that he understood "asshole," but his fist in my eye was harder than the blows thrown by his larger friend. I fell off of the chair and had to grab the edge of the table to get back up. I sat and scooted my chair again.

"Give me something to confess to, you prick!"

When nosepicker drew back his fist, I scooted the chair away. He stepped forward, and I scooted again. My eye was swelling shut, but I could see out of my good one that he was becoming agitated at my scooting. He began to mutter, and I assumed that I wasn't supposed to be scooting my chair.

As I was deciding whether or not to just let him close my other eye and be done with it, the door opened. A tall thin man wearing evening dress stepped confidently into the room.

"Hello. What have we here?" he asked with a deep British accent. "These chaps are knocking you about a bit, it seems."

He launched into what I assumed was Vietnamese although it looked like lip-synching in a bad movie. Quang nign gyen yuen, throat clearing sound, nguen, hey, nonny ding dong, and so on. It had the desired effect. Nosepicker retreated behind the table and stood silently with the other two junior goons, looking the Vietnamese version of sheepish. Through my one good eye I saw all three bow their heads slightly.

The well-dressed fellow turned and addressed me.

"Well, now, you must be Almost Captain Gearheardt."

"If I were Almost Captain Gearheardt, I would strangle myself. That's how much I am not Almost Captain Gearheardt," I replied, gingerly feeling the swelling under my left eye. "Almost Captain Gearheardt is in the basement with Butty. Who are the three stooges here with us? That's the better question."

"Yes, well, these gentlemen are apprentice interrogators, I believe. Not all that experienced but hoping to move out to the main POW prison at some point." He sighed. "I've tried to explain to their superiors that a basic understanding of English really is a necessity in these proceedings. By the way, you didn't confess to anything did you?"

"I may have confessed to bombing a hospital."

The gentleman laughed. "Oh, no problem there. Everyone confesses to that one. No, I'm referring to those 'women and children' missiles and the like. One Air Force major confessed to dropping a gas that caused women to grow enormous bosoms. Had the male populace tossing their wives into the street willy-nilly during air attacks, I'm afraid. Beat him bloody silly when the hoax was discovered. No, a hospital bombing or two is quite acceptable. Here, let me look at that eye of yours. Rather a nasty bruise."

"Who the hell are you?" I asked as he bent toward me, probing my left cheek. "You seem awfully familiar with the North Vietnamese."

"Lord, I *am* forgetting my manners. Whifferly Nelson Poofter, sir. At your service. Take my kerchief and hold it against that cut, and I'll instruct these buggers, if you'll excuse the language, to summon your friend."

Dinner man and the civilian came forward and wanted to shake my hand, which I reluctantly agreed to. Nosepicker sensed correctly that I would not extend that courtesy to him. They left and I heard them bickering angrily in the hall.

"Are you Whiffenpoof then?" I asked. "We were told to look for a Whiffenpoof when we arrived in Hanoi.

Whiffenpoof, if it were indeed him, perched one leg on the edge of the table and after straightening his pant seam, smiled and took out a cigarette case. He offered a cigarette to me, and I accepted.

"Yes, that would be me. I have been expecting the contact for some weeks now. You no doubt know that I have been *representing*, unofficially of course, your government in Hanoi for some time. A rather curious set of circumstances finds me perhaps the only Westerner allowed to operate openly in Hanoi. A long-ago love affair with a Vietnamese girl had me speaking the language like a native while I was still at Oxford. I was in the area arranging a gin distribution situation when the war began to heat up, so I just passed myself off as a Vietnamese, and, well, here I am."

"You passed yourself off as a Vietnamese? Could I point out that you must be over six feet tall, blond, with a large mustache?"

He smiled. "You don't know these oriental chaps very well, do you, Almost Captain? Polite to a fault. Wouldn't think of actually coming out and calling me a liar, now would they? Since I speak their language extremely well, I'm afraid they must take me at my word or cause us both a great deal of embarrassment. Rather unorthodox, I'll admit. Once the first few accepted my Vietnameseness, the others had little choice, actually. Are you feeling better now?"

Before I could frame a reply the door opened and Gearheardt waltzed in, his arm around a smiling Butty.

"Hey, what the hell happened to you?" Gearheardt asked, dropping his arm from Butty's shoulders and coming to me. "You been fighting again?"

"I held out as long as I could, Gearheardt, but I finally had to ram the guy's fist with my face." I lowered my voice. "What's with you and Miss Hanoi?"

"She held out as long as she could, too," he said. He noticed Whiffenpoof, who was beaming like a professional matchmaker. "Don't tell me," he said, offering his hand, "you're the Poof."

Whiffenpoof's jaws tightened, but he smiled quickly.

"That would be me, sir. Almost Captain Gearheardt, I presume." Enormous show of teeth.

"You presume correctly, my friend. Now we're getting somewhere. Jack and I are on a mission, you know. Time's wasting. Got a war to stop. Presume yourself over to the Main Minh's quarters and set up a meeting for us. And get our boots back while you're at it. These sandals must be the reason the Viets feel cranky all the time. And chow would be nice."

"I'm not sure that you're cognizant of the potential peril of your situation, Captain Gearheardt. I was asked to be of assistance to you and your friend, but given no instructions beyond that. What exactly is your plan?" As he spoke, the Brit was staring at Butty, who was looking quite comely in her North Vietnamese uniform now that the top buttons of her tunic were undone and her pith helmet was cocked jauntily. She was humming a vaguely familiar tune and studying her fingernails.

Whiffenpoof's lower lip was trembling, and I felt it was not on account of the comeliness of Butty. Something was bugging him.

Gearheardt stared him down.

"Yes, you would be hungry by now. I'll see what I can arrange."

He spoke rapidly to the two soldiers who had been standing just outside the door. They nodded and hastily left down the hall.

"I've given them your requests, and you will be taken care of."

"What's with the monkey suit?" Gearheardt asked.

The Brit looked down and smoothed his tuxedo jacket, then adjusted his bow tie.

"I was at a reception for the visiting Chinese, if you must know. Purely social affair, with atrocious food, I might add. This Hanoi assignment is not all that you would assume."

"I guess I would assume that living in Hanoi when the most powerful country on earth is bombing the shit out of it wouldn't be all that great," I said, beginning not to like Whiffenpoof.

His smile covered the distaste his eyes signaled. "I suppose you have a point."

We looked at one another for a moment and then he drew himself up. "I'll take Miss LaFirm to a hotel so that she can freshen up. When I return, we can discuss your mission. I'll need to know the details if I'm to assist you. Good evening, gentlemen."

Gearheardt stepped aside so that Whiffenpoof could open the door. Butty took his arm and left, smiling over her shoulder at Gearheardt.

"Miss LaFirm?" I said.

"Everybody's got to be somebody," Gearheardt said. He sat down behind the interrogation table, took off his sandals, and began to rub his feet. "So what do we do now?"

"I guess we have to trust Whiffenpoof. The President said to find him and let him help us. So here we are."

"The President also said to kill him if we wanted to. That doesn't give me a lot of confidence in relying on old Poofy," Gearheardt said.

I rubbed the cut below my eye gingerly. I was beginning to be able to see out of it, which was a relief. "I won't dignify the situation by asking you if you have a better plan."

"Jack, the Poofter is obviously a goddam spy. You can't just—"

"As was everybody else you have met since we got off the boat, Gearheardt. Of *course* he's a spy. He spies for *us*. We're sitting on our fat asses in downtown Hanoi with our dicks in our hands, and you're looking for spooks under the table. Figure something out, for Chrissakes!"

Gearheardt rose from the table and walked to the wall opposite the door. He studied a calendar hanging at eye level. After flipping through the months quickly, he dropped back into the chair. "Jack, every damn month is a different picture of a piece of Russian farm equipment. We can beat these guys, Jack." He slammed his palm hard down on the wooden table. "And their furniture is *shit*."

"I'm sure that was a consideration in the Pentagon, Gearheardt. But listen, did you notice how Butty walked out of here?"

Gearheardt grinned. "Well, I don't want to brag, but—"

"Oh give me a damn break, Gearheardt. I mean the way she just walked out with a guy that she supposedly had never seen before. Didn't that strike you as odd?"

"Well he did have on a decent-looking tux. And he wasn't a slope. That's two pretty good reasons."

"Don't call them slopes, Gearheardt. You know it bugs me. I know it's stupid, but—"

"But it's okay to waste them with a daisy cutter or a few napalm cannisters."

"Let's get back to Butty and our current situation. I assume that Whiffer—"

"You mean Poofer."

"You know who I mean. I assume that he will be back soon. Let's say he *is* able to fix up the meeting with Ho Chi Minh. Then what are we going to do?"

Gearheardt dropped the front legs of his chair to the floor. The sound was loud in the room. After a moment of staring at me he picked up the chair and brought it to my side of the table, sitting down facing the back, his knees almost touching mine.

"Jack, you really haven't figured it out yet, have you?"

"Evidently not. And I suppose *you* have?" I leaned back in my chair and folded my arms across my chest.

"We're here to waste him, Jack. We're assassins. Double-O-Sevens. Hit men. Executioners. Our mission is to see that Ho Chi Minh is a martyr to his cause. Are you getting the idea?"

"We're supposed to *kill* him?" My mouth was trying to give my brain time to catch up.

Gearheardt nodded and smiled.

"How about making a deal with him?"

"We can try that. What do you think our chances are?"

Starting with the fact that neither of us spoke Vietnamese, I had to admit to a low probability.

"But theoretically we could? Right?"

"You're a good human, Jack. Sure. I suppose so."

"But say we can't and we have to kill him. Then the assumption is that the North Vietnamese will just not have the leadership to continue the war, or—or what exactly?"

"I would imagine that is the assumption, after we bomb the piss out of them for a while longer. *And* assuming that we kill Giap too." I could see Gearheardt losing interest in the conversation. He was no longer looking at me but studying his fingernails, biting at a cuticle occasionally.

"We have to kill *Giap?*"

"He's the strategist for the war, Jack. Plus I've heard he's an asshole." Gearheardt was clearly getting impatient now.

I took a deep breath. Maybe a part of me had always suspected this. I knew that I would begin to worry about the logistics in a short while, as in we had no weapons at the moment, but I was still grappling with the enormity of being hours away from assassinating a world leader. Even if he was the leader of a little pissant country, as the President called it.

"But we *can* try to make a deal, right? We don't just walk in and start shooting. Assuming we have something to shoot with. Right?"

I didn't think that Gearheardt was even listening by this time, but he answered.

"Oh, sure."

"We'll have to get the Poof to help us," I said. "Maybe he can find the gunny. That would be a *big* help."

"And get our guns," Gearheardt said. "Got to have some guns."

The door opened, and Whiffenpoof strode in. He was followed by two Vietnamese army officers, who grinned and saluted.

Marines don't salute indoors, but they were grinning so I returned their salute.

Whiffenpoof beamed and held his arms out wide. "Let's get the rest of your gear and then you'll dine. Tomorrow you will have your meeting with Ho Chi Minh. And I understand that General Giap will attend also."

Gearheardt looked over at me and winked. "Goody," he said. "Let's go eat."

Outside the room we found all of our gear. It felt better to be dressed and booted. Even our weapons were there, my Walther PPK—I had long ago thrown away the Marine Corps–issued .38— and Gearheardt's .357 Magnum Police Special. These were carefully handed to us by the Whiff.

Whiff smiled as we laced our boots and strapped on our weapons. "At the curb you will find your driver. He will take you to your quarters. Not very luxurious, unfortunately, but after all you *are* knocking the locals about a bit with your bombing. Tomorrow morning you

will be picked up by the same man and I will meet you at Ho Chi
Minh's condominium and headquarters."

"Ho Chi Minh has a condo?" Gearheardt was always surprised at
the strangest things.

"Godspeed, chaps. I'll see you tomorrow."

He turned to the soldiers and spoke seriously to them. As the door
closed behind me I was sure that I heard the Gunny's name.

The street was dark and deserted, quiet except for the steady
grumble of the car that stood at the curb.

"What a shit car," Gearheardt said. "Leave it to the French to
build this damned thing. It looks like the winner of Madame LeFeu's
'draw a car' contest."

"Get in," I said, tired, hungry, and my needle bouncing on the
don't-give-a-shit mark.

Gearheardt squeezed into the backseat, such as it was, and I
dropped wearily into the passenger seat in front, looking in the dark
at grinning white teeth, black wavy hair, and an extended hand.
"Gon Norea," the teeth said, slurring the syllables into one word. "I
will drive you to your quarters and also fetch you food, no? Did your
president send a message for me?"

"He told us to kill you," Gearheardt said from the backseat.

The driver threw back his head and laughed as he pulled away
from the curb. He seemed familiar.

"He is a funny man," he said.

"It was Whiffenpoof he said we could kill, Gearheardt," I said,
behind my hand. "Do you actually know the President of the United
States?"

"Oh, I know many people, many people. I am a triple agent you
should know. I am a Cuban, although I was born in Panama. Trained
as a Cuban agent, torture and traffic control my specialties. But I tired
of the communist. So much learning and talking. Talk, talk, talk. I
take boat to Florida. America send me back to Bay of the Pig. I swim
back to Florida. They put me in the jail. So I agree to work for the

British intelligence on behalf of the Americans. Good idea, no? But as they say in Mexico, where my mother is from, *ay caramba*. I had the misfortune to make my deal with the British intelligence who worked for the Russians. So now I must work for the Russians too. And since I have such knowledge of the Cuban operations, the Russians have assigned me to work for the Cubans and spy on them also. Sometimes it is confusing, no?" He was jolly as a farmer as we drove through the Hanoi night. His mood darkened when he discussed his pay—the Brits insisted on ten percent off the top, since they had gotten him the job—but he brightened again as we ran over a dog.

"Tonight the streets are very quiet. It is easy to drive and very fast. But during the day . . . Ay yi yi, as my mother would say. The people, the traffic, the bicycles, ai yi yi the bicycles, and during the air raid, well, it is impossible to move. They do not understand traffic control. And you do not want to know their methods for torture. Simple peasants in my country, even without the training and certification that I have achieved, could torture many, many times better. But that is why I here."

From the backseat I heard the click of Gearheardt cocking his .357, which, from the range of two feet, would have pretty well vaporized the driver's head.

"Hold it, Gearheardt. Driver, do you mean that you are here torturing American pilots? My friend is about to remove your head— watch the old man on the bicycle—and I thought maybe you should have a chance to explain yourself."

The man was a pro. In fact he threw back his head and laughed again. "Oh no, no. You have caught me, my friends. I will have to admit to you that I am very recently become a—what would you call it— *cuatro* agent? Quadripple? Something like that, no? You see, I work for the Americans once again. Full circle, as you say in the great America. I would never hurt them. I am an honorable man, my friends. In the spying business I am what you would call a whore. But in the business of life, the business of my friends, I am an honorable man."

"Of course you are, señor," Gearheardt released the hammer

slowly. He then settled back against the seat and closed his eyes. "Wake me when we're there. This is an honorable man."

"You said the magic word, driver." I was exhausted, anxious, and hungry still. The drive through downtown Hanoi at night with a Cuban quadruple agent was anticlimactic.

"That I am an honorable man?" Gon asked.

"That you are a whore," I answered, leaning my head against the back of the seat and closing my eyes. "Gearheardt trusts whores."

I heard the driver laugh again. "I am the best," he said. "The *número uno*."

Once again, adrenaline depletion caused me to doze off. When we stopped in the suburbs of Hanoi, a light clicked on in a first floor window of the nearest villa. A skinny man in his underwear opened a door, greeting us with the charm of one who is gotten out of bed by authorities and ordered to accommodate two people who had been bombing his country.

"Bon soir," I said as I approached him, hoping to lighten the scene with my schoolboy French.

His response was in a universal language. He hawked and spat at my feet, then turned to go into the cramped, tiny, littered office. Gearheardt hurried to catch the door. As I stepped behind him, I felt someone pull on my arm.

"Señor," the driver said. He was out of the car, standing in an awkward, stooped position on the sidewalk. "Some advice from a friend. The Whiffer is not always to be trusted."

"The Whiffer?" There was something very American about calling someone the Whiffer.

"Señor Poofter. Something is not quite right, my friend. And in Hanoi he is often seen with my countryman, Juanton NaMeara. Perhaps you know all this, but you should be very careful."

"And what's all this to you, driver? What's your angle?"

"Because you have many weapons and very good infantry, I have placed many pesos on the Americans, my friend. For you to lose would be a financial disaster for me and my poor Mexican mother."

His thin brown face was pulled long; his brown eyes glistened in the dim light from the open door. Then he smiled and stuck out his hand.

"But how could that be, my friend? These people"—he looked around at the deserted, dark streets—"they have no such weapons and they eat foul, rotten fish. We will beat them, no?"

Tired as I was, the driver was strongly familiar.

"Driver, if you don't mind my asking, what in the hell is the story on your back? How can you walk around looking like you're tying your shoes all the time?"

The man turned his butt away and looked back through his legs at me. A gold tooth flashed in the light of the open door behind us.

"Devil of a war, ain't it, mate?" He grinned beneath his butt.

"Gon! You're the British spy we saw in Qui Nhon. Jesus, what— Oh, hell it was those damn Koreans with their barrel, wasn't it? Jeez, sorry about that, Gon."

He grinned again.

"Oh, it is a danger of the spy trade, my friend. And not so bad in the morning. As the day goes on my back begins to be a pretzel, no? By nighttime I am kissing the ass."

He laughed and patted himself on the butt.

"Is tough business, spying. I also was forced to give up eating spicy food. Ay yi yi. I learn my lesson." With a great effort, he straightened himself enough to return to his car and get behind the wheel. Now I noticed that his feet were on the dash on each side of the steering wheel and wondered how he braked and accelerated. And he seemed not particularly concerned with what Gearheardt and I were up to.

The thought crossed my mind a few inches below consciousness that Gon was not up to speed on what Gearheardt and I had in mind here. Or was he? Did everyone in the chain know that we were going to kill Ho and Giap? I had just found out, and I hated to think I was the last to know.

Gon started his Citroën—it sounded more like a motor scooter than a car—and was gone. Inside the building I found a scowling woman with a lantern waiting to show me to my humble, very humble, quarters. I was asleep almost as soon as my head hit the wooden pillow.

19 · Hanoi Hoche the Perfect Host

Gearheardt burst into my room.

"What happened to that dinner that Poofter promised us last night?"

I sat up and saw my night's bunkmate skitter through a hole in the wall, a large strip of the tongue of my flight boot trailing. I felt terrible.

"Remind me where we are, Gearheardt, and please don't tell me we're in some shit-hole hotel in Hanoi with plans to kill Ho Chi Minh today."

I rubbed my eyes and tried to move my neck around to work out the stiffness.

"Ix-nay on the ill-kay stuff, Jack. We're in the land of the enemy you know."

He sat on the edge of what I had used for a bed, a wooden bench covered with a threadbare grease-rag. Grease being the most hopeful description I could imagine at the time.

"I talked to Gon this morning. He came by to see what time we wanted to head over to Ho Chi's headquarters. Did you know that he was that British spy that came to see us in Qui Nhon? Damn good accent. I told you he was a Mexican."

"Cuban."

"Anyway, I told him to go rouse the Poofter and come back and get us and bring some chow for us to eat on the way. You look like shit."

"Thanks. I was afraid that I looked a lot worse, like how I feel. So what's the plan?" I swung my legs to the floor and picked up my gnawed flight boot. Gearheardt watched me as I began to put on my boots.

"Well, my boy," Gearheardt said in a low, serious voice, "we got guns, we're Marines, and we're going to meet the leader of the band."

I searched in vain for a cigarette and finally took one of Gearheardt's.

"Gearheardt, listen to me. It's time to get serious. Why is this so easy? Why are they letting us run around Hanoi with guns when they have scores of guys just like us caged up in prison not a mile from here? Don't you think there's more to it than that?"

Gearheardt got up and shut the door after craning his head down the hall. He sat back down on the bench, close to me.

"Jack, you're my best friend. Probably my only friend. I'm going to go back on an oath and give you the scoop. Promise you won't tell a soul." He put his arm around my shoulder. "The fix is in, Jack."

I waited for him to go on. He didn't, but kept looking at me squarely.

"The fix is in. That explains exactly what?"

"You never heard of fixes? Look, you know the President asked me to meet with Ho Chi and offer him a deal to stop the war. What you don't know is that there are secret peace talks going on in Paris. That's right. Surprised you there, didn't I? Problem is that Ho Chi wants a side deal or it's no go in Paris. Right now they're hung up on furniture, but that's none of our concern—"

"They're hung up on what?"

"They want the Americans to sit in highchairs and wear little bibs. Shit, I don't know. I told you that it's no concern of ours. The real deal is here. You and me, pal. We're going to make a deal that Ho Chi can't refuse. Or at least we were."

Gearheardt looked away and I didn't like it.

"What does that mean? Were?"

"The President got overruled is all. We got other orders."

"From who, for Christ's sakes? He's the damn commander in chief. What the hell are you talking about?"

"From the agency."

"The CIA?"

"Kind of."

"Kind of?"

"It's an agency of the agency. They think it would be better if we just kill Ho Chi Minh. And they were pretty damn persuasive. The President's too far into the bog, they said. Way too far."

"Jesus, Gearheardt," I said, hanging my head and trying to think, "this is worse than I thought. Too far into the bog? Are you nuts? Who are these guys?"

"Jack, guys like that don't tell you who they are. They couldn't be guys like that then, could they?"

My hands were shaking. The only guy in Hanoi that I could kill to stop any kind of madness was sitting beside me.

"Why didn't you tell me all this before? You knew I wouldn't be a part of all this crap, didn't you?"

"To tell the truth, I felt that you're the kind of guy that would do what had to be done. Like me. You're a loyal man. A good Marine even if no one in the squadron likes you. It's because you're a good guy."

He put his hand on my shoulder and gave it a squeeze.

"No, I didn't tell you everything just for that reason, Jack. I knew that if we fucked up and this went bad, they'd be ripping our nuts off and feeding them to us. They can break anybody, Jack, and if you broke and told the real story just to save your nuts, I knew you'd feel bad about it. I know you, Jack." He squeezed my shoulder again and then dropped his hand. He stood up.

I looked up at him. He didn't look at all like a raving lunatic.

"What's all this about, Gearheardt? I'll do what I have to do, but just tell me what all of this is about." I was resigned and calm. I wished *I* was a raving lunatic.

Gearheardt went to the door and rested his hand on the doorknob. He turned, sighed, and bit his lower lip while he looked at me. Then he said, "Beer, Jack. It's about who hauls the beer."

An hour later we were ushered into the office of Ho Chi Minh. The fix must have been in for sure. Gon had picked us up and deposited us without challenge at the entrance to a prewar, two-story French villa with a tile roof that had been red before decades of dirt, soot, and fungus had despoiled it. Shutters hanging loosely from the windows were thrown open, and had they been painted would have given the building a friendly, country look.

The office, in the front of the building on the second floor, was empty. It was large and filled with souvenirs from Paris and various Southeast Asian battlefields. A cheap plank desk almost eight feet long was at the center of the room, and behind it sat a rocking chair.

I sat in one of the hard-back chairs in front of the desk but Gearheardt wandered the room, peering closely at the photos and memorabilia.

"Look at this, Jack, Ho on a pony. Ho with a dog. Here's a diploma from LaSalle Law School. Isn't that that correspondence thing?"

He continued along the wall and to the trophy cases.

"Can you believe this, Jack? This trophy is from the goddamned Hanoi Rotary. *Ho Chi Minh, First Place, Dien Bien Phu, May 1954.* Wasn't that where the Viets beat the hell out of the French? They give *trophies* for that kind of shit? Look at all these books in French."

"He went to school in France, Gearheardt. He worked as a waiter or something before he came back here and—"

"And started all this trouble." Gearheardt sat down beside me.

"I doubt if he looks at it that way." I leaned closer to him. "Gear-heardt, do we just start blasting away when he comes in or what? I'm a little new at this shooting-dictators thing, you know."

"No time for that sarcastic attitude, Jack. But no. Follow my lead. We try to negotiate a deal along the lines the President briefed me on. When we back him into a corner, we blow his fucking brains out."

"Why bother with the negotiating for God's sake?"

"History, Jack. History." Gearheardt smiled as if he had explained something. "And this way we're kind of doing what the President and CIA each want. Kind of."

Gearheardt looked sheepish, and I wasn't sure he believed it.

"And remember, we've got to get that Giap guy in here too. Ho Chi won't make a move without consulting with Giap. So that's how we get them both in the room."

The door opened suddenly behind us, and a small, goatish man walked briskly into the room. The door shut behind him. Gearheardt and I rose to our feet as Ho Chi Minh made himself comfortable be-hind his desk and began rocking slowly back and forth, looking from Gearheardt to me and then back to Gearheardt. He was wearing huge baggy shorts topped by a ratty T-shirt with a stretched-out neck. On the front in faded letters it read LA MORT AUX GRENOUILLES. His thin hair matched the famous wispy goatee.

"Be seat, genermen," he said with a dismissive tone. He began thumbing through a stack of papers on his desk. Occasionally he would mutter to himself, wad up a document, and toss it to the floor. The room began to get hot even though a three-bladed ceiling fan turned slowly overhead. Gearheardt rose and walked to the windows behind us. He grasped the latch and began to push.

"Leave shut," Ho Chi Minh said without looking up from his paperwork. As Gearheardt sat back down, Ho Chi Minh opened a desk drawer and took out an abacus. He moved the discs back and forth with hypnotic precision until Gearheardt began tapping his shoe lightly on the wooden floor. I glanced over at him and caught his eye. I shook my head slowly. Gearheardt grimaced but said nothing.

Ho Chi Minh took a pencil from a coffee cup on the credenza behind him, opened a ledger, and began laboriously to enter numbers in columns. Trying to read upside down, I could only make out the headings, a North Vietnamese flag and an American flag. The North Vietnamese flag was ahead by a large margin. He began muttering to himself again and threw down the pencil in evident disgust. Then he leaned back in his chair and began his slow rock again, looking at first one then the other of us but saying nothing.

"Mr. Minh—" Gearheardt began.

"Ho."

"Yes, Ho, Mr. Minh. I think that you know—"

"Mr. Ho. Not Mr. Minh."

"Fine, Mr. Ho then. My President has asked Captain Armstrong and I—"

"How many my men you kill, Captain?"

Gearheardt stopped and looked at the old man. Then he smiled and I knew I should kick him but I didn't.

"Not nearly enough, Mr. Ho," Gearheardt said. "But we have plenty of ammunition left."

"That military secret, Captain. You give enemy military secret very quick." Now the old man smiled.

After a moment Gearheardt shrugged and held out his hands palms up. "You are too shrewd for me, Mr. Ho. You tricked me."

"Can bullshit, Captain. Lay out brass tacks. What the offer?"

I was beginning to notice that although the Communist leader was relaxed, he kept looking over our shoulders toward the door as if expecting someone. I felt the hair on the back of my neck begin to tickle.

"Okay, Mr. Ho," Gearheardt scooted his chair to the edge of the desk, "first the syndication. No deal. No Wall Street firm is willing to put North Vietnam into a limited partnership and make you the general partner. Won't work, end of story."

"Racist pigs," Ho Chi Minh said without real rancor.

"Yes, well, thirty billion dollars is a lot of money. I don't think race had anything to do with it."

The phone rang, and Ho Chi Minh turned to his credenza and lifted the heavy black instrument and put it to his ear. The receiver looked like it weighed about five pounds. After listening a moment, Ho Chi Minh began a rapid, singsong diatribe into the mouthpiece.

Gearheardt leaned toward me and I turned my ear to his whisper.

"Five Street firms offered a firm underwriting at that price, but the President vetoed the whole thing," he said. "Wall Street would lick a dog's dick to get these fees, but the President said ixnay."

I settled back in my chair wondering how Gearheardt suddenly had become a financial genius. If a pig had flown out of his nose I couldn't have been more surprised.

The phone was slammed down, and Ho Chi Minh swung his rocking chair back around. His face said that the phone call hadn't been good news. He opened the ledger and angrily wrote another number in the Vietnamese flag column then slammed the book shut.

"So, no syndication. What offer?" he asked.

"You got the girl, right? Barbonella, you got her. The President didn't let you down on that one, right?"

"Ha! You think Ho Chi Minh give up country for pussy?"

"Lots of guys have." Gearheardt looked to me for support of that position. I shrugged.

"Bullshit. What offer you?"

"Okay, but you got the girl. And the rest of the list is yours too. Complete set of Barbie dolls, with clothes and the Ken doll." Gearheardt looked up from the list he had taken from his pocket. "Guess that's for the niece, huh?" He smiled.

Ho looked out the window and blushed.

Gearheardt continued. "Molokai, okay. The five percent thirty-year fixed on the penthouse condo, okay. The—"

"Not Molokai. Molokai home for leper people. Want Maui or no deal."

"I am not authorized to make that trade, Mr. Ho. I can tell you that Lanai is a possibility, but Maui could be a deal killer." Gearheardt stopped and fixed his gaze into the eyes of his opponent in the best tradition of a car salesman. I expected him to say he needed to check with the manager next. But the Communist dropped his gaze first.

"Lanai, okay," he said as if it wasn't important. He waved his hand "go on."

"Bank of America card, okay. Like I said, you got the whole list. But there is one last item that the President insists upon. You have to—"

The door slammed open against the wall, and a blast of angry Vietnamese came through it. Gearheardt and I both jumped up, and even Ho Chi Minh seemed startled. The shouting came from five feet of North Vietnamese general. He stopped when he saw Gearheardt and me and pulled out an enormous revolver. He began waving it around, all the while shouting, his face contorted and full of rancor.

Ho Chi Minh rose slowly from his chair and sighed.

"Genermen," he said, "I present number one hero of Vietnam. Generer Giap."

Ho came around the desk, pushing the gun down toward the floor. He put his arm around the general and led him from the room, talking softly but firmly.

When the door closed I let out my breath and sank back into my chair.

"Holy shit, Gearheardt. What the hell is going on? Unless that pipsqueak queers the deal, we've made a bargain. I assume that he is agreeing to stop the war. We gave him every damn thing he asked for."

Gearheardt smiled and held out his list. I knew that smile, and my short-lived hopes sank. Taking the paper I turned to the back page. I read the last item and looked up at my still-grinning friend. "He'll never agree to this. It's disgusting. It's—it's . . . obscene. Who thought of this? Your 'guys,' I'll bet. They want us to have to kill him, don't they?"

"I told you they did, Jack. But I want to see the look on his face when I tell him this is what the President demands. It's symbolic don't you see?"

But when Ho Chi Minh returned with a calmed-down Giap, we didn't get the chance to tell Ho Chi Minh that the President wanted him to agree to anal intercourse with Mickey Mouse in front of Sleeping Beauty's castle on the Fourth of July.

Ho Chi Minh led the quiet but seething Giap to a chair and then returned to his rocker. He picked up a small bell, and its ring was answered almost immediately by a bowing waiter bearing a tray of tea and cups before him.

When we all were served, Ho Chi Minh held his cup toward Gearheardt and me and offered a toast. "Here to you, Marine. You gave gallant battle. Now you must be generous in defeat." He sipped his tea.

I saw that Gearheardt had not taken his cup to his lip. "Well, to be perfectly honest, Mr. Ho, the U.S. has not lost this war. Don't mistake our being here with—"

"You are finish! Your men all die!" Giap was on his feet again, the teacup dropping to the floor, his arm extended toward Gearheardt, pointing a finger in his face. "John Wayne love duck! Bomb all day hospiter never mind! You are finish!"

Ho Chi Minh made gentle shushing noises and gestured Giap back into his chair. He spoke to him quietly in Vietnamese.

Out of the corner of his mouth Gearheardt said, "John Wayne love duck? What the hell is that supposed to mean? This guy's a raving asshole."

"No asshole, Captain," Ho Chi Minh said reprovingly. "Very brave generer, number one Vietnam hero."

The room was quiet for a moment with no one taking the initiative to begin conversation. Finally Gearheardt spoke. "So where were we, Mr. Ho? If we agree to the terms that we have dis—"

But Ho shook his head and tilted it slightly toward Giap, who was playing with his pistol, opening the chamber and then jerking it so that the cylinder clicked closed again, and muttering to himself. I assumed, and hoped that Gearheardt did also, that Giap was not in on the deal that Ho Chi Minh was committing to.

"Yes, Mr. Ho, I see your point. There is one other item that I need to relay to you, but we can cover that later. Perhaps we can schedule a meeting this afternoon. If that would be convenient."

Ho Chi Minh sat forward and put his elbows on his desk. "Yes, Captain, I sure that is arranged. There is no deal"—he glanced over at Giap, whose eyes were darting suspiciously from one face to another—"but I thank Captain for bringing proposal from President." Ho Chi Minh sighed. "We must continue killing now. It must be freedom in all Vietnam."

"FREEDOM FROM ALL FOREIGN COUNTRY!" Giap leapt to his feet again and waved his pistol wildly. Gearheardt and I both started and shrank back.

"I have beaten Japan people! I have beaten French people! I beat now American people!" He paced back and forth in front of us. I glanced at Ho Chi Minh, who rolled his eyes and shrugged.

Giap launched into a new tirade in what I took to be French. Although I could not understand many words, it seemed that he was more comfortable in that language. After a few minutes, he stopped abruptly and looked at Gearheardt. *"Parlez-vous français?"*

"No speakee," Gearheardt said.

This set Giap off again, back in his fractured English.

"John Wayne number ten. Our battalion kill all! Dien Bien Phu come now again! You bomb, bomb, bomb, we scare no! Brave Viet people die many times. Ten thousand die, we fight, ten million die, we fight!" He sat back down and straightened the tunic of his dark olive uniform. He held his jaw firm and glowered at Gearheardt, who looked back to Ho Chi Minh.

"Mr. Ho, I don't need to remind you that the U.S. has the finest military and equipment in the world. We haven't even started to really fight. I'm sure that our leaders are prepared to do whatever it takes to win this war. But it is our—"

Napoleon was on his feet again. "Leaders shit! No strategy. Vietnam have big strategy." He took a step toward Gearheardt, who did not flinch even when Giap reached inside his tunic and withdrew a book and shoved it in his face. "Wesmorlan, shit strategy. I read book. Shit strategy!"

He slammed the book on the desk and sat back down. A trickle of sweat rolled down his brow.

The pages of the beaten paperback rippled in the slight breeze from the overhead fan. The book was *Catch-22*.

"Mr. Ho, what I was trying to say was—" Gearheardt began.

"No give damn what you say!" Giap was on his feet again. "U.S. beaten! Viet—"

"Would you shut the fuck up!" Now Gearheardt was on his feet. He squared off with the little fireball, who pulled his giant pistol out and pointed it at Gearheardt's nose.

Gearheardt pulled his .357 and stuck it in Giap's nose. I jumped to my feet and pulled out my PPK. I wanted to point it at my temple and just pull the trigger, but I felt like I needed to support Gearheardt. The three of us stood grim-faced in front of Ho Chi Minh's desk. My arm was shaking.

Ho Chi Minh gave his tea one last slurp, set the cup lightly on the saucer, and rose to his feet.

"So, gennermen," he said softly, "shall we now finish meeting? No more meeting today. Tonight we will go to dinner and talk."

"Capital idea, gentlemen. Capital idea. Sorry we're late." It was Whiffenpoof, who strode confidently into the room with Butty beside him. Ho Chi Minh's face lit up. He wiped his mustache again and came around the desk. He shook hands absently with

Whiffenpoof and kissed Butty on the cheek. He began whispering in her ear.

"What's all this?" Whiffenpoof said, seeming to notice for the first time that three of us were standing in the room pointing guns at one another. "Some sort of misunderstanding, it appears. General Giap, pleasure to see you sir. I see you've met Captains Gearheardt and Armstrong. Sorry I'm so bloody late. Try finding a 36C bra in Hanoi sometime. What say we put away our weapons for a moment and make plans for this evening? There, that's capital. Capital."

I exhaled and heard Giap do the same. Gearheardt didn't seem at all perturbed as he holstered his .357. He continued looking at Giap.

Ho Chi Minh had disappeared with Butty. I heard her laughter from the hall. Giap said something in French to Whiffenpoof, who looked over at Gearheardt and me and then replied to Giap in French. Giap snorted with disdain, put his pistol away, picked up his book from the desk and started to the door, bumping Gearheardt with his shoulder as he passed.

"Tonight, genermen. We see who is soldier first time." He left.

"Talk about a complex," Gearheardt said. "Fucking Hitler. Willing to lose ten million men to save his sorry-ass country." He snorted with similar disdain.

Whiffenpoof rubbed his hands together like a maître d'. "Let me see you to your quarters then, gentlemen. You can rest up a bit and then we'll reconvene this evening. On the town with Ho Chi Minh is quite an event, I will warn you." He laughed and took Gearheardt's arm and moved him toward the door. I heard him ask softly, "Did you discuss the beer situation?"

Gearheardt shook his head. "It didn't come up."

"Well, all in good time, then. All in good time."

When Whiffenpoof stopped in an office to inquire about better accommodations for Gearheardt and me, I looked at my friend and noisily let out my breath.

"Whoooey," I said. "What in the hell was all that in there? I thought Giap was going to shoot you."

Gearheardt smiled and patted my shoulder, watching Whiffen-poof arguing with a soldier vehemently, "That was just the boys playing 'good cop, bad cop,' Jack. They're just dicking with us." He turned now and grinned into my face. "Didn't I tell you this was going to be fun?"

20 · Going Dutch in Hanoi

Our new quarters in Hanoi were an improvement from the previous evening.

"This is the life," Gearheardt said as he plopped down on the metal cot covered with a thin green blanket and put his hands behind his head. "No dog turds on the floor, and the cockroaches are less than an inch long. Must be the VIP suite, don't you think?"

I sat down on the adjacent bunk. The room had four beds and appeared to be a transient facility. Cigarette butts littered the floor, and a crude wooden table with matching chair sat empty of ornament. Afternoon sunlight filtered through a dusty, cracked window. The walls, like all of the other walls in the two-story, French-style building, were a faded yellow.

"You seem to be enjoying yourself, Gearheardt. You think this is fun, don't you?"

"Jack, if I'd known Vietnam was going to be this much fun I'd have come over here five years ago."

"We weren't at war in Vietnam five years ago."

"We would have been if I'd of come over here and started bombing the shit out of them. Wars are pretty easy to start, you know."

"Look, Gearheardt, when are you going to level with me? What in the hell is this *beer* thing that you and Poofy are whispering about? And *hauling* it? What's that got to do with anything? I'm almost beginning to like the idea of just shooting Ho Chi Minh and Giap. They're the enemy, we're Marines, we have guns. At the risk of sounding like you, why isn't that our plan?"

"You'll never make a politician, Jack."

"If I'm going to die, I'd like to know what for. Is that too much to ask?"

"So you could die happy?"

I thought about it. "No."

He sat up on the cot and scratched his head vigorously.

"You're not going to tell me, are you, you asshole?" I said.

"Tell you what, Captain Armstrong?" Whiffenpoof came into the room carrying packs of cigarettes and two bottles of beer. He sat the lot on the desk and dropped into the chair. "Not easy to find Winstons in Hanoi, old boy," he said to Gearheardt.

"How the cow ate the cabbage," I answered.

The Brit looked puzzled and turned to Gearheardt.

"The cow—yes, well I'm afraid I haven't much knowledge of that event. I suggest we take advantage of the opportunity to do a spot of planning. Several items to get 'straight,' as you Americans say. First off—"

"First off, hand me one of those bottles," Gearheardt said. "Next off, why don't you tell us what old Butty the Bomber is up to?"

"Butty the—oh you mean Miss LaFirm. At this moment she is, I assume, with General Giap on route to an anti-aircraft emplacement."

"You're shitting me," Gearheardt said.

"If that means having you on, as I suspect, then no, I am most assuredly not 'shitting' you. One would assume from the bits of conversation that *Butty* had with Giap, she will attempt to fire on an aircraft if one enters the airspace above Hanoi this afternoon. Rather odd behavior, don't you think? She seemed quite serious about it."

"The bitch," Gearheardt growled. "And after I spent half the night indoctrinating her. So help me, if she shoots down an American airplane, I'll disembowel her. Whiffy, what's your role in all this? I haven't figured you out yet."

"I say, would it be altogether too much trouble to determine just what name you prefer to call me and utilize that? Whiffy, Poofy, Poofter. Really. I may be the only friend you—"

"Whiff."

"Pardon?"

"Whiff. We'll call you Whiff. As in 'get a whiff of that.' That okay with you?"

"Goddammit! Could we get on to this *planning* that someone mentioned?"

They both turned their heads toward me, and I got the notion that Whiff was a kindred soul to Gearheardt in more ways than I would prefer.

Whiff smiled, looked at Gearheardt with raised eyebrows, then back at me.

"Well, not much use in beating the badger at this juncture I'm sure. Your companion—"

"Beating the badger?"

"Could you just let him talk, Gearheardt? I foolishly would like to have some idea what is going on. If it means dying happy, as you put it, so be it."

"Dying? That's a rather severe undertaking. Not ready by half to go that way if I can help it," Whiff said. "Your companion has no doubt told you that I am a distributor of spirits, in addition to performing a spot of spying—on behalf of friends, of course." He looked back at Gearheardt, who was inspecting his .357. "Please put that away if you don't mind, old chap. Thanks, that's better." He looked relieved, and later I was to find out just why. But now he startled me when I would have sworn my startling centers were hopelessly burned out.

"Simply stated, your president has promised me a major beer franchise for Vietnam. Seems that your friend Gearheardt has no knowledge of that fact, although I was told that he would bring documents to that effect."

"A major beer franchise." My mind was spinning wildly in neutral.

Out of his tuxedo Whiff looked a bit seedy. His socks were without elastic and bunched loosely above his shoes. His blue wool jacket, shiny at the elbows, was missing a couple of sleeve buttons and in dire need of a cleaning.

Whiff went on, although he seemed to take notice of my scrutiny and shrugged his jacket about his shoulders and pulled one frayed cuff farther from his sleeve.

"Yes, I wouldn't think it too much to ask, given the lengths I have taken to assure a civilized reception for you and Almost Captain Gearheardt. Copious amounts of the beverage are consumed by your troopers here, and it doesn't seem out of sorts to benefit one's purse by attending to their supply."

"Why aren't you importing some of that warm piss you sell in England?" Gearheardt asked.

Whiff drew a wounded expression and then gently cleared his throat as if shutting off the bile that he would prefer to deliver. "Well then, I'm afraid the *warm piss* that you refer to so generously, has a flavor and character that is somewhat stymied by the near-frozen state that you Americans prefer in your beverages. In any case, that isn't the point. The point is—"

"You're saying the Americans can't appreciate the finer *character* of your English brew? My friend, you've never—"

I jumped to my feet. "Jesus, Mary, and Joseph! Now we're going to sit here and argue over the goddam *beer*! I won't have it! I don't give a shit! There is *no* point!" I sat back down and exhaled, trying to calm myself. "I'm taking charge here. I'm the senior officer—don't even start, Gearheardt. I don't think either of you have a plan, so I'm making one. *Comprende?*" I was back on my feet.

The Brit looked at Gearheardt before he spoke. "Well, I say, as a commercial activity this is not a situation that lends itself—"

"It's a war, shit-for-brains. War." I pulled out my pistol and pointed at his British nose. "Are you in or out, Whifferpooferpooftersham?"

"Oh, decidedly in, Captain. First things first, I always say." He threw up his hands in front of his face when I shoved the pistol closer to his nose. "Blood before beer, I always say." He laughed and motioned my pistol away from his face. His cool surprised me. I really would have liked to shoot him. I was wanting to shoot *somebody*.

Gearheardt was lighting a cigarette. "You've got the controls, buddy," he said.

"Good. First you, Whiff, what's your game? And don't give me that beer franchise crap." I sat back down on my bunk, keeping my PPK in my hand.

"Actually, my primary mission is to support your efforts, Captain Armstrong. Beyond that, old man, I'm afraid I'm completely in the wool. It was my impression that you and Captain Gearheardt were here to make some sort of bargain with the old chap and that he would then instruct his minions in Paris to cooperate in the conclusion of the hostile activities. Butty the Bomber, as you call her, most whimsical I might add, was to be a diversion of sorts."

"Who's this Gon Norea guy? He work for you?"

"Decidedly not. I assumed that he worked for you. Through one of your other contacts here I mean." The Brit was sounding more defensive. "By the by, I believe that he may have hooked up with your Gunnery Sergeant Buckles."

Gearheardt looked up from polishing his boots with a strip of blanket he had torn off.

"He what? If that's the case why doesn't Gon bring him here? What do you know about the gunny anyway, Poofy? Jack and I haven't discussed him with you."

"Whiff, you mean," he replied with a nervous laugh. "Certainly you did. Or perhaps it was Miss LaFirm."

"You didn't answer my question." I watched the Brit's face carefully.

"Yes, I suppose that would make sense. But you see—"

Outside, an air-raid siren began wailing. We heard the sounds of running in the building. Gearheardt dove over a bunk and looked out the window.

"Uh oh, sounds like the boys are coming. Stay away from the hospitals, Jack."

"Very funny. What can you see out there?"

"My first actual Chinese firedrill. Except with North Vietnamese. Whoa. Listen to that AA fire. That'd better not be that Butty bitch!"

"Shit. What next?"

I stood at the window beside him and watched the scurrying crowd below us.

"Don't ask me. You're in charge, remember?" He searched the skies. "Man, would you look at that flak? These fuckers throw up some lead, don't they?"

"Whiffer, what do—"

But the Whiffer was gone when I turned around.

"I don't like the looks of this, Gearheardt. Do you think that Brit is on our side?"

Gearheardt was still looking out of the window.

"Do you suppose I could pick off a couple of these little bastards with my .357 and they would blame it on the airstrike?" He was fingering his pistol.

"Something tells me that wouldn't be a good idea."

A blast nearby drove Gearheardt away from the window, which rattled but did not break. Gearheardt stepped to the side and looked at me.

"Jack, that's what we call cowering," he said with a smile. I was nearly under the desk. "Make room for me, pal."

The explosions and anti-aircraft fire continued for ten minutes and then moved farther away. Finally, we heard another siren which we took to be the all-clear signal. Gearheardt moved cautiously to the window.

"I see some smoke but that's all. If we lost any aircraft today, I'm ramming this pistol up someone's—"

"If I see that damn Brit again . . ." I trailed off, not sure what I would do.

"I think he's okay. He's just a hustler, Jack. Doesn't mean that he's against us. He's helped us so far, hasn't he? No one has skinned us.

He got our weapons back. And he seems to have arranged the meeting with Ho. That's all that we could ask at this point."

"Maybe so, but if he found out that we're going to kill those bastards, he might not be so helpful. Seems he has a cozy little racket running here." Although I wasn't quite sure what it was and was only repeating something I had heard in a movie.

"Nothing to do now but wait, Jack me boy. Get some rest. This should be quite a night."

"If the Brit knew that we planned to kill Ho and—"

"But he does know. I told him."

Gearheardt had his eyes closed.

"That *is* our plan, is it not? We're wasting those two, right?"

Gearheardt didn't open his eyes. "It's all right with me."

"What do you mean it's all right with you? Isn't that the plan? Gearheardt, look at me. I don't get a lot of comfort out of 'It's all right with me.'"

He opened his eyes and sat up now. "Jack, it's a complicated situation. Yes, that's *one* plan. As a Marine officer I'm committed to pretty well killing everybody foreign and domestic or however that oath went. But as a spy I have to take into consideration America's reputation in the intelligence community, and as a businessman, well we have certain contracts—"

"You're not a goddamned businessman, Gearheardt! Where in the hell did you get that idea? We need to find the gunny, do our duty and then, if possible, which I doubt, get our asses out of Dodge."

Gearheardt sat by me and offered me one of his cigarettes.

"Jack, think about it. If we were able to really make a deal with Ho Chi Minh. A deal that would cause him to send the signal to Paris to stop dicking around and negotiate. Think what that would mean. Thousands, maybe millions of innocent lives might be saved. And yes, we could go down as the guys who did it."

I jumped up and stepped away from him. Gearheardt making sense. Gearheardt spewing humanitarian clichés. Gearheardt thinking beyond beer and women.

"Weren't you the one that not twenty-four hours ago was telling me that our mission was to Double-O-Seven these two? Remember that? Assassins? Hired guns?" This was a nightmare. I wished I were back with Barker and that other guy, lying in a landing zone with North Vietnamese trying to kill me.

"Jack, all I am saying is give peace a chance."

I stared hard at him. Something was different. He looked away.

"Oh shit. Oh holy shit. Gearheardt, you bastard. You poor alcoholic, good-for-nothing low-life, chickenshit bastard. It's Butty, isn't it? You think you're in love. You're pussy-whipped. You were only with her a few hours, and you're willing to give up killing. And what about strafing? You're willing to give that up too?"

"Now, Jack, don't give me a lot of grief. The woman is—"

"What about all that disembowel, shove a pistol up her—?"

"Hold on, Jack. Don't get personal. Sure, she has a few hangups. But I've done some pretty stupid things myself. And she's not a bad person. Her career needed a little something, and the next thing she knew—voilà, parachuting naked into North Vietnam. And, I might add, I talked her out of killing you."

"She was going to kill *me*?" I pulled even farther away from him, back against the wall by the window.

"Well, actually she wanted me to do it. But I didn't even hesitate, Jack. No fucking deal, I told her. I was ready to offer to just wing you, but she backed off the whole thing."

He smiled and I didn't have the slightest idea whether or not he was kidding. "Look, Jack. She is just a little mixed up sometimes. Demonstrating against a damn good war and all that. You know I respect people like that."

"This anti-war stuff is great, Jack," Gearheardt told me after one of his trips to the Bay Area. "You get the girls all fired up, and they have to release that emotion. I'm there, Jack. I'm there."

"But doesn't it ever bother you? I mean you're taking advantage of these girls, aren't you?"

"Jack, these girls are trying to destroy my way of life. How can I be taking advantage of them? Remember, I'm the one making the world a safe place for me to screw them."

"Yes, there is that, I guess."

I slid down the wall until I was sitting on the floor. After a moment Gearheardt went back to polishing his boots. He began to hum softly, a Beatles tune.

"Well, as my old dad would say 'this is a fine fettle of kish.' "

We sat that way, me against the wall and Gearheardt on the side of a bunk polishing his boots. After a bit I began to hear the noises of the city outside. My old dad. And my old mom, and old brothers and sisters. I began to get melancholy. The light now came into the room in a slanted, lazy rectangle, the floor darkening as the sun went below the window sill. I considered shooting Gearheardt, but the thought of being in Hanoi with no friends was too depressing. I thought of lying on the thin bunk with Mickey Mouse, or Penny, not making love but just holding her. Gearheardt walked to the window, patting my head as he passed me. I heard him straining to open the window and then felt the breeze when he succeeded. The city noises were louder.

"Pontius Pilate on blue rubber crutches!" Gearheardt yelled.

In the courtyard below us, standing beside an idling 1966 red Corvette convertible, Ho Chi Minh grinned up at us.

"You come down, Marine. Painting town." He waved and then sat back down in the Corvette and revved the engine and let it back off. He grinned up again.

Gearheardt pointed at the gate through which a bright yellow Boss Mustang was creeping, looking ready to attack, its pipes blasting and rattling off the courtyard walls like a dragster on nitro. When it reached the Corvette, the driver, Giap apparently, revved up to max

RPM and let it back off, popping and sputtering in Ho Chi Minh's face. The old rascal stuck out his hand and raised his middle finger. Then he looked back up at us.

"Get ass hauling. Honey's in ville."

Gearheardt was at the door in two bounds. As he opened it he looked back at me, still standing at the window. "You heard him. Honey's in ville."

21 · The Blue Daisy Summit and Beer Bust

As soon as I got in the passenger side of the Mustang, Giap, who could barely see over the steering wheel, threw it in reverse and flew backward; the tires screeched as he turned the wheel expertly so that we ended up facing the courtyard gate. We were airborne briefly over the gutter at the side of the boulevard, turning ninety degrees and screaming up the street, Giap shifting into second before we reached the corner, near seventy miles an hour. I heard Ho Chi Minh's Corvette burn out of the courtyard behind us and evidently over the median in the boulevard as he drew alongside us on the other side of the landscaped island. Gearheardt gave me a thumbs up from the Corvette's passenger seat.

Giap downshifted suddenly, throwing me into the dashboard. He squealed around a corner, sending bicycles and pedestrians flying to the walls of the adjacent buildings. At ninety he shoved the screaming engine into third and accelerated through a market area. I ventured a look behind us and saw the Corvette gaining.

"Imperialist enemy America unnerstan history no. Neba beat Vietnam. Our country die, never mind and America go home." He laid on the horn as an old woman, a pole across her shoulders with baskets of vegetables suspended from each end, ventured into our path. The windshield on my side clipped one end of the pole and spun the old lady like a top.

"Russia like keep gun airplane, send old. Forget Lenin. I know him. Not forget. French army drink drink never mind." Ahead I saw what appeared to be a dead end. We were not slowing down that I could tell. Ho Chi Minh and his Corvette drew up to our side. Giap and Ho began yelling at one another in Vietnamese, occasionally smiling, then looking back at the road. Just before the dead end, Giap braked and downshifted, allowing the Corvette to shoot ahead and turn into our path, its turn signal blinking. The force of the turn threw Gearheardt onto Ho. When Gearheardt straightened back up, he was laughing. A beer can flew out of the Corvette and bounced on the Mustang's hood, setting Giap off on an orgasm of Vietnamese shouting. He laid on his horn again.

"Drink drive no good evil. South Vietnam no South all Vietnam. Revolution same all country no want foreign people tell—" The Corvette slammed on its brakes in front of us, causing Giap to run up on the sidewalk to avoid hitting it. I looked back again and saw the Corvette disappear around a corner. "—government. Stupid Ho Chi Minh shortcut no good bomb road. Ha!" We accelerated again, and I was pushed back in the seat by the power of the Mustang engine. It was almost dark and hard to see people in the road until they jumped out of the way.

"Have you got lights?" I yelled over the engine roar.

Giap turned toward me as if I had insulted his ancestors.

"No light! Have new seat. No smoke now." He patted the white Naugahyde seat.

"No! I mean *lights! Lights!* You know see dark." I pointed toward the dash on his side where I thought the light switch would be. "LIGHTS!"

We were approaching a narrow bridge. An ancient army truck was entering it from the opposite direction. Giap hit his horn again, then flicked his lights on, flashing from bright to dim rapidly.

The truck stopped in the center of the bridge and the driver and his passenger bolted out its sides and ran back the way that they had come.

Giap slammed on the brakes and screeched to a halt. The engine died. Giap jumped out of the car, drawing his huge pistol and firing at the two men disappearing in the dark. He got back in and started the car. I braced myself for a gut-wrenching peelout, but Giap slowly turned around and drove alongside the river at a modest speed.

"No need hurry. Ho win first time. Corvette shit never mind."

When we rounded a corner minutes later, I saw the Corvette parked at the curb and Ho Chi Minh and Gearheardt leaning against it. We parked and got out. Ho rubbed his thumb rapidly against his fingers until Giap threw a wad of bills at him.

We followed Ho Chi and Giap into the Blue Daisy. They were greeted with shouts and raised glasses. Perhaps fifty soldiers, plus the bar girls that were attached to them, filled the small room. Ahead of us was a dark stage, to the right a bar that ran the length of the room. Tables and chairs filled the remaining space except for a very tiny dance floor in front of the stage. An American jukebox blared Vietnamese music, tinny and shrill. I hated these places.

Ho Chi beckoned Gearheardt and me to tables hastily shoved together by a team of obsequious waiters.

"You sit. Drink on me yes. Mustang number ten." Ho Chi laughed at Giap who sat down in his normally grumpy mood. Ho yelled at the bartender. "Hey you, beer my friend."

Gearheardt was in his element. "Yes, beer my friend too, Ho Chi. Need lots of friends, right?"

"No call Ho Chi. Name Hoche. More friend, no? My friend they drink me, call Hoche."

Gearheardt grabbed a beer from the tray being brought to the table. He took a swig and spewed it out on the floor. "Whoa! The horse who pissed this is seriously ill."

Hoche took a bottle to his lips, turned it up and drained it without stopping to take a breath. "Drink too slow, Marine."

Gearheardt tilted his head and chugged the beer. He let out a long breath. "You know, pal, you're right." He grabbed another and saluted Hoche. "What do you say we call number one hero *Geepster*?"

Hoche looked puzzled for a moment, then smiled at General Giap. "Helloooo, Geepster."

Geepster nursed a beer and kept looking from Gearheardt to me to Hoche.

Ho Chi Minh was a different personality in a bar. His eyes twinkled and he grinned as he rested his forearms on the table and surveyed the room. Spotting a woman standing near the end of the bar, he raised his beer bottle and waved her to the table.

"This mama-san Blue Daisy. Number one mama-san." He pulled her giggling onto his lap and began to whisper in her ear.

Giap, now Geepster, took an offered cigarette from Gearheardt and lit it with a Zippo engraved with the outline of an aircraft carrier. He turned his chair slightly away from the table, excusing himself from the group.

"Gearheardt, I need to have a chat with you," I said.

"Okaaay. Now we're talking," Gearheardt said, ignoring me.

The mama-san was heading back to our table leading two young women. She was grinning. The women weren't.

Both women sat down beside Hoche on chairs drawn from the adjacent table, displacing two soldier patrons, who grumbled and moved to the bar.

"Hey, what kind of socialist are you, Hoche?" Gearheardt laughed. "Where's the sharing attitude?"

Ho Chi Minh was nuzzling the neck of one of the women. "Women no like America. Bomb too much."

"Well, what kind of hospitality—"

Giap broke in, "American unnerstan nothing! Socialis share shit. French all time want Vietnam women. Beat French. Now we beat—"

Gearheardt took another beer and downed half of it, then looked at me.

"Can you keep that little twerp quiet, Jack? He's beginning to piss me off."

"Heaven forbid you should get mad at the enemy, Gearheardt."

"Jack, you're bound and determined not to have any fun, aren't you?"

I sat staring at my friend. I decided that I would feel better if I really believed that Gearheardt had knowledge of a plan of action that for reasons unknown he was keeping from me. I suspected, however, that he had come to Hanoi with no real conviction and, through sheer arrogance and an ultimate belief in himself, was certain that things would just "work out."

I sipped my beer and watched Hoche snake his hand up the dress of the woman on his lap. Looking over at Giap, I saw that he was watching the same thing. He caught my eye and I saw disgust. He hissed and turned away.

A commotion at the door caught my attention. A man had entered, and the Vietnamese soldiers were moving out of his path as he strode into the room. He was Hispanic, tall and slim, dressed in what appeared to be a tailored military uniform of indeterminate origin. His face was twisted in a scowl directed at the soldiers who averted their eyes. He was handsome and evil-looking. I knew it was Juanton.

He spotted our table, breaking into a smile as he started to make his way to us.

A screaming three-foot queen in a pink dress flew into his path and smashed his testicles with a small black purse.

"Ay yi yi!" Juanton doubled over and clutched his groinic region, his face twisted in pain and anger. When he was able to straighten up, he judo-chopped the midget queen across the neck sending her head over tiny high heels under a table. A miniature Uncle Sam burst through the crowd and I stood to watch the attack, but he was jerked short of Juanton's crotch by a choker and the four-foot chain held by a one-eyed Vietnamese beauty.

"Juantono, you miserable rotten bastard," the girl said, slacking the chain to allow the Chinese midget to rub the red mark across his throat.

"By golly, she speaks American, Jack." Gearheardt grabbed my elbow as I started to the couple, now slowly circling each other. "She looks like she can take care of herself."

"You think I was in countryside giving important show. I get ride to Hanoi and at prison they tell me you finish torture early and having beer with American woman who jumped from Yankee airplane."

Juanton looked around at the mostly silent crowd.

"I theenk this is for later, my little Cyclopa. Yes, I was having beer with American woman, but not what you theenk. Is business."

"Cyclopa" spit on the floor and stepped in front of Juanton.

Juanton cold-cocked her with a blow that could be heard in the street. The midgets dragged her to a table, their beady eyes flashing at Juanton as he rubbed his knuckles. He turned to our group.

"Venerable Leader," he said, "how wonderful it ees to see you this evening. ¿Cómo está? my friend?" He held out his hand and waited, smiling, while Hoche untangled his hand from the bar-girl's clothing.

"Juanton, you have washed blood from hand?"

The Hispanic laughed and threw back his head.

"Meester Ho, you are so very comical. Another of your leadership good traits. It is why the people love you so, no?"

Hoche looked down the table and caught my eye. He winked.

"Juanton, you have known Gennerer Giap, Vietnam number one hero. Also my friend Almost Captain Armstrong, United State Marine, you maybe not know."

The Hispanic's face kept the smile, but his eyes hardened as he looked at me. He walked to my side and stuck out his hand again.

"Juanton NaMeara, Capitán. It is a pleasure, no?"

"Creo que no, shithead."

It was Gearheardt, who now stood beside Juanton.

Juanton took a small step back. He wasn't smiling now.

"So you do not think so? And why would that be? We are all soldiers, are we not?"

"I'm not a soldier, I'm a Marine. And you're not a soldier. You're a slimy sick bastard here to torture American pilots."

"Who told you this terrible thing, *Capitán*?"

"Why do you Mexicans always talk in questions?" Gearheardt asked. Juanton bristled. He glanced back at Hoche.

"I am Cuban. I am here because my country is a friend of those who fight against American imperialists."

"American imperialist fight no—" Giap began, getting to his feet.

Gearheardt whirled on him. "When I want your opinion I'll knock it out of you, you little—"

Guns were drawn again, and I expected someone to call someone else a yellow-bellied varmint any minute. Giap looked ridiculous with his large revolver, Gearheardt foolish with a beer bottle in one hand and his .357 in the other, the Cuban uncertain with a large Russian .45. A number of the North Vietnamese soldiers dove behind the bar. I stepped between Gearheardt and Juanton.

"Gentlemen, gentlemen. Let's not be childish, we have a war to discuss." I didn't know where that had come from, fear or stupidity. I was pretty sure a shootout in the Blue Daisy was not our mission. The three gunslingers holstered their weapons and sat down.

Juanton raised his hand and a beer appeared in front of him. It was a San Miguel. Juanton squinted across at Gearheardt.

"You are pilots, no?" He caught himself. "You are pilots."

"Was it the flight suits or the wings on the jackets that gave it away, Einstein?"

"I know many American pilots. Today I have . . . interviewed a number of them." The bastard smiled, and I got ready for the .357 to appear again. But Gearheardt returned the smile.

Juanton smiled at me now, his eyes quickly darting toward the midgets who were tending Cyclopa. She was sitting up, holding a bloody rag to her nose.

"These women, you live with them and have baby and they theenk they own you, no? But there are two sides to all stories, no? And Cyclopa only see one side, yes?"

He threw back his head and laughed. Looked at me and winked and then laughed again. Gearheardt put his hand over mine as I grabbed the handle of my PPK. But the reality was that my ardor for Cyclopa was cooling as quickly as it had started.

"They say that torture is a substitute for sex. Is that right, Juanton?" Gearheardt asked pleasantly.

Giap choked on his beer and spewed the table.

"You okay there, Geepster?" Gearheardt asked. Giap ignored him.

"Sex is war, Captain." This from Hoche, who had to raise his face from a female bosom to make the statement.

Gearheardt rested his arms on the table, glaring at Giap when he realized how much beer the General had spewed. "Shit," he said, then, "I mean, my Cuban burrito-burner, that guys that get their rocks off sticking sharp instruments into other men usually don't have an interest in sticking other instruments into womenfolk. Kemo Sabe?"

"I don't think 'Kemo Sabe' means what you think it means, Gearheardt," I put in. "Try 'comprende.'"

Juanton swung his still smiling face around the table, stopping at Hoche for a moment, then back to Gearheardt.

"You are wanting to pick a fight, no?" He launched into a tirade barely audible, in a language that was mostly Spanish. Then, "But I have no need to fight you now. You are a guest of Ho Chi Minh, the finest leader in Asia, and General Giap, the—"

"Yeah, yeah, I know. Number fucking one Vietnamese hero. But I still say that you couldn't get it up with one of the cuties here, Juantono. Already had your jollies today, right?"

Juanton's jaw tightened. He picked up his San Miguel and drained it. He turned his chair toward Hoche and began talking to him, ignoring the fact that Hoche was fully engaged and only grunting vague replies.

A waiter appeared at the table balancing a tray of bottles. "From the Russians. Beer free."

Sure enough, near the back of the dark room sat a table of four Caucasians, ill-suited with loud, wide ties and short haircuts. They grinned at us and raised their glasses. Gearheardt and I raised our bottles in return. The Russian nearest to us (we could only see his back) raised his middle finger over his shoulder. The other three laughed and went back to their drinking.

"Goddam Russians," Gearheardt said loudly. "Anybody that would take help from those sonsabitches deserves to lose their pissant country." He saw Juanton looking at him and made a face of surprise. "Oh, shit, sorry, Juanton. I forgot you bastards are on the Russian teat."

The Cuban's jaw quivered. He and Giap both looked down the table to Ho Chi.

Gearheardt stood up. "I've got to take a leak," he announced. He nodded his head at me. "You've got to take a leak too."

The bathroom was a small cell to the rear of the bar. Ancient tile with two holes in the floor. Four million gallons of pine-scented disinfectant would not have helped.

Gearheardt lit a cigarette, oblivious to the chance that the air could ignite.

"What do you think?" he asked me.

"You're asking *me*?"

"Mama-san told me that this Juanton character comes here all the time bragging about the pilots he's broken. Gives vivid details to impress the girls." He dragged heavily on his cigarette, then flipped it expertly into one of the holes. I moved back.

"I'm not making any deal with that asshole," he said.

"Why would we make a deal with the Cuban? Who the hell is he, other than what we know he is?"

Gearheardt rubbed the bridge of his nose. In the dim light from the ten-watt bulb hanging from the ceiling he looked tired. He took out his .357 and opened it, checking to see that it was fully loaded.

"He's the representative that we were supposed to meet. You know, on behalf of the 'businessmen' I told you about."

A Vietnamese soldier stumbled in the door, already fumbling at his fly. He saw Gearheardt and the pistol and hurried back out. My eyes were burning from the smell.

"Gearheardt, this is as good as time as any. What are we supposed to do?"

"NaMeara has represented to the Teamsters that he can deliver a contract on the trail haul. They want a piece of that action. They have someone's nuts in a vise, someone high up in the government—"

"Ours?" I asked, my mind skipping over the revelation that somehow a truckers' union was involved in negotiations having to do with the conduct of the Vietnam War. Before Gearheardt answered, I went on.

"Okay, of course it's ours. The Teamsters want to unionize the peasants carrying supplies down the trail?"

We heard a loud raucous roar from the bar. Gearheardt turned his head toward it and hesitated. I grabbed his arm.

"Gearheardt, is there anybody on the planet that thinks about this war in black and white, good and evil, right or wrong? Am I the one who's nuts?"

"Jack, you're the one who is hopelessly naive. That's why I like you."

"And what are you, Gearheardt? Nuts, naive, or just . . . just . . ." I waved my hands. I couldn't describe what the others, seemingly everybody, were. There was no plan. There was no fix. There was no deal. In fact, there was no war. There was a disagreement over a beer franchise. There was a union power grab. There was a political one-upmanship. There was a furniture battle in Paris. Maybe this was all about furniture.

"Jack," Gearheardt said, "when the time comes, we'll do the right thing. Okay?"

He walked out and I followed him, bumping through a dozen or so soldiers glaring at us, hands pressing their beer-bloated bladders.

She may have been an unwilling spy. Possibly a woefully misguided patriot. But when she entered the Blue Daisy, you felt the star presence. First, the buzz over the loud conversation and screeching Vietnamese jukebox. The cigarette smoke parted and there she was—Barbonella. Her reddish blond hair glowed. Her angular angelic face was art, her body luscious and full. And was she *pissed*.

Juanton rose to his feet, holding his arms to the star barreling toward him.

"Ah, my sweet Buttee. You are lovely in your . . . you are wearing *black panties? Ay caramba*. Where did you get these panties?"

"Panties? *Panties?* What in the hell did you expect me to put on? All you had was a drawer full of these damn black panties and Cuban uniforms. I'm *tired* of wearing communist uniforms. What I want to know is what happened to my clothes and where the hell you disappeared to this afternoon? It better be a good story you Latin son-of—Mr. Ho-OH, how are you, Venerable Leader?"

Hoche had come up behind Butty and goosed her. Gearheardt watched all this while snorting into his fist, barely able to contain his mirth.

Hoche calmed Butty and coached her into a seat near him.

"You rooking ve'y ruvry tonight, Butty." His English was suffering from his first six-pack.

"Buttee, did you not find hot bath pleasurable? I was returning with your clothing, but duty was calling. I am so very sorry," Juanton smiled.

Gearheardt found his opening. "Butty, there are three tank repairmen up in Dihn Nyge province that haven't slept with you. How much longer will you be in town?"

Butty's smile, as she looked up, missed Gearheardt at first and froze a cockroach on the wall behind us.

"Oh, Captain Gearheardt. How nice to see you."

"*Capitán* Gearheardt, as distasteful as it may be, I would perhaps speak to you outside. You also, *Capitán* Armstrong." Juanton stood and pushed through the crowd.

Gearheardt smiled big teeth at Butty, who smiled big teeth back. "Let's go, Jack me boy. Duty calls."

We caught up with Juanton outside the front of the bar. He stood with one foot propped on the bumper of Hoche's Corvette, lighting a small cheroot.

"I would prefer to kill you, *capitanes*. But I have business, and that is what business is about, no?"

"Brilliant," Gearheardt said. I elbowed him.

"Let us move ahead. Do you speak Spanish? It would be easier if you were fluent."

"*El gato bebe leche,*" Gearheardt said.

"Quit playing the fool, *Capitán*. Here is the offer. The war will last three more years. My clients will have the hauling contract and the beer contract, which, I might add, may not be American beer."

"And would that beer be British beer, taco face?"

"It is none of your concern. The Hoche and I are prepared to deal now, tonight, or there is no deal to be done." He threw his cheroot down, ground it with his boot, and went back into the bar.

"British beer, Gearheardt? Could this damn thing get any more confusing? I say we kill them and try to make it out of the country."

"That would be the reasonable thing to do, Jack." He looked at the ground and rubbed his chin. A thoughtful Gearheardt. "I think the commies are in with the Brits on this deal."

"No way, Gearheardt. You have a lot of crazy ideas but—"

"Jack, they have a damn special commuter train to run Brit spies over to Moscow when they defect. I'm not talking about *regular* Brit spies."

He slapped me on the shoulder. "We'll figure it out. Let's go back in."

Hilarity had broken out. Hoche was on the table, shirtless, doing a dance that was a cross between the twist and a Highland fling. He had a bra tied around his head—a big one. Giap sat muttering to himself, slumped over a beer. Juanton was smiling and clapping, egging Hoche to higher kicks and faster twirls. And topless, above borrowed black panties and totally swanked at the end of the table, sat Barbonella. Grinning, singing, and squirming on the lap of Gon Norea, he with teeth a mile wide. He had appeared at the bar in good spirits and only at half-mast. I admired his stoic acceptance of a rather debilitating run-in with the Koreans.

22 · N. VN Minh-e Fini

on Norea was in seventh heaven. At least he was in the Blue Daisy in Hanoi with a topless American movie star squirming on his lap. His only difficulty seemed to be an uncertainty about where to place his hands. He was a gentleman, no less.

Gearheardt and I had rejoined the group. The music had changed from the grating Vietnamese to screaming British and American rock. Hoche, his thin chest heaving, was holding his baggy shorts up with one hand while adjusting the 36C bra on his head with the other so that the cups fit more or less over his ears. I looked at Gearheardt and shook my head.

Giap saw my look and leaned toward me, shouting in my ear above the sounds of the Animals.

"Ho Chi let steam off."

The bar was crowded beyond capacity now. Most of the soldiers and their companions were ignoring Hoche and staring at Barbonella's admittedly luscious breasts as she clapped and sang along with the music.

When a new record started, Hoche jumped down from the table, with amazing nimbleness, and indicated that it was Barbonella's turn. Barbonella was a darn fine go-go dancer, it turned out. Certainly more attractive than Hoche. Of course, he hadn't been wearing black panties.

Back in his chair, Hoche stepped up his rhythm of lift and drink. When he finished a beer, he threw the empty bottle over his shoulder, a signal for another to be placed in front of him. Giap had moved to a chair at his side and talked unceasingly into his ear. Hoche moved to leave, but Giap kept him at the table. When Giap rose and walked by, I grabbed his arm.

"Does Hoche want to leave?" I asked, wanting to find out if we were going to get back into the cars. I had decided that I needed to do what I thought I had come to Hanoi to do.

"Ho Chi always wanting halass pilots."

"Halass the pilots? Our pilots?"

Giap grimaced at my hand on his arm and I let go.

"Throw rocks at prison. Talk loud and sing on bullhorn. Halass." He pulled away and went toward the bathroom.

Watching him walk away, I saw mama-san catch Gearheardt's eye and motion him over.

"I'll be right back," he said. "I've got a surprise cooking for our pal."

A minute later I saw Gearheardt approaching the table, leading an enormous woman. An enormous *nude* woman. He was talking into her ear and pulling her along with him, smiling broadly.

"Oh my God," I said out loud when he finally broke through the soldiers and drew up a chair for his companion.

Gearheardt grinned at me, shoving a beer in front of the Vietnamese Amazon, who sucked the liquid from the bottle and then belched.

"Is that a woman?" I asked, shouting over the Doors whining about sage. The woman was the most powerful-looking creature I had ever seen.

"Kind of," Gearheardt shouted back. He gave me a surreptitious thumbs-up, rolling his eyes toward Juanton, who was mesmerized by the swinging and swaying of untethered 36Cs. He was much less handsome with his eyes bugged out.

Gearheardt leaned close to my ear. "Legend has it she was captured by some Chinese bandits a few years ago. When her villagers caught up with them, three of the bandits were tied up in a pile, scared shitless and whimpering. The Gorilla Girl was squatting next to a fire, gnawing on a thigh bone and turning a spit, roasting another one of the bandits." He chuckled.

I froze as a huge hand reached up and roughly pinched my cheek.

"She likes you, Jack." Gearheardt chuckled again. "Mama-san used to use her as a bouncer, but she won't wear clothes, and she scared the crap out of the customers."

I rubbed my cheek and tried to look inedible. "I can't imagine why," I said as I gingerly pulled the hand away from my face.

Gearheardt positioned himself one chair away from Juanton with the Gorilla Girl between them. Juanton seemed to be trying to ignore them both, although he would occasionally look with disbelief at the girl and then quickly back to Butty.

Our circle was complete when Whiffenpoof arrived. He looked unsteady and glassy-eyed. I had seen the look in people drifting out of opium rooms in Saigon. Whiff peeled one of the Vietnamese girls off of Hoche and took a chair at his side. The girl hurried away, and Hoche gave Whiffenpoof a sour look, then busied himself with the remaining girl.

The music began to slow down, as if the Mamas and the Papas were drowning in molasses. Then the jukebox emitted an electronic belch and a bright flash of light and went dead. Barbonella jumped from the table and sat back down. A T-shirt was offered her, but she declined with a shake of her head, and breasts, that looked more arrogance than exhibitionism. She *was* a stunning creature.

Giap had returned and began nghing, nying, and presumably spitting in Hoche's ear, the one that wasn't being used by Whiffenpoof. Gon Norea was sulking behind his beer bottle, staring hungrily at Barbonella. Juanton was turned in his chair now, half-facing Gorilla Girl, who was picking something from the plastic tablecloth and nibbling it. Gearheardt was into a hard sell to Juanton over God knew what. As I watched, Juanton pushed his chair back from the table and led Gorilla Girl away, over loud—and, I presumed, fake—protests from Gearheardt, who grinned at me and gave me an "okay" signal with his thumb and forefinger. He motioned for me to lean across the table.

In my ear he said, "Listen closely and you can hear the sound of a man getting his nuts caught in a grinder." He laughed.

"How did you—"

"Mama-san's a spy. Works for us," he whispered. "Been promised a major whorehouse in Saigon and stock options."

"Of course." For once I didn't doubt him.

He started to lean back away from me into his chair. I grabbed his flight suit at the collar.

"Gearheardt, I'm doing it." More than anything, I wanted out of the madhouse bar.

"I'm with you, Jack."

"We'll never get out of here."

"War is hell, Jack. Can't live forever. Gotta break some eggs—"

"What about her?" Barbonella was holding her beer glass toward the stage spotlight and pointing out a spot on her beer glass to the intimidated waitress.

"She really can be a bitch, can't she?" Gearheardt said wistfully. He turned back to me. "An A-4 was shot down today."

"You think she—"

"Couldn't find her ass with both hands. But she was willing to try." He looked back at Butty. "Puts her over the line in my book. Good tits, though."

He paused, then said, "Here's what we do. When Geepster goes— What the hell is going on down there now?"

A commotion at the end of the table brought Giap to his feet. He was obviously trying to talk Hoche out of something. Hoche had the fixed grin of a drunk man. He looked directly at Gearheardt and me, his eyes unfocused and twinkling at the same time.

"Have fun now. You listen." The bar had quieted except for Butty loudly berating the mama-san who had been called over to mediate the dirty-beer-glass dispute.

A long wire was brought to the table with much jabbering and gesturing by animated soldiers, each anxious to do well for their leader. A wooden box was placed on the table and the wire attached to a connection protruding from its end. Whiff rose from his chair next to Hoche, shook his head with his mouth fixed in disgust, and headed for the bar.

A speaker device was attached to the other end of the box. Hoche arranged the speaker with the concentration of an inebriated man, then flipped a switch. A dial tone was heard for a moment and then a ring. The phone device rang ten more times until the smile left Hoche's face. Just as he angrily reached for the box a voice was heard.

"—lo."

Hoche stifled his laughter with a hand over his mouth and motioned for everyone else to do the same. The voice came on again.

"Hello-o?" It was clearer.

Hoche leaned over until his lips almost touched the bulbous microphone.

"Here Prince Albert." He sat back giggling.

"What? What in the hell? Who's this here I'm talking to?"

Hoche leaned in again. "Prince Albert here."

Groans and mechanical squeaks. A throat cleared.

"Aw for chrissakes. Ho, you little turd, the joke is supposed to be that you say 'Do you have Prince Albert in a can?' You're not supposed to *be* Prince Albert. I might goddam point out that you're not supposed to use the hot line to make joke calls either."

Hoche's smile turned watery. I thought about Gearheardt telling me of his first meeting with the President in the White House, when he, Gearheardt, was a CIA pizza man and the President supposedly didn't even know where the hell Vietnam was.

"Mr. President, your bombing is only making things worse. In my opinion—"

"Who in the hell is that?" The President sounded alert now.

It was Butty, who, upon hearing the President, had rushed to the end of the table. She leaned toward the microphone.

"You know damn well who I am, Mr. President."

The President's voice came through weaker, as if he were holding the phone away from his mouth.

"Dammit, this is presidentin' business. Quit listenin' in."

Whiffenpoof now came hurriedly back to the table.

"Mr. President, your men claim no knowledge of the agreement that you promised. I must demand that—"

"Jumpin' Jehoshophat! *Now who in the hell is this?* What happened to Ho Chi?"

"America all die! You send many more men. Kill all. Never mind. Imperialist learn lesson nothing. Beat French, beat—"

"Fuck America!" This from the Russians, who had joined the crowd around the speaker.

"ROOSKIES! I'd know you sonsabitches from anywhere. If this isn't the party line from hell. Let me tell you a thing or two, you commie—"

"PresiLarry Bob!"

"Gear—Narsworthy! Don't tell me you're on this damn line too!" The President's voice became faint. "I *SAID* get your ass out if you can't let me do a little work here." Then stronger again. "Now, Narsworthy, what in the old Blue Billy heck is goin' on over there? Speak to me, son."

"Everything's under control, Mr. Larry Bob."

An ear-splitting scream from above us temporarily quieted the room.

Giap recovered first. "America all finish. We kill all soldier," he sputtered.

"Mr. President, the peace-loving people of—" Butty yelled.

"I have to tell you, sir, in all honesty, that the Guinness people have contacted me." Whiffenpoof was whining.

"Babe Ruth eat shit!"

"Will somebody *please* shoot that goddam Rooskie?" the President demanded.

"Mr. President, sir, I have to run upstairs for just a moment," Gearheardt said.

"Have you people gone plumb loco over there? Put that damn Ho Chi back on. I'll bomb his ass from here to Sunday before I'll take this kind of crap. Hold on a minute. Woman, I'm tellin you one last time. This ain't her. I ain't seen her since Denver, and if you hit me in the back one more time, the Secret Service will be in here so fast it'll make your head swim. Okay, boys, where were we?"

"You big nose bully man!" Giap yelled toward the microphone. It sounded like "U be no burry man," but I was beginning to understand his pidgin English.

Gearheardt came back in the middle of another tirade from Giap. The President was humming loudly into the phone.

"I can't *hear* you. Hmmdehmmmdededum. Can't hear a word you're *sayin*."

Gearheardt nudged Giap aside. "I wish to report that we are going Plan B immediately. Deep code, you understand, Mr. President."

"If that's the one where we shoot the shit out of everone in sight I do."

Gearheardt and I looked at one another and around the table.

"Roger that, Larry Bob." Gearheardt spoke low, his mouth close to the speaker.

Whiffenpoof turned from his animated argument with one of the Russians over vodka prices.

"It was never proved," Whiffenpoof moaned to no one in particular.

"What in the hell are you talking about, Whiffenpoof?" Gearheardt asked, never one to let a world crisis interfere with an opportunity to rub salt into the wound of an enemy.

"You know very well, Gearheardt. The Denver beer family isn't going to let a franchise go to someone who—who has deviated from the sexual norms."

"*Now who was it that brought up Denver?* I'm gettin mighty pissed here. Little woman comes outta the john and hears me talking Denver and my ass is grass. Next call I make is the United States Navy orderin up some serious bombin, I hear any more of that talk."

"There is a family that sells something that makes men want to try to piss across a road and drive into trees, and they won't let homosexuals sell it? Is that what I heard?" Butty stood with her hands on her hips, disgusted at the hypocrisy.

"I'll thank you to keep your questions to yourself, Miss Show Your Breasts All Over Town." Whiffenpoof was almost crying.

"Is Nixon with you? Is that Nixon talking? Goddammit, this better not be the Republicans pullin' my chain on the Hanoi hotline."

"No, Mr. President. This is Almost Captain Armstrong. Gearheardt and I want to say that it's been an honor serving you and our country. Sometimes it has seemed—"

"Could you make it snappy, Captain? I got about five sonsabitches on the line I need to kill."

Gon Norea grabbed the microphone to complain about the British taking ten percent off the top of his spying pay. He was C-shaped by now. Giap began a shouting match with Barbonella over her lack of respect for the Vietnamese women, something about tits.

A gunshot one-upped the cacophony of screaming, demanding, whining, and political discussions. I ducked behind the Russians. Juanton was at the bottom of the stairway, clutching his crotch in one hand and a large pistol in the other. He continued to fire wildly, the pain evidently blinding.

Half of the bar patrons unholstered their weapons. Some began firing into the roof. The bar-women were screaming. The midgets had revived Cyclopa and were helping her to her feet, their beady eyes wide with fear. Uncle Sam was holding a large Bowie knife.

"What in the goddamned Sam Hill is going on over there, people? Gearheardt, you better answer me, boy."

Everyone screamed at the microphone at the same time. Except for Geepster, who took aim and blasted it to kingdom come. There was moment's silence, and then sound exploded to a new and painful level.

Meanwhile, Gon had pulled out the elastic band of the raving Butty's panties and was leering at her butt. He caught my eye and grinned. A soldier slugged him, and he fell into Geepster, who turned and whacked the soldier, which set off a chain reaction of slugging. Uncle Sam was slashing at knees to beat the band.

I saw Hoche slouched over the table, muttering into the top of a beer bottle. He was why I had come to Hanoi, and he was why I was still sitting in this crappy bar. I lifted him to his feet and began walking him to the door. He was light as a feather and didn't resist.

The street was deserted. In the darkness I could just make out Hoche's Corvette. I walked him to it, opened the driver's side door, and dumped him behind the wheel. The car seemed to be the final thumb in the eye of the American soldier. Behind me I heard the bar door open and I drew my 9mm PPK. It felt good to finally have it in my hand.

Gearheardt marched toward me, Giap in front of him. He had a giant pistol firmly against the back of the fuming general's head.

Gearheardt leaned down, "Tell me about 'kill all America,' you little shit."

"Colonialism all dead. America live memory. Think France. Think British."

"Think dead, you murdering bastard," Gearheardt said as he dragged him toward the yellow Mustang, evidently feeling as I did about the communists' use of American sports cars. "You're going to get to be one of those millions of your countrymen that you don't mind losing." He opened the door of the car and forced Giap into the backseat.

I heard someone scream "New seatcovers never mind" just as Hoche began to stir. My pistol bothered his temple, and he brushed at it with a weak hand.

"I Prince Alber' *his* can. Give me phone. I Tet his ass to Sunday." His opened his eyes. They were cold as a reptile's. "No shoot me. Take Butty back. Go home."

His head dropped again and, after a large belch, he threw up in his beard. I put my pistol back against his temple.

I had a vision of the 9mm slug entering the chamber as I began to squeeze the trigger. "Tet his ass" zinged around my schizoid cranium.

Nothing clicked. No bouncing ball settled in a red or black pocket. I should have a vision of this act meaning something, accomplishing something.

When I looked up, Gearheardt was backing out of the Mustang, holding Giap's long pistol. Fire jumped at least a foot from the end of the barrel. I heard a scream from the backseat. Gearheardt fired twice more. Then he calmly pointed the pistol at the hood of the Mustang and pulled the trigger three times. He tossed the pistol into the car through the window and turned to me, smiling.

"Is this fun?" he asked.

The door to the Blue Daisy burst open, and one of the Russians rushed out. His wide, ugly tie glowed in the thin light of the Hanoi street. I aimed my pistol at the tie.

"Not so fast, Captain. Unless you don't want a ride to the airport."

"Gunny! Where in the hell did you get that tie?" Gearheardt yelled.

"Gon Norea isn't going to be able to hold everybody in there much longer, Captains. I suggest we didi our asses over to his Fiat and get!" He grabbed my arm and began pulling me along. As we passed the Corvette, he looked through the windshield, and looked back at me for just a moment. Gon's shitty little pretend car was parked across the street. I felt like clowns at a circus as we all tried to get in at once. The engine sputtered and coughed and we pulled away. White smoke, or steam, rose from the hood of the Mustang. I couldn't see the Corvette from my spot in the backseat of the Fiat and I really didn't want to look.

The door to the Blue Daisy burst open. All three of us turned and pointed our guns. But it was Cyclopa, a midget under each arm. She ran toward the car.

"Take midgets. Take midgets to America," she yelled.

The Fiat engine screamed and we rocketed up to about twenty-five miles an hour, leaving her in our exhaust. She dropped the midgets and extended her finger. Uncle Sam threw his Bowie knife. It clanged in the dark street behind us.

"I don't want to complain, Gunny, but weren't there any other cars you might have chosen?" Gearheardt asked.

The gunny laughed. "Not to worry, Captain. The aircraft we're taking isn't going to leave without us." He looked back at me and then back to the road. "The fix is in. My Russian buddies have taken care of everything. They're back there holding your friends at bay for you. And I got the vodka franchise from Singapore to Vientiane. By the way, you *can* fly an Ilyushin, can't you? Old twin-engine job. I'm not sure what model it is. I don't know much about airplanes."

"They haven't made a plane I can't get airborne, Gunny. Who are these Russians—"

"Gunny, what will happen to Barbonella?" If Gearheardt didn't care, I did. Somehow we were supposed to be part of her plan. Now she was half dressed in a crap bar after midnight in Hanoi surrounded by North Vietnamese, treacherous Cubans, and a sexually confused, beer-franchise-deprived Brit.

Gearheardt spoke up before the gunny replied. "I think Gon has his nose sufficiently up her butt, Jack. Or she may marry the Second Regiment of the People's Army."

"Don't go all sentimental on me, Gearheardt. I'm just saying, you insensitive prick, that we might have—"

Gearheardt turned around in the seat. In the dark I couldn't see his face. "Jack, I'm just saying that no one is going to shoot prime tits and twat if she plays her cards right. She knows how to take care of herself." He turned back to the front.

"Uhh-hmm." I was beginning to get deeply depressed as I watched and listened to Gearheardt work himself up to highly manic. If he'd had one, Gearheardt would have lit up a large cigar. If I'd been a real CIA agent, I would've been chewing on a cyanide pill. I had accomplished exactly nothing.

As we approached the Hanoi airport I was dimly aware of Gunny Buckles filling Gearheardt in on his adventures in Hanoi. He had been able to play the visiting Russian very easily, as the Asians were not quick to question Westerners who seemed to have a purpose in

Hanoi. The Russians that the gunny had hooked up with really didn't give a damn one way or another.

The airport was lightly guarded. The gunny had no trouble getting the little car through the gate and up to the side of the aircraft. As Gearheardt and I climbed aboard, the gunny hung back.

"Get in, Gunny!" I yelled as we made our way to the cockpit. I scrambled into the co-pilot's seat beside Gearheardt and stuck my head out of the small side window. "What do you think you're doing? Get in here!"

I saw the gunny give a lazy salute. As the engines popped and sputtered alive under the expert hand of Gearheardt, the gunny smiled and began directing us with his arms, indicating the way to the runway. He yelled something that was lost as Gearheardt gave power to the engines and we began to roll.

"Can you tell what he's saying, Gearheardt?"

"He said, 'See you in Danang.' He already told me that he didn't want to go to the Philippines with us."

"Is that where we're heading? The Philippines?"

"Promised the President that no matter what, we'd meet him in the Cave Bar in Olongopo. He's probably got his fat ass, no disrespect intended, on Air Force One right now." He was comfortable in the cockpit of the small Russian cargo aircraft, flicking switches and turning dials as we taxied to the runway. He brought the hand mike to his mouth as we turned onto the end of the runway.

"Hanoi tower, Narsworthy One requests permission for an immediate takeoff from your pissant country. Sayonara, motherfuckers." He applied full power and we were airborne before we reached the middle of the field, our wheels barely clearing a flatbed truck carrying Brits, tits, midgets, five-foot generals, a Cuban in a Kotex, and an old man with puke in his beard. They were firing every imaginable weapon at us.

I felt sad as I watched the frustrated Cyclopa hold the midgets toward us. Why did she want to get rid of two perfectly good Chinese midgets so bad?

Gearheardt was elated. "Man the gunnels, men, they're loading the M-6 Midget Launcher." He laughed. "Nam-a-rama!"

Which I suppose was about right.

We made a climbing right turn into the dawn showing on the eastern horizon. But instead of leveling off, Gearheardt continued the turn until we were heading back to the field. He shoved the nose of the airplane over and dove at the tower, pulling up at the last moment just as we saw little people abandoning the tower platform.

Then we made another hard turn and headed east, Gearheardt trimming and adjusting as he taught himself the vagaries of the ancient communist aircraft.

"You sitting on your hands all morning, Jack, or do you want to give me some help here? See if you can find any kind of manual. A map would be helpful. Take your mind off your troubles."

I searched the cockpit, went back into the cabin, returned and strapped in. "Not much," I said.

We leveled off at ten thousand feet. Gearheardt set the engines at cruise power, gently manipulating them until their roar was without audible conflict.

After a few minutes, I let out the breath I had been holding ever since I had grabbed Hoche and dragged him out of the club.

"I didn't kill him, you know."

Gearheardt made a minor adjustment and listened to the engines for a moment.

"Yep, I know."

I looked at him. "What do you mean you know? Gearheardt, you bastard—"

"Take a look at your PPK, Jack. Pull back the slide and tell me if you see a firing pin. I assume when Whiffer brought back our weapons, they had already been fixed."

"But, how did you . . . when did you—"

"I found out just before you went off half-cocked and grabbed old Hoche. Figured if I'd yelled at you that your pistol wasn't working, that might have been a little embarrassing. So I just grabbed that Number One Vietnam Hero and followed you out." Gearheardt looked over at me and grinned. "Not much for planning are you, Jack?"

I was hardly listening, trying to figure out what I had done. Gearheardt went on.

"I took the old pistola from Number One Vietnam Hero, so I could back you up."

Silence in the cockpit except for the comforting rumble of the engines. I felt sick to my stomach. I wanted a cigarette.

"So you just wasted Giap and let Hoche go? Why would you do that if you knew I couldn't kill him?"

Gearheardt made more maddeningly minor engine adjustments. Ahead of us the coast appeared below, the new sun touching the white edge of the shore.

"Nope. I didn't kill him." I couldn't tell from his voice what he was feeling, regret or remorse. "Never does your career any good to put a bullet in someone's head," he went on. "Not up close, anyway."

He looked toward me. "I made him shit himself though. That first round went between his legs. Then I blew a couple of holes in his white Naugahyde interior. He won't be tear-assing around Hanoi with that engine either." He paused. "I probably *should* have shot the little commie. No right to drive a Boss Mustang."

The ocean below us was dark, whitecaps only visible where the rising sun broke through the high clouds here and there. Gearheardt put the aircraft in a gentle right turn, heading south toward clearer weather and supposedly friendlier shores. The sun rose to a height that gave gold to the billowing clouds on the horizon.

Finally Gearheardt spoke. "Did you pull the trigger, Jack?" When I didn't answer or look at him, he continued, as if he didn't want to hear my answer. "Wouldn't have made any difference you know. And no one knows but you."

I opened my mouth to say something but closed it again. Gearheardt reached out and tapped the glass on the sticking engine heat gauge, then flipped open the cowling door to cool the engine more. He watched the gauge and after a moment, flipped closed the cowling switch. He leaned back in his seat.

"Jack, I know you like a book. You're sitting over there wondering if you did your duty. Aren't you? Were you prepared to kill Hoche for your country? That's what you're thinking."

It wasn't. I wasn't sure that Gearheardt would understand, but what I had really been thinking was, "Screw the bastards who wanted me to kill Ho Chi Minh and take the fall. No one had the balls to just tell me to kill him. And he had asked us to call him Hoche."

Gearheardt leaned toward me and pointed ahead and down. It was an aircraft carrier. From our position we could see the launch of jets from its deck. I searched the sky and found the fighters that had already launched were bending in a shallow turn so the wingmen could join up. Against the low sun a flight of four Phantoms climbed toward us. The sun hit their wings and flashed against the dark water. The best fighter pilots in the world.

A second pig flew out of Gearheardt's nose as he said, *"C'est magnifique mais ce n'est pas la guerre."*

I found my sunglasses in my jacket pocket and put them on before I turned and raised my eyebrows to him.

"Marshall Bosquet on the self-destruction of the British at the Charge of the Light Brigade," Gearheardt said.

For a moment I wondered if the Phantoms would rise up to shoot us down. Certainly the airborne command ship had us on radar and had tracked us out of North Vietnam. I was calm. I didn't care, for one thing, and I figured if I mentioned it to Gearheardt he would say, "The fix is in."

"This was a hell of a scheme you and the President cooked up, Gearheardt."

"Jack, this little twerp country doesn't even have toilet paper. And they need to keep their commie hands off of Saigon. Remember that. Hoche couldn't leave well enough alone after the 'Frog feast.'"

I rested my boot on the instrument panel, leaned back in my

uncomfortable Russian chair and closed my eyes, daring myself to think about what lurked behind my lids.

Gearheardt spoke to me. "You want to take it, Jack?"

I shook my head. I wanted to think. I wanted to fully plumb the depths of my failures and insecurities. "No, thanks, Gearheardt. I'll just let you keep it for a while."

"Well, I was kind of hoping you knew how to get us to the Philippines."

23 · Sucker-punched by the Pres

*I*t's because she showers in her underpants, Jack," Gearheardt said. He held out his hands and wrinkled his brow as if everybody should know that.

"I still don't get it," I said. "Why would that make her the most popular girl in the bar?" forgetting that I was the one that had started the story in the first place.

The bars in Olongopo are considered by most military pilots to be among the most dangerous in the world. Gearheardt and I sat in the Cave sipping whiskey and watching the women. We had resolved not to indulge in womanizing, a promise that we made to ourselves when we were lost and running out of fuel in a thunderstorm over the South China Sea. We had also given up smoking, swearing, wearing loud socks, and talking ill of our superiors. In fact we had finally told God that if He would make a list appear in front of us, we would sign it without hesitation. When a list *didn't* appear and we broke out of the storm and found the Cubi Point Naval Base in the Philippines, Gearheardt argued that the absence of a list was a sign from God that we were on our own and there was no deal. I finally got him to agree that we would not sin until after we met with the President. The whiskey was medicinal, Gearheardt successfully argued, since he didn't really like it, but just used it to get inebriated.

The Shore Patrol treated us with some suspicion after we landed. In fact, before we landed they threatened to shoot us out of the landing pattern. We called their bluff and made a reasonably good landing in the Russian airplane, taking out a row of runway lights and smashing into the fire truck, which helped slow us considerably after we found out that the Russians evidently didn't believe in airplane brakes.

We left the base commander with a seriously throbbing temple vein. If Gearheardt hadn't tried to pay for the damage to the fire truck with a bundle of North Vietnamese dong he found in our airplane, the interview might have been shorter.

"I'll bet I can make him cry," Gearheardt whispered to me as we were being led by a band of burly seamen into the base commander's office.

He did. After jacking the poor guy around for a few minutes, Gearheardt requested a phone and got someone in the Pentagon to confirm that the President of the United States was meeting us in the Cave Bar, on his way to meet the president of South Korea. The Pentagon only knew because they had a flight plan for Air Force One, and they had loaded a case of nylons and lipstick on it, the President being from another era. It was during the discussion of where one would find nylons that the base commander more or less lost control. He seemed already a bit nervous about the President visiting his base. Careers are lost over lesser issues than the President getting clapped up or into a bar fight while under your jurisdiction.

"Just get out of my sight," the captain said finally, dropping his head in his hands. Gearheardt wanted to wait around to hear him sob, but I pulled him away.

Tiptoeing up to the edge of our resolve while waiting for the President to show up, Gearheardt had asked the mama-san to point out the most popular girl. The girl was chubby, had frizzy black hair, beady eyes, and interior lineman legs. Her name was, the best I could make out, something like Lizzado.

"What do you think he'll say?" I asked Gearheardt. "Do you think he knows what happened?"

"Who? The President? Who knows? He's kind of a pisser. Not a bad guy really. Likes his troops."

"But—"

"Jack, the day after we left Hanoi, the North Vietnamese attacked every damned city in South Vietnam. The President has bigger problems than what the hell to do with us."

"But Hoche, I mean Ho Chi Minh, attacked them *because* of us."

"We don't know that. They might have been planning that all along. Devious little bastards, you know. Table shape, my ass."

"But don't you think—"

"JACK! Damn it! Stop worrying about shit you can't change. We went, we saw, we fucked up. Forget it. Relax. Have another whiskey. *Mama-san, dos whiskeys, por favor.*"

I did relax. Or at least did my best impression of it. I looked around the darkened room. I tried to imagine the marketing meeting where the entrepreneurs of Olongopo discussed the merits of serving alcohol to U.S. servicemen sitting in a cave. It was lost on me. But it was a very popular bar.

I looked up from my sorrows to see two black-suited men staring down at me.

"Are you Almost Captains Armstrong and Gearheardt?" the taller one asked. He had a wimpy mustache and acne scars.

"Who's asking?" Gearheardt replied.

Two wallets appeared. "U.S. Secret Service. I'll ask you again, sirs. Are you Almost Captains Arm—"

"Yes, yes, don't mind him. I'm Armstrong and that's Gearheardt. Are you from the President? Is he here?"

"That's not for me to say, sir."

Both agents turned away. In a loud voice the taller one said, "I'll have to ask you all to immediately leave the bar. Mama-san, please get those girls out of here. I don't care where you take them. This place is off-limits until further notice."

He turned back to Gearheardt and me as his partner helped shoo the women, a few patrons, and the bartender out the back of the club.

When the bar was empty except for the four of us, one of the agents went to the front door and stood by it. Almost immediately the door was opened and the President of the United States strode into the room, grinning from ear to ear. He wore a Hawaiian shirt, khakis, and sandals.

The grin fell quickly to disappointment and then to pretty pissed off, if I knew my grins.

"Where in the Blue Billy Hell *is* everybody?" the President asked. His huge jowls closely followed the face he swung around the room, his eyes blinking as they adjusted to the semidarkness.

The senior Secret Service agent stepped forward. Three aides to the President had now followed him into the bar. They stood blinking in their dark jackets, identical attaché cases in their hands.

"The bar is secure, Mr. President," the agent said confidently.

"Well, son," the President said, beginning slowly, "do you think that I flew eleven thousand miles over here so I could set in a goddam bar with a papier-mâché stalagmite up my ass—and no women?! You ain't got the sense God gave a chicken. Get them women back in here, and get somebody behind that bar. Hell, son, the kind of folks that want to do harm to the President don't hang around Olongopo *bars*, for Chrissakes. Now, get on with it." He grabbed the stunned agent and spun him around. Then he turned to his aides.

"You boys spread out and watch my back. Soon as I say there ain't nobody in here wants to harm me, some idiot will shoot me and I'll look like a fool."

He looked at Gearheardt and me for the first time. We were standing at attention beside our table.

"Well, what have we here?" The President ambled over, a smile on his face that wouldn't have cheered the sick. "Is this my old friend Gearheardt? I believe it is."

I could smell bay rum aftershave.

"And this must be Lieutenant, excuse me, Almost Captain Armstrong." I wouldn't have thought it possible, but his smile became colder.

"Yes, sir, Mr. President," I said.

"Oh, you don't have to be so formal, boy, does he, Gearheardt? What say we all sit down and have us a drink." The aides scrambled to pull a chair up to the table where Gearheardt and I had been sitting. Seconds earlier and the President would have sat on thin air.

"Oh, lookee here. Hello ladies." A crowd of people including maybe twenty bar-girls was streaming back into the club. The patrons followed and the room was transformed. A Filipino band began playing a Beatles song. The President watched them and hummed along with them while a glass of whiskey and ice was placed in front of him. He took and raised it. We raised our glasses.

"Here's to success, boys. God knows I need some." He drank deeply from the glass, blew out breath, and then wiped his mouth with the back of his hand. He raised his glass again and we followed. "And here's to that son-of-a-bitch Ho Chi and that Gip fellow."

He drank again, and a waiter appeared and refilled his glass. I wasn't prepared for how subdued Gearheardt remained. No wisecracks. No PresiLarry Bobs.

"I suppose you boys don't know the latest."

We both shook our heads.

"Son of a bitch up and died this morning. Rotten little bastard."

"Who, sir? Ho Chi Minh?" I asked.

The President looked at me like I was retarded. "Naw, I'm talking about Mortimer Snerd. Of course I meant Ho Chee, the old boy you were supposed to make a deal with."

He slammed his glass down on the table. "Now what the hell

happened and it better be good. Couldn't you boys follow a simple plan? Do I have to do ever' damn thing myself in this country?"

"Sir, we tried to—"

"Tried don't get the hogs slaughtered, boy."

"Sir, Captain Gearheardt and I received some conflicting orders, and also—"

"What the hell is that supposed to mean, conflicting orders? Let me call one of my aides over here and see if I ain't still President. Co-mander in Chief last time I read the constitution or that other deal. Shit-fire, son, did you try to make a deal with him *or not*? I got about twenty-five hundred lepers floating around on Navy boats, and I per-sonally guaranteed a damn condo loan. Wasn't like I didn't give you boys a hell of a hand to deal."

"He wouldn't go for the Molokai deal, Mr. Larry Bob." Gear-heardt said.

"Oh, he wouldn't, would he? Mr. High and Mighty wouldn't trade a few shit-covered rice paddies for a hundred and seventy five miles of beachfront?" He paused and looked at the go-go dancers, all of whom were watching him as they gyrated on their little platforms.

Gearheardt was fully engaged. "Sir, we offered him just what you suggested. We were kind of playing him along, you know. I think he was about to go for it but that damned Geepster—"

"Am I supposed to know who the hell 'Geepster' is?"

"I mean Giap, Mr. President. Anyway he barged in, and Hoche, I mean Ho Chi Minh, kind of gave us the signal that the Geepster wasn't in on the deal. We had agreed to meet again the next day and I think that we'd of struck a deal. I really do."

"Mr. President—" I began.

He turned on me sternly. "This better not be some of that whinin' you're famous for, Armstrong."

"No, sir. I was just going to ask what difference it would have made if we had struck a deal. I mean since he's dead anyway, wouldn't we be right where we are now?"

The President scrooched up his lips like he was trying to control a harsh reply. "You got State Department experience, son? You sound like some of those pointyheads over there in Foggy Bottom." He squared himself around in his chair so that he was facing me. "If you'd of made a deal it would have been binding even if he dropped dead on the spot. He might have been a raggedy-assed commie leader of a pissant country, but he *was* President. I know a bit about presidentin', you might notice, and that's the way these things work. If he gave the word to those boys in Paris, and I know he wouldn't have wasted no time doin' that, then wham bam we got ourselves a real peace talk. And I got me an election that I might have a chance to win. Way it is now, I ain't got a chance in old Billy heck unless the Republicans dig up the corpse of Joe Stalin to run against me. Hell, my boys tell me I can't even beat Nixon! Lord, what is this world comin' to?"

Against my better judgment I had to continue. "But I still don't see what or how—"

"Goddamm it, son, do I have to sit here in this bar and be fussed at by a Marine almost captain? The day I let soldiers tell me how to run a damn war is the day Flipper marries the Pope." He drained his glass. "Anybody got a decent cigar around here?"

Gearheardt jumped in. "Jack means no disrespect, sir. He is kind of a worrier. Likes all the little details crossed and dotted. He was just—"

"See if those Mexicans know 'Sentimental Journey,' John," the President said to a hovering aide.

"Filipinos, Mr. President. I'll check for you, sir."

"Filipinos? They look like Mexicans. 'Cept these boys play real well. None of that 'Cucaracha' shit." He rose up in his chair and clapped his huge hands head high. "Nice goin', boys!" he yelled above the noise of the bar.

He turned back to Gearheardt and me, face sober. "Now, for the sixty-four-dollar question. Why in the hell didn't you boys shoot him? I didn't hire myself a couple of pussy boys, did I?"

I raised half out of my chair. *"Shoot him? Did you say shoot him?"*

Gearheardt grabbed my arm and pulled me back into the chair. The President didn't change expressions. I leaned across the table toward him. I could feel myself shaking. My voice was a low growl that caused the President to tilt back in his chair and catch the eye of one of the Secret Service men.

"Weren't we just getting our asses chewed out for *not* making a deal with him? Wasn't that what we were just talking about fifteen seconds ago? Goddammit! Before I die I would just like for someone to give me a straight answer. *Were we supposed to shoot him or make a deal with him?"* I stopped, panting from stress and anger.

The President studied his fingernails. He raised his eyebrows at Gearheardt now, who shrugged. Finally he took a deep breath and blew it out at his chest.

"You through, son?" He looked up at me. "Let me tell you a little story about a chicken my daddy gave me to raise once. Seems it had two—"

"I don't want to hear about a damn chicken. I don't want to hear about your damn childhood or your daddy or about *anything else!* There is a war going on and my pals are fighting it. I've had it, Mr. President. No, don't make excuses for me, Gearheardt. And tell that Secret Service man if he comes one step closer I'll ram that pistol up his asshole if I can figure out which end it's on." I slumped back in my chair, feeling beaten, exhausted.

"—so my daddy said, son, either way the chicken is going to be dead, and you don't lay eggs." The President looked at me. "I'll ask you one more time, son. Are you about through?"

I weakly shook my head.

"Plan B was for you to shoot the son-of-a-bitch which—don't interrupt, I know he's dead—would have thrown the Vietnamese into such a tizzy that they would have done something stupid and we'd have bombed them into the by-God Stone Age."

Gearheardt was drawing circles on the tabletop with his swizzle stick. He looked embarrassed. For me or for the President?

I closed my eyes and spoke softly. "With all due respect, sir. Ho Chi Minh *is* dead. The North Vietnamese *have* launched a stupid military initiative. The North Vietnamese *live* in the stone age."

"And who gets the credit, Mr. Smart-ass Almost Captain? Who gets the credit?" After a moment he squinted his eyes and looked directly at me. "A little birdie told me you couldn't pull the trigger anyhow. Is that right, son?"

I sat up straight and looked at Gearheardt, but he looked as shocked as I felt.

"But I—I—it was the weapon, my pistol—"

"That's what the military always says." He raised his voice and mocked, "But we don't have the right weapons. Not our fault. Hmmmph." He gave a dismissive wave of his hand. "And if puttin' up with those prima donnas weren't bad enough, I got ever' news hack in the world runnin' around takin' pictures and discoverin' that people get killed in wars. Now there's a flash for you. And the *hippies*! You know any hippies, son? They think old Ho Chi's gonna give up if we just talk nice to him. That's 'fore he's dead, of course. They think we can just sit over here and screw our sisters and smoke marywanna and the Rooskies, and Chinese, and North Koreans, and Cubans and everbody else with a bug up his butt 'bout the United States will just go their merry way and we'll all have a peace-in or some shit. How'd you like to walk into the Oval Office ever mornin' and have so many situations that you don't know whether to shit or go blind?" He snorted and craned his head around. "John, what in the hell does a man have to do to get some women over here?"

His aide hurried over, escorting the mama-san, who was dressed in her Sunday best. She snapped her fingers and five Filipino girls quickly appeared in front of our table. A grinning President stood up and shook the hand of each. "Howdy, ladies."

He kept his grin wide as he leaned behind the five and spoke to the mama-san. "Fine, fine. You got anything with tits?" He held his hands out six inches from his chest.

The mama-san lowered her head in shame and snapped her fingers again. Five more girls replaced the five in front of us. The President was gazing around the bar. His eyes landed on Lizzado. She was sitting in a chair by the ladies' room, cleaning her toenails with a sliver of bamboo. Her bare-midriff blouse exposed multiple rolls of fat protruding as she bent over to reach her toes.

"What about that young lady there?" the President asked.

His aides, the Secret Service men, and the mama-san were momentarily speechless.

I stood up. "I'm afraid that one's mine, Mr. President. That's Lizzado." I lowered my voice and spoke confidentially into his ear. "She showers in her underpants." Lieutenant Riggens had told a story about a fat girl in the Cave Bar who insisted she shower before getting into bed with a customer. But she wouldn't take her underpants off. For no reason at all, she became an object of my desire. And I needed to not let the President win every round. After all, it was him who had sent Gearheardt and me to Hanoi on the lunatic excursion.

The President swung around to face me. He was a big man. He set his jaw tight and I saw it begin to quiver. "Jack," he said reasonably, "I got just a bit more info for you and Gearheardt. You ain't Marines anymore. The CIA figured out that you boys are also Dexter and Narsworthy, and they got you under contract." He smiled. "I fixed it with the chiefs over at the Pentagon so you boys will be flying in Lay-ohs from now on. And I do mean now on. They got a little piddly-assed war goin' over there, and you boys will fit right in."

Gearheardt was on his feet. "But Mr. President, what about my career?"

"Same as mine, son. Shit."

He was looking back at Lizzado. She smiled at him and patted a frizz or two back into place on her head. She was missing a tooth in front. Remembering, she held her chubby hand in front of her mouth.

"Jack," the President said, "you and Gearheardt should know that I don't have no hard feelings. I've screwed up a time or two myself.

'Course this will be the first war I screwed up, but that's no never-mind of yours. You boys be careful."

He stuck out his hand. After a moment I reached for it. "Well, sir, it may seem—"

He coldcocked me with a roundhouse right to my jaw.

When I woke up Gearheardt and the mama-san were kneeling beside me. Someone had put a seat cushion under my head, which hurt like a bastard. They gave me aspirin and told me that the President had left with Lizzado in the presidential limo. Gearheardt and I were to have our asses on an airplane to Danang in one hour and from there we would go to Vientiane, Laos. In the taxi back to the airfield, the driver told us that the U.S. forces had killed more North Vietnamese in the last two days than in all the time since the war had begun. I felt good about that.

Then he told me that the U.S. Congress had declared the war officially insane and demanded the U.S. pull out of the war because the North Vietnamese refused to fight fair. The Pentagon revised their official body count downward and declared that we actually hadn't killed many people after all and sent out an order forbidding anyone in the military from slicking their hair straight back.

We sat in the cold, equipment-laden cargo aircraft, wishing that we had earplugs. An hour out of Cubi Point, Gearheardt, looking like he had lost his best friend, leaned close so that I could hear him. "What does it mean, 'She showers in her underpants'?"

"How should I know?" Of course I *did* know. Girls who had no home but the one which was provided by the guy paying to screw them that night, often would shower in their underwear, just to get clean. The squadron chaplain had overheard me telling this sad fact in the bar and tried to build it into a sermon about not chasing women who showered in their underpants, but no one got the point, and trying to find someone who showered in their underpants became a legendary chase for the Holy Grail. I went back to sleep. I dreamed of black panties. It was the last thing I heard Juanton cry when I was leading Hoche out of the bar.

Gearheardt and I were on our way back to Vietnam to be drummed out of the Marine Corps and inducted into Air America. An airline for pilots with more balls than sense.

In Danang, Gearheardt and I scrounged up clean flight suits and polished our boots as best we could. We were to report to the wing commander's office at 0900 in a ceremony dismissing us from the Marine Corps and transferring us to Air America, the CIA's airline in Southeast Asia. It was now 0855. Gearheardt put a final touch to his wet, slicked-back hair and then tossed his cigarette into the sink.

"Where did we go wrong, Jack? We did—"

"We did shit, Gearheardt. Let's go in and get this over."

We knocked sharply on the wing commander's door and then let ourselves in.

The wing commander, a massive lieutenant general who wore a specially sewn-on shoulder holster for his pipe, looked up quickly. His face turned red.

"Get out of my Marine Corps!" he bellowed. "Sergeant," he yelled through the door, "get these traitors"—that hurt—"out of my sight. Chase them off the base!"

Gearheardt and I left the Marine Corps by running down the dusty road behind wing headquarters with the military police throwing rocks at us and the small children of the whores who operated just outside the base running alongside us, laughing gleefully and calling "Geelhot, Geelhot," "You give me money number one."

It was not the separation from the Marine Corps that I had hoped for.

PART 4

We go to gain a little patch of ground that hath in it no profit but the name.

—William Shakespeare

War is hell and all that, but it has a good deal to recommend it. It wipes out all the small nuisances of peacetime.

—Ian Hay

Eat your crusts so the soldier boys won't go hungry.

—Grandma

24 · Dénouement, Certainement Excrêtement

After our journey to Hong Kong, where we didn't find the British spies, settle with the Cubans, or get our commissions in the Marine Corps back, Gearheardt and I settled into the routine of flying in Laos for Air America. Live up, dead back. Lots of resupply. The occasional infill or extraction of mercenaries that lined our pocketbooks and took years from our lives. And the squandering of seed and lucre in various Asian capitals. One of which was where I searched for Gearheardt after he finished flying for the week and went ahead to get the "lay of the land."

I found him in Max's Club on Pat Pong Road in Bangkok, apparently unconcerned that we all were curious as to why he wore only a red kimono and had a naked girl riding him piggyback. He was arguing with Max, the proprietor, about the official diameter of baseball bats.

"Who is that on your back, Gearheardt?" I asked him.

"I lost her clothes. I'm taking her to get new ones."

The few days that followed, bars and baths, added to the desultory aura that Gearheardt had assumed. I was hoping that he would snap out of it. War without Gearheardt's craziness was making me seriously consider knocking the crap out of him.

But one evening he changed to the old Gearheardt.

"I have had a vision," he said over a late night meal of fried rice at the Montien coffee shop. "We're pissing away our resources in Vietnam, and God wants me to move on to better opportunities."

"I guess I didn't realize you were having these conversations with God," I said. "Did He mention what He might want me to be doing?"

Gearheardt ignored my skepticism.

"He spoke to me through Max. That's when—"

"You mean Max the guy who owns Max's Club, right?"

"Max was throwing me out for wearing his wife's clothes, Jack. When he threw my clothes out after me he said, 'Maybe you need to find new place, Geelhot.' "

Gearheardt looked at me and I couldn't detect any madman's drool dripping down his chin.

"So this is your new vision?"

"Clear as a fucking bell."

The next morning Gearheardt and I headed back to Udorn Thani, our Air America base in northern Thailand, in time for me to pick up an aircraft and leave for a mission in Luang Prabang, the sleepy royal capital of Laos on the Mekong.

"I'll see you in Vientiane in a couple of days, Jack. I promised the chief pilot I would meet with him tomorrow. Take care of yourself."

I hopped in the little Air America shuttle bus and left for the base. He had never said that to me before. He never worried about either of us.

After flying a couple of days in the Sam Nuea area, I headed to Vientiane and that evening met up with Gearheardt at the White Rose.

Gary, the Operations Genius—everyone assumed he gave himself that nickname—came in the bar, waving a fistful of papers.

"Hey, naked night. No one told me," he whined.

"No one likes you, Gary," Gearheardt said from his booth, without looking up.

"Gearheardt, just who I was looking for. We need you to extract some Nungs from the trail. Tomorrow night. You up for it? Special pay."

"Yeah, I'll do it."

"Gearheardt, if we take a team of Nungs in there, we get our asses shot off. There are fifty thousand North Vietnamese trucks coming down the trail. What are these guys going to do? Let the air out of their tires? It's crazy."

"The Nungs are already in there, Jack. This is the extraction."

"Oh, crap. That's even worse. They'll have guys chasing them all pissed off."

Gary broke in. "No wingman, Gearheardt. We just need the one bird. Picking up two guys."

"Yeah, okay," Gearheardt said absently, not looking at me. He motioned for Gary to get lost.

"What the hell is that all about?" I asked. "We never do extractions with one aircraft. Who's your SAR?"

Gearheardt said nothing until after Gary left. He kept his eyes on the table in front of him.

"I can make five grand tomorrow night, Jack. Five grand. I'm going to buy every whore out of the White Rose and send them back to their villages rich women."

He looked up at me and I shrugged, smiling at the thought of the girls in the villages.

"Can I go with you?" Peter asked.

He was a reporter that Gearheardt and I had been hauling around the mountains of Laos, at great danger from the enemy and the U.S. ambassador to Laos, not necessarily in that order. We had hoped that he would make us famous.

"Not this time, Peter," Gearheardt said. "This is crash and dash at night. Believe me, you don't want to go pick up a bunch of smelly Chinese mercenaries."

Peter started to protest, but Gearheardt cut him off. He laughed and slammed the table with his palms, spilling Peter's beer and causing the naked ladies to look.

"No story this time, you hack," Gearheardt said. "You won't be riding my coattails to publisher." He laughed as Peter got up and began bugging Bald Fred to take him to the PDJ, a high plains area in the center of Laos, the next morning.

Gearheardt ordered another beer and motioned me to a booth in a dark corner of the bar. He looked different. I wasn't sure why, but he seemed almost subdued, resigned.

"What's up, Gearheardt? By this time you're normally arranging the bar women in the Gearheardt pyramid you call the *Hanging Wall of Tits*. You worrying about the trail mission?" Knowing that he wasn't.

He looked at me and smiled. "They're going to disappear me, Jack."

I swallowed hard, knowing what he meant and not wanting to believe it. Without Gearheardt, the war in Laos wouldn't be bearable.

"Have they told you or are you just surmising?"

Gearheardt looked at me closely, the slight smile still on his face. His eyes caught the glare of the flashlight the pilots were using to examine God knew what on the women. The eyes twinkled but looked slightly distant.

"They wanted me to take you, Jack. Bongo Congo. I told them to go screw themselves."

I wasn't sure what to say, but started to protest. "Wait a minute—"

"You need a real life, Jackie," he said. "Don't fuck it up."

He rose and joined the pilots at the bar who were chanting, "Give us spoons. Give us spoons."

"Disappear me" meant that the Company would make Gearheardt not exist. Every record and trace would be erased and replaced. Bongo Congo meant Africa, where a new Gearheardt would appear and be his amazing self for a different but exactly the same cause, real or imagined.

And he had never called me "Jackie." I felt a chill. I saw Gearheardt walk to the door of the White Rose, his arms around the shoulders of two Lao women. He looked up in the mirror, saw me watching him, and winked.

I sat alone in the booth, stunned. I sipped my beer slowly, feeling sorry for myself without a sure sense of why.

Murdock (so named by Gearheardt because the real Murdock, a pilot in the Army, was a pussy, he said) stopped by my table to show me her new breast implants, the latest thing among bar girls who could save the money to make it to Bangkok. She was disappointed that I didn't feel like rubbing them for good luck.

"Go have Bald Fred rub them, Murdock. I'm trying to get drunk. They're very nice, though." I went back to being morose.

"Hey, Jack, you still mooning over Gorilla Girl?"

It was Gearheardt, grinning as he slapped my shoulder.

I shuddered involuntarily at the thought of Gorilla Girl, looked up at Gearheardt, and started to tell him that I was going to insist that Gary schedule me to fly his wing on the extraction.

But Gearheardt squeezed my shoulder and said, "Do you have a bundle of kip you could spot me? These girls won't take a check on an out-of-town bank."

He laughed. Later I would remember that none of the White Rose girls ever charged Gearheardt for anything.

"You're a heckofa guy, Jackson. We were golden." He patted my shoulder again, grabbed the kip I had in my hand, and left, stopping to give a good luck rub to Murdock's new breasts.

As I watched him leave the White Rose, I felt my stomach knotting. The other way the Company "disappeared" people had occurred to me. Giving someone an assignment that was impossible. Like a single helicopter extracting mercenaries from the Ho Chi Minh Trail at night.

If Gearheardt were being sent to Africa, surely he would have taken me with him.

Back in Udorn the next morning, I opened the door to the chief pilot's office without knocking. He looked up from a mountain of paperwork.

"This better be good, Armstrong, or I'll kill you."

"Where's Gearheardt?" I asked firmly.

The Chief Pilot stared blankly at me. He took a cigarette from the carved wooden box on his desk and lit it deliberately.

"Who in the hell are you talking about?"

I didn't need to hear anything else.

"I'm going to Bangkok this afternoon," I said, turning for the door.

"Try to get sane while you're there, would you?" He took a document from the top of his desk and leaned back in his chair. "And don't ever, ever come in here again without knocking. What I have you do up there is confidential."

I had my hand on the doorknob. "So even we can't know about it while we're doing it?"

"Exactly. Now close the goddamned door."

In Bangkok I found Gearheardt's girlfriend, Dow. We talked about Gearheardt, drinking wine and then Mekong, the local whiskey, until she fell asleep in her chair. At Max's I bought drinks and tried to hold a memorial service for Gearheardt, complete with my drunken toasts, but everyone acted like I was crazy.

I wandered back to Dow's apartment and drank the rest of the Mekong, then climbed into bed with her. "Jack friend Geelhot," she said, putting her arms around my neck. I knew that in the morning she would ask me for money.

"That's the story, Dr. Boon," I said, exhausted on the couch, my shirt wet against the almost-leather couch. "Sometimes I'm pissing in my pants just thinking about all the fun we had. And sometimes I want to just put a gun to my head and pull the trigger."

"Is ho'se for Loy Loge's, chi mai?"

"Is holse for . . . You mean horse for Roy Rogers? Shit, doc, haven't you been listening?"

"I know story, Jack. I hear Gearheardt. He same same you."

I seemed to have offended his professional standards. I sat up. Ms. Boon was sleeping on a mat beside the couch.

"Gearheardt is not same same me, Doc. Gearheardt is mok mok brave, chi mai? He isn't in here pissing and moaning about the price of tea in China." I looked up at him.

"Did Gearheardt tell you this same story, Doctor Boon?" I asked.

The good doctor smiled and patted me on the shoulder.

"Gearheardt, he—"

"Yeah, I know. Gearheardt he same same me." I was getting tired of that.

"You good man, Jack. Number one. I shitty Doctor tell you Vietnam you fault. Not you fault you fuckup." He began to cry, a habit that was beginning to irritate me. I lay back, feeling the patterns tooled into the almost-leather couch, waiting for Dr. Boon to continue. Mrs. Boon awoke and began rubbing my stockinged feet. After a long while, during which the good doctor sobbed and the massage parlor/bar beneath the office filled with loud gaiety, I patted his knee.

"I would like Mrs. Boon to finish my bath now, Doctor," I said.

The doctor didn't remove his hands from his eyes.

"Yes, that would be good idea," he said, not sounding as if he knew that was why I continued to visit his office even after he confessed that he had never gone to medical school and had been paid by Gearheardt to hang out his shingle. I wanted to be near people that had been close to Gearheardt, and I still suspected that the lovely Mrs. Boon was one of them.

I forgave Dr. Boon for confirming that I had indeed probably prolonged the war in Vietnam, caused countless deaths, and ruined the President's chances for reelection.

"Thank you, Jack. Maybe you feel better McWatt too." He fumbled through his bookcase and pulled out a well-worn book. After thumbing through it for a few moments he found what he had been looking for, on page 333.

"McWatt say, 'Oh, well, what the hell.' You say too, Jack. Oh well, what hell."

I stood and took off my clothes, my watch, gold Air America bracelet, everything, and let Mrs. Boon lead me to the tub. The water was hot and rose up around my chin when Doctor Boon's wife joined me.

I closed my eyes and the war went on without me.

Epilogue

South of the airstrip, one of the longest in Laos, the jungle city of Luang Prabang dozes in the Asian sun. The Mekong River runs brown and powerful along one side, and to the east the mountains that eat pilots in the rainy season are green and tempting. A temple sits on a single knob near the center of the town where during the day the North Vietnamese and the Pathet Lao come in to visit the markets. In the evenings the American pilots drink beer and eat Vietnamese noodle soup on the lawn of the lovely French-owned Laing Xaing Hotel. The King of Laos, Savang Vatthana, lives in Luang Prabang, and one day I had tea with him. I was in my Air America uniform, walking in the town after a short day in the air. When I asked the guard if I could see the King, I was just being another American wiseass. I didn't expect to meet him, thinking kings must stay pretty busy.

But I found myself on a quiet, tree-shaded terrace on the Mekong side of the palace. Tea was served and the servants retired. The late sun hit the river and almost made the brown monster pretty. Across the river the jungle running up the hills was wild. It was pleasant with a late afternoon coolness to the light breeze flowing over the patio.

The old man must have known that if we failed to hold the North Vietnamese back, he would be the last king of Laos.

"You friend Gearheardt?" he asked. His smile almost made me think he knew something that I didn't.

"Yes," I said. "I friend Gearheardt."

We sat watching the sun disappear behind the hills across the darkening river. Behind us, the rooms in the modest palace grew dark, and in the courtyard, candles were being lit. The servants moved quietly in the dark rooms, wearing soft slippers and whispering silken gowns. Cooking fires tainted the air with Asian spices. Faintly, I could hear a television.

After tea the King dozed, his head bobbing and then settling to his chest. He looked older than his years. In the twilight, the Mekong noise seemed louder. I had always feared fast water at night. The pilots' and the CIA advisors' voices occasionally carried from the veranda of the Laing Xaing Hotel, down the road south of the palace. Certainly the loud laughter was clear. When I rose, the King awoke and clapped his hands gently, bringing a bowing servant bearing a small silver drum, about seven inches in diameter and ten inches high, a replica of the Kao drums of northern Laos. The King lifted and offered it to me. The small frogs decorating the top and sides were powerful symbols in the kingdom, the King explained in broken but competent English.

"When they get hungry, they eat moon. America gives many guns to us to frighten the frogs trying to eat moon," he said.

Unkindly, I thought how ridiculous it was for a nation's leader to believe that firing a few guns would keep a flying frog from eating the moon. But I took the drum.

The soldier at the gate demanded money for letting me in to see the King. I tried to brush by him but he stepped in front of me and stuck his carbine into my nostril. He wanted seven hundred million kip, but was happy as a pig when I gave him ten dollars. The intricately etched silver drum was just the size to wear on my head, so I put it on and walked down the dark, pungent street to join the laughter at the Laing Xaing. Hoping I might find Gearheardt.

O Lord our God, help us to tear their soldiers to bloody shreds with our shells; help us to cover their smiling fields with the pale forms of their patriot dead; help us to drown the thunder of the guns with the shrieks of their wounded, writhing in pain; help us to lay waste their humble homes with a hurricane of fire; help us to wring the hearts of their unoffending widows with unavailing grief. . . . For our sakes who adore Thee, Lord, blast their hopes, blight their lives, protract their bitter pilgrimage, make heavy their steps, water their way with their tears, stain the white snow with the blood of their wounded feet! We ask it, in the spirit of love, of Him Who is the Source of Love, and Who is the ever-faithful refuge and friend of all that are sore beset and seek His aid with humble and contrite hearts. Amen.

—Mark Twain

War is an ugly thing, but not the ugliest of things: the decayed and degraded state of moral and patriotic feeling which thinks nothing worth a war, is worse. A war to protect other human beings against tyrannical injustice; a war to give victory to their own ideas of right and good, and which is their own war, carried on for an honest purpose by their own free choice—is often the means of their regeneration.

—John Stuart Mill

In war there is no substitute for victory.

—Douglas MacArthur

Afterword: Heroes

The term has become almost valueless in today's media. That speaks more to an American desire to admire courage and the willingness to sacrifice for the good of others, than it does to denigrate the term or the individual. We want to believe that men and women will place loyalty, honor, and doing the right thing above their own well-being.

The most indelible memory I have of Vietnam is witnessing heroism and courage on a daily basis.

The infantrymen were magnificent. I still cannot imagine the amount of courage it took to head into the hell of the jungles and rice paddies knowing that mortal danger could come from any direction, at any time.

I worked a great deal with Army helicopters. Searching for a word that tops "fearless" has been fruitless, but it must be there somewhere. Their air crews were superb.

Navy pilots, the best fighter pilots in the world, took off in danger and landed in peril. What happened in between was all in a day's work. No one else was as arrogant as the carrier pilot, and maybe no one else had the right to be.

My personal description of Air Force pilots in Vietnam can be summed up in a single name—General Robbie Risner. If you can lead your men into a game of death and have them love you, you will be honored above all fighting men. As a fighter/bomber pilot and a POW, Robbie was the epitome of the greatest fighting machine history has ever known. (A-1 pilots are saints, by the way.)

A special word for the medics and corpsmen—your place in heaven is secure.

And for my beloved Marines, you don't need my accolades; you're the best of them all. Every day in the uniform of a United States Marine is a gift from God. You embrace duty. You seek challenge. You are faithful—to each other, to your country, and to the Corps.

In the end, a hero is a common man who performs an act of heroism. Nothing more. Nothing less. The strength and beauty of our Vietnam commitment was the common man doing what his country asked.

God Bless America.